W9-CTE-883

"Are you my enemy still?" Lucas asked, his eyes seizing hers,

burning into them until they seared her very soul.

"No," Alanna said solemnly, breathless in spite of the brevity of the response.

"How badly did he hurt you?" he asked, finding it difficult to swallow as he awaited her answer and the stilling of his own rebellious desires.

"He didn't. But you—did this incident open your wound?" Alanna asked quickly, allowing her fingertips to light softly on his shoulder, like a delicate butterfly upon a hardy flower.

"No, only my heart," Lucas replied, the touch of her skin upon his crumbling his resistance. Even bedraggled as she was by her ordeal, Alanna O'Donnell somehow beckoned to him. She was forbidden fruit, temptation and the glimmering promise of paradise. She was all that a man needed to be wary of in a woman, and all that he craved, as well....

Dear Reader,

Our featured big book this month, *The Honor Price*, by Erin Yorke, is a stirring tale of adventure and forbidden passion. One of Harlequin Historical's most popular authors, Yorke brings readers the story of Alanna O'Donnell, a young Irishwoman whose flight from her uncle's treachery brings her into an uneasy alliance with Spanish nobleman Lucas del Fuentes— a man she should by all rights hate.

Cheryl St.John's first book, *Rain Shadow*, was part of our March Madness 1993 promotion. Don't miss *Heaven Can Wait*, the gripping prequel to *Rain Shadow*. Heartland Critiques gave both books a GOLD ★★★★★ rating!

Aisley de Laci is wed to a knight rumored to be in league with the devil in *The Devil's Lady*, a remarkable medieval by Deborah Simmons. And finally, Laurel Pace's *Winds of Destiny* is the long-awaited sequel to *Destiny's Promise*.

We hope you enjoy all of these titles. And next month, be sure to look for the new Theresa Michaels, *Fire and Sword*.

Sincerely,

Tracy Farrell
Senior Editor
Harlequin Historicals

Please address questions and book requests to:
Harlequin Reader Service
U.S.: 3010 Walden Ave., P.O. Box 1325, Buffalo, NY 14269
Canadian: P.O. Box 609, Fort Erie, Ont. L2A 5X3

ERIN YORKE

THE HONORPRICE

Harlequin Books

TORONTO • NEW YORK • LONDON
AMSTERDAM • PARIS • SYDNEY • HAMBURG
STOCKHOLM • ATHENS • TOKYO • MILAN
MADRID • WARSAW • BUDAPEST • AUCKLAND

If you purchased this book without a cover you should be aware that this book is stolen property. It was reported as "unsold and destroyed" to the publisher, and neither the author nor the publisher has received any payment for this "stripped book."

ISBN 0-373-28839-5

THE HONOR PRICE

Copyright © 1994 by Susan McGovern Yansick & Christine Healy.

All rights reserved. Except for use in any review, the reproduction or utilization of this work in whole or in part in any form by any electronic, mechanical or other means, now known or hereafter invented, including xerography, photocopying and recording, or in any information storage or retrieval system, is forbidden without the written permission of the publisher, Harlequin Enterprises Limited, 225 Duncan Mill Road, Don Mills, Ontario, Canada M3B 3K9.

All characters in this book have no existence outside the imagination of the author and have no relation whatsoever to anyone bearing the same name or names. They are not even distantly inspired by any individual known or unknown to the author, and all incidents are pure invention.

This edition published by arrangement with Harlequin Enterprises B. V.

® and TM are trademarks of the publisher. Trademarks indicated with ® are registered in the United States Patent and Trademark Office, the Canadian Trade Marks Office and in other countries.

Printed in U.S.A.

Books by Erin Yorke

Harlequin Historicals

American Beauty #58
Forever Defiant #94
Heaven's Gate #124
Dangerous Deceptions #152
Bound by Love #176
Counterfeit Laird #202
The Honor Price #239

ERIN YORKE

is the pseudonym used by the writing team of Christine Healy and Susan Yansick. One half of the team is single, fancy-free and countrified, and the other is married, the mother of two sons and suburban, but they find that their differing lives and styles enrich their writing with a broader perspective.

For Helen T. McGovern, a courageous woman in a sometimes unkind world, and for all the Robinson, Fleming, Cavanaugh and McGovern women who came before her and passed their strength along to the next generation.

and

To Anita Disanza, fluent in English, Latin, Spanish and shopping, and Marta Recarey, who commiserates on the tough days—*muchas gracias para la amistad*.

Chapter One

Ireland, September 1588

The angry slam of wave against rock continued unchanged, but the feral howling of the wind seemed to have lessened. It was hard for Lucas to be certain, however, over the incessant murmured chant of his companions, huddled around the meager flames of the fire they had lit to stay warm.

"Dios te salve Maria, llena eres tu gracia..."

Though he was as religious as the next man, Lucas Rafael del Fuentes turned his back on their desperate supplication of the Virgin. Deciding that God and His saints helped those who helped themselves, the tall Spaniard moved easily to the mouth of the cave for a closer view of the fierce storm that had raged for nearly a day. But almost instantly a sharp voice called him back.

"You might not need anyone, del Fuentes, but can't you spare your frightened men some solace, an encouraging word, a prayer? Your lack of faith unsettles them further."

"If it weren't for your chasing miles inland after that boar, we wouldn't need prayers, Alvarez. We would have been at our rendezvous on time," snapped Lucas. As leader of the shore party to replenish their battle-worn ship's dwindling supply of food, he deeply resented missing his appointed return to *La Rata*.

"Perhaps it was not my actions, but the *captain's* desire to rid himself of you at all costs that sees us stranded here," taunted the other man. He never missed an opportunity to provoke del Fuentes.

"*La Rata* wouldn't have sailed without us if Alonso could have avoided it," retorted Lucas, irritated at the arrogance and incompetence of his companion, whose only qualification for anything was being godson to Spain's Philip II.

"And I suppose it's my fault that Carlos is dead, too?"

"You'll have to answer for that yourself, but I wouldn't have sent him into the brush alone after an injured boar, no matter how strongly I craved fresh meat," Lucas drawled softly. Yet as he spoke, his emerald eyes showed no complacency. They glinted with a fire reminiscent of that used to temper the finest blade of Toledo steel. At no time was Lucas del Fuentes less than an imposing figure, but now, with tension clearly evident in his nearly six feet of well-muscled strength, few men would think it wise to challenge his authority. But then, few men had as little sense as Alvarez.

Although Lucas had done his best to avoid criticizing the other nobleman in front of the seamen, he had lost all patience with Juan's arrogant judgments, particularly since they were usually misjudgments, producing only more aggravation. Yet Juan Felipe Alvarez, not astute enough to notice the manner in which Lucas's lean jaw clamped in fury, continued his goading.

"No, I should have realized you would have no heart for the hunt. Your *inglés* blood has always held you back from real danger, hasn't it, *señor*? Being only half Spanish, you haven't the stomach for a man's sport," mocked Juan. He was surreptitiously called *El Pavoreal*. Though stocky in build and possessed of bullish manners, his overly proud nature and constant strutting had nonetheless earned him the title of peacock.

"The only so-called sport in which you are an expert, Don Juan, is whoring," Lucas answered, his voice soft and deadly with warning. "As for fighting, unlike you, I believe in *leading* my men ... not following after them, as is your habit."

All at once the long-smoldering friction between the two men sparked, filling the shadowy cave with the furious heat of conflict, the smell of blood. Even the terrified sailors busy with their beads were distracted from salvation by the exchange between the officers.

As *El Pavoreal* adopted a fighting stance and kicked at the sand of the cave, Lucas's mouth tightened in a grimace, his eyes narrowing in thought. He and Juan had tangled before and undoubtedly would again. While he preferred to avoid such a scene in front of his men, today it would be a pleasure to release some of his anger, which burned hotter than ever since the defeat of Spain's Great Enterprise at the hands of the English. Let Alvarez witness the real del Fuentes, unhampered by the emotional restraint demanded of an officer aboard a ship at war, he decided, flexing the muscles in his hands.

"If you are man enough, try it," Lucas suggested quietly, watching Alvarez preen for the benefit of his audience. The fool had no doubt of his success, Lucas realized, relishing the thrashing he was about to deliver as much as the humiliation it would cause.

But suddenly, before Juan could reply, the ominous atmosphere in the belly of the cliff eased as, outside, Nature's savagery quieted. In the startling silence, the sound of a bird's cry penetrated Lucas's concentration, and he looked past Juan toward the cave entrance.

Perhaps his luck had changed and they could set out at once to meet up with their ship, *La Rata Santa Maria Encoronada*, he considered, thrusting aside his own concerns. The captain, Alonso, would have stayed as close to shore as he possibly could, ready to attempt the rendezvous whenever it was feasible. Everyone knew the dangers in landing on Irish shores, and all would be anxious to leave.

The landing party had drawn their small boat ashore and emptied it when the heavens opened so furiously last night, but if they divided the stores they had salvaged, and everyone helped, the reloading shouldn't take too long. There was still some light left in the sky, and after being in the cave nearly a full day, they'd all welcome the exercise.

"We have no time for this foolishness now. As much as I would prefer to settle our disagreement once and for all, Juan, we must bow to duty and try to rejoin *La Rata. Vamos.*" In his natural role as leader, Lucas hadn't even thought to consult the other officer, an oversight Juan pounced upon.

"I thought the safety of your men was always paramount with you?" he challenged. "Have you forgotten Alonso's warnings that the local barbarians could be dangerous? You're ordering us to venture out with no weapons except our knives."

"I don't see that we have much choice. If we remain here, Alonso will never find us and the Irish might. Besides, Alonso will have *La Rata* offshore as soon as the seas subside; we had best be ready."

"*Bueno, señor,* but the matter between us still stands. For now, you lead the men, I'll follow," taunted Juan, claiming the last word. "I wouldn't trust you at my back."

In the tranquil aftermath of the storm, Alanna Desmond O'Donnell stood, a lone figure paused midway on the path that led from the rock-strewn beach below to the somber, gray stone keep at the edge of the cliffs above.

The savage winds and raging ocean had quieted two hours past, and the ensuing silence had enticed Alanna to comb the beach, as she had in childhood, for any treasures Mananaan MacLir, the ancient Irish god of the sea, might have cast upon the shore during his latest tirade. And now, as she departed empty-handed, a playful breeze tugged at Alanna's thick blond hair as if the appeased deity wished to tease her into believing that he could be as gentle and loving as he could be cruel.

Caressed by the tangy salt air, Alanna had succumbed to temptation and stopped her climb to survey the watery majesty below. Its awesome splendor caused her to understand why the earliest Celts had believed the ocean to be a mighty being.

No matter what the Church taught, the continuing roar of the waves made certain that the primitive ocean god would never be forgotten. But just as important, a feeling for the land and waters of Ireland ran in the blood of all of its people. It kept the ancient beliefs alive, the elders passing them on to the next generation in whispered tones on a Sunday afternoon following Holy Mass. And sometimes, heretical as they were, the superstitions of the old ones proved true. Hadn't the beach been alchemized into a stretch of gold by a yellow sunset yesterday? And today, hadn't an avenging Mananaan MacLir transformed the sea into a wrathful giant, ready to snatch and devour whole ships in his powerful foam-flecked jaws?

Though she put little stock in the age-old tales of her forefathers, Alanna knew them by heart, having heard the lore of Irish gods and heroes ever since she could remember. They were so much a part of her that she had instinctively gone to the coastline when the thundering rain had subsided, not really expecting to be the recipient of Mananaan MacLir's largess, but curious all the same to see what the waters had deposited upon Irish soil.

A wry smile curved Alanna's full lips as she considered her folly. Unless its mists shrouded some secret breeding ground for men more heroic than the ones who shared her world, what could the sea give her that would fill her battered heart with joy? No, a gift of such magnitude was beyond even Mananaan MacLir's power to grant. Yet, while she conceded the falsity of Ireland's legends, Alanna realized they would always be a part of her, the way the land itself would be. It mattered not what foreign power claimed Ireland, the lithesome blonde thought with determination, her eyes suddenly flashing the same stormy blue as the waters below.

Giving in to a sigh so small that it almost defied detection, Alanna shifted her gaze to the forbidding stone walls above and knew that she should be on her way once more. However, the distinctly British atmosphere awaiting her at the keep dissuaded her from renewing her climb.

Once she had loved the walled habitation that sat at the rim of the cliff and seemed, when viewed from the water's edge on an overcast morning, to be floating on a cloud. But in those days, her mother's childhood home had been known as *Radharc Alainn,* or Beautiful Place. Now, as the residence of her mother's brother and his wife, the small fortress was called Castlemount, a name as English as its present mistress, though the woman had been born on Irish soil.

At the thought of her uncle Grady's Anglo wife, Alanna's delicate features wrinkled in distaste. *Radharc Alainn* was no more, and the keep no longer a haven for her, no matter that her uncle was its lord. Was it any wonder that she was glad tomorrow's sunrise would see her leave Castlemount behind? It truly was time to get back to the Irish way of things, to move once more beyond the pale into the wild heart and soul of her beautiful homeland.

Taking one last look around her, the young woman realized that her present location on the cliffside—halfway between the craggy Irish shoreline and the Anglicized citadel—reflected her existence as clearly as any lake could mirror her image. It was her fate to be caught in the middle, pulled by desire to the free, Irish life with her foster father, Kevin O'Donnell, and yet drawn by familial obligations to the MacWilliams of Castlemount, though Grady had allied himself with the English in order to retain the MacWilliams holdings.

Such conflicting loyalties forced Alanna to divide her time between the Irish rebel stronghold up north and the Anglicized establishment in the south. She spent her life traveling from one to the other but, widowed as she was, had never really found a home in either one.

However, things were not all that bad, Alanna consoled herself as she scanned the horizon once again, praying that if one of Kevin's small boats had been scavenging in these treacherous waters, it had ridden out the storm safely. At twenty-four, Alanna had seen enough of life to know that she was more fortunate than most women who found themselves widowed in Ireland. She had two protectors in Kevin and Grady, two men who loved her, so she had not been forced to remarry or enter a convent in order to survive.

And if, at present, she had tired of Castlemount and its English ways, if she chafed at wearing the English fashions that Cordelia decreed all within the keep's walls must endure, her time here was almost at an end. Tomorrow she would leave both Castlemount and her uncle's wife behind and return to O'Donnell lands. There she would take up the old ways, residing with the O'Donnell himself, the man to whom her parents had given her in fosterage when their own home had been ravaged by war. And she would be content to stay in the place he made for her beside his hearth, at least until her longing for Grady and her mother's people brought her back here once more.

Alanna lifted her skirts and continued her trek up the cliff side, the movements of her tall, slender body as graceful as the surrounding seabirds playfully riding the wind.

By the time Alanna had made her way back to her room within the central tower of Castlemount, she had lost the consolation the sea had afforded her. Not even the sight of old Moira was enough to dispel her ill humor.

"Tsk, tsk, lass, it's rare your comely face is marred by such a scowl," the loyal retainer chided as she bustled around the young widow, taking her cloak and then stirring the fire that burned in the brazier.

In the soft shadows of the room, the elderly woman's still-black hair and violet eyes hinted at the good looks that had been hers so many decades before. But more than that, Moira's coloring suggested that she was a *pisoque,* a teller of tales, a weaver of spells. However, unlike those of most of her kind, the old woman's narratives were more often than not concerned with Curran Desmond, Alanna's father, rather than Ireland's age-old heroes. And if she wove spells, they were ones of pure enchantment as she related the particulars of Curran's warrior days or told the story of how he had abducted Alanna's mother in order to make her his bride.

Prodded by the affection she felt for the old woman, Alanna attempted to replace the expression on her delicate features with a smile of sorts. But Moira MacReynolds was not to be fooled.

"It matters not a whit if you found nothing worthwhile during your amble on the beach," Moira said, noting Alanna's empty hands and mistaking the reason for the girl's frown. "I told you when you were but a wee one that Mananaan MacLir might sometimes cast up a treasure on the rocks only to take it back in a trice, just when you think it's yours."

"Oh, Moira, you forget I'm long past being a child," Alanna said with a laugh. "In truth, my exploration of the beach was quite enjoyable."

"Then what is it that has you upset?" the ancient servant persisted. "Is it herself again?"

"Isn't it always Cordelia?" Alanna replied. She abandoned all pretense at lightheartedness as she sat near the fire and took the cup of *scailtin* Moira had pressed into her hand, knowing the hot flavored milk and whiskey would taste good, indeed.

"That one!" the older woman snorted in contempt. Age had made her comfortable enough to pour herself a generous amount of the draught without asking her lady's leave, and she did so, continuing to voice her opinion, though Alanna hadn't asked for it. "*She* knows nothing of our ways and cares much less. Why let such a one as she bother you?"

"Sometimes my uncle's wife is a difficult woman to ignore," Alanna responded before drinking deeply from her cup.

"What has the hag done now?"

"She accosted me as I came back to the keep through the small gate near the stables—"

"That's where she belongs, with the rest of the horse manure," Moira interjected, the fire in her eyes belying the wrinkles of her many years.

"Be that as it may, I was trying to avoid her, but the great lady of Castlemount had just returned from a ride to inspect her lands. When she saw me and guessed where I had been, she began one of her tirades, telling me that if I had a decent husband, one loyal to the English Crown, of course, I'd have no time to engage in such unseemly activities."

"I hope you told the old biddy that if you wanted a man to warm your bed you'd take one, and an Irish one, at that," Moira replied indignantly after she had drained her cup. "Imagine, trying to settle you with an English husband!"

"Yes, but there's more to it than that, and I'm on to her plotting. Though she has broached the idea of marriage before, this time she hasn't let the subject rest. Childless as she is, I suspect Cordelia hopes to wed me to one of her numerous relatives so that MacWilliams lands will stay in her family after Grady passes on. But she can try all she likes to promote such a match. I'll have none of it!" Alanna vowed defiantly, the tilt of her head exceedingly feminine, even in the throes of her anger. "Since Sean's death, there's not a man drawing breath who can tempt me, and certainly not one with Anglo blood flowing in his veins."

"There, there, lass. She can't force you into such an arrangement, so just ignore her. By this time tomorrow, you'll be far from her carping tongue. Now let me dress your hair before you go down to sup and bid your uncle a proper farewell. If you don't make an appearance at table soon, I'm sure Cordelia will feed your meal to the hounds. Come along with you, now."

Though not a docile creature by nature, Alanna smiled and did as the old woman bid her, the shimmering gold of her tresses coming alive under Moira's competent hands. As the comb wielded its magic Alanna reflected that there were very few problems Moira MacReynolds couldn't help alleviate, and Grady MacWilliams's niece counted herself fortunate to have such an ally.

Long after she had returned from the bothersome task of farewells, Alanna awoke at the first touch of a hand on her shoulder. Her fingers curled instinctively around the small dagger ever present at her side. Though she felt secure in her uncle's household, the ongoing troubles in her homeland had taught Alanna that there was no such thing as certainty regarding possession of a keep. To survive, one had to constantly be on guard, even in the relative privacy of a bedchamber.

Surreptitiously opening one eye, Alanna was both relieved and annoyed to see that the intruder was only Cordelia, though why her aunt should be standing there in a nightdress at this hour, Alanna couldn't fathom.

"Get up, girl, get up!" the woman was saying. That she spoke in English made the demand seem all the more harsh and unreasonable.

"What is it, Cordelia?" Alanna asked, not attempting to hide the exasperation tinging her voice. She'd been called upon to deal with this harridan twice already today. Surely she shouldn't have to suffer such a tribulation again. "Is this to be yet another sermon on the sacred bonds of matrimony and my obligation to take a husband?"

"Your uncle requires your presence in the Great Hall immediately," Cordelia replied curtly, not rising to the girl's bait. "If you are disinclined, however..." she drawled, only to halt suddenly when the bedcovers slipped from around her niece and revealed the utterly indecent short tunic the girl had donned in place of the fine English nightclothes that had been supplied for her. At the sight, Cordelia's usually pinched expression became extraordinarily sour. It seemed to the mistress of Castlemount that despite all of her efforts to Anglicize Alanna Desmond O'Donnell, the girl was barely above painting herself blue, as her heathen ancestors had done.

"No matter how urgent my husband's command, you certainly can't go below wearing *that*," the woman contended. Without asking permission, she turned to rummage through the chests that held the English clothing Alanna was called upon to wear when residing in Cordelia's household but which would have to remain behind when she left. The garments might have been presented to Alanna, but Cordelia felt that they, along with everything else in Grady's possession, were her own. After all, if it hadn't been for her, wouldn't all of the MacWilliams lands now belong to the English Crown?

Almost instantly, the older woman withdrew a proper, heavy nightrail, which she proceeded to drape across Alanna's bed. "Just imagine the commotion if the kin of Castlemount's lord appeared clad in such a mere Irish rag!"

Throwing aside the intricately embroidered bedcovers, Alanna rose from the bed, biting back the stinging comment that sprang to mind. Mere Irish rag, indeed!

As Alanna fingered the soft wool of the old tunic, she knew she couldn't answer Grady's odd summons thus attired, but *not* because her apparel was Irish. Rather, the problem was her bared shoulder and exposed thighs. The garment had been created for a man, a fighting man. In fact, she had made it for Sean, her husband, but a few short months before he had been slain.

Turning her back on the grim-lipped Cordelia, Alanna shed her clothing and replaced it with the stiff, confining English nightdress. She hastily tied the ribbons that fastened the material across her bosom and turned to Castlemount's mistress once more. The picture the woman presented made Alanna more cognizant than ever of the daily sacrifice her mother's brother suffered to keep the family lands intact.

"Is Grady in his cups, then, and wanting to bid me one last sad goodbye before I leave tomorrow morning?" Alanna asked quietly. "Or does he think to talk me into staying here? I can guess no other reason for him to require my attendance in the Great Hall when the entire household should be abed." Nor, she thought while she waited for Cordelia to complete her dour inspection of the nightgown's propriety, could any man have a better excuse to be drunk than to have such a one as you to wife.

"Your Uncle Grady does not drink to excess," the tall, angular woman stated in clipped tones, her posture as rigid as her words. "Though I must add that I couldn't fault him should your unsettled life eventually drive the poor man to such overindulgence. Still, as it is, my husband didn't send for you to try to change your mind or to effect another tearful farewell. Much as it pains me to say this, Grady has need of your services. Some captives have been brought in who speak neither English nor your own strange Celtic tongue. Perhaps the education you so foolishly received at the insistence of your convent-reared mother can finally be put to some use. Grady feels that you may be able to communicate with these foreigners in Latin."

"Wouldn't Friar Galen be better able than I to undertake this task?" Alanna asked.

"As usual, the MacWilliams trusts none but his own, and certainly not that papist charlatan who traveled here in your company. I, myself, see no reason for an unmarried woman to be present at such an interrogation. If you wish, I would be willing to convey your regrets to the lord of the household, and we can proceed with the executions of these men without disturbing you further."

"Cordelia, you are well aware that I am no green girl to be spared the sight of captive males," Alanna said, stepping over the bundles that had been prepared for her departure the next day. Her aunt looked to be all too anxious to witness the demise of Grady's prisoners. The thought occurred to Alanna that perhaps these strangers were not from the continent after all, but Irish rebels clever enough to feign ignorance of their tongue in an English household. And so she hastened from the chamber to see whether she could be of assistance to them if these were indeed her countrymen, or to her uncle if they were not.

Walking past the disapproving Cordelia, Alanna lifted her chin proudly. The English cat's-paw might have turned *Radharc Alainn* into Castlemount, and transformed the *flaith*, the chieftain of the MacWilliams clan, into the lord of an Anglicized keep, but the iron-haired hag would never extinguish the Irish spirit that had shaped and nurtured these lands, Alanna swore to herself . . . never!

The numerous torches that filled the confines of the cavernous hall with flame and smoke made the prisoners feel they had entered hell itself, surrounded by demon captors. Being held under such barbaric condictions had intimidated the seamen and incensed the two Spanish noblemen. Juan Alvarez, however, had soon lost his pomposity when his sputtering and swaggering had earned him a blow to his jaw from a tightly clenched fist. Now he stood, fearful, with the rest. As for Lucas del Fuentes, he had thus far managed to control his temper and to view the situation with the distance of a seasoned soldier. Freedom and perhaps life itself depended upon his ability to seize any opportunity for escape.

For this reason, he had pretended ignorance of English from the moment he and the others had been set upon and taken. After all, the patter of these individuals bespoke allegiance to Elizabeth of England, and Lucas and his men were her foes—her vanquished foes. Hadn't they been returning from Philip's attack upon England, failed though it was, when the ferocious storm had stranded them on the shores of this primitive land?

Should these people discover he could speak their language, Lucas knew he would only be leaving himself open to the possibility of torture. It was better to allow the ruffians to think there was no way they could compel him to impart information about the Spanish fleet and his own ship. But more importantly, Lucas's ploy gave him the one advantage available. His captors spoke freely before their prisoners, thinking none of them understood what was being said. And that, Lucas realized, provided his one chance to extricate himself and his men from their present humiliating situation.

Willing his flesh to ignore the dampness while he stood awaiting the lord of the keep's pleasure, Lucas blessed his father's wisdom in marrying an Englishwoman, Anne Talbot. If it had not been for the affection that had sprung between his parents in the court of Mary Tudor and her husband, Philip of Spain, Lucas had no doubt that he would be a man without hope. The question remained, however, could his knowledge of his mother's native tongue help him conquer this present threat of death?

For the moment it appeared these rowdy Irishmen who played at being British in their isolated, sparsely furnished castle, had given up hope of communicating with the foreigners in English. Lucas knew, however, that the Irish had not yet completely abandoned the idea of finding out just who their prisoners were or why they had come to be there. In a final attempt to converse with the captured men, the head of the household had sent a dour-faced female to fetch someone who spoke Latin.

It was likely that this new interrogator would be some kind of prelate, and Lucas considered that if he communicated with this man of God, there was the possibility Lucas could win him to the idea of recommending mercy to his barbaric lord. After all, noblemen were usually given the opportunity to be ransomed by their families. It was a practice accepted throughout Christendom. And if Lucas vouched payment for the seamen, might not their lives be spared, as well? Certainly there was no one better to receive his appeal than what Lucas hoped was a kindhearted clergyman...if, that was, the man answered to the Papacy and not the Church of England.

Though English law prohibited the faith of Rome in Ireland, Lucas knew from Irish rebels visiting the court of Spain that the religion still flourished. Many houses kept their own priests just as they had always done. It was simply a matter of doing it quietly. Such might be the case in this house.

Suddenly the men around Lucas grew noisier. Scanning those standing near, the Spanish nobleman noted that no one had joined the group surrounding him, and then he raised his eyes to the stairway and saw a young woman descending. White gown floating around her and blond hair shimmering in the torchlight, she presented an image of goodness and innocence. In fact, under the present circumstances, she looked like some merciful angel swooping into Satan's lair. Lucas fervently prayed as he watched her draw closer that the young woman would indeed prove to be their salvation.

Though this was no priest, Lucas concluded that the softness of a female heart would stand him in as good a stead. And as he was wont to do when dealing with women for any reason whatsoever, he determined to take command from the first, completely ignoring the shame with which his present nakedness was supposed to fill him.

Chapter Two

Following the cold stone steps down into the smoky dimness of the Great Hall, Alanna could barely discern Grady and his fighting men clustered at the opposite end of the oversize chamber. Their agitated voices, however, rebounded eerily off the bare, soot-covered walls, and Alanna hastened her step across the rush-covered floor.

"I am here, Grady," she announced. She stopped beside the gray-haired man who stood at the center of the fracas, his face a study in consternation.

"Yes, and they are there," Alanna's uncle responded. With a nod of his neatly trimmed head, the lord of the keep indicated a scarcely illuminated corner. His voice was calm, in order to hide the terror building in his heart. As he scrutinized the men yet again, Grady MacWilliams prayed that his suspicions would prove groundless. But he swore these were men of Spain, and not Italians or Portuguese. Spaniards found on his own coastline! After all of the rumors he had heard about Philip's fleet, what else could it mean but invasion?

Alanna's steady gaze followed that of her kinsman. There, in the dark recess of the hall, cowered Castlemount's newest captives. Surprised by what she saw, Alanna worked to suppress the small degree of satisfaction she felt. Celtic blood still ran in Grady's veins, try as Cordelia might to civilize him. Clinging to the old ways, Grady had stripped his prisoners of their clothing, leaving them totally naked. Alanna could only guess at what the prim Cordelia thought of that.

Unclothed though they were, Alanna knew by the look of them that these were no natives of Ireland. Their complexions were too dark, and the cut of their hair and beards too foreign. Not one of them sported a *glib*, the forelock favored by Irish freemen despite a futile English ban.

"I suspect they may be Spanish," Grady said gruffly. "Find out who they are and what they are doing here. One or two of them were dressed as nobles. Someone must be educated enough to understand Latin."

Glad that the prisoners were not loyal sons of Eire and that she would not be called upon to choose between betraying either her uncle or her countrymen, Alanna walked forward to do Grady's bidding.

There were four of them, the young widow noted, huddled together to find warmth as well as to hide their shame. And then she saw him. One man stood apart from the rest. His presence brought the total of the group to five, and his carriage contrasted sharply with the pitiable quality of the others. From the look of him, the stranger was an aristocrat as well as a soldier. No one else would take so grand a stance nor bear so jagged a scar across one hip, undoubtedly the result of a sword taken in battle.

Judging him in a detached manner as she would a prize horse, Alanna noted the clean, hard lines of his flesh, appreciating the length of his legs and the breadth of his chest. His well-defined features were proud, his expression hinting at a fiery spirit. Begrudgingly, she marked him a magnificent figure of a fighting man even if the possibility existed that he might have been spawned in Spain. Her blue eyes followed the fine, dark hair that covered his chest and narrowed downward to a slender line only to fan out again. Alanna was struck once more by the man's well-proportioned body, though it was apparent that in some aspects, nature had been most generous.

The fact that he was being held prisoner in a hostile keep had not cowed him one bit, nor did his nudity. Instead, he returned Alanna's cool, appraising stare with one of his own, causing the young widow to feel as though she were the one who stood unclothed before his green, probing eyes. She blushed and pulled the modest English nightgown to her more closely, whereupon he issued a lazy smile and a nod of his head.

Alanna silently cursed him for his arrogance and was about to voice her feelings when Grady's insistent words brought her back to the task at hand.

"On with it, girl," her uncle commanded. "Find out who they are, and more importantly what they are doing here. And God have mercy on them if I like not their answers."

"God's mercy will be all they can hope for," added Cordelia, who had joined her husband and stood perched like a hawk at his shoulder. "They won't get any from us."

"*Qui estis?* Who are you?" Alanna inquired in stilted Latin, choosing to ignore the insolent man who had so unnerved her and to address the remaining cluster of prisoners instead. It had been years since she had uttered this ancient tongue in anything other than prayer or hymn, and concentration was a necessity.

"We are but poor seamen who have lost our way." The husky voice forced Alanna's attention back once more to the man who had elected to isolate himself from the others. Like his form, his Latin was distinctive.

"You are the one who will speak for all?" Alanna asked quietly, fighting to control the breathy quality of her voice that the man's presence seemed to inspire.

"I am," he responded simply. His piercing green eyes locked Alanna's to his own, commanding her attention so that she was unable to look away.

Being the daughter of Curran Desmond, and so related to Gerald Fitzgerald himself, Alanna's life among her own people had always been a free one. But in addition, her beautiful face and fine hair had persuaded men to treat her as though she was special, a woman to be cossetted and given her head. No man, not even her husband, had ever dared to attempt imposing such strong-willed control upon her as this prisoner did now. Unused to an attitude such as his, Alanna desperately fought the sensation this man called forth. She felt like a salmon in the icy stream fighting the line meant to pull it to shore where it would be devoured as surely as this stranger would devour her if given the chance.

His hair with its wayward curls, dark as any raven's wing, marked him as a creature of the night, but the golden skin of his face, chest and arms, sun kissed as it was, proclaimed him an entity of the day. He was a study in contradictions, this stranger, with his alluring good looks and the spark of danger that glowed in his eyes. It was the easy air of dominance he wore so casually, however, that troubled Alanna the most, and she shivered in spite of the warm material enveloping her.

What did she have to fear? she chided herself, trying to gain control of the situation once more. This was merely a weaponless, unclad man whom she faced in the safety of her own kinsman's hall.

Yet all the same, it *was* danger that lurked in those sea green eyes of his, and Alanna was not fool enough to ignore it. Mustering her strength, she composed herself to start the questioning anew, but was interrupted before she could begin.

"What is this place where my fellows and I find ourselves so shabbily treated?" he asked boldly, as though it were he in control.

"I will ask the questions here," Alanna responded, determination glinting in her eyes. "Now what is your name, and which nation claims you as her own?"

He regarded her for a moment, as though considering how he should answer. And then he spoke, his rich, deep voice echoing slightly in the stillness of the hall.

"I am Lucas Rafael del Fuentes," he said with a proud jut of his chin. "My homeland and that of my fellows is Spain. And who are you? The daughter of the household?"

"Who I am is of no importance," Alanna retorted, her hatred of the Spanish wiping away any consideration she might have had for a band of outsiders who found themselves in such perilous straits.

"Ah, but you underrate yourself," Lucas intoned smoothly. The girl was obviously educated, though there were things Lucas would have enjoyed teaching her. She had the face of a Madonna, but there was something of the temptress about her nonetheless. Her rich, honey-colored hair, disarrayed from her slumber, curled around her face and hung unbound down her slender back. No matter how primly she was clothed, an air of wildness and freedom clung to her, as though she had galloped with the wind. And yet for all her untamed beauty, Lucas was aware that he had never seen a woman more regal, not even at Philip's court. Had their positions been reversed and she were his captive, Lucas del Fuentes knew he would be tempted to ask her questions of a far different nature than the ones she was demanding he answer.

"Let me assure you, Spaniard, I neither underestimate myself nor you. What has brought you to Irish soil?" Alanna managed to stay aloof while struggling to keep memories of Sean and her father at bay. Yet how could she not recall their unnecessary deaths eight years ago? How could she fail to remember that it had been the Spanish who were ultimately to blame?

Lucas keenly observed the different emotions that played across the girl's exquisite face. Right now his life and those of the others depended on his wits and his warrior's instincts, not on the enchantment cast by his interrogator's large blue eyes. He could not allow himself to be distracted into revealing something that would destroy them all. Now was the time to exercise extreme care, and as the experienced soldier he was, Lucas knew nothing should matter but survival.

"I will ask you once more," Alanna snapped, her disposition becoming more fiery in the face of this man's impudence, "what brings you here?"

"After a fierce storm blew us off course, it was the promise of fresh water and food that lured us to your beautiful homeland," Lucas said. Then he raised one mocking eyebrow and added dryly, "However, it was the hospitality of your own home that persuaded us to stay."

The man had to be mad, Alanna decided, to treat his situation so blithely, either that or admirably brave. But such a possibility was one she wished to disregard, just as she wished to ignore Mananaan MacLir's capriciousness, if the Spaniard was to be believed, in bringing this newest peril to Ireland's shores rather than the riches his legend promised.

"What have you learned?" interrupted an anxious Grady. "Who are they and why did we find them on MacWilliams lands?"

"He has admitted they are Spanish," Alanna told her uncle, switching to English. "As for their purpose, he has still told me nothing other than to offer mundane excuses for their presence. He says they landed only to replenish their supplies."

"Spanish, did you say? I told you!" Cordelia exclaimed. "How dare they invade MacWilliams holdings? Let us put an end to their miserable existence as quickly as possible." The eerie shadows cast on the walls by the torches and the renewed growling of the dogs made her demands seem all the more macabre.

Studying Lucas del Fuentes, Alanna was satisfied that her aunt and uncle had been correct in their assumption. None of the foreigners understood a word of English, not even their educated spokesman. The Spaniard hadn't flinched at Cordelia's demand for the immediate execution of the prisoners, so Alanna discounted the need for caution when her uncle or his wife spoke their minds in front of him.

"We cannot execute them, Cordelia, until we find out why they are here," Grady said. "We've all heard word of the fleet Philip sent against Elizabeth. If these men are part of that enterprise, I want to know what has happened.

What if they have been successful in their attack on England and have now turned their attentions here?''

"All the more reason to slay them," the mistress of the keep countered.

While Grady and Cordelia debated the issue, Alanna watched the group of prisoners. Most of them were fearful about their fate, and appealed silently to her for some sort of aid. Before she could stop it, Alanna felt a small stirring of pity, but she fought against the unsettling emotion, combating it with the loyalty she held to the memories of her father and Sean. They would be alive today, living prosperously in their own land, had Philip of Spain kept his promise and sent reinforcements to Smerwick when James Fitzmaurice, Captain of Desmond, had taken his rebellious stand against the English. As it was, Spain had sent only empty words and one small, inexperienced company of men, and they had been mostly Italians, at that. The result was that the British had easily wrested a victory. And the Queen's forces had been quick to make an example of the insurgents. Smerwick had become the site of a slaughter so brutal and dishonorable that even Ireland had never seen the like. From that day on, Alanna had hated Spain as much as she hated England.

Her heart must be growing soft, she rebuked herself amid visions of the horrible deaths suffered by her father and Sean, to have ever felt an inkling of sympathy for these treacherous Spaniards. Still, something within her resisted her desire to add her voice to Cordelia's demand for their deaths. Perhaps it was her sense of honor, of right and wrong, or at the very least her natural inclination to disagree with her uncle's wife on any issue. This was a possibility emphasized by her aunt's very next words.

"Let them know that we are loyal subjects of Elizabeth and not *mere* Irish," Cordelia insisted without any regard for the feelings of either her spouse or his niece. "That might put the fear of almighty God into them!"

"Perhaps, my dove, it would be best to lead them to believe we have rebel leanings," Grady insisted with patience worthy of any saint. ''Then their information might flow more freely.''

''No sacrifice is too great to make for our most gracious sovereign, but that is still a tremendous request you ask of me, Grady MacWilliams. Besides, why try to pass yourself off as some unholy rebel lord when a Spaniard who is a friend is no more to be trusted than one who is a foe? Even your argumentative niece would say aye to that.''

Though he desired nothing more than to wrap his fingers around the yapping woman's throat, Grady won the battle to control his anger, his thoughts now on Smerwick as he tasted the bitter memories and cursed beneath his breath. So many dead, and for what? Alanna's father and husband may have been rebels, but no Irishman deserved the death they had suffered, and all for believing Philip of Spain. As he continued his conversation with his wife, Grady vowed not to make the same mistake. ''Mayhap you are right, dearest love. The Spanish are not to be trusted. I merely sought to learn as quickly as possible whether the men in our grasp plan our destruction through invasion or friendship. However, I will accede to your wishes and not play the rebel for their benefit.''

At Grady's groveling words, Alanna became incensed. Who cared if her uncle's wife was a distant relative to Black Tom, Earl of Ormand and cousin to the English Queen? That fact did not make Cordelia the Queen of Ireland, nor did it give her the right to have her every whim granted. And it certainly didn't entitle her to besmirch the honor of *Radharc Alainn,* call it by any name the harridan would. Though Alanna judged both English and Spanish to care little about integrity, she was not about to allow this Anglo witch to further desecrate the ancestral MacWilliams home by ignoring tradition. It was an accepted practice to offer families of captured noblemen the opportunity to ransom them, no matter their nationality.

But Alanna knew deep down inside that it was not merely tradition that concerned her. Though the riches themselves meant little to her, she regretted that no *eraic,* or blood money, had ever been sought for the deaths of her

husband and father. Compensation for sparing the lives of
these foreigners could take its place, honoring as they
should be honored the memories of Curran Desmond and
Sean O'Donnell, the man who had been her foster father's
son and her husband. With this possibility before her, it
would be unseemly if the slaughter of the men she had
loved was now to be paid for by the execution of this
wretched group of Spaniards. Her father and Sean were
worth more than that. It was this feeling that caused
Alanna to attempt to thwart her uncle's wife and her insistence upon death for the prisoners.

"Surely I have less love for the Spanish than either of
you," the young woman began. "However, I have a very
practical nature. Why murder these pathetic beings, when
surely at least the nobles could be held for ransom as befits
their rank? Why soil your hands with their blood when you
can line your pockets with their gold?"

The comment elicited a gleam of greed in Grady's eyes
and gave Lucas a sense of satisfaction. The girl had brought
up the idea of ransom without his prompting. That was
quite promising. But before the issue could be discussed
between uncle and niece, one of Castlemount's men burst
into the hall.

"My lord," he managed to get out between gasps for
breath, "I have news. We have learned that a Spanish ship
called the *Santa Maria Encoronada* has put into Blacksod
Bay. And, my lord, she is a ship of war! The captain has
disembarked his men, and they have taken a small fortress. There are also rumors that other ships have been
sighted along the coast. Mother of God preserve us, but the
Spanish are attacking!"

Alanna wheeled around to confront Lucas del Fuentes,
all thoughts of his redemption forgotten. But she only received an insolent though questioning stare in return. She
had forgotten that he did not understand what had been
said in English, and so she reverted to Latin once more.

"On your way home when a storm blew your ship off
course, were you?" she hissed. "Then why is a warship

sitting in Blacksod Bay, northwest of here? Were you under orders to take Ireland?"

"My pretty Irish maiden, what I told you is the truth. We were sailing back to Spain when we decided to put in here for food and water."

"I don't believe you," she yelled, "and don't call me your pretty Irish maiden. I am no maiden at all, but a wife made a widow at Smerwick by the empty promises of Spain!"

"For that," he said quietly, his voice sincere for the first time in their conversation, "I am truly sorry."

"What is he saying?" Grady demanded.

"Nothing," Alanna replied, brushing off the foreigner's sympathy. "He only repeats his story and denies an invasion."

"I don't care what he says," Cordelia argued. "While there is the slightest doubt as to what has happened, allowing these men to remain alive might be construed as an act of treason. Then even my connections with the Earl of Ormand will not be enough to save you."

Cordelia paused, noting with satisfaction the look of uncertainty on Grady's face. "Besides," she added triumphantly, "the ransom means little. What need have you of Spanish gold when you are certain to be rewarded by the Crown for so loyal an action as disposing of the Queen's enemies? Death for them, I say!"

Grady weighed his wife's words. Though he doubted he would ever see so much as a single coin from the parsimonious Elizabeth, if indeed she still ruled England, the execution of his prisoners was perhaps the safest course of action. After all, who but his own people even knew these men were here?

"Very well. We will hang them in the morning," he decreed, surprising his niece, though she offered no resistance to his decision. "Alanna, tell them so."

Yes, tell me, Alanna, Lucas thought bitterly, though he managed to hide his emotions in the face of understanding all that had been spoken in his mother's native tongue. Yet a part of him nonetheless pitied the young woman who had thought to offer the idea of ransom as an alternative to their deaths.

Lucas had a sense she would be sorry to see them dead despite her bitter feelings concerning Smerwick. He fancied he saw traces of compassion in her eyes even now, while she struggled to find a way to inform him of their fate. How strange, he decided, to find such a jewel in so rough a setting as this semibarbaric keep.

For her part, Alanna swallowed deeply as she somberly studied the Spaniard's handsome face. He deserved execution for his duplicity, she told herself. Hadn't the messenger's speech proved just that? But still, it was difficult to release the words that would seal Lucas del Fuentes's doom.

"What are you to me?" Alanna murmured softly in English, more to herself than to him. "I will forget about your demise more easily than I have forgotten about the deaths of so many others."

"Stop mumbling in that barbaric tongue of yours and speak to me in a civilized language that I can understand," Lucas said arrogantly in Latin, his pride unable to bear her pity. Though he deplored the fact that it was she who had to pronounce his death sentence and those of his men, he found that now it was established, he wanted it over with, and quickly.

"Do not seek to command me," Alanna retorted, her sympathy turning into temper at being prompted to perform a task she found distasteful. "You'll find out what I have to say all too soon, and be none the happier for it."

"There is nothing you can tell me that would make me any unhappier than finding myself detained so crudely in your desolate and godforsaken country."

"Know then, Spaniard, that you and your men are scheduled to die come morning," Alanna replied quietly. A whimper from the other prisoners alerted her to the fact that at least one more of them understood Latin.

"So this is Irish honor?" Lucas asked. "To murder foreign noblemen rather than ransom them as is only fitting and right? What they say about the Irish is true."

"The only honor I know is what it takes to survive. The Irish have become very good at that these last few decades, and we will do whatever is necessary to maintain that honor, such as it is."

"Including the killing of innocent men?"

"Whatever."

"Can't you reason with the lord of this keep?" Lucas demanded, trying to build an alliance with this woman. "What he is doing defies civility and morality. It is against the laws of God and man. Will you do nothing to save us, gentle lady?" Lucas asked. His voice grew soft and warm even as the chill of Castlemount's stone walls pierced his unclad flesh.

"I am disinclined to undertake fruitless tasks," Alanna responded coldly, desperately trying to block out the emotions of the moment, emotions that arose both from the situation at hand and from the effect the Spaniard's deep voice and well-muscled form had upon her.

Lucas misread the reason for her seeming callousness. All he knew was that he was a man condemned to death, a man who had stupidly pitied the woman forced to inform him of the fact. Yet she appeared to be unbothered by the telling. He felt betrayed by a pair of blue eyes, and he gave way to the anger welling within him.

"What is it to be, hanged, drawn and quartered?" he asked with a condescending sneer that said more than words ever could about his opinion of Irish integrity. Damnation, he thought as he regarded Alanna dispassionately, he could have sworn he had seen some compassion lurking in the girl's eyes, or at least a degree of regret. Yet here she stood, an ice maiden who had just calmly announced their executions with as little feeling as she would command the slaughter of a sheep to grace her table. Her demeanor dashed all Lucas's hopes. There would be no help from her quarter.

"I believe you will simply be hanged," Alanna replied. Once more ambivalence in the matter swept through her heart, and she gave way to the only gesture of solace she was willing to make. "If you like, I will send you my confessor."

"Keep your priest," the proud Spaniard growled in response.

"Think before you answer," Alanna cautioned. "He may be of some comfort to your men."

"My men want only what I allow them."

"And you? Have you no need to be shriven? Have you never done anything wrong?" she asked with growing disdain. How dare this man make her the object of his wrath? Was it her fault he and his men had landed on Grady's beach and been captured? Ireland was cruel to those who called it home. Should foreigners fare any better?

"I have sinned like most men," Lucas said, his words and manner chilling, "but unlike the rest, I do not regret any of it."

"Then farewell, Lucas del Fuentes, and may God have mercy on your soul."

"And may God have mercy on your children, my lady, if they resemble you in their heartlessness or your kinswoman in their looks," Lucas rejoined with a nod in Cordelia's direction.

Alanna's steely glare was the only response he received before she turned her back on him as he and his band were led away to the dungeon in the belly of the keep.

It *was* only fitting that the Spaniards be executed, Alanna tried to convince herself as she sought to ignore the sounds of their being herded from the central chamber. Still, she couldn't deny that the events of this night had proved most disturbing. Now, all she wanted was to flee the Great Hall and depart Castlemount as soon as possible. But suddenly, a dreadful realization struck her. If Spain was attacking the western coast of Ireland, Grady would never allow her to leave his protection.

The thought of remaining at Castlemount during a war, when the possibility of a rebel alliance with Spain was a very real one, was more frightening to Alanna than the consequences of war itself. She had seen death, she had experienced uprising, but she had never known what it was to be in an Anglo keep during such a time. How could she stay here if her uncle Grady joined forces with the English and the rebels supported the Spanish? How could she stand helplessly by while her countrymen were slaughtered? God above, she had to persuade Grady to permit her departure as scheduled. She *had* to!

"Uncle," Alanna began tentatively, "you don't really believe these rumors of an attack by Spain, do you?"

"That remains to be seen," the MacWilliams said gravely.

"But I'm certain the men in your dungeon are not part of an invasion force."

"Are you asking my husband for clemency?" Cordelia snapped before Grady could reply. "Because if you think to do so—"

"That's not it at all," Alanna interrupted.

"Why speak of the captives, then?" the MacWilliams asked, his manner softening when he recognized his sister's likeness imprinted on the girl's lovely features.

Alanna hesitated. How could she tell this man that in the event of war, she wanted to be among the rebel O'Donnells? But, it was something she had to do. Perhaps, though, she could couch her desire in words Grady would find acceptable.

"Dear Grady, you have been most good to me," Alanna said gently, ignoring Cordelia's snort of agreement. "And it is because of your generosity that I feel I can no longer impose. We have received no word of any skirmishes or approaching army. Surely circumstances are safe enough for me to travel to my foster father's home. I must leave tomorrow as I proposed to do."

Alanna found that with these last words she was unable to meet Grady's questioning gaze, and she stood quietly, mustering her arguments and waiting for the objections that she was certain would follow.

"What poppycock!" Cordelia spouted, her loud, rasping voice reminiscent of a screeching crow.

"But—"

"There are to be no buts about it, girl, no buts at all. You must do as you had planned, and be on your way tomorrow. Though if you were safely wed, there would be no question of your needing protection. Your husband would see to it. Am I not right, Grady?"

"Why, y-yes," a scarlet-faced Grady sputtered in agreement. "What I mean is of course you must go. After all, we cannot hoard you all to ourselves. It wouldn't be meet to deny Kevin O'Donnell your company," he added, the shameful secret he kept causing his face to grow redder still. "I've no doubt but that it will be safe enough for you to travel. There will be no danger..." He faltered before going on resolutely, "No danger at all from the Spanish."

Alanna's eyes widened slightly in disbelief. She had thought it certain that Grady would have forbidden her leaving. But apparently Cordelia was as anxious to see her gone as she, herself, was to quit Castlemount. Not stopping to question her good fortune, Alanna once more bade her uncle farewell and turned to make her way to her chamber, hoping to salvage some sleep during what remained of this tumultuous night.

"Oh, Alanna," came Cordelia's strident voice across the now empty hall, "one moment."

"Yes?" queried the young woman.

"Will you be staying for the hangings in the morning?" Her tone and demeanor were the quintessential embodiment of the perfect hostess except for the grim smile that played about her thin lips.

"I think not," Alanna responded, her voice chillier than any winter's freeze.

"Ah, 'tis a pity to miss such an event." Cordelia sighed. "But I suppose as time goes on, there will be plenty of executions for you to see."

Chapter Three

Lucas sat alone in a cramped, filthy cell. Pounding his hand into his fist, he once more sought a plan of escape.

Before the thought had even formed, however, he discounted making his English heritage known to the lord of this obviously Anglo-Irish keep. No matter his mother's nationality and his ability to speak her native tongue, he was Spanish and had taken part in Philip's Great Enterprise against England. To attempt to claim otherwise in an effort to save his life and those of his men would be a breach of honor, and for Lucas, his honor was something that belonged to Spain. It was not his to give away as he chose, regardless of the reason.

The darkness of MacWilliams's dungeon was no worse, no more distasteful to him than the blackness of Irish hearts. And the girl, the fair Alanna, was the worst offender of them all. What was it about this dismal land that could so embitter such a beauty? Or was her lack of sympathy and charity a natural state for women bred here? Whatever the answer, she was nothing like the warm and loving women he had known. Yet Lucas couldn't help but suspect a capacity for love smoldered beneath her cold exterior, just waiting to be fanned before it burst into flames hot enough to consume any man.

No matter which way he considered her, she was an enigma. At first, he had thought to use her tender years and gentle sex to his advantage, but she had proved too hard-

ened, too elusive for that. True, she had been the one to
broach the topic of ransom instead of execution, but she
had acquiesced quickly enough when her suggestion had
been dismissed. Then there was that business of her husband. If she blamed Philip for his death, that meant the
man had fought with the Irish against their English mas-
ters. Yet here she was, a rebel bride residing in a distinctly
Anglo keep. Just where did her loyalties lie, or did she have
any at all? Was she the sort to give herself to the victor, not
caring who or what he was?

But what was he doing thinking of that wench? Alanna
was no concern of his, and if things progressed as Mac-
Williams had ordained, Lucas knew he would never have
to deal with her again. She was nothing more than a bitter
memory to be forgotten while he struggled against the approaching dawn, desperate to find some means of escape.

However, no matter how Lucas tried to evade images of
the bewitching Alanna, they assailed him all the same. In
frustration he berated himself. What he needed now was a
sympathetic accomplice, and Alanna would never willingly be that. She might look like an angel, but without
mercy, as she was, the woman lacked a soul. Yet perhaps,
he thought, a lazy smile spreading across his face as this last
idea sparked another and a plan began to form, she *could*
be of use, after all, she and her offer of a priest. Quickly,
he set about working out the details.

"*Gracias*, Alanna," he whispered, "for all of the help
you are about to give, unwilling and unaware as you may
be."

"Lady Alanna, wake up," spoke a hesitant voice in the
darkness broken by a single taper. As a scullery maid, Me-
gan was not permitted in the main keep, but Padraic had
convinced her that this was an emergency. Even so, if the
MacWilliams found her, she would be beaten for certain.
Anxious not to awaken the sleeping Moira, Megan touched
Alanna's shoulder gently and repeated her whispered cry.
"Milady, wake up, please."

For a second time that night, Alanna became aware of an unwelcome voice and moaned softly. Though she would be the first to admit she had slept little since returning to her room, she was certainly not ready to rise for the day. As often as she had attempted to banish the image of Lucas del Fuentes from her mind, the memory of his bold green eyes and aristocratic stance haunted her. He had acted as fiercely as if it were her life at stake rather than his. Indeed, the few minutes' sleep she had snatched were wrought with nightmarish scenes of Sean waiting for the promised Spanish troops, which never arrived to help defend Smerwick. Then, bewilderingly, in the last minute of the dream before her husband was killed by the British, his clean-shaven face and bright blue eyes disappeared and she was weeping for the golden Spaniard with the black beard and trim mustache.

"Lady Alanna, you must pay me some heed." Megan's voice took on a pleading note as MacWilliams's niece murmured insensibly and nestled farther into the bedclothes. "Milady, them foreigners is making a terrible row, all hollering and yelling at once, calling your name. Cedric, the head guard, is drunk and says he'll kill them himself and not wait for morning. My man, Padraic, says maybe you could help since you talked to them before. Please hurry before Cedric starts his bloody work."

When the serving girl's words penetrated Alanna's drowsy haze, she was up and moving in an instant, her feet finding her soft kid boots. Pushing her hair away from her face, she laced the English nightdress she hadn't bothered to change, perhaps another reason sleep had been so elusive. Squeezing the maid's hand, Alanna spoke reassuringly.

"I'll do my best, but I don't understand the Spaniards all that well."

"Padraic said you were the only one who could get any sense from them," whispered the lass as she lighted the way through the darkened corridor toward the back tower. At the top of the stairs that led down to the dungeon, Megan

halted and handed the candle to Alanna. "Padraic is waiting for you. God be with you."

Inching her way cautiously downward, Alanna shook her
head at the strident calls she heard before she had taken
even a dozen steps. Despite the thick stone walls of Castlemount, the men's voices were easily audible, though barely
intelligible. Her name was mentioned, perhaps, and was it
padre or *pater?* Had Lucas reconsidered the need for a
priest, after all?

How common it is, thought Alanna, that the most
steadfast of men grow panicked at the approach of death.
In war-ravaged Ireland, she had seen more than enough
butchery, and though she understood that the enemy might
deserve death, she was glad that she would be gone before
these prisoners were hanged, no matter how treacherous
their deeds.

As she reached the last step and entered the confines of
the MacWilliams prison, Alanna realized that Lucas's voice
was not to be heard among those caterwauling. Had Cedric already killed him? Then Padraic led her forward and
she saw the foolishness of her concern. Lucas Rafael del
Fuentes was standing proudly aloof in a separate cell, both
physically and emotionally removed from those bellowing
men he commanded.

"*Silencio!*" His sudden bark cut the sounds like a knife
through fresh-churned butter, and at once the men quieted, moving away from the bars to the rear of their cell.

Waving Padraic and a sullen Cedric aside, the Irish
woman went toward the last of the dungeon's cells, the one
that quartered Lucas. As she approached the isolated male,
he made an exaggerated bow. Obviously he did want
something, after all.

"How kind of you to come calling, gentle lady. I am
sorry I cannot entertain you properly, but my circumstances are rather strained at present." Above the bearded
cheeks, Lucas's eyes seemed to laugh at her. His Latin was
much less stilted than hers had been earlier, but he might
have rehearsed his greeting.

"I venture to say *restrained* might be a more fitting description," she corrected softly. In another setting, Alanna would have found him an interesting man. The combination of emerald eyes and honeyed skin was as fascinating now as when she had first seen it. But once again his glance arrogantly devoured her, making her feel as though she had no secrets from him. If he had but known the dreams that had haunted her...

What was she thinking? The two of them were foreigners, barely communicating in a language natural to neither. Yet, as he licked his lips, his tongue briefly edging the hairs on his upper lip, and began to speak again, Alanna reacted as a woman to a man, his very presence dominating her thoughts until she barely heard his words. Idly she wondered again about the scar at his hip, feeling the strangest impulse to trace its jagged outline, when she caught mention of her name and tried fruitlessly to recall what he had said.

"I—I'm sorry, I'm afraid I did not understand that last," she said. "Could you repeat that?"

"Lady Alanna, I have reconsidered your offer of a priest and ask that you send your friar to hear our confessions before we die today. Since but a short time remains before dawn, I think it best we take care of the matter at once."

"Oh, then you've reexamined your conscience and decided to repent? I'm surprised," Alanna admitted with a touch of disappointment. She had believed the Spaniard beyond second thoughts, determined and consistent, never the sort to look back with regrets. Perhaps, she realized, that was what had drawn her admiration, no matter how unwillingly she gave it.

"Don't misunderstand. I am only sorry for the things in life I *haven't* done, not those I have. However, I feel a certain responsibility to my men, and they crave the services of a cleric. Your heretic uncle ordered their rosaries taken away, and at this point, they deeply need the comfort of their faith. At least the priest can offer them the consolation of everlasting life even if he can do nothing for them in this world," he explained sardonically.

"Then I shouldn't direct Friar Galen to *your* cell?"

"Given a choice, I'd prefer the welcoming arms of a beautiful female to the prayerfully folded ones of a balding, judgmental cleric any day. But I don't suppose you would provide a confessor for the others and a courtesan for me, would you?" While his stance and the tone of his voice were exactly proper, even formal, the corners of Lucas's mouth curled upward as his emerald eyes provocatively traveled the length of her once again. Before Alanna could respond to this latest outrage, he shook his head and frowned.

"No, of course not. I can see this soggy climate would dampen the desires of any female bred here. How could I expect an Irish woman to warm a man when the only ones I have seen are so very cold? And I won't spend eternity in the hellfires of damnation for a less than satisfactory coupling. Of that I assure you." When only silence greeted his condemnation of Eire's womanhood, Lucas heaved an exasperated sigh. "Since I appear to have no other choice, you may as well send the priest."

"I'll dispatch my friar at once, Lucas del Fuentes. You sorely need his prayers, despite your opinion otherwise. It is clear the state of your soul is in dire peril."

"No more than my physical being is, but thank you, milady, for your concern. Actually, I rather imagined you would want me to rot in hell, but from the way you've stared at my unclad body, I believe the image of it in flames would distress even you."

Leaving Alanna open-mouthed at his implication, Lucas turned his back to her and moved slowly toward the pallet near the wall. He was content that his plan had worked. The more irreverently he acted, the more determined the lovely Alanna had become to send him her confessor. The priest was coming; that was all that mattered. In truth, though, if he really was going to die in a few hours, Lucas reflected, he would certainly prefer to spend the night sinning with Alanna than repenting with a clergyman.

"Bastard," muttered Alanna in English, as Padraic approached. "Of all the insensitive, arrogant, lewd creatures I have ever encountered, that one is the worst. He deserves to be hanged, but slowly, after being torn limb from limb by animals as wild as himself. Still, I will not condemn his soul to hell if he hasn't already done so himself.

"Padraic, go and awaken Friar Galen. That man is especially in need of a priest, and if we don't hurry, the sun will rise and set before he finishes listing all his sins. Tell the friar that I know it is early, but he is to come at once and hear these confessions. If he complains too bitterly, inform him he should consider it penance for the fine food and drink he's enjoyed here at Castlemount. When he's finished hearing the confessions, he is to rouse my men. Moira and I will pack and see to the necessary provisions and we'll join him in the courtyard. I want to be away before the sun is fully up." Without a backward glance at the Spaniard who surreptitiously watched her departure, Alanna gathered up the skirt of her nightdress and departed.

Padraic was about to follow when Cedric stopped him.

"Once you've gotten the cleric, get yourself a few hours rest, Padraic. This crew is quiet now, and for sure they won't give the priest no trouble," the head jailer instructed, swaying slightly as he took a sip of *poitin* and wiped his mouth with the back of his hand. "At least, nothing I can't handle."

On her return upstairs, Alanna smiled at the lightly snoring figure of Moira, still undisturbed despite the visitor to her chamber. How unfortunate that when her serving woman was nearly deaf, her only nighttime callers were females, the pretty widow thought with a frown. Undoubtedly, if there ever came a time she wanted privacy for a rendezvous, it wouldn't be hers.

Shaking her head at the mysterious twists the threads of her life had taken, Alanna decided to dress and see to the staples they would need for the journey to the O'Donnell holdings. Since her party was not due to leave for another hour or two, Moira might as well sleep as long as possible. The four-day trip south to Grady's keep had been hard on the old woman, insisting as she had on still sitting a horse rather than riding in a cart. The dear thing admitted to having seen seventy summers, so only the Lord knew how old she really was, though Alanna had decided this was the last journey her father's nurse would make with her, no matter what her protestations. It was well past time for Moira to take her place by the warmth of the fire in Kevin's keep and snooze or gossip as suited her fancy.

Removing the harsh cotton gown that Cordelia had foisted on her, Alanna bound up her blond tresses and reached for the glazed ewer and bowl to freshen up. She washed quickly, wanting only to erase the feel of the Spaniard's eyes roving over her body. Yet even as she ran the damp cloth lightly across her breasts, her nipples stood proudly as if for his ardent inspection. Damn, would she never be rid of image of that man? She had thought him gone from her life twice already tonight, but her body evidently didn't discount him so easily.

Shortly after dawn, answered an unbidden thought, he'll be removed from your life and his own, when he mounts the gibbet your uncle's men are fixing even now.

By all that is holy, what is that Spaniard to me? bristled Alanna. No matter how attractive, he was *still* Spanish! Besides, she would be gone before his last breath was taken.

Once again reassuring herself that the Spaniards deserved death for allowing her husband and father to be massacred on that cold November day at Smerwick, Alanna deliberately closed her mind to Lucas del Fuentes. Fingering the soft cloth of her Celtic dress, so simple in its sheathlike cut, so symbolic of the strength in simplicity, she began to mentally list the foodstuffs she wanted from the kitchens.

On his way to the MacWilliams dungeon, Friar Galen grumbled, descending the stone steps to a chamber even damper than his own. He had helped Curran Desmond's daughter with many unusual charities since being appointed her confessor, but this had to be among the strangest requests she had ever made of him. A tinker's dam these confessions would mean when he could not understand the penitents and they would not be able to grasp his admonitions, counseling or penance!

Still, the priest reflected as he motioned for the drowsy-eyed, inebriated Cedric to go to the farthest cell, death seemed penance enough for any sin, and the fact that the men wanted absolution had to be taken into consideration.

Besides, maybe it was better he didn't comprehend their soldierly wrongdoings, he thought suddenly. After being accustomed to the confessions of Alanna and her serving women, he wasn't certain he was prepared to hear men's sins again. But he had no choice, he supposed. Draping the sacramental stole about his neck, Friar Galen motioned Cedric to unlock the cell, stepped inside and waved the guard away, surprised when he resisted.

"Privacy is the preferred condition for a true confession," he reminded the jailer. "For the sake of this man's immortal soul, be off with you. I will call when I'm ready to go on to the rest of them."

Nodding reluctantly, Cedric backed away after locking the cell and eying Lucas carefully, though he saw nothing untoward in his demeanor.

Acknowledging the prisoner with a nod, Galen knelt on the damp stone floor, praying he would be able to rise again. When the Spaniard remained seated on his pallet, he gestured for the man to kneel before him.

Lucas complied with the friar's direction, but remained silent, prompting the cleric to begin.

"In nomine patris, et filii et spiritus sancti, amen." To his surprise, the prisoner answered in Latin.

"Benedicemei, Pater . . . for I have sinned." The formula was traditional, and while Lucas did not intend to complete the rite of confession, the words came automatically. Keeping his eyes downcast as he spoke, Lucas did his best to appear remorseful and nervous.

"Our Lord has promised all sins will be forgiven if you sincerely repent and promise to avoid such wrongdoing in the future, short as yours may be. In what way have you failed to live a good life?" Relieved that he would be able to offer comfort to at least one of the men, Galen was more vocal than usual.

"I am sorry to admit them, Father, but please remember that mine has been the raucous life of a soldier, though most recently I have fought for the honor of Our Lady." When the friar made no reply, Lucas continued. "Well, in addition to the usual cursing, fornicating and killing that most soldiers engage in, the Lord must also judge me for striking a cleric." Still in the role of penitent, Lucas had to fight back a chuckle at the friar's gasp.

"My word, what would induce you to do such a thing?" Galen asked, wiping his brow with the purple stole of his office. "Why ever would you attack a holy man?"

"Only to save my life." For the first time Lucas looked directly at the cleric, his green eyes surprising the priest.

"And when was this?"

"Now!" In a single fluid motion, Lucas was on his feet, but the blow he delivered to Galen started from the kneeling position and effectively lifted the man off his knees, throwing him backward onto the pallet against the far wall. Without wasting a moment, Lucas stripped the friar, donned his sandals and habit, short as it was, pulled up its hood and called for the guard, speaking English for the first time in the MacWilliams keep.

"Cedric!"

It was almost child's play, acknowledged Lucas with a grin as he met the guard with a hard left hook to the jaw, knocking him to the floor with great pleasure. Quickly he scooped up the keys that had fallen from his hand and secured him in the cell with the priest, who, though unconscious, was breathing normally. Now, he thought, moving hurriedly, to release the others and find some horses.

"Pedro, there is a pile of clothes over by the guard's station. See what you can find for everyone to wear and then meet me in the stable yard. I'll wear the cleric's robe for the time being, but be quick if you want to get out of here alive. And, Juan, don't hold us back."

"But these are peasant's rags, del Fuentes. How can I dress in something so unstylish, not to mention filthy, as this?" protested the king's godson.

"Does it make any more sense for me to wear the clothes of a religious?" snapped Lucas, angered once again by *El Pavoreal*'s imperious attitude. "Look, I've gotten us free of the cells, but we've yet to escape these walls. If the clothes don't suit you, stay behind."

Alanna moved about the kitchen comfortably. Though she doubted that Cordelia would be able to locate even a tub of butter, Alanna enjoyed domestic chores. To her aunt's constant dismay, the girl was often found talking to the servants and learning a new method of curing meats or preserving game. Living as she did, dependent on the age-old skills of hunting, fishing and gardening instead of seeking favors from the English, Alanna had cause to master the art of managing a keep. Though widowed eight years now, she had declined various offers of marriage, preferring instead to oversee her foster father's household rather than marry a man who could never compare to her lost Sean. Being a contributing member of Kevin's family made her feel much more useful than sitting by Cordelia's fire embroidering yet another sheet.

At the thought of her uncle's wife, Alanna silently gave thanks for whatever it was that prompted Grady's acceptance of her departure. She certainly wasn't about to question her good fortune that rumors of the invasion would

not keep her at Castlemount even one more day. She had
been among the English long enough. Now she craved the
cooler air and friendly warmth of Ulster, where Kevin's
people at Donegal Bay were dear to her.

As she acknowledged the vast difference between her life
with the MacWilliams and her life with Kevin O'Donnell,
Alanna moved off toward the cold cellar for cheese, potatoes and roots. She passed the door to the outside and was
amazed to see her horse, Piobar, saddled and ready in the
courtyard. Going to the outside step of the kitchen, she was
even more startled to see Friar Galen leading two more
horses out of the stable. Had the Spaniards' confessions so
shocked the man that he forgot his distaste for chores not
directly church related? Perhaps he didn't know it was not
yet five and too early to depart, but if he wanted to be
helpful, he could raise her men and let them see to the
horses.

Alanna was about to call out to him until she realized
how her voice would echo in the stone courtyard. Grabbing the cloak she had worn from the main tower to the
kitchens, she decided it would be better to go out and speak
with the cleric rather than scream like a fishwife and wake
the entire household.

But as the young woman reached the horses, there was no
sign of her priest. He had apparently gone back into the
stable to ready the other animals. Since when had he become so efficient? Alanna wondered again, unless he, too,
wished to depart *Radharc Alainn* before the executions.
After all, how could he shrive men and feel no bond for
them?

Entering the area of the keep that served as the stable,
Alanna spied the clergyman in a corner stall and approached him.

"A Galen cade ta cearr?" she asked, relieved to be using
her native tongue again. "What devilment are you up to
this morning, unless you are doing penance for some secret sin?" she speculated with a soft laugh.

It was not until the last words escaped her lips that Alanna realized the man wearing Galen's habit was far too tall and dark to be her confessor. As she opened her mouth to scream for help, Lucas turned and captured her in an iron grip, one hand clasping her jaw and forcing her to silence as the other pulled her body close to his.

"Silencio," he whispered, his voice nonetheless as forceful as when he had bellowed to his men in the dungeon.

Nodding as much as his hold on her would allow, Alanna feared not for herself, but for Friar Galen. Suddenly the reason for Lucas del Fuentes's change of heart regarding religion became apparent. She did not care if he escaped or not, so long as her priest was unharmed. It had been she who had sent the poor man down to the dungeon, she who had felt compassion for the foreign devils when her aunt had screamed for their blood and her uncle had spurned the suggestion of ransom demands. Yet who had been hurt by her foolishness?

As the Spaniard stood motionless, Alanna grabbed a piece of the brown cloth of his robe and looked at her captor beseechingly, hoping he understood the question in her eyes.

"He lives," the devil's spawn answered her in Latin, "as does the guard, but they won't for long unless you cooperate."

"Why keep her alive at all?" protested Juan, also in Latin, as he and the other seamen came forward from the shadows. "What good can she do us? Better we kill her now in retaliation for MacWilliams's hospitality and be on our way to join Alonso at that Blacksod Bay."

"Speak Spanish," cautioned Lucas. "The more she knows the more dangerous she'll be to us."

"What difference, since she's going to die anyway?" Juan retorted, still speaking the ancient language of the Roman Empire. He treated Alanna to a taunting sneer.

"Spanish, I told you! *She's* not our enemy. Besides, she's only a female," snapped Lucas, motioning Pedro forward to keep the woman quiet. Taking the woven cincture from around his waist, the nobleman bound her hands together.

While it went against her very being to be docile in the face of threats, neither was Alanna a fool. Five men against one woman in a deserted stable provided odds even she wouldn't gamble. Her best chance for raising the alarm would be in the courtyard when she could perhaps make enough noise to rouse some of Grady's retainers. Until then, it was wiser if the Spaniards thought her cooperative.

When Lucas finished tying Alanna's hands, he motioned Pedro away, grabbed her upper arm in his iron grip and shook her, warning her to maintain her silence.

"One sound, milady, and I swear it will be your last. I can't afford to take any greater risks than absolutely necessary and I fear your uncle won't be very understanding of our wish to leave, let alone take you with us."

"Once he catches you, he'll hang you all and I'll watch the ceremony with glee," Alanna promised softly, her quiet tones all the more effective than hysteria. "Don't imagine you'll get away with this."

"He has to take us first," said Lucas, "and from what I've seen of him, his ability to do so is questionable. I suspect his wife possesses more manhood than he. But, be that as it may, you are coming with us, no matter what you threaten."

"Del Fuentes, this woman translated for that sad excuse of a man and his bloodthirsty wench. And, as I recall, your prisoner there is the very one who pronounced our death sentences. Are you so starved for a woman's embrace that you would risk our lives for a chance to lift her skirts?" mocked *El Pavoreal*.

"As *I* recall it, Alvarez, Alanna is the one who argued for a ransom, and unwittingly as it may have been, she also gave us the opportunity to escape. I hardly think such actions merit a death sentence." Though his Spanish words were directed at his fellow officer, Lucas permitted his eyes to study his captive, outwardly calm and unstruggling in his grip. There was a strength in the way she stood quietly, not shifting her weight or trembling, yet seeming to gauge the activity about her as though alert for a chance at freedom.

"You've got to silence her permanently. She knows where we're heading—"

"Thanks to your unguarded tongue, Alanna could well know—"

Though she did not understand the Spanish words, Alanna had to struggle to keep herself from reacting to the soft tone Lucas used when he said her name. To be unable to do anything while awaiting his pleasure was galling.

"Oh, now this is my fault, too. It's not enough that you blame me for Carlos's death," whined Juan.

"Stop your complaining and saddle yourself a horse. We'll take her with us, at least until we're safely away from here. If necessary, she can be a hostage to assure us safe passage, though I wouldn't bet on the aunt paying much in the way of a ransom. We can leave her at a monastery or convent when we're out of the area. There are supposed to be plenty of them hidden in this godforsaken land, English law to the contrary. Pedro, bring the sorrel and the gray horse back in here. No need to advertise ourselves by mounting in the courtyard."

Turning to Alanna, Lucas was again impressed by her outward expression of serenity. He had witnessed her fire last night, but she had herself strongly under control now. As much as she must loathe him, she was intelligent enough to know her fate was in his hands, and she met his gaze without flinching. Switching back to Latin, he addressed her in what he hoped was a soothing tone.

"I fear, Lady Alanna, that you have no choice but to give us the honor of your company for the next few hours. Since you were leaving this morning anyway, I trust we won't inconvenience you overly much. I swear to you, on my honor, you will be as safe with me as if it were your own friar riding beside you."

Somehow Alanna doubted that, but she bit back the anger so overpowering she could taste it. Despite his sophisticated manner, the man was an animal, and she'd give herself to eternal damnation before she provided him with an excuse to put his hands on her and discover the knife she always kept strapped to her leg. Instead, she nodded passively and asked the question that worried her most.

"Friar Galen? Is he truly unharmed?"

"Merely sleeping, though his jaw may be somewhat tender when he awakens," Lucas confirmed, oddly touched that her first words would be of concern for one other than herself. Still, after her demeanor last night, he knew she wasn't completely soft of heart. Taking a cloth he found on the floor, he moved to gag her.

As soon as she understood his intent, however, Alanna began to struggle violently, kicking out with her feet and tossing her head back. How could she cry out for help in the courtyard with a filthy rag stuffed in her mouth? Leaning forward, she gnashed her teeth deeply into the golden skin of Lucas's hand, tasting his blood.

As foreign curses filled the air, the Irish beauty twisted away from him and turned to run for the main keep, opening her mouth to scream. But suddenly, she was confronted with the other Latin-speaking prisoner brandishing a pitchfork in her direction. Realizing that this Spaniard presented more danger to her than del Fuentes, she closed her mouth and abandoned her dash for freedom.

"Going somewhere, milady? I think not." Juan laughed as Lucas grabbed Alanna's hair and yanked her back to his side. This dominance over a female excited *El Pavoreal*, and a lewd smile curved his lips. "Since the old man kept us naked, del Fuentes, don't you think it fair we strip the girl? Of course, riding might be awkward for her, but it would give us something to look at, and you do seem to want her alive."

Alanna ignored the spouting poppinjay, her eyes brimming with unshed tears she fought to keep from spilling. Lucas's touch was no longer gentle as he caught her hair in the gag he was fixing in place.

"I should make you suck the poison out of my bite, you little viper," he snarled, "but we haven't the time. Now, move over to your horse. No, not the gray, you'll ride the sorrel."

Obviously the Spaniard knew horseflesh well enough to choose her mount as his own, Alanna realized, regretting that Moira's Baibi would never give her enough speed to escape, but she had no choice now. Or did she?

As Lucas attempted to lift her onto Baibi, Alanna once again resisted, wriggling and fiercely kicking out against him until at last he lost his hold on her, allowing her to fall to the dirt and muck on the stable floor, her breath knocked from her.

"I told you she's more trouble than she's worth." Juan laughed while Lucas rubbed his bruised thigh. "Just kill her and hide the body in the hay. Nobody will find her for hours."

"I said she was traveling with us, and she will," snapped Lucas in an icy tone more frightening to Alanna than the loud anger of most men. Reaching down, the Spaniard grabbed her arm and jerked her to her feet, thoroughly shaking her slender form in the process.

"Until now, milady, I've resisted Juan's suggestion that you ride naked, but since you're not in the mood to cooperate, I may have to consider that option," he stated coldly in Latin. "Or I could just leave your body here as carrion for the vermin to feast on. I am certain it would not take long for your sweet flesh to attract a hungry crowd."

Gathering as much dignity as she could without being able to brush the filth from her gown, Alanna gritted her teeth in an effort to stop shaking. Though he might be mad enough to carry out his threats, she would not allow this demon to know he frightened her.

Then, without warning, she was in his arms as Lucas called out softly to his men in Spanish. Before she could anticipate what was coming, he had taken a half dozen steps across the stable and she was tossed across Baibi's back, facedown, like a bag of grain. Lucas's heavy hands held her in place while his men tied her ankles together and secured her flailing feet with a rope tied under the horse's belly and around to the bonds confining her wrists.

"Enrique, you're the smallest of us. Take her cape and put it on. Pull the hood up over your head and go first to signal the guard to allow us to pass. Pedro, grab a blanket from the stall and toss it over her so we don't arouse suspicion," Lucas ordered as he grabbed the sorrel's reins and mounted the gray beauty. Regardless of his gentlemanly instincts, he had no more time to waste seeing to the girl's comfort. Besides, he told himself, this way, by the time they stopped in a few hours, she might be chastened enough to ride normally.

Nodding to the sleepy-eyed guard who watched them unlatch the gate without challenge, Lucas gave the man benediction, then, looking over his shoulder, led his men to freedom. In minutes, they had escaped the confines of the keep, and all save Alanna seemed to breathe easier. To confound their eventual pursuers, Lucas chose to travel inland rather than along the shore where sailors might be expected to go. Moving as quickly as possible, he urged them onward, pushing the horses to their limit, hoping to make the most of the time until they were missed.

Moira had always cautioned her to be careful of what she prayed for, Alanna thought dismally, swallowing the dust that Baibi kicked up. She hadn't wanted to be at Castlemount for the Spaniards' deaths and she wouldn't be. But she would see them die all the same. No one did this to Alanna Desmond O'Donnell and lived!

Chapter Four

It was an eternity until the horses finally slowed to a walk, but even at the slower pace Baibi's rocking motion did nothing to decrease Alanna's discomfort. Bound as she was across the mare's back, her arms and legs joined by a rope under the animal's stomach, Alanna jounced against the hornless leather saddle with every step Baibi took, making her chest and midriff raw and tender. Were it possible to scream for help, Alanna doubted she would have the breath to do so as the air was systematically squeezed from her each time she slammed into the saddle. Initially she had tried to avoid the stench of the horse's sweat, but since she had been unable to brace herself, such an attempt only slid her body more distressingly earthward until she was afraid her feet would be caught by Baibi's long stride.

By all the saints, why had she ever felt sympathy for that foreign fiend in the first place? She should have known better. Why hadn't she just curtly dismissed Megan and ignored the Spaniard's plea for a priest? At the very least, Alanna reflected sadly, if she had done as her hindsight now urged, she would have enjoyed a few more hours of sleep, a decent meal and her own steed en route to Kevin's lands. Instead, her sympathetic idiocy had seen her trussed like a calf being led to slaughter. Her father, Sean, Kevin and even Devlin, his gallowglass, had oftentimes chided her for her impetuous nature and soft heart, but where were the men in her life when she needed their help?

And what about Grady? Surely he must have missed her by now, Alanna thought suddenly. Judging from the sun, it had to be well into morning. Even Moira couldn't sleep this late. The old dear would have sought help as soon as she realized her charge was missing, and once they had found Friar Galen and the guards, Grady would understand what had happened. Maybe he had already sent word to Kevin and dispatched search parties himself.

Alanna tried to raise her head sufficiently to see the direction in which they were traveling, but her proximity to the trotting hoofs made it impossible to view anything as the dust of the road burned her eyes. Despite the gag in her mouth, the dirt from the path constantly filled Alanna's nose. The loamy grit, mixed with the bitter gall of being del Fuentes's captive, made her want to retch. Had it not been for the foul rag stuffed between her teeth, her stomach would have purged itself miles back. Instead, as she had done before, Alanna once more swallowed the sour bile of her helplessness and swore bloody vengeance on the golden devil who, somewhere up ahead, held the reins of her fate.

"I told you we should have killed them last night. Then we wouldn't have all this trouble. Why did you have to let them live until dawn?" berated Cordelia in her most aggravating manner. "Now, Grady Seamus MacWilliams, that poor sweet girl, your dear departed sister's only child, your own innocent niece, is at the mercy of those bloodthirsty foreigners. And whose fault is it but yours? I do hope you're satisfied!"

Biting back the urge to remind his wife of the harsher opinions of Alanna's virtue Cordelia had expressed on other occasions, Grady shook his head and looked across the Great Hall to where Moira was tending an outraged Friar Galen. If the Spaniard had no scruples about attacking a man of the cloth, how safe could Alanna be? Yet del Fuentes must realize the girl's life was more valuable than his own. Maybe he would send a ransom demand....

Sadly Grady recalled his own adamant refusal to seek payment in exchange for the prisoners. He hoped the Spaniard wouldn't do likewise. Of course, he didn't have a woman like Cordelia supervising his every action.

"Well, husband, what have you to say for yourself?" came his spouse's harping voice once more.

"We don't know for certain that they have even taken Alanna, dearest. She may have been abandoned in one of the outbuildings or left with some of our tenants once the prisoners escaped from our immediate holdings. Remember, the man at the gate just assumed it was Alanna's contingent leaving this morning. He didn't get a good look at the figure in the front."

"Then why in heaven's name did the idiot allow them to open the gate? He should be flogged! With men like him standing watch, we could all be murdered in our beds. You must double the guard at once in case those filthy Spaniards come back."

"I hardly think that likely, Cordelia. John said they took six of Alanna's mounts, and with solid horseflesh like that, I'd wager they are miles away from here by now. Besides, we are short of men since I've sent all we had available to track those dastardly foreigners and hopefully find my niece."

"Oh, so you care more about her than your wife? Not that I'm surprised, but it's inexcusable when it is my English blood that permitted you to keep the MacWilliams lands in the first place," the shrewish female reminded him for the thousandth time since he'd married her. "And what about our neighbor, Lord Bravingham? You know he was expecting Alanna today. I do hope you've decided upon a plausible story for him."

"Not yet. I don't think we should worry about his reaction right now. He doesn't even know Alanna is gone yet. First and foremost, we need to get her back unharmed," said the man of the house, desiring nothing more than a strong drink and the peace to enjoy it.

"Well, see that you do, and quickly. If she's not found within the hour, he will have men hunting for her under every rock and boulder before nightfall, and he'll be none too pleased," warned Cordelia, turning on her heel and leaving. She had better things to do than sit with her useless husband all day.

"I pray to God it's that easy," sighed Grady. Groping for the jug beside his chair, the weary head of Castlemount poured himself a cup of fiery Gaelic *poitín*. He saw the liquid not so much a drink as potent, painkilling courage, and quickly lifting the cup, he drained its contents in a single swallow.

It was nearly midmorning when Lucas began to watch the countryside for somewhere to stop and rest his men and horses. Judging from the position of the pale sun, they had been on the road for at least three hours, and even his Irish hellcat must need a respite by now.

A quick-running stream had meandered through the mist along their route for the last few miles, but he wanted some natural cover if they were to dismount and stretch their legs in safety. It would be foolhardy to lose their advantage over MacWilliams by blatantly advertising their presence in what might still conceivably be his lands. And Lucas swore he'd take no more chances with the lives of his men. It was enough of a miracle that they had escaped MacWilliams's bloody plans.

Gradually the scenery changed as small rocks on the left of the road became crags. A copse of oak trees appeared on the right, effectively screening the stream from any journeymen happening by.

"Stop here," he commanded abruptly, jumping down from his mount and leading the men and animals into the green alcove provided by nature. "Pedro, drink quickly and let Luis water your horse. You climb the tallest tree and inform me if anyone approaches. Itinerant peddler, monk or soldier, I want to know at once, understand?"

"*Sí*, Don Lucas. *Inmediamente*."

"Enrique, you take charge of the other horses. Don't let them drink too much or they'll bloat, but we owe them a healthy rest. Juan, once you've had your fill of water, I'll need you to help me untie our prisoner," Lucas continued, squatting by the stream to dip his hands in the cool liquid and splash it on his face.

"Me? I'm not your servant. Do your own nursemaid chores," snapped *El Pavoreal*, but he moved toward Baibi and yanked the blanket off Alanna all the same. "You are the one who insisted on bringing her along, and a sorrier sight I have never seen."

For once, Lucas could not dispute Juan's judgment. The girl lay unmoving across the mare's back, the unmistakable odor of horse clinging to her, her face streaked with grimy sweat and traces of tears, her hair more untamed than many a wild horse's mane.

"Well, tell me that she's worth our trouble," sneered Juan arrogantly. "Turn the horse loose and maybe it will improve the scenery and take her back home. If the animal doesn't make it, at least her death won't be on your tender conscience, and we'll have one less worry until we meet Alonso."

"*We?* Since I didn't see you orchestrating our escape from MacWilliams's dungeon or getting us this far, you'll pardon my disregarding your words of wisdom." Lucas's tone cut sharply through the man's braggadocio. "When I have need of your advice, I'll ask for it. Until then, keep your thoughts to yourself and cut the rope that binds her hands and feet together. Watch the knife around her face. I don't want her marked," warned Lucas as he came around Baibi to brace Alanna.

Putting his hand on her bottom to prevent her falling to the ground, he was momentarily distracted by the womanly feel of her curves. In other circumstances... When he smacked his hand soundly against her posterior to banish such ideas from his mind, Lucas was startled to feel her jump.

"*Ahora,*" he called to Juan.

Alanna's lack of Spanish left her totally unprepared for the sudden swat on her backside and, more distressing, for the abrupt appearance of a Spaniard in front of her, waving a knife twice the size of hers. What was he going to do? And why was del Fuentes holding her so familiarly in place on Baibi's back, let alone slapping her? Fearing the disgruntled look on the foreigner's face and the flash of sunlight on the blade in his hands as it moved closer to her, she began to thrash about as much as her restraints would allow, kicking back and trying to roll away from the descending knife at the same time.

Her feet hit an unseen target, and a low grunt told her she'd made a solid impression on her rear guard, but before she could enjoy the satisfaction of victory, she felt a sharp throbbing in her wrist. Yanking it toward her mouth, the rebellious captive was amazed to find it bloody yet moving freely. But then she was rapidly sliding backward, only to land in a heap at the feet of Lucas del Fuentes.

"*Madre de Dios,* she is a hellcat. I did not mean to cut her, but she jerked and twisted," explained Juan uneasily as he rounded the horse.

"Go and wet your neckerchief so we can wash her wound and bind it," snapped Lucas in disgust. Could *El Pavoreal* never do even the smallest chore without creating a problem?

Looking at his bedraggled prisoner, Lucas, a man who had led countless men through the hell of battle, was uncertain as to his next move. Should he take the offensive and turn her over his knee for her constant troublemaking and her kick to his groin, or apologize for the discomfort he and his men had caused such a delicate lady? Lying as she was in a small lump, nursing her bleeding wrist, he might almost have believed her forlorn and helpless until he noticed the flashing spots of light in her sapphire eyes and realized more trouble might be ahead. Even after hours as a prisoner, the girl had enough spirit to struggle!

Respecting her strength of character if not her fighting tactics, Lucas knelt down beside her and gently lifted the arm in question, somewhat surprised that it was still tethered to its mate. Cursing beneath his breath, he began to undo the knots as Alanna watched, wide-eyed, until Juan returned with a dripping cloth.

"Cut the rope here, without cutting us," ordered Lucas. This time, as the blade moved closer, Alanna understood its intent and didn't flinch. Seconds later, she stretched her arm toward the wet rag. Lucas nodded and gingerly wiped at the bloody wrist. It was only a scratch, he was relieved to see, but it should never have happened in the first place. He lost no time telling Alvarez just that.

For her part, Alanna knew only that she was off that blasted animal and mere feet from the icy promise of a country stream. First she had to convince the Spaniards that she was docile, and then, when they were off guard, she could raise hell and escape.

Attempting to stand for the first time in hours, she was startled to find her legs trembling from the effort. Maybe it wouldn't be so difficult to persuade the men she was helpless, after all. She glanced toward Lucas, who was apparently sending his man to climb a tree, and motioned toward the water. When he nodded acquiescence, she began to pull at her gag, but before she could undo it, he was upon her, clasping his hand over her mouth.

"One sound, one scream, the gag goes back on, and I guarantee you'll never scream again," he cautioned in Latin, dark green eyes piercing. "We have come too far to be taken now. No matter what the cost, I will see my men to safety. Understood?"

Nodding, Alanna found herself admiring the man's determination as well as his vigor. He had lived with the certainty of death at her uncle's keep, yet had planned and executed a daring escape and ridden over unfamiliar terrain for hours. Still, his hand, unlike her legs, betrayed no hint of weakness or hesitation. She had no doubt that Lucas del Fuentes would kill her or, at the very least, beat her senseless if she risked his life or those of his men. For the moment, however, cool water to drink and wash in was her

primary need. After that, well, Kevin had not raised her to
be a coward, but neither was she a fool. She would bide her
time and wait for the right opportunity.

Too pleased with the woman's docility to question the
fire that had burned in her eyes earlier, Lucas removed the
gag and guided her gently to the stream. There he helped
her sit on a rock near enough to the water so that she could
trail her hands in the soothing liquid without danger of
falling in, but accessible enough so that he could keep hold
of the rope binding her feet. Not that there was anywhere
for her to run, but why take chances?

He had found a temporary haven of peace and was in no
hurry to rush onward. He could not feed his men or
Alanna, but at least they could steal a half hour's ease.
Juan was now standing watch while Pedro, Luis and Enrique rested. They would all be the sharper for the interruption of their journey, he decided.

Watching Alanna through half-closed eyes, Lucas was
startled to find he wanted her. The way she rested her hand
on her cheek and stroked the water with long, slender fingers made him ache for her touch. The saffron woolen
gown she wore concealed her charms as effectively as the
prim nightdress had done the night before, yet his fingers
itched for the feel of her beneath his exploring hands. As
he remembered the curve of her bottom when he'd held her
over the horse, Lucas could almost taste the honey of her
lips made salty by her tears.

Fortunately the friar's garb hid his growing interest, a
chagrined Lucas noticed. Like the robe's true owner, he had
been celibate too long. Perhaps he should have availed
himself of the services aboard the women's ship that had
accompanied the Armada, but he had never found much
pleasure in such episodes. They were too businesslike and
impersonal for him. For now, perhaps he should wade in
the stream before he did something he would only regret
later.

"Do you intend to drown me, then?" asked Alanna as
she saw her captor remove the friar's sandals and step into

the stream still holding her tethered. He had been watching her too intently for her liking, and she needed to put some emotional distance between them. There was no need for him to pity her. After all, his pity could all too easily turn into an interest that was far more dangerous. "Isn't it enough that you took advantage of my compassionate nature so you could attack my priest and escape, that you abducted me and tortured me on horseback for hours? Now you want me to go to a watery grave? Whether I survive or not, Spaniard, know that my uncle will hunt you down for this and kill you, slowly and painfully. He will never rest until you've suffered the way I have."

"He'll have a hard time doing that, I am afraid." Lucas shook his head and chuckled. Angry as she was, his prisoner's voice was but a hoarse whisper. Either the dust she'd swallowed had weakened her throat or she was taking his threats to heart. In either case, as long as she didn't start screaming to attract attention, she could complain as much as she wanted. Her cries would never match those brittle tones of Maria Elena, his contracted bride who had considerately died of the plague before their arranged wedding. Sorry as he was that she had passed away, Maria Elena was a handful Lucas didn't miss.

"Del Fuentes, I am speaking to you. Will you stop grinning like an idiot and have some regard for my needs?"

"Your needs?" the raven-haired male repeated in surprise. Aside from her freedom, which he wouldn't grant, and food, which he couldn't, what else could the woman need?

"Yes, my bodily needs...that is, some privacy is wanted, sir." Damn it, no wonder Latin was a disappearing language. How could she tell her abductor she needed to relieve herself in such a formal tongue? Fortunately he suddenly seemed to grasp her meaning and motioned her toward the line of trees.

"You expect me to walk that far with my ankles bound?" the blonde snapped as arrogantly as her voice would allow.

"All right. I will untie your feet, but the rope stays around one ankle so you don't disappear on me," the Spaniard agreed, stepping out of the stream and rearranging her bonds.

"By your leave, I would prefer to go behind the rocks rather than under the trees where your men will enjoy the view," she stated with a modest downward glance.

"Very well, come along."

Like someone taking a pig to market, Lucas moved at his own pace, pulling the rope behind him and permitting Alanna no freedom to wander. He crossed to the other side of the road, led her behind one of the larger outcroppings of rock nearby, and stopped.

"You are not going to stand there watching, are you?" she protested. "Go around the rock and turn your back. The cord is long enough to allow me that much privacy, isn't it?"

Lucas ran his questioning eyes over his captive in a slow, deliberate manner, searching for some hint of falsity in her request. Finding none, he finally nodded slightly and stepped a few feet back around the crag.

Realizing that was as much of a compromise as she was likely to get, Alanna moved into action quickly. As if to answer nature's call, she squatted and found her knife, unsheathed it from her thigh and carefully cut through the offensive rope, weighing it down with a rock so the sudden slack would not give her away. Then she was gone, heading up into the hills, more at ease than she had been in weeks. This was her land, and she would use it to her advantage.

Five minutes passed before Lucas felt sufficiently impatient to interrupt her, but when he called out, there was no response. Rounding the crag at a run despite his bare feet, he caught his breath at the sight of the untethered rope.

Knowing that if she had headed back toward the horses his men would have spotted her, Lucas concluded his prisoner's only logical route had to be upward. Furiously, he began to climb the rocks after her.

For a big man, del Fuentes moved quietly, determined to avoid giving her notice of his pursuit. A sudden spurt of pebbles drifting down from his left was enough to tell him the direction she took, and he moved steadily on, using his anger for energy. She could not have gotten too far ahead of him, especially not with her legs so unsteady, he reasoned.

Then he caught sight of his prey. She had crawled into a slight depression behind some boulders, and he would have missed her altogether but that the yellow of her gown attracted his eye. Pretending not to have seen her, the hunter climbed steadily past her hiding place.

Alanna slowly released her indrawn breath, careful not to make any noise but feeling relief nonetheless. However, just as she slipped the knife she had been concealing back into its sheath unobserved, his iron hand gripped her shoulder and began to shake her.

"I told you not to try anything or you would regret it," Lucas snarled, yanking Alanna's slender form out of the rocky crevice that had sheltered her.

"Oh, I suppose I should meekly wait to be slaughtered whenever the mood strikes you," Alanna snapped back, more angry at herself for being taken than at him for besting her. "Why don't you murder me now and get it over with? My uncle wouldn't ransom you, so I expect no mercy. But I swear that if not Grady MacWilliams then my foster father, Kevin O'Donnell, the man who sired my husband, will see you hanging from a gibbet yet. No one abducts me and lives."

"I won't kill you unless you leave me no choice, Alanna," the nobleman attempted to reason, regretting his previous harshness. "I want no innocent blood on my hands, but my men and I must reach our ship and return to our lives and our families. Is that asking too much?"

"What price is life? My husband and the others were promised their lives when the Italian commander at Smerwick surrendered to the English, but Sean and the rest were

slaughtered anyway. Why should I trust you not to kill
me?''

"Because I am not disreputable, nor am I your enemy."
Lucas's words shocked Alanna into silence. "I could have
killed you in the stable and your priest, too, but I didn't, did
I?'' Pulling her about to face him, Lucas held Alanna fast
against his chest, enjoying the feel of her and stroking her
wild curls as he continued. "Besides, you helped save our
lives. Can't we call a truce, at least for the duration of this
journey?''

The Spaniard's quiet plea touched a place in Alanna's
soul that she had thought closed forever. The last time she
had felt so vulnerable, Sean O'Donnell had stolen her
heart. She'd been but sixteen. Having lost him after only a
few months of marriage, she had sworn then she would
never commit herself again. She meant to keep that vow.
How dare the Spaniard talk to her as a man to a woman
instead of as soldier to foe?

"Take your filthy hands off me, you uncivilized dog. Do
you think I meant to save your life? Beat me if you want,
tie me up, kill me, but I'll consign myself to hell's fires before I agree to peace with you. The MacWilliams and
O'Donnells are undoubtedly searching for you already, and
I'll enjoy watching what they do to you when they catch
you.''

Pushing against his rock-hard chest, Alanna managed to
break his hold on her, but only for an instant before his
long arms reached out to catch her once more. Lucas del
Fuentes glared silently at his prisoner, his eyes stagnant
chips of glacial ice, and fought to bring his temper under
control. He had been right about her all along. She was a
coldhearted bitch! He had offered her friendship of a sort,
and she had refused it.

Finally, without acknowledging her insult, the nobleman grabbed her arm and started the trek back to where his
men waited. He and Alanna were nearly to the road when
they heard a shout.

"Don Lucas, es peligroso. Muchos hombres vienen."

Before she knew what had happened, Alanna found herself thrown to the ground and held there by the Spaniard's strong grasp, his left arm coming across her shoulders and pinning her small frame to the damp earth as he positioned himself beside her. He clamped his hand over her mouth before Alanna had regained the breath knocked out of her by the fall. Not only did the maneuver keep his hostage in place, it freed Lucas to use his weapon should the need arise.

When Alanna began to squiggle and squirm at her predicament, he threw one strong leg atop her calves, restricting her even further.

"One troublesome move," he whispered fiercely in her ear, "and I vow that it will be your last."

Move! How could she move at all, Alanna reflected, with this great lummox half-astride her? Truce, indeed! The Spaniard had thought to lull her with soft words and warm promises, but when given the opportunity, he demonstrated he was as heartless and full of treachery as any of his countrymen.

Mother of God, the man had to have the power of six warriors, Alanna thought, to be able to hold her fast with such seemingly little effort. Raised in a land where strength often meant survival, the young widow couldn't help but be impressed by the granite muscles in her subduer's arms and the powerful hardness of his thigh, digging so mercilessly now into her legs. Conceding the Spaniard's muscular prowess spawned unthinkable reactions in her body that both surprised and shamed her, Alanna struggled as desperately against them as she did against being held prisoner.

As for Lucas, he was almost unaware of the feminine qualities trapped beneath him, so intent was he upon remaining hidden from those traveling the dirt road a mere twenty yards away. Concealed though they were behind tall grass and an outcropping of boulders, he was nevertheless concerned that he was cut off from his men, who, he assumed, had secreted themselves as best they could on the opposite side of the roadway. Listening for approaching horses, he prayed their own appropriated steeds would remain quiet.

At the distant sound of hoofbeats, Alanna's efforts at liberty became more resolute. Almost instantly, she heard Lucas mutter softly Spanish words that could have only been an oath. He tightened his hold on her, but not before Alanna inched apart the side slit in her tunic and found the hilt of the dagger she had strapped to her upper leg.

It had taken all of her might to shift her weight ever so slightly within Lucas's restrictive grip, but the exertion had been a fruitful one. If she could put but a slight space between them, she could bring her forearm up hard and fast enough to plunge her blade into the unguarded ribs resting alongside her own. With any luck, the target her dagger found would be the Spaniard's black, unfeeling heart.

The dull thuds of the hoofbeats were louder now, though their slow rhythm bespoke no urgency, and the closer the riders came, the more anxious Alanna felt. She couldn't allow them to pass her by, and the only person who could hinder her signaling them was Lucas del Fuentes.

All it would take would be a slight roll to her left in order to give her right arm the freedom it needed. Looking up as best she could into Lucas's strong profile, Alanna saw how engrossed he was in the danger at hand. The nearer the horsemen came, the more he ignored her in order to concentrate on them. Surely when the travelers were directly in front of them, he would be so absorbed in their actions that it would be much easier to strike than it was now. That, Alanna decided, was what she would do. Once the plan was formed, her heart pounded so loudly she swore surely Lucas would hear it, too, and be forewarned. She tried to calm herself, but it was a difficult task to accomplish when she kept envisioning her blade ripping into the body of the man lying beside her.

Soon distinctly English-speaking voices preceded the riders and Alanna realized joyously that these were indeed Grady's men, sent in search of her.

"Castlemount's lord will be sorely disappointed if we return without the girl, though I don't expect to find the Spaniards this far inland. They'd be traveling along the shoreline," Alanna heard a soldier state with certainty.

Slowly, with Lucas focusing intently on the enemy nearby, she managed to dip her left shoulder down and raise her right one, giving herself scarcely the latitude demanded for what she was about to do. Carefully steadying the knife in her hand, she poised it so she could drive it, with all of the might her cramped position would allow, into the man imprisoning her. Though it was a pity to mar the clean lines of flesh she had viewed in the dimness of the Great Hall, Alanna decided that del Fuentes deserved that and more for the indignities he had forced upon her.

"I call it lunacy," replied another of the riders, "bringing the girl back to the keep just so she can be stolen once more. Considering what's in store for her, she'd be better off if she wasn't found at all."

Muscles tensed in preparation for the thrust, Alanna barely heard the surprising words and took little note of them until they began to penetrate her concentration where they roared like thunder. Their meaning took her so aback that she paused in order to pay heed to what was being said.

"I still don't understand why we have to save her from one abduction so that she can be seized again," grumbled a third man.

"Do things have to be drawn out for you, simpleton?" asked the original speaker. "The other kidnapping is to be done with Grady's blessing. The Englishman, Bravingham, was supposed to steal the wench, wed her and bed her, though not necessarily in that order, and thus relieve the lord of his unwed niece. After the fact, what could the girl or that rebel, Kevin O'Donnell, do other than agree to the match? The lord of Castlemount is a shrewd one, indeed! O'Donnell wouldn't connect him with the incident. Besides which, you can't say that it wouldn't form a nice alliance to unite Bravingham's lands with the MacWilliams's own."

Alanna froze in horror. She forgot her situation, her surroundings and even the dagger she clutched. Her uncle had schemed to betray her, to have her kidnapped on her journey to Kevin's holdings in Donegal. No wonder he and Cordelia had insisted she leave Castlemount as planned despite rumors of invasion. Although Alanna was certain Cordelia had instigated the conspiracy, it was all too obvious Grady had agreed, attempting to force his niece to follow the path he had chosen for himself, alliance with the British. Alanna didn't care how good her uncle's intentions might have been. The Spaniard had been right. Grady's household knew nothing of honor.

Suddenly, Alanna was brought back to her immediate circumstances by the violent shaking of del Fuentes's shoulders. Not certain of its cause, she nevertheless doubted he was quaking in fear of Grady's laconic men. The movement, however, served to recall both the blade she held and her designs on Lucas del Fuentes's life, and she found that she wanted to strike out at him viciously in order to erase the hurt caused by the words of the soldiers.

She began to bring the knife upward, but her moment's hesitation had undone her. With the instincts of a man familiar with danger, Lucas sensed her purpose and removed himself swiftly from the dagger's path, shifting completely atop his captured Irish vixen as he delivered a threatening glare. His unrelenting grip around her wrist cut off the blood from Alanna's hand, and her fingers involuntarily dropped their weapon. Lucas retrieved it and placed it outside her reach before settling himself once more to await the passage of the last of Grady's soldiers.

Again, Alanna could feel an odd tremor emanating from Lucas's chest as it traveled up and down against her back. Though she could still discern no reason for it, the motion of his frame against hers was disquieting in the extreme. Alanna began to feel the heat of Lucas's body penetrating first through his clothing and then her own, to set her senses on edge. Needs long denied demanded to be satisfied, incited by the proximity of this man, the feel of his breath against her neck and the touch of his skin where it covered hers.

They lay in this manner waiting for the final plodding horseman to ride by, and then a while longer, until Lucas deemed it safe to rise and rejoin his men. Although in reality a short time, it seemed an eternity to the tortured Alanna. She was furious with herself for the traitorous reactions of her body, and she was even more enraged with Lucas for causing them, memories of his unclad form coming unbidden to disturb her further. By the time he pulled her to her feet, she was a hellcat, all hisses and claws.

"Damn you, Lucas del Fuentes!" she snarled.

"You tried to send my soul to damnation, all right, just a few moments ago," Lucas stated calmly as he fingered the knife Curran Desmond had given his daughter. But to Alanna's amazement, her abductor didn't kill her. He didn't beat her or even berate her. Instead, he threw back his head and laughed, amused that such a tiny bit of womanhood would have the audacity to attempt dispatching him to his eternal reward.

His reaction goaded Alanna all the more. How dare he treat her as though she posed no serious threat, as if she were no more than a bothersome fly to be brushed aside and ignored! She threw herself against him, fists flailing, in a state of frustrated fury, only to have him push her away as gently as she allowed.

Regarding her with an amused expression, Lucas had to admit to himself that he liked the woman's fire; indeed, he found it slightly arousing. But he also knew he had to teach Alanna that she was not to attempt such a foolhardy undertaking again.

Studying the dagger, he knew what he would do. Holding the weapon at both ends, he proceeded to break it over his knee, snapping off its blade in one swift motion. The cracking sound of metal separating from metal echoed in Alanna's heart and spoke more loudly and succinctly than any threat the Spanish nobleman could have made. Not yet finished with his lesson, he presented her the hilt with exaggerated courtliness compounded by a mock bow, as though she were a lady of the court who had dropped a handkerchief in order to attract a suitor.

"Milady, I believe this is yours," he said without a trace of anger.

Of all the reactions Alanna had anticipated when Lucas del Fuentes had disarmed her, this had not been one of them. Her wide-eyed expression of disbelief increased Lucas's light mood, and he laughed again as he grabbed her wrist and began to drag her behind him up a small incline to the road where the horses were waiting.

The familiar movement of Lucas's chest when he chuckled captured Alanna's attention. Suddenly she knew the reason for the mysterious tremors. He had been *laughing* when Castlemount's soldiers had ridden by! But at that point, he couldn't have known about the dagger. What had he found so humorous? Then it dawned on her. He had fathomed what Grady's men had said about her uncle's scheme to marry her off! Lucas del Fuentes understood English ... that bastard!

The realization gave Alanna a strength she hadn't known she possessed, and before they had taken another two steps, she dug in her heels. When Lucas turned around to find out what was amiss, Alanna attacked with the fury of a summer squall, addressing him in the language of Castlemount.

"You speak English, you devil's scum. Don't bother to deny it, I'm convinced of it!"

"You're as intelligent as you are pretty," Lucas said, switching to his mother's native tongue as he barely managed to suppress a smile at this woman's continued fiery temper. *Madre de Dios,* but she was beautiful when her face was flushed with anger.

"Don't you dare laugh at me!" Alanna demanded.

"Correct me if I am mistaken," Lucas said patiently, "you *did* tell me that your uncle was devoted to you, didn't you? That this very same uncle would move heaven and earth to keep you safe? And you threatened me with all sorts of dreadful consequences should this man catch up with me? Why, Alanna, I fail to see how he could be annoyed with me for abducting you when I simply did what he was going to do himself."

"I'm glad you find it amusing, Spaniard, because I swear to you, Grady MacWilliams will never kill you. Neither will the O'Donnell. I'll have done it long before either of them ever get the opportunity."

"Yes, milady," he said in richly masculine placating tones. "Of course you will." With that, he tossed her over his shoulder as though she were a common bundle of hay and began carrying her the remaining distance to the road.

"I'll allow you to keep your pride and satisfy your curiosity without your asking," he called good-naturedly over his shoulder, his breath coming evenly in spite of the climb and the squirming weight he carried. "I speak the language because England is my mother's birthplace. She was a lady-in-waiting to Mary Tudor, and my father a court attendant to her husband, Philip of Spain."

"Now I realize, del Fuentes, why I find you doubly hateful," Alanna stormed, her voice muffled against Lucas's broad back. "English and Spanish! I should have known. How dare you play me for the fool, deceiving my uncle—"

"I would venture, Alanna, that from what I've heard, the man is very adept at deception himself."

"Don't you dare interrupt me," she raged. "Having me struggle to communicate in Latin, all the while probably snickering up your sleeve—"

"Might I remind you, madam, that I wasn't in possession of any sleeves when first we met."

"Lucas del Fuentes, you'll pay for this, you wretch. When you put me down, I'll prove to you just how sorry you'll be."

Then, without warning, Alanna found herself plummeting downward when he dropped her in the middle of the dusty road at Baibi's feet. The impact bruised her ego as well as her posterior.

"I must crave your pardon, sweet lady," Lucas said, towering over her, an indolent smile tugging at his mouth. "I couldn't hear what you were saying just now. Would you care to repeat it?"

But Alanna discovered when she opened her mouth to speak that she was unable to utter a word. Suddenly everything overwhelmed her, the abduction, her uncle's betrayal, her father's dagger broken, this unbearable man's attitude and her own exhaustion. Sitting in the dirt, feeling trivial and forlorn, Alanna found tears slipping slowly down her cheeks.

Lucas was taken aback. He had thought to allow his hostage a chance to vent her anger, and to perhaps tire herself out in the process so that she would be more manageable. He had never expected, and was not at all prepared for, her silent weeping. Its effect on Lucas del Fuentes was more devastating than any tirade Alanna could devise. Immediately he was down on one knee, gently wiping the tears that still clung to the soft contours of his hostage's face. But no matter how solicitous he was, another tear fell, and then another.

"*Dios!*" he muttered, running his hand through his raven black hair. A frustrated scowl darkened his countenance when he saw that his ministrations were to no avail. He rose quickly to his feet and strode to his horse without a backward glance, barking orders to Pedro to see to the woman.

Looking at the other two seamen, Pedro heaved a sigh and shook his head in exasperation at the nobleman's hasty retreat. It didn't seem right that Lucas del Fuentes, brave and ferocious in battle, should be quickly undone by the tears of this one small, defenseless woman.

Chapter Five

"Del Fuentes, where are you going? You cannot be thinking of leaving. I have not yet had time to wash," whined Juan, coming quickly from behind the hedges that had hidden him as he watched the interplay between his compatriot and the woman. Nothing but trouble with a female could put storm clouds in his leader's eyes, now dark and brooding. Juan had known she was trouble from the start, and she had proven him right.

"We must move on before the patrol returns," Lucas said, determined not to let Alvarez's carping irritate him. It was enough that the girl had unsettled him; this preening peacock was a burden he didn't deserve. None of them was comfortable or clean in the clothes they wore, but at least they were still alive and on their way to freedom. "If you have any complaints about my orders, I suggest you swallow them or prepare to set out on your own."

"But the men, we are not fully rested—"

"If we are captured, there will be plenty of time to rest after you've swung from an English rope," snapped Lucas, his harsh words contrasting oddly with his religious habit. "Now, unless you want to be left behind, see that Alanna is properly cared for and then mount up. I will scout the road ahead and wait for you to join me."

"Can we not be rid of her? Kill her or tie her up and leave her for her people to find?" suggested Juan.

"They already know she was our prisoner, you pig-headed dolt! Would you have them realize we traveled this road? No! Do as I say and stop trying to think. It doesn't become you."

Lucas turned his horse toward the road and the temporary solitude it would allow him until his small band caught up with him. Although he had never regretted the role of leader, some days the responsibility seemed overwhelming. Now especially, when not only his men but an innocent woman fell under his protection. A woman he had recently brought to tears, he admitted with annoyance.

Still, there were moments of great reward, he thought with a grin, remembering Alanna's shock and fury at the realization that not only had Grady sold her future to an Englishman but that *he,* Don Lucas Rafael del Fuentes, knew it. Yes, she was a virago, he mused, but one he wouldn't be averse to taming, if only circumstances and time allowed. Unfortunately, however, he needed to see to his men before he could contemplate such activity; thus was the price of duty.

Back in the camp, Juan Felipe Alvarez stared angrily after Lucas del Fuentes, hatred shining brightly in his black eyes. Outraged at being treated like a common servant, *El Pavoreal* looked down at the woman still sitting in the dust. She affected del Fuentes strangely, he considered sullenly, and that might be used to advantage. Besides, she wasn't all that difficult to look at. He stepped forward to halt Pedro's movement toward the woman.

"Never mind, I'll see to the prisoner," he informed the sailor. Though at the moment the Irish beauty seemed to offer more in aggravation than pleasure, night would eventually approach, and one as passionate as she had been in struggling against Lucas would no doubt be a joy to bed. Licking his lips in anticipation, Juan reached down to catch Alanna's quivering chin in his hand and forced her to look up at him.

"That's enough time for weeping," he announced brusquely, his Latin poorly formed even to Alanna's inex-

perienced ears. "Stand up and prepare yourself to ride so
we may escape from here before the search party returns."

Alanna, however, was too disheartened to obey even the
simplest of commands, and stayed unmoving.

Her world, her confidence in its orderly working had
been shattered as the one man she had unhesitatingly called
enemy had turned out to be her savior, unwittingly freeing
her from a forced marriage to the cursed Bravingham. For,
inconceivable as her mind still protested it was, her beloved Grady, her mother's brother, whom she'd devotedly
visited despite his wife's waspish ways, had betrayed her to
satisfy Cordelia's avarice. Only her abduction by the
Spaniard had saved her from the degradation planned by
her own blood, she mourned.

Yet it was equally incomprehensible that she could owe
her life to one whose country's inaction had condemned
Sean to death. Too weary to accept such an overwhelming
realignment of her loyalties, Alanna preferred to remain
where she was, trusting fate to see to her safety. Freeing her
chin from the rude Spaniard's touch, she tried to contain
her revulsion as well as her sorrow, but her body betrayed
her as tears continued to fall.

El Pavoreal snorted with fury at her disobedience. Juan
had never been patient with female emotions under the best
of circumstances. Now, though, knowing his life was in
greater danger every minute he had to spend dealing with
Alanna's reluctance, the nobleman was even more abrupt
than usual. If she wouldn't cooperate of her own will, then
he would force her to do so. Clearly Lucas didn't care, or
he wouldn't have abandoned her.

"Enrique, Pedro, *ayudame pronto,*" Juan called, jerking the blonde roughly to her feet and pulling her stumbling after him as he moved toward the horses. Despite del
Fuentes's insistence that she might prove a valuable asset
should they need to buy their freedom, Juan had still to be
convinced that bringing her along hadn't been a grave mistake in judgment. He would deal with her as one did an
enemy, he decided grimly. Besides, if he treated her poorly

now, later she would be all the more thankful for his kindness and reward him appropriately.

Of course, in the meantime, she would be a nuisance. But then, if he ordered that she ride with him, there could be pleasure in such closeness. Del Fuentes had apparently finished with her after their outing alone together among the rocks. Tonight would be his turn.

"Pedro, hold my horse. Enrique, restrain the woman while I mount and then lift her up to me," he instructed briskly in Spanish. Turning to Alanna, he shook her slight form to be certain he had her attention and then continued in a Latin far less graceful. "I will tie your hands and gag you. Then you will share my horse, Irish, and make no effort to fight me or cry out. Should you be difficult, I will cut your throat with no regrets."

As if to leave no doubt as to his meaning, the pompous Spaniard pulled out a knife, undoubtedly stolen from Castlemount along with the ill-fitting clothes he wore so poorly. He brought a finger to his mouth, licked it and then ran it lightly over the shiny blade, only inches from Alanna's eyes.

"Your skin would be like butter for a knife such as this," he said with a leer. "And I am man enough to use it. Do not believe otherwise."

For a brief instant Alanna hesitated, contemplating the pilfered dagger. It would be simple to force this jackass to end her misery. But then her Irish fire caught anew when she recalled the vengeful debt she owed Cordelia, and Alanna realized she could never choose such a cowardly fate.

Maybe Sean had died for lack of Spanish support, but she'd not allow this filthy excuse for a man to drain her lifeblood. Until she could free herself from her unwanted escorts, she would be an ideal prisoner. Then, once away from them, with or without Kevin's assistance, Alanna Desmond O'Donnell would see her mother's relatives were well paid for their damnable perfidy.

The weary blonde nodded in acknowledgment of her captor's threats.

Juan chuckled, clearly pleased with what he perceived as his skill in dealing with the previously uncooperative prisoner. Within moments Alanna's wrists were tied together and she was properly silenced, mounted on his horse, his arm steadying her body against his own. Motioning for the others to follow, Juan turned down the road Lucas had taken, certain the future could offer no further blows to his welfare, not when he had such a soft and pliant female well in hand. With a bit of luck, they'd not encounter del Fuentes for miles.

As they rode together, with Alanna's lush curves fitting easily against him, Juan found himself uncharacteristically relishing each uneven step in the horse's gait. Never a willing horseman, he delighted in this day's events as he felt himself truly coming alive for the first time since the shipwreck. For every jostling movement gave him greater contact with the woman's body, thrusting her more urgently against him until he found it difficult to sit comfortably in the saddle. Perhaps, he considered, running a suggestive hand along Alanna's thigh as he allowed the one holding the reins to brush her breast, a fifteen-minute reprieve in the shrubs would ease his predicament. After all, she had made no protest thus far, though judging from the fierce red coloring of her neck, she was not unaware of his urges. Besides, since they had not met up with del Fuentes, he could take his enjoyment without that demon's being the wiser. First, however, he would send the other men on ahead.

"Alvarez, what are you doing?" challenged an unwelcome voice, hard with anger, as Lucas came riding into view. "I told you to see to the woman, not molest her on horseback."

"But I—I do nothing," the godson of Philip II argued, moving his hand quickly back to his own leg. "The easiest way to prevent your prisoner's escaping was to guard her thus, keeping hold of the reins and her at the same time. I couldn't very well throw the woman over a horse again and expect her to stay there, not while she was alert and cooperative."

"I only wonder how cooperative," muttered Lucas. He noticed the furious blush on Alanna's face and the quick way she shifted forward to distance herself from the man who held her. No woman deserved to be saddled with such a villain, he decided, raising his hand to signal a halt.

Jumping down from Piobar, the tall Spaniard reached up and removed Alanna from Juan's grasp, setting her on her feet even as he kept one arm about her waist to steady her. He should have known better than to entrust her to *El Pavoreal,* Lucas castigated himself. When would he learn?

"We will water the horses in the stream around the bend of the road and rest briefly," he instructed the sailors before he turned to Alvarez and announced curtly, "From now on, Alanna will ride alone, though I will control her reins. *You* will not go near her again."

Hearing Lucas speak her name in a softer voice than his other words, Alanna tensed, wondering what was being planned. Clearly Lucas was not pleased with the other Spaniard's behavior. She was grateful for that but, more important, would their dispute give her a chance to slip away? Her hands were still bound, but that would present no difficulty, given a sharp rock, if the men remained sufficiently distracted. Taking a half pace backward, she felt a sudden shiver of hope as Lucas's hold failed to tighten. Maybe one small step at a time would see her to freedom.

"Haven't you more important tasks, del Fuentes, than pretending you truly belong in those pious robes?" challenged Juan, thoroughly irritated and not a little pained that Lucas had interrupted his pleasure. After the female had tantalized him for hours, surely he deserved his reward. "Why aren't you off foraging for food, unless you fancy the prisoner yourself? We haven't eaten since yesterday in the cave."

"Damn it, Alvarez, do you think of nothing but satisfying your appetites?" demanded Lucas, his anger tensing the muscles in his arm about Alanna's waist. "It was your blasted concern with your stomach that got us captured in the first place."

"I didn't lead us straight into the path of a party of scavengers on the beach."

"No, but if you hadn't chased that boar, we would have made the appointed rendezvous and been aboard *La Rata* instead of on that beach," snarled the leader of their small shore excursion. He turned abruptly away from Juan's mocking face only to notice Alanna's suspiciously downcast eyes and slow, stealthy retreat from his side. Giving a short chuckle, he switched to English and addressed her, dashing her dreams to dust.

"Sorry, milady, but you are *not* free to leave us just yet. However, if you give me your word that you will neither sound an alarm nor try to escape, I will permit you to sit your own horse, though, of course, I'll control its lead. Otherwise, my dear Alanna, you will stay bound and ride with me... or, if you should prove recalcitrant, with Juan again."

Alanna closed her eyes and considered his words, though she knew already she had no choice. Still, for a desperate man trying to escape death, Lucas Rafael del Fuentes was a great deal more noble than his compatriots.

Annoyed, she shook such thoughts aside and returned to considering her dilemma. If she were to signal for help on the road, it would mean allowing herself to be taken by Bravingham or Grady's men. On the other hand, if she stayed with del Fuentes and his men, she could travel farther north and escape them when there was some likelihood of encountering O'Donnell forces. As galling as it might be, she would yield to the Spaniard's offer.

Opening her sapphirelike eyes, Alanna looked up at Lucas's bearded face and found him smiling at her as if he knew her mind already. Despite his monk's robes, she thought, this man was fiercer and more passionate than most. It was just too bad he was Spanish. It might have been enjoyable to try to tame his uncivilized moods. Then she nodded regally and gestured for him to untie her.

* * *

By late that same afternoon, after hours of struggling to
remain upright on a horse she didn't command, a weary
Alanna was thrilled to see Lucas tighten the reins on Piobar
as well as Baibi, calling a halt to their progress. Simulta-
neously, he signaled the men behind them to stop. Pedro,
the sailor he had sent to scout the land to the west, appeared in the clearing before them, excitement in his voice
and his posture.

"*Señor, una casa religiosa,*" he began, breathless with
the news.

Whether the information was good or bad, however,
Alanna could not be certain. She noted only the confused
murmuring among the shipmates as they looked to Lucas
for guidance. Led from the certainty of death at Castlemount by the sheer audacity of the brazen del Fuentes, the
sailors evidently had no doubt that he would lead them
through hostile territory to the safety of their ship, as well.

And, from what Alanna could judge, it was quite possible they were correct in their belief. Lucas Rafael del
Fuentes was a man of single-minded determination, concentrating on their continued flight, escaping detection. Yet
even as they had journeyed that afternoon, Alanna had felt
his searching glance caressing her, making her incredibly
warm when his green eyes traveled her length, an occasional smile gracing his full lips, just visible within the soft
strands of his beard and moustache. He had kept her near
to him the rest of the day, twice reprimanding Juan for
riding too close and attempting a conversation, as if she was
off limits for all but himself.

It seemed del Fuentes felt some responsibility for, if not
interest in, her well-being, and well he should, Alanna
thought irritably. She remained his hostage, and though she
couldn't count on Grady to avenge her kidnapping, Kevin
was certain to exact just punishment for his foster daughter's ill treatment. Yet Juan was more the villain than Lucas. Del Fuentes had saved her from a marriage to that oaf

Bravingham. Of course had the marriage been to an Irish-man as strong and handsome as her captor...

"Del Fuentes," she called out, suddenly impatient with the turn her thoughts had taken. "If we are stopping, I wish to dismount and stretch my legs. I am stiff from riding all day."

"Ah, the Irish princess speaks," mocked *El Pavoreal*. "Shall our lives be forfeit, *señor*, while you satisfy her, or, as you have always claimed, is your first concern still your men?"

Lucas turned swiftly on Juan, giving full voice to his fury, his words like a braided whip cutting through the tranquil air of twilight. Diplomatically, the other sailors looked away, preferring not to witness Juan's humiliation, but Alanna found she hadn't the power to turn from the sight of Lucas demonstrating his authority.

The angry del Fuentes was a tantalizing sight, she marveled again, cursing the fates that had made him Spanish. Sea green eyes snapping, nostrils slightly flared, the muscles in his neck and shoulders corded in rage, he was the vision of masculine strength barely held in check, an energy tugging at the leash of its control, frightening but at the same time fearfully attractive. Even the sharpness of his tone bespoke confident dominance.

"Since we left the ship, you have done nothing but whine about missing your comforts and carp at my efforts to save your scrawny neck from the rope, you pitiful excuse for a man. Despite your own beliefs, I tell you, the smallest mouse scurrying across the road is more of a man than you, and no woman, let alone one as lovely as Alanna, would willingly have anything to do with you," reviled Lucas as Juan blanched at the smoothly delivered insult. "Given the hindrance you've proven to be, the only reason I don't abandon you to find your own way is that I am certain you'd not only be captured within hours, but that you'd try to buy your life at the expense of ours."

"You forget, del Fuentes, I am godson to Philip—"

"Our king has nothing to do with this. He is a strong leader and a brave soldier whose relationship to you is no fault of his. Philip's name ought not be spoken by a dog such as you. In fact, I no longer wish to hear your voice at all. Enrique, Pedro, if *El Pavoreal* opens his mouth again tonight, fill it with dirt and gag him," Lucas ordered. "You will make camp out of sight in the woods ahead and await my return."

Turning toward Alanna, he softened his anger, allowing himself the momentary pleasure of simply gazing at her, enjoying her presence. Indeed, she had been so amazingly cooperative since he'd rescued her from Juan's attentions, he couldn't bring himself to leave her to that devil again. She would accompany him, he decided thoughtfully. Her knowledge of the Gaelic tongue might be useful.

"A few minutes more, and you will not only be off your horse, but able to wash and enjoy a meal in safety."

"But how? We are nowhere near the shore yet—"

"Later, you will see," he said, leaning forward to stroke her riotous curls in reassurance. "I shan't abandon you to the English forces, Alanna, but you'll have to trust me."

He asked too much, her soul protested. As she licked her dusty lips, his green eyes held her blue ones captive with a single glance and brought back memories of his proud, golden body awash with the light of the fire in Castlemount's dungeon. She had provided him with the means of his escape, and still he wanted more from her! Just how much could she give, she wondered, and yet be true to herself? Lucas had adhered to his word, though, protecting her thus far, she acknowledged, trying to justify the inexplicable impulse to obey his request for trust.

"All right, but I shall no longer be silent when I consider it wiser to speak," she bargained. "And I want my own reins."

"I have no objection to hearing your voice. Indeed, I would welcome it, provided you are not giving a signal to my enemies. But since you do not know where we are going and I do, I shall take us both there." With a quick jerk of his hand, Lucas signaled their horses forward at a fast step, relieved to be free of the others in his party. They rode in companionable silence for a while until he saw her studying the surroundings with interest.

"Does something strike you as familiar? Pedro spotted a small abbey situated on a lake a few miles northwest of here. Though I would not ask them to hide us, whether they be nuns or friars, I am certain we can expect a ready welcome and some food for my men."

"No!" Alanna had thought this dreadful day could become no worse, but she had been wrong. "I will not visit there."

Startled at her vehemence, Lucas swung about, amazed to find Alanna attempting to bring one leg over her saddle as if to jump from the moving horse.

Reining in both animals, he was on the ground before his golden-haired hostage and easily captured her in his arms. It was clearly fury, not fear that motivated her, a glorious female warrior intent on vanquishing her foe and escaping. With her deep-set blue eyes, the splashes of crimson coloring her cheeks, her head held high and her chin jutting forward in defiance, Alanna resembled a modern-day Athena, Lucas mused.

"Damn you, del Fuentes, let me go," demanded the Irish vixen, continuing her battle for freedom. Thrusting her body first right then left to loosen his grasp, she kicked out sharply against the Spaniard's legs, but his close proximity prevented her from striking a more desirable target.

All at once, however, his right arm snaked itself around her tiny waist and she found herself suspended in the air, her head resting against his chest, as he stroked her wild curls and murmured gently. His voice echoed only concern, and that, more than anything else, was Alanna's downfall. She ceased her struggle.

"Now then, I've said I won't let you come to harm, Alanna, and I meant it, but you must warn me if we are heading into some heathen ambush or English stronghold." He managed to control his impatience, though he wanted to shout. "Can't you tell me what is so fearsome about the abbey? Do they worship Satan and his followers or perform human sacrifice, perhaps?"

Alanna couldn't help but laugh at the absurd image of Mother Columbine standing over a boiling kettle, stirring human entrails into her preciously guarded recipe for Friday's stew. Then she looked up at Lucas's face to find the worry lines etched across his brow easing.

She had been so shocked by the idea of returning to St. Bridget's, she had foolishly permitted her memories to take over. When she looked at the situation reasonably, however, more than fourteen years had passed since she had been at the place. She was far different from the innocent child cloistered within those unyielding walls for her own good and a proper education. Besides, how could del Fuentes know she had been imprisoned there for nearly two years of her life? He promised her safety, after all, and he wouldn't abandon her now, not when he still might need a hostage.

"Well?" he asked softly, a large hand stroking her cheek in a soothing rhythm. "You obviously know more about the abbey than I do. Shall we seek sustenance or turn back?"

"I... The abbey is a convent, St. Bridget's. It is a safe enough place. At least it was fourteen years ago when my parents sent me there—"

"They expected you to be an nun?" He didn't even try to hide the amazement in his voice. Alanna, the passionate, fiery female who had taunted him in person and haunted his every moment since they had met, a nun? Either she had changed drastically in the last fourteen years, or her parents never knew their daughter.

"No, not really, but they believed it safer for me there than on the Desmond estates, which were often under siege by the English. I disagreed, however, and ran away or tried to so often that I spent nearly every hour I was at St. Bridget's on my knees, praying, studying or scrubbing floors to work off my penance. I thought at the time that

Mother Columbine was so intractable because she was the devil's mistress.''

"And now?"

"I suppose some part of me still balks at entering those walls, but..."

Alanna hesitated briefly as Lucas scowled. He had already considered the possibility of entrusting his captive to the care of the nuns. If he made it clear her stay was only to be a temporary one, perhaps he could still guarantee her cooperation.

"Well, go on," he urged quietly.

"I realize she was only doing as my parents asked, and that is where I learned Latin," she admitted. "Without Mother Columbine, I might never have unwittingly saved your detestable hide, so if we go there, you will ask for food, not steal it or demand it. But let us hurry, your men are not the only ones who are hungry."

Pleased with Alanna's trust, Lucas found himself lowering his lips to hers—just a quick kiss, a token of thanks and reassurance, he told himself, wanting to explore the velvety texture of her mouth, to have her dainty lips accept his own with a soft, tantalizing quiver. But he had to restrain himself, Lucas realized suddenly, or he would lose his soul to the sweet taste of her. Abruptly, the green-eyed Spaniard released her from his arms and pulled back, finding it difficult to swallow, let alone speak, for the unyielding lump in his throat.

For her part, Alanna had no qualms about giving voice to her words, if not her true feelings. Thoroughly unsettled by the rushing in her ears and the trembling of her heart at the feathery brush of Lucas's mouth on hers, the young widow could not help but remember Sean and the similar way he had oft teased her, knowing full well how easily he could reduce her to a quivering mass of desire in minutes. Well, Lucas del Fuentes was not Sean, and he would never know such a privilege, she vowed silently.

"Evidently, del Fuentes, gentlemanly behavior is as foreign to you as my Gaelic tongue, but, I assure you, despite your best efforts, *that* will remain forever beyond your reach,'' she snapped, unaware of the blush coloring her face in the early twilight. ''I may be your prisoner, but I shall never choose to be your amusement. You would do well to remember that, especially since you are still many miles from your ship in *my* land.''

The Spaniard's emerald eyes darkened briefly as he considered the deep chasm between the truth expressed by Alanna's body, held so close to his own, and the words she angrily spouted. Still, it was not his place to challenge her, not now when they were about to enter a house of God. He would behave.

''You have my word of honor that it shall not happen again, my lady Alanna. I can only say I was bewitched by you and didn't consider the offense I might give. When you realize how far from death you've led me today, perhaps you will forgive my desperate grasping at life.'' He led her to the grazing horses. ''Will you accompany me to the abbey?''

''I, for one, do not go back on my word,'' the blonde chided, accepting his hand up onto her horse. ''We shall tell Mother Columbine you are my priest, recently arrived from the Continent. Hopefully, that and old reminiscences will forestall any awkward questions.''

Chapter Six

The thick stone walls surrounding the abbey surprised Lucas somewhat, unaccustomed as he was to a land where religion, though offering eternal salvation, often saw the spilling of blood when leaders changed churches. Having rung the bell for admittance, he eyed the woven wicker basket at the gate with curiosity.

"That's for people to leave their offerings for the sisters," explained Alanna nervously.

"Offerings? You mean money?"

"In Ireland, money is a rare commodity, Lucas," disputed the blonde. "Those who can feed their families may share bacon, potatoes or cabbage, but the poor often leave their babes."

"They give up their children?" Lucas was astonished. In Spain, one's offspring held the promise of honor and distinction. Boys grew up to be well-appointed soldiers or members of court, and girls made good marriages. Indeed, a man's seed was the summary of his life's ambition. And the Irish threw that away? No wonder he had heard them called savages.

"When the choice is between watching a beloved infant starve to death or knowing he will be cared for by the church, a mother has no choice. It is difficult enough to keep oneself alive at times, let alone be responsible for another mouth to feed," defended Alanna, her irritation at the foreigner's insensitivity barely hidden. How could he, raised in a noble household of plenty, understand her people or their ways? No, the Irish and Spanish could never be compatible, Alanna thought with a frown, not when they were so very different in their history and in their hearts.

Then a small door in the wooden gates of the abbey opened and there stood Mother Columbine, a tall, spare figure whose expression was far from friendly. To Alanna, the woman hadn't changed at all. Her dark eyes were as hard, her mouth compressed as ever into a thin line, her face as stern and uncompromising as when the nun had confronted her delinquent charge so often, ready to mete out punishment. Yet the words from the abbess's lips were far from the accusing ones Alanna expected.

"Are you travelers in need of food and lodging? I am Mother Columbine, and on behalf of St. Bridget's Abbey, I open our doors," she began, her eyes widening slightly at the sight of the small blond woman accompanying the tall friar. "Of course, you are more than welcome, though we haven't a proper stable for your horses, just an old shed for a few sheep and chickens."

"Your kind heart will one day see you blessed in heaven," replied Lucas, extending his hand in benediction over the nun. Given Alanna's attitude toward this place, she certainly had never visited here with her priest, he mused, so that man's name should be a safe one to borrow. "I am Friar Galen, and we will ask your charity but briefly."

"As you wish. Sister Mary Patrick, open the gates at once," instructed the seemingly ageless nun. "Then, while you arrange our guests' supper, have Sister Mary Matthew assist the friar with the horses."

"We do not wish to burden you, Mother. We can tend to them ourselves," protested Lucas, already leading Piobar and Baibi into the abbey's courtyard.

Built in the manner of most monasteries, the church was laid out with the altar facing east, abutted by the cloister, which connected it to the chapter house, the individual cells and the refectory. At the far end of the property were the kitchens, the guest house and the makeshift stable. It was in that direction Lucas moved, motioning for Alanna to follow.

"Nonsense, this young woman is pale with exhaustion. She will come inside with me and wait for your meal," Columbine chided. Quickly, she stepped forward, wrapped an arm about Alanna's shoulders and turned her toward the refectory. "You may join us when you have finished."

Lucas frowned, too surprised by the woman's taking charge to protest. He had not expected to be separated from Alanna, but he saw no way to avoid it since the abbess showed absolutely no regard for his authority as a cleric. Well, he would have to trust that Alanna would not reveal his secret... and hurry the care of the horses as never before.

"Of course, Mother, as you say," he agreed. He led the animals away while he considered keeping them saddled in case he had need of a quick escape. No, if it came to that, he could always ride bareback. Even their mounts needed some respite from labor, he decided, looking over his shoulder to the door through which the women had disappeared. How he would love to hear their conversation!

"Now, my child, tell me all that has befallen you since you left us," invited Columbine, settling her charge at the empty table in the dining hall while she fetched their drink. "Surely you are no longer Alanna Desmond, not as striking a young woman as you've become. Indeed, I saw the promise of your beauty even then, when you were but an angry child."

"You remember me so well?" the blonde asked softly, somehow not startled at the nun's recognition. Columbine had always known much of what should have been hidden. "Why, when I was such a problem, would you care?"

"Have you not yet learned that the problems and worries of life are what enrich us and challenge us to reach new heights?" murmured Columbine. She brushed Alanna's hair away from her face with a gentle hand. Pressing a cup of homemade liquor into her hand as she poured one for herself, the abbess continued. "But that was long ago.

Know only that you were never a burden, and I have prayed often that you would find happiness. Have you?"

"Briefly," admitted Alanna, smiling at memories. "His name was Sean O'Donnell, and we loved each other mightily from the day we pledged our troth until he was massacred at Smerwick."

"I'm sorry. May he rest in peace," Columbine muttered. "And since then?" When Alanna did not respond, the old nun sighed deeply. "It is sad to lose one's husband so young, but that was nearly eight years ago, child. Have you been alone all that time?"

"Aye, but not unhappily. I live with the O'Donnells most of the year, but for a few months at Castlemount with my mother's brother."

Suddenly recalling the insidious betrayal she had escaped, Alanna was silent, uncertain how much to reveal of her current circumstances. If she wanted to get farther north and remove herself from Grady's grasp, Alanna knew she could not inform Columbine of her situation. The nun would insist Alanna remain at the convent, and that would only place her in peril.

Slowly she raised her cup and sipped at the *poitin* within. As Lucas opened the door to enter, she again found her tongue. "There was some trouble on the coast with rumors of invading Spanish ships, so I was dispatched northward to the O'Donnell lands for safety."

"Unfortunately an English party waylaid us this morning and confiscated our provisions," added Lucas, pleased with Alanna's half-truth. "The barbarians had no respect for the sanctity of the cloth or my lady Alanna."

"They—they didn't harm her?" The abbess was horrified at the very thought of it.

"No, not at all," soothed the young woman, reaching out to pat the nun's wrinkled hand.

"No man would dare while I am alive," declared Lucas, revealing more than he realized as his jaw muscles tightened with resolution. "She is under my care."

"Spoken like a soldier," observed Mother Columbine. She carefully studied the friar where he stood in the shadows thrown by the candles. Not only his words, but also his muscular physique marked him a man of force and physical strength rather than prayer and contemplation, she decided.

"A soldier in the service of our Lord," Alanna defended quickly, hoping Columbine's powers of intuition had dimmed over the years. Since Lucas *had* saved her from Bravingham, she knew her conscience wouldn't stand for him to be discovered now, not when it would leave her stranded here at the abbey. "Friar Galen has just returned from a long pilgrimage on the continent."

"Ah, a man of wide experience and true devotion. How marvelous you found him to be your confessor, child," said the abbess softly. Her dark eyes missed nothing of the looks that passed between her guests. Still, they had not asked her advice or confided in her. She would be silent and bide her time. "Here is Sister Mary Patrick with bread and hot soup for your supper."

"Friar, why don't you sit beside me and offer the blessing?" suggested Alanna as Lucas unthinkingly reached for the bread.

A blessing? For a moment, he froze, remembering only the Spanish prayers he had learned at his mother's knee. Well, fresh from the continent, Lucas hoped he'd be excused a less than orthodox Irish litany.

"Gracious Father, we ask Your blessing first on those who prepared this meal and offer us their hospitality and then on us who are so fortunate to enjoy it. May we always know and obey Your will," he said solemnly. He was inordinately pleased when Mother Columbine uttered "amen" rather than "imposter."

"Enjoy your meal, my children," invited the abbess. "I will see about beds for you."

"No," protested Alanna. "We couldn't trouble you."

"That is not necessary, Mother. The rest of our party awaits us in the forest," Lucas explained, realizing how unorthodox it was for him to be eating his fill while his men sat hungry in the darkness.

"But why did you not journey together?" pressed the nun in surprise. She could barely accept the idea of an English party overpowering the athletic Galen, let alone Galen *and* others. Clearly she had not yet heard the truth.

"They were too weary to travel farther," replied Alanna, her guilty look giving evidence to the lie, "but we promised to bring back supplies. That is, if you can spare them."

The young woman was in trouble, that much was evident to Mother Columbine, but whether the trouble originated with her friar or was eased by him, she could not decide. Indeed, she strongly suspected he wasn't a friar at all—or shouldn't be, given the sparks in his eyes when he looked at Alanna. Still, they hadn't asked for any assistance other than a few days' provisions, and the charity of her order dictated that much be done no matter who requested it.

"Of course, we can oblige you," the nun was saying when the bell at the front gate began to toll angrily at the same time a rhythmic pounding sounded. "Sister Mary Alphonse, see what that noise is all about. Alanna, you will change into a habit at once."

"But, Mother—" protested the young widow as Columbine went to a large chest and thrust the clothing and veil of their order into her arms.

"Only English soldiers or a raiding party would dare to create such a disturbance in a religious house," the abbess explained. "In either case, the sight of such a lovely woman as yourself would tempt even the strongest man to sin, let alone his weaker brothers. If you are clothed in the uniform of St. Bridget, the church will be your protection."

Still Alanna hesitated, again envisioning an eternity spent on her knees at this abbey. Then Sister Mary Alphonse returned, her face worried, her quiet voice trembling with apprehension.

"Mother, a group of soldiers is at the gate, demanding to search the abbey for a band of escaped Spanish prisoners and the Irish woman they kidnapped," reported the young novitiate. Lucas and Alanna exchanged troubled looks. "They must be Protestants because their captain says he will torch the gates if you do not give permission for them to enter promptly. What shall I tell him?"

"What shall we tell him, Alanna?" the abbess asked meaningfully.

"Nothing," Alanna said, her heart thumping in her chest.

"You heard the girl. Don't say anything. I will handle the captain, and you may ring the bells to call the sisters to *complin.*"

"But it is too early. The clock has not yet struck nine."

"You may inform the others that Friar Galen will lead us in prayer this evening, so we may not follow the usual service. Now, Sister Mary Alphonse, if you will show him to the chapel." Mother Columbine's icy tones overrode the young nun's confusion, and quickly she set about doing as ordered, waiting by the door for the cleric.

Lucas stood quietly, his emerald eyes carefully studying the abbess's face. Then he nodded and rose to follow the younger nun, hesitating briefly beside Alanna's chair.

"I know you are frightened, but our only hope is to obey Mother Columbine, Alanna. I believe she is worthy of our trust," he murmured, praying that his judgment hadn't failed him.

"My dear," pressed the abbess, closing the door behind the friar, "if he is holding you against your will, you have only to tell me and I will let the soldiers take him."

Alanna's eyes widened apprehensively at the nun's words, but she quickly shook her head. "Of course, Friar Galen is doing no such thing, Mother. If you permit me, I'll put this habit on and join him in the chapel."

Columbine nodded. She had offered protection and Alanna had declined. Now the matter rested with God.

"The sisters are gathered in the chapel for evening prayer, Captain. You and your men may search the abbey unencumbered by our presence, though I assure you we harbor no escaping prisoners or their hostages within our walls," declared Mother Columbine haughtily a few minutes later at the gate of St. Bridget's. As she admitted the small band of soldiers, she was relieved to see from their motley uniforms that they did not actually represent the English Crown, but were mercenaries, available to the highest bidder. She hoped their Irish blood would keep them from committing blatant sacrilege of the abbey. "I must inquire first, however, by whose authority do you seek these foreigners?"

"The reward the girl's uncle is offering is authority enough for any man in the county," said the group's leader. "If you must know, my name is Denton. My men and I have, this day, joined in the service of a neighbor of the MacWilliams's, a noble named Bravingham. He wants us to find the girl and rescue her from invading Spanish devils who carried her off so MacWilliams can marry her to him as promised."

"Hmm, well then, I'll leave you to your quest, but mind you, gentlemen, this is a house of God, not a storehouse to be looted. When you depart, I expect you to take nothing with you but our prayers." Columbine fixed each man with a warning look. "In the meantime I shall be at chapel."

"We only want the Spaniards and their prisoner," the soldier assured her, gesturing for his men to disperse and begin the search. "In fact, while the others explore elsewhere, I will accompany you to personally inspect the chapel and your nuns, Mother. I understand there are nine and yourself."

"Myself and ten," corrected the abbess, outraged at his implication, "but how can you suspect my nuns?"

"A habit wouldn't be a bad disguise for a small man, now would it? We don't have descriptions of the fugitives, but your outfits and headdresses do cover a lot of territory."

"And I assure you, Captain Denton, not for you nor any man will that territory be uncovered as long as I am Abbess of St. Bridget's," snapped the nun indignantly. "You will have to be satisfied with the fact that none of the sisters sports facial hair or deep voices."

"If each of them is as pious and committed as yourself, Mother Columbine, you've nothing to worry about," said the soldier, his voice echoing loudly in the chapel as he opened the wooden door and stepped into the rear of the nave.

Lit only by the candles on the main altar, a few wall sconces and the sparse moonlight entering through the lantern tower, the church was filled with more dusky shadows than patches of brightness, observed Denton. It was simple enough, however, to discern the friar waiting in the chancel area and the sisters kneeling quietly in the double row of prie-dieux before the altar.

No more than sixty feet in length, he gauged, and twenty in width, the small church was modest in adornment and design, with nothing worth stealing visible. The place lacked formal columns and transepts and was possessed of few statues. Most of the alcoves were empty, their sacred images already carted off.

Indeed, at first glance, it seemed that only the sanctuary or perhaps the inevitable crypt beneath its altar might offer a reasonable hiding place, unless, as he had joked, the nuns were the men for whom he hunted. Before he could move toward them, however, the abbess interfered, calling the cleric to attention.

"Friar Galen, if you don't mind, let us say a decade of the rosary for the safe return of a missing woman. If you will begin, each of the sisters will offer an *Ave* in turn," decreed Mother Columbine, trusting such a blatant distraction would deter the captain from perusing the individual nuns too closely. They hadn't time to cut Alanna's hair, nor would she possess a properly meek demeanor if challenged. Her voice, though, was clearly feminine and melodic in tone and should dissuade the man from suspicion of her, or so it could be hoped.

At Mother Columbine's instructions, Lucas glanced over his shoulder and nodded, moving toward the foot of the altar where he knelt to intone the *paternoster* that would open the requested prayer. Only one soldier accompanied the nun, and he seemed more interested in the sisters than their priest, he observed. He recited the Latin verse by rote without hesitation. Still, kneeling as he was with his back to the nave, the hood of his robe drawn over his head, Lucas felt perilously exposed, his position indefensible to whatever might befall him.

"Very good, Mother, an excellent gambit to satisfy my curiosity, though I will, of course, watch and listen closely to be sure that each sister speaks her words of worship," warned Denton.

Lucas reached the point in the prayer where they responded, and he gratefully fell silent, weighing the possibility that the abbess might betray him. Was it possible that the hope of the reward and the acts of charity it would endow was enough to sway her loyalty away from Alanna? Casting a quick glance over his shoulder, Lucas found the nun staring at him, a stern look on her face as she nodded for him to turn around. Damn it, he fumed, facing the altar once more, how could he protect Alanna or himself if he didn't know what was happening behind him?

The *paternoster* was finished and the sisters began their *aves,* but Lucas could not recall where Alanna was. Resisting the urge to glance behind him again, possibly targeting her for the soldier's attention, he concentrated on the voices. No, this was not his captive. Two other sisters spoke the prayer, and he responded as did the rest, his voice successfully hiding his growing trepidation. Then, as his patience was rapidly disappearing, he heard Alanna's voice, sweet and untroubled as she offered her Hail Mary for her own safety. The irony of it galled Lucas. Fitfully he waited for their inevitable discovery, but the soldier remained silent, somewhere in the darkness, as the fifth nun continued the decade.

Lucas feared the strain of the deception was telling on him. He was glad his face was turned from view when he felt icy perspiration scale down his back, drop after drop crystallizing his frustration at being not only powerless but on his knees in the face of danger. His had always been a life of action, quick and decisive, on the battlefield and off, not one of stealth and concealment, and this duplicity did not sit well with him. Indeed, the bitter struggle to stay silent and do nothing while an enemy lingered outside his field of vision was one of the fiercest battles Lucas had ever fought. He required a valiant effort to fend off the silent accusations of cowardice sounding in his brain. When had he, a soldier and defender of the faith, ever taken refuge behind a skirt?

Then, as the door to the chapel slammed shut, he heard Mother Columbine finish reciting the Gloria and he took the opportunity to stand and face his audience. Acknowledging the abbess's angry glare and the shaking of her head, he nevertheless gave a curt nod and continued to approach the pulpit. If he was about to be taken, at least he would see it coming. He counted seven men now grouped around their leader at the rear of the nave.

Bowing his head briefly as he stood before them, Lucas scanned the church and watched the captain deploy the newly arrived soldiers to search the area thoroughly. As the men spread out, they moved between the kneeling nuns, in and around the occupied and empty prie-dieux, exploring the small alcoves that dotted the walls, even going down into what he supposed was the abbey's crypt. He searched for the proper words to give the frightened nuns reassurance without giving himself away. He was the cause of their distress. He ought to be able to lessen it. Yes, he recalled suddenly, he would share the psalm taught them by the Bishop of Killaloe, an Irish prelate, before the battle with the English. If nothing else, it was apropos of events in his life.

"Sisters, until these men permit us to resume our nightly prayer uninterrupted, I invite you to let the words of Psalm 116 comfort your heavy hearts.

"'The cords of death encompassed me; the snares of the nether world seized me. I fell into distress and anguish.'"

His eyes sought Alanna's and sent her his calm strength even as the captain approached the altar with a purposeful stride.

"'Then I invoked the name of the Lord. Gracious is the Lord and just. I was brought low and He saved me.'"

"Nothing down there, Captain," called one of the men coming up from the small crypt, stopping to stand behind Lucas.

"Not here, either, sir," announced another. One by one the men made their way forward to the altar, forming a loose circle in the chancel area, effectively cutting off any chance for Lucas's escape.

"'Return, oh my soul, to your tranquillity, for the Lord has been good to you,'" Lucas continued, his eyes moving away from Alanna's so as not to single her out.

Suddenly the captain wheeled forward, swooped past the friar and lifted the altar cloth, but was disappointed to find only a stone facing behind it. Still, his men lingered, their attention focused totally on the friar who stood so very tall and unmoving despite their disruptions.

"'For he has freed my soul from Death, my eyes from tears, my feet from stumbling. I shall walk before the Lord in the lands of the living!'" Lucas's prayers were one with the words of the psalm even as he wondered at his own temerity in expecting help from on high.

"If you please," interrupted the captain, suddenly standing at Lucas's side, one hand reaching out to touch him.

For a moment Lucas hesitated, his hand itching to draw a weapon he no longer carried. His fists might serve well enough to delay the inevitable, he considered, but then he crushed the self-preserving urge, which could only endanger the women before him. He turned obediently to his accuser.

"Yes, Captain?" he replied, quietly awaiting his end.

Watching the brief exchange but unable to hear the precise words, Alanna tasted fear in her throat and knew she had to act. But as she started to rise to her feet, she felt Mother Columbine kneel beside her, forcing her back to her knees.

"Hush, child," the abbess whispered vehemently. Her fingers were a vise grasping Alanna's arm so tightly it felt her blood no longer flowed. "Don't reveal yourself if he is taken. He would not want it. Think of that, and of us, as well."

Stunned at the nun's words and helpless against her iron grip, the young widow stared at Lucas, offering her soul for his deliverance. After all, she told herself in an attempt to explain her concern for the Spaniard who had abducted her, if he was captured it was likely she would be, as well.

"Oh, Lord, please save him," she murmured.

"If prayers mean anything, Friar, ask your God to keep the Spanish from ravishing the girl. Should they do so, no one will want her," observed the mercenary to Lucas. "I hear those Spanish are particularly bloodthirsty savages with no regard for women. If I were you and they showed up at my gate I wouldn't take them in. However, I'll send word to Bravingham's regular forces, camped on the south ridge, that your community has already been searched and nothing found."

"They are close enough to protect us should we be attacked by the foreigners?" Mother Columbine asked shrewdly, to ascertain their exact location. Perhaps she could provide Alanna not only with food but a safe route, as well.

"Only a few miles south from here, near Braddock Hill."

"Very well then, Captain. I will see you and these men out while the sisters finish the *complin*," announced the abbess, scurrying to lead the way.

If ever a prayer of thanksgiving deserved completion, this one did, Lucas vowed as the soldiers stomped out of the holy chamber.

"'Precious in the eyes of the Lord are the lives of his faithful ones. Oh, Lord, You have loosed my bonds. To You I will offer sacrifice of thanksgiving and I will call upon the name of the Lord in the land of the living,'" he recited, his voice resounding throughout the chapel.

"Amen," answered Alanna and her companions, rising from their knees at Mother Columbine's return.

"Sisters, you may retire," the abbess announced quietly. Turning to Alanna and her friar, she put a hand on each of their arms, but waited for the nuns to leave before speaking. "You will be glad to hear the soldiers have gone away fully satisfied. You may rest your heads in safety at the abbey tonight if you wish."

"Though I can never thank you enough for your help, I must decline and return to my men," Lucas said. "I am Lucas del Fuentes, a soldier, not a friar, and as you have guessed, we are who they seek. But permit me to assure you that the Spanish are not invading your shores, we are merely on our way home from Philip's Great Enterprise against England. The swifter we gather some food and depart, the safer you and the others will be."

Mother Columbine nodded and led the two fugitives from the chapel along the convent's quiet and dark hallways, her veiled figure blending into the haze of shadows through which they traveled. Suddenly, she stopped before a door set deep in the gray stone wall.

Like the pantries of all who had refused to make their peace with the English, accepting neither their sovereign nor religion, St. Bridget's was sparsely stocked these days. Nevertheless the abbess was bent on sharing what she could spare, and begrudged nothing to this Spaniard who had boldly breached her gates demanding sustenance. Lucas del Fuentes was still a son of the church, and had dedicated himself to a rightful attack upon England's heretic queen.

But more importantly, he had earned Mother Columbine's respect by exhibiting both resourcefulness and bravery.

After striking a flint to light the candle stub always waiting in a niche outside the storeroom, Mother Columbine held the heavy door open and watched her visitors closely as they entered.

Though he still held his body stiffly and a certain male arrogance crept out from beneath his priest's robes, the abbess could see that the Spaniard had visibly relaxed now that the English soldiers had departed and he was assured not only of escape but the provisions he had originally come seeking.

As for Alanna, the girl appeared more nervous than a hind fleeing the huntsman, though the defiant scowl that puckered her lips was meant to signal otherwise. But now that she was safe, what was there to be afraid of unless it was the yearnings of her own heart? The abbess had been witness to the girl's reluctant concern for del Fuentes. Could it be that such confusing emotions caused her fear?

Stepping into the center of the small chamber, Mother Columbine observed del Fuentes's reaction when the candle flame flickered and cast its weak light over the foodstuffs hoarded there. His expression, though impassive to most, betrayed a great hunger to the abbess's watchful eye, and the nun wondered sympathetically how long he had been without food prior to the simple meal she had served him. But when his gaze came to rest on Curran Desmond's daughter and lingered overlong, Mother Columbine was witness to a much fiercer appetite. Lowering her eyes for an instant, the abbess feared this also was the result of a prolonged deprivation even as she prayed it was something of a higher nature blossoming there beneath her convent's roof.

Quickly her attention shifted to Alanna. The girl's head was tilted as defiantly and proudly as ever she had held it while living within these walls years ago. In fact, Alanna was so caught up with her fiery show that she failed completely to notice the devouring flames in Lucas's eyes whenever he looked in her direction.

Yet, unaware as the two were, Mother Columbine continued to see the sparks that flew between the young pair, threatening to ignite and burst into a blaze. All this Mother Columbine saw and more. It was there in the surreptitious glances Lucas sent Alanna's way as he inspected the food spread upon the shelves, just as it was there in the studied manner in which the girl ignored her captor. Would it be a bad thing, then, to nurture such a grand passion to fruition? the abbess wondered.

A match with the Spaniard would save Alanna from the spouse chosen for her by her despicable uncle, Grady MacWilliams. And it would keep her from the harm certain to one day befall the stronghold of the reckless Kevin O'Donnell. More important, hadn't the girl's own mother been abducted from this very convent twenty-five years ago? And she had found happiness, or at least as much joy as any woman could find in this land so beset by war and troubles. Why, wedding Lucas del Fuentes might solve even that dilemma if he took his bride home to Spain and away from the turmoil that was Ireland.

But, Mother Columbine mourned, how could she, an outsider, promote something both of these obstinate intruders seemed intent on disregarding? Yet the abbess was not a woman given to despair. Her faith rose up before her. If it was to be, God would provide, she decided. Her thoughts were interrupted, however, as Lucas finished his survey of the shelves and addressed her.

"I will not overtax your generosity, Mother," he said gently, "but will take only what we require to sustain six for a day or two."

"There are only five of you," Alanna objected quickly. "There's no need to be greedy."

"Are you telling me, Alanna, that you will not feel hunger's gnawing pangs before you are released? How generous of you to offer to fast so that we do not deprive the good nuns of more than they can spare," Lucas said lightly but his tone held a note of warning that he was in no mood for her aggravation. It was a warning, however, that Alanna chose to ignore.

"What I am saying, del Fuentes, is that there will be five traveling north and not six," she stated with finality. Concerned by her recent fears for Lucas del Fuentes's safety, Alanna had decided to separate herself from him as quickly as possible. Though she hated St. Bridget's, how much more would she come to hate herself if she betrayed her memory of Sean and gave in to the temptation this handsome Spaniard seemed to stir in her? Since the English had already determined the abbey was not her hiding place, staying behind when he left would serve her needs well, and put an end to her peculiar reactions to him. He was, after all, but a man, and an enemy at that. "I will not accompany you."

"Is that so?" Lucas asked softly though his eyes glinted with hard determination. "Am I to understand that the woman who refused to give me away to the English just a short while ago is now balking at guiding me to Blacksod Bay? I will not believe it. Had you wanted to be rid of me, you had only to open your mouth when the soldiers were in the chapel. So what game is this you seek to play with me, Alanna?"

" 'Tis no game, *señor*," she replied with the coldness of a gale blowing in from the North Sea, a coldness that could not combat the cursed warmth he ignited in her. "I did not betray you only because it did not suit my purpose at the time. Rest assured, if it had, I would have done so. As it was, I had no wish to be taken, as well, and delivered to the bridegroom my uncle has chosen for me."

"That might very well be," Lucas said at last, his voice husky with the effort to convince himself that he wanted this comely female with him only to serve as guide and hostage. "But as it is, you are still mine until I release you, and I say it is time we move on."

"Say what you like, Lucas del Fuentes," Alanna shot back, "but I am telling you, now that the moment of danger has passed, we will part ways. You can return to your men, and I will stay here for the time being."

"Not bloody likely," Lucas said with a chuckle, though the dangerous gleam always lurking in his dark green eyes burned hotter than usual. "You're coming with me."

"By all that's holy, I'm not," replied Alanna adamantly. She perched herself on a stool in the corner of the room as though to demonstrate her point.

Mother Columbine looked from Alanna's challenging demeanor to Lucas's rising anger, evidenced primarily by the building fire in his eyes and the tightening of the muscles along his strong, lean jaw. Even in a rage, he was a man who could restrain himself, and thus one to whom she could entrust Curran Desmond's daughter. And though the rugged Spaniard was displaying the hardened features of a warrior at present, Lucas del Fuentes could not hide from Mother Columbine the basic decency and caring nature that existed beneath his fierce surface. For that reason, the abbess decided not to interfere.

"In the name of God and all his saints, madam," Lucas said with deadly quiet, his patience at an end, "we will gather what we need and be on our way now!"

"No," said Alanna simply. She settled herself more comfortably upon the stool and demurely arranged her skirts as though this man's temper was of little consequence to her.

"Listen to me, Alanna, and listen well. I have no time for your games or childish fits of pique, not when the lives of my men and our duty to Spain are at stake. Now either divest yourself of that nun's habit and make ready to travel, or I swear by the Virgin, I will rip that garb off you myself, and none too gently," Lucas bellowed, allowing his anger to run away with him in order to still the excitement that images of tearing off Alanna's clothing aroused.

"I do not expect any man, even a sinner such as yourself, to profane holy cloth," Alanna retorted.

"Then tempt me, Alanna, and see how much I dare," Lucas whispered hotly, his tall frame looming over her as he bent to place his face only inches from her own.

"Surely there is no need to rend what our order has worked so diligently to fashion," Mother Columbine interjected quickly. "Can't you threaten the girl with something else?" she asked, earning a snort of laughter from Lucas and an angry glare from Alanna.

"You are right, Reverend Mother," Lucas agreed gallantly after a moment's reflection, a wicked smile curling about his lips. "Why cause your sisters to be deprived of the fruits of their labor by this one's petulant obstinacy? Alanna, if you continue to defy me, I swear before the throne of God that I will throw you over my shoulder and carry you out of here. And since you appear so reluctant to part with religious robes, I will not leave you here in Ireland as I have promised to do, but instead will carry you back to Spain. Once home, I will find some isolated convent and deposit you there, to spend the rest of your life in quiet prayer with no hope of ever returning to your native land. Now either do as I command, or I will make good my threat."

Suddenly, in spite of herself, Alanna began reliving the interminable boredom she had experienced at St. Bridget's during her childhood. The silent tranquillity had all but driven her mad. There was no way she could ever again turn her back on the world and all it had to offer. But she would burn in hell before she would apprise Lucas del Fuentes of that fact, and so she looked at him with mockery in her brilliant blue eyes. "You wouldn't do such a thing," she scoffed.

"Oh, but I would, though 'twould be a great pity to forever lock you away from men behind convent walls, especially when your temper tells me you are a woman of deep passions. Why, not even your nun's veil can give you an air of innocence, Alanna O'Donnell. You are not a woman who was ever meant for abstinence. Yet, refuse to do as I say, and I will act as I must."

"Mother Columbine will never surrender me to you against my will," Alanna rejoined heatedly, taking the abbess by surprise.

"You didn't want to come here to begin with," Lucas argued despite himself, unable to fathom this fiery Irish lass.

"That is beside the point," Alanna stated, calmly brushing his objection aside.

"But child, this is not the place for you," the nun asserted quickly, not willing to have this match end before it began. "Do you forget how intolerable you found the quiet life? During those scarce two years that your mother entrusted you into our care, how many times did you try to run off? It was after your fourth or fifth attempt that Curran decided this was not the place for you, and sent you north instead to be fostered by Kevin O'Donnell."

"If I had such a willful daughter, I'd send her north, too," Lucas muttered. He was glad that Columbine agreed with him, though why the woman did so, he had no idea.

"But I don't mean to stay forever," Alanna protested, sending Lucas a fierce glare meant to wipe the smug, mocking smile from his face. "I wish to remain only until I can get word to Kevin as to my whereabouts and he sends someone to fetch me."

"Why he would want to is beyond me," Lucas answered, looking to Columbine for her response.

"Think of what you are asking, my daughter," the older woman replied. It was obvious from Lucas's glib remarks that he harbored no suspicions of the plans the nun had for him, so she could afford to concentrate all her efforts on Alanna. "This man appears to be a match for a whole company of soldiers if he so chooses. Do you really think a small band of nuns could keep you safe from him when he wants you with him? Besides, think of the danger into which your presence here would plunge the good sisters in my care. We were fortunate once, but if the soldiers return and learn that we are harboring you, it could mean the end of our small convent, if not our very lives. Is this what you want for St. Bridget's?"

"No, of course not," Alanna admitted reluctantly, remembering the kindness the nuns had shown her in her youth, despite her rebellious ways. Yet tears of disappointment welled up in her eyes all the same.

"Then what recourse is there but that you go with Lucas del Fuentes?" a pleased Mother Columbine encouraged with a benevolent smile. "Trusting in God, of course, that you will be kept safe," she added piously when Alanna's look of unhappiness turned to one of outraged disbelief.

"What the abbess says is right," Lucas commented, beginning to fill a sack with provisions. Glad though he was that Mother Columbine had been reasonable, he continued to be perplexed by the nun's cooperation all the same. And the girl, why was she weeping now? First she did not want to enter St. Bridget's and now she balked at leaving. Damn, but whether they be in the convent or out, he did not understand Irish women!

A short while later, St. Bridget's abbess led Lucas and a sullen Alanna to the gates, where the older woman quietly lifted the latch and made ready to bid the young couple farewell.

"Thank you, Reverend Mother, for this, and for everything else, as well," Lucas said, holding the sack of food aloft.

"Godspeed, and take care of her, my son," the abbess responded meaningfully. "But before you go, a word with Alanna, if you please. It will not take more than a moment."

"I have not long to spare, Mother, but the time you seek is yours," Lucas said. He moved a few feet away to give the women a bit of privacy. The abbess had been helpful to him in more ways than one. Surely a goodbye to the woman who had come to the convent as a child was not something he could deny her.

"Farewell, Alanna Desmond O'Donnell," Mother Columbine began, taking the comely widow's hands in her own. "Do not judge me harshly or think me overly concerned with the welfare of St. Bridget's, putting its future above your own. The truth of the matter, my dear, is that it *is* your future that has prompted me to send you off with your Spaniard. And if truth be told, he may be more your captive than you are his."

"What do you mean?" Alanna asked suspiciously, glancing over her shoulder in Lucas's direction.

"Only that Curran Desmond abducted your mother, and that worked out well enough."

"You can't be serious, Reverend Mother!" Alanna objected in a furious whisper. "This man is not only half Spanish, but half English, as well, all that I hate in this world, the spawn of the two nations that caused the deaths of both Sean and my father!"

"Before he is anything else, Lucas del Fuentes is a man, Alanna, a good, honorable and decent man," Mother Columbine counseled, oddly enough echoing the thoughts Alanna refused to recognize.

"I can't believe that he has deceived you into viewing him in that light," the younger woman uttered in amazement. "You, who are always such a good judge of character, who see people as they really are."

"If you do not see him as I do, consider that mayhap it is you who are deceived, my daughter," the abbess said softly, bringing Alanna to Lucas's side once more. "It is with love that I caution you. Do not allow the ghosts of the past to interfere with the future of the living."

Quickly ushering the pair through the gate, she whispered into the darkness, "God go with you. God go with you both."

Chapter Seven

Though the journey to rejoin Lucas's shipmates was a short one, it was fraught with conflicting emotions for Alanna nonetheless. Mother Columbine's words rang in her ears, battling her natural reluctance to see Lucas Raphael del Fuentes as anything other than the embodiment of all she abhorred.

Yet as they traveled across starlit fields and into the forest, Lucas's sure hand holding her reins and his proud, rugged profile holding her attention just as tightly, Alanna couldn't help but once again be aware of the handsome Spaniard as more of a man than an enemy.

In the moon's silvery glow, his looks were gentled, transformed into something much softer and more attractive than the scowl he wore so often under the sun's harsh glare. And with the mists that rose from the damp ground and swirled about the powerful thighs he clamped tightly against the sides of his horse, he looked like some phantom monk, though surely it had to be a sacrilege for a man of his vigorous and bursting virility to wear the robes of one who had vowed to follow the path of chastity.

"I could not have left you in Mother Columbine's care," the haunting figure riding at Alanna's side said suddenly, breaking into her thoughts and destroying the spell the night winds had woven about her.

"I know," she replied. Her guilt for indulging in ridiculous fantasies made her response sharp and clipped. "It would have put the convent in jeopardy had I remained."

"It would have placed you in danger, as well," he said gruffly, stung by the tone she had used with him, and not at all sure why he felt compelled to explain himself to this Irish rose who had more thorns than petals. "That is, unless you really have no objections to marrying Bravingham," he added, looking at her pale, moon-bathed face.

"I said I had no wish to wed the man, didn't I?" Alanna snapped.

"So you did, but I wondered if perhaps your reluctance stemmed only from wounded pride, and anger that you had been bartered away without your knowledge," he continued, unable to let the matter drop.

"Aye, it's true enough that Grady's deception fired my temper," Alanna admitted. Her mouth drew in tightly as her emotions flamed anew.

"And Bravingham?" Lucas pressed.

"He's more beast than man. I'd rather throw myself from Castlemount's cliffs than become his wife!" Alanna fumed, her contempt for the Englishman momentarily diverting her anger from Lucas and his second successful abduction.

"I see," he said with no trace of the manner in which his spirits were inexplicably soaring.

"Why this sudden interest in my future, del Fuentes?" Alanna demanded, noting a hint of a smile haunting the corners of her captor's well-formed mouth.

"It eases my conscience to know I have not ruined your chances for happiness by removing you from Bravingham's reach," he replied.

"Well, then, why not cleanse your soul entirely by releasing me now?" Alanna countered impudently as they entered the small clearing where the others awaited their return. "And before you answer, don't think to paint yourself as my savior for rescuing me from Bravingham.

I'm not some fool to believe such a tale. I know 'twas by accident and not design. And while I realize I might have some little value as a hostage, I cannot help believe the aggravation of dragging me with you is not worth the effort. In fact, I definitely think it is not, especially when you enjoy my company no more than I do yours.''

"Woman, I grow weary of your clattering tongue," Lucas muttered as he helped her to dismount. He pushed her ahead of him into the clearing, perhaps more roughly than he had intended. "If you cannot keep still, I will gag you once more."

"Have a care, Spaniard," Alanna hissed, "or I swear I will plunge a blade into your black heart yet, long before you ever reach your captain."

"Try it, little she-wolf, and I will see that you regret it." The planes of Lucas's face hardened as he regarded the woman before him. *Dios,* but she was an enigma! To a masculine eye she appeared all softness and femininity, her enticing form promising more joy than could be imagined. But beneath that exquisite exterior lay the spirit of a warrior queen, and a heart so brittle that any man who sought to claim it could only be doomed to disappointment. Still, that was no business of his, he chided himself. Alanna Desmond O'Donnell was like the land that had seen her birth, lush but primitive, alluring yet destructive, and at the moment, Lucas del Fuentes cursed the fate that had brought them together and placed her in his keeping.

"Distribute some of the food," he ordered curtly, dropping the heavy sack at her feet. He paid no heed to the furious sparks lighting her eyes, just as he discounted the odd emotions flaring within his own chest.

"Speak to her in Latin, a language I can understand," reminded Juan, coming forward to join the pair. "Otherwise I might suspect that you and she are plotting against the rest of us. Such an observation would have to be reported to de Leiva."

"Are you always a fool, Alvarez?" asked Lucas brusquely, but he slipped back into the ancient tongue all the same. He had no wish to deal with *El Pavoreal* now, not after the emotional upheaval his adventure with Alanna had cost him. "I merely commanded her to give each man a portion of bread and drink."

"Ah, most commendable. It is always pleasant to have one's appetites appeased," Juan replied, his glittering eyes resting on Alanna's slender form and not the provisions brought forth from the rough linen bag.

Absorbed in her task, Alanna was not aware of the attention she was garnering from Juan Felipe Alvarez. But Lucas noted it, and the blood that normally ran hotly through his veins began to boil.

"Gather round," he abruptly ordered his men in Spanish, partly to draw Juan's attention from Alanna. "I learned much during my short visit to the convent, and I need to share it with you quickly."

Soon the sailors were being apprised that bands of soldiers—other than MacWilliams's—were searching for them. It made their predicament more perilous than ever, and no one, not even *El Pavoreal*, demurred when Lucas explained his plan to steal upon Bravingham's sleeping soldiers, camped within striking distance.

Yet dire though their circumstance might be, Juan's focus consistently wandered from Lucas's strategy to Alanna, who sat near the small campfire, flickering flames bestowing golden caresses upon her flawless skin.

Nibbling gracefully at a bit of bread, she was the epitome of all that was erotic as her small, pink tongue darted from between her pouting lips to daintily lick a bread crumb from the corner of her mouth.

Santa Maria! Lucas thought in frustration when his gaze also fell upon Alanna. The woman was a trial even when she did nothing. God was testing him sorely. Not only had he been forced to deal with Alvarez, the storm and their capture, but he had his attraction toward this wench to contend with, too. Surely no man could be expected to bear more, he decided, until Juan's continuing preoccupation with their prisoner and the predatory gleam in his eye raised Lucas's ire to even greater heights.

"It is agreed, then," he stated with finality, exerting iron control over the rage he felt when Juan's eyes once more slid lazily over Alanna's feminine curves. "We will allow ourselves some sleep and the horses more rest, and then we leave to attack the English soldiers on the other side of the mountain."

The men agreed in quiet, somber tones and began moving off to find what rest they could. But Lucas's granite hand on Juan's shoulder stayed the peacock.

"Understand, Alvarez, that our situation is little better than hopeless. I will not have our chances for survival done away with because of your baser instincts. You will feast on nothing but the food and drink contained in the sack," Lucas growled.

"We'll see," Juan replied smoothly, his silky voice and lecherous smirk nearly driving the other nobleman to violence.

But Lucas, well trained in the ways of battle, knew that now was not the time to fight Alvarez, expending energy and hatred that would be better directed against the enemy. Summoning his last vestiges of restraint, he managed to contain the pulsing urge to wrap his hands around *El Pavoreal*'s throat. Instead, he uttered a curse when he realized that he had but one way to keep Alvarez from defiling their proud and beautiful hostage.

Though he had thought to keep his distance from Alanna and thus safeguard his own sanity, Lucas nevertheless rose and stalked to the middle of the encampment. Grabbing Alanna's hand in his, he roughly dragged her to her feet and pulled her to the far side of the clearing. He did not utter a word of explanation until her struggles told him that she thought him guilty of the same sort of plans for her that Juan had devised.

"In a few hours we leave to attack Bravingham's men. Until that time, we rest. You will sleep by my side," he commanded impatiently.

"I'll do no such thing," Alanna hissed. Outraged by this latest affront, she tried to squirm away as Lucas lowered himself upon the mossy ground, bringing her with him.

"You don't have a choice," he muttered. He draped an arm over Alanna's wriggling body, despairing of the discomfort her shifting bottom was having upon him as she tried to wrest herself from his grasp. "Besides, you have nothing to fear from me," he added with a heavy sigh of exasperation. "Haven't you told me yourself that I care for you no more than you do me?"

"Then prove it. Allow me to move to the other side of the fire."

"So you can escape and inadvertently inform the English of our whereabouts? Nay, Alanna. I am no more a fool than you are," Lucas answered, trying to settle himself comfortably, but knowing peace would be impossible. *Madre de Dios,* but what he needed now, he thought angrily, was rest, not his warming blood pounding in his ears or his senses coming alive at the touch and fragrance of this wild Irish hellcat.

"Then bind me to a tree. Even that is preferable to suffering your nearness," Alanna retorted, frustrated by her inability to successfully fight Lucas's infuriating physical dominance.

"If you do not stay at my side, you will suffer even more at the hands of Juan Alvarez. Damnation, haven't you noticed, woman, that his eyes have not left you since our return from the convent? Do you think I enjoy this tussling? Now be still, or I will be tempted to hand you over to that bastard simply so that I might get some sleep!"

Alanna ceased fighting in an instant. Her instinct for self-preservation was strong, and she had not managed to survive in her turbulent homeland only to meet harm at the hands of one as despicable as Juan Alvarez. Still, her fiery nature would not allow her to meekly obey the edict of the golden Spaniard pinning her to him so casually.

"My foster father, the O'Donnell, will see you dead for what you have done to me," she whispered.

"First it was your uncle, then your foster father. So you have told me again and again," Lucas murmured into her hair.

" 'Tis a real threat I make," she insisted, not at all pleased by his unimpressed response.

"Hush, Alanna. If it will make you feel any better, you can dream of O'Donnell, Grady and the loving bridegroom all coming together to garrote me while you look on gleefully. Conjure up any vision you like, but only be silent and go to sleep."

"You don't take me seriously," she accused. How could Mother Columbine ever have hinted that this boorish lout was worthy of consideration as a man, never mind a husband?

"You're wrong, Alanna," Lucas replied despite himself, a deep sigh underscoring his words. "I consider you a very serious matter, indeed. But so is the question of the soldiers. Having them nearby is as much a danger to you as it is to me. Now, for the love of God, go to sleep so that I will be capable of dealing with them for both our sakes."

The weary sincerity in Lucas's deep voice gave Alanna pause, and soon the words he had spoken became oddly comforting. True, Lucas del Fuentes would benefit as much as she if her proposed husband's forces could be overcome. But still, it had been a long time since any man had taken care of her.

At Castlemount, she knew, her well-being was secondary to that of the keep, and on O'Donnell lands, Kevin granted her such independence that she fared remarkably well. But this golden-skinned Spaniard, with his English blood flowing through his veins, offered his protection and demonstrated concern for her even when beset by monumental troubles of his own. Resist though she might, Alanna found such a realization very warm and comforting indeed.

It was almost as warm as the heat generated by Lucas's hard, masculine body lying against her own. But while the sensation was pleasant, it was unsettling, as well. It awakened in her the desires she had denied herself these eight years since Sean's death. The masculine scent of Lucas del Fuentes and the vivid memory of his strong, lean lines stirred embers she had thought turned to ashes long ago.

Lying beside Lucas, conscious of the rise and fall of his powerful chest, feeling his breath as it wended through her hair, Alanna discovered she still possessed all the yearnings any woman would experience when confronted with the magnificent specimen of masculinity that was Lucas del Fuentes.

But, dear God, what was she thinking? Alarm suddenly pulsed through Alanna's body with such force that she jumped, causing Lucas to stir and murmur in his sleep. She had been Curran Desmond's daughter and Sean O'Donnell's bride. How could she be tempted to forget that, especially by this man who was half Spanish and half English? Hadn't those two nations stolen the lives of those she had held most dear? And wouldn't the surrender to the longings Lucas aroused within her brand her a traitor of the worst sort?

Yet as she fought to subdue thoughts of Lucas, Alanna discovered the task to be most difficult. Upon reflection, her handsome abductor had done much more than awaken the desires asleep for so long. Though he was overly proud, domineering and frequently insufferable, Alanna had to admit that there were things about him that demanded her admiration, reluctant as she might be to give it.

There were his bravery and cleverness to admire. The cool implacability under circumstances that would have another man quaking in terror. And then, too, he was possessed of gentleness at times. And honor. Hadn't he offered her, an enemy, his protection?

This awareness of Lucas del Fuentes as a man of soul as well as body disturbed her greatly. In fact, it turned her world completely upside down. Where there was once hatred, attraction was blossoming. Betrayal of Sean and her father threatened to replace her loyalty to them. But worst of all, memories of her past were being torn from her as she was being thrust into imagining an impossible future. Dear Lord, but she had not felt this miserable in eight years, and certainly she had never been so terribly confused.

Exhausted though she was, sleep proved elusive for Alanna. No sooner was she finally able to close her eyes than she was awakened, forced from the warm security of a masculine embrace into the all enveloping chill of the predawn air.

Colder still was the atmosphere of the camp itself. Though Alanna was no green girl and had seen men ready themselves for battle before, the preparations going on around her when she woke that morning were nevertheless discomfiting.

The sailors were grim as they went about their tasks, but Lucas del Fuentes was the most serious of them all. Gone was the protective, almost chivalrous man of last night, and in his place was a determined warrior so intent upon readying his men for battle that he spared neither word nor glance for the woman he had only recently held in his arms.

She had been a fool to have imagined that he might be different, Alanna berated herself. He was like all the rest of the males she had known, always ready to run off in pursuit of violence. Yet Alanna noted one important dissimilarity as she watched his sure hands saddle Piobar. He appeared fiercer than the others, his concentration greater, his tightly controlled aggression more lethal. As he stood there, seeing that his orders were carried out, he was the quintessential commander, no, the Prince of Blackness himself, the darkness of his good looks and raven hair relieved only by the anticipatory flames of battle flickering in his deep green eyes. He was, in short, the enemy, fearsome and merciless. And though Alanna could not help but respect his warrior's demeanor, she wondered how she could have ever considered betraying Sean's memory for the likes of such a demon.

"Be ready to ride in a few moments. I can't afford dawdling this morning. If you have any needs, see to them now," he barked in Latin, his voice icy, when he finally completed his tasks and deigned to address his hostage.

His decision to forgo the English he had used when speaking with her privately eroded any lingering traces of last night's intimacy. Instead, it nurtured Alanna's already burgeoning resentment of her near fall from grace.

"The only need I have is to escape you," Alanna retorted, the frostiness of her words a match for his own.

"Del Fuentes, the woman does not seem to be very enamored of you, even after a night at your side," Juan said with a cruel laugh as he came to the center of the encampment. "Surely that does not speak well for your prowess. Perhaps now the wench will be more willing to accept a real man."

"Mayhap I would, were I to find one," Alanna pronounced coldly.

"You bitch!" Juan spat, taking a menacing step forward only to be halted when Lucas planted himself in the aristocrat's path.

"There is no time for this now, Alvarez," he all but growled. "Remember that you are a nobleman in the service of Spain and act accordingly."

"'Tis exactly how he is behaving," Alanna mocked.

"You get to your horse and be quiet," Lucas directed sharply, his eyes flashing fury. "There will be no fighting until we encounter the English. Do I make myself clear to you both?"

While Pedro and his fellow sailors had no knowledge of the ancient tongue the trio used, they understood the tension that had developed all the same. More than one of them heaved a sigh of relief when a glowering Juan and a fiery Alanna finally did as they were told. Don Lucas and Alvarez had been at each other's throats since their party had landed on Irish shores, and now the woman had become an additional point of contention between them. Her presence could only portend eventual disaster. The men wished her gone. Yet there was something in the way Lu-

cas del Fuentes looked at her that made each and every
sailor afraid to suggest such a thing.

The cautious ride to the crest of the hill was a quiet one,
each member of the small band wrapped in thoughts too
personal to share. Fear itself dogged the hoofprints of their
horses as they journeyed through the still, dark forest, but
Lucas's presence somehow kept it at bay and did not allow
it to join their ranks.

Finally they came to the edge of the line of trees and dismounted. Enrique crawled forward on his belly to count the
number of guards and to ascertain that most of Bravingham's score of men still slept.

"You have but one knife among you," Alanna stated
calmly when Lucas came to untie her wrists and to help her
dismount. "If you had not broken my blade, I could have
wielded that."

"At my back while I faced the English before me?" Lucas inquired with a laugh, his eyes brimming with amusement. "No one but you, Alanna, has ever considered me
such a dullard!"

"I meant I would have used it on the English," she replied, annoyed that not only did this man refuse to take her
seriously, but that he was given to casual humor at such an
inappropriate time.

"You! But surely you do not think you are going into the
camp!" he exclaimed in genuine surprise. "I would not
permit it."

"Don't you fear my running off while you're engaged in
the fighting?" Alanna asked curiously while he led her
away from the horses in the direction of a small tree.

"Not at all," he stated matter-of-factly. "You'll wait for
us right here."

With that, he came purposefully forward. His inscruta-
ble expression was so unsettling that before she knew what
she was doing, Alanna retreated until finally she found her
back pressed against rough, ridged bark.

Suddenly Lucas's strong arms were reaching out toward her own and forcing them behind the tree, where he swiftly tied them together in one adroit movement.

"I told you that you would wait here," he said, a smug smile pulling at his mouth.

"You can't mean to abandon me and leave me tied to this damnable tree!" Alanna objected, her vulnerability completely wiping away her anger.

"That's exactly what I purpose. And before you decide to cease being the reluctant bride and try to scream out to the groom's men, I will gag you before I go."

"What if you are killed?" Alanna protested, worriedly eyeing the cloth Lucas was wrapping around his knuckles.

"Are you telling me you are concerned for my well-being, *querida?* I am touched," he said mockingly.

"No! 'Tis my own safety I am worried about, you great lout, and well you know it," she insisted, as much to herself as to him. "What will happen to me if you are slain?"

"If that is all that is bothering you, then you have nothing to fear," he said. "I *will* be back."

With that, he bent over her, bringing his face to hers, wanting to once more kiss this bewitching Irish temptress before going into battle. No matter what he had told her, he was experienced enough to know that he might very well die within the hour. And inexplicably, he could not think of enduring eternity without ever having tasted her lips again.

But just before his mouth found hers, he stopped himself. This was not how he wanted her, taking what he would rather than accepting that which she offered freely. Besides, he thought with determination, he would not allow himself to perish at the hands of the English, not with this woman dependent upon him.

Living, however, would present another difficulty should he kiss her as he wanted to do. He feared he would not be able to survive a lifetime with the memory of Alanna's lips pressed to his own without wanting more, wanting but not having because such a desire must never be fulfilled, not with circumstances as they were. Spain and his duty had to come first. If not, he would never be worthy of any woman, much less one such as Alanna Desmond O'Donnell.

While Lucas struggled to control his mounting desire, the beauty who unconsciously tempted him stood breathless, her blue eyes widening as they regarded him intently. Just as she could almost taste his mouth upon her own, she felt his breath hot upon her lips. But he was speaking to her, not tendering what his actions had promised.

"Fool that I am, I trust you, Alanna, at least to a point," he said wearily. "There will be no gag. Now stay out of trouble until I can rejoin you. You will see me again shortly."

"Damn you, Lucas del Fuentes!" Alanna whispered fiercely to his broad, retreating back. Damn all men and their inflated confidence in times of war, she thought miserably, tears welling up in her eyes. Hadn't Sean told her the same thing when he had kissed her goodbye that final time? And he had never returned, despite all his fine promises.

Once the attack was underway it did not last overlong, though to Alanna it seemed to go on indefinitely. At the first cry of alarm, she began twisting her wrists in an effort to escape. And as screams of pain and shouted orders filled her ears, she discovered that with sustained effort she could soon be free of the leather thong that bound her. It was careless of the Spaniard, she mused in surprise, until she realized that a man as prudent as Lucas would never make such an error. He had purposely left her some slack. Should things not go as planned, he had given her the opportunity to flee before the English found her. She thought such generosity odd, but then Lucas del Fuentes was the most puzzling man she had ever encountered.

Furiously Alanna worked at the leather imprisoning her. The sounds of fighting and death in the distance grew more intense until they reached a haunting crescendo and then fell away to near silence. It was done, and she was almost free.

But just when she was near to claiming her liberty, footsteps rustled nearby. They were not the tread of stealthy approach nor those of hasty retreat. They were loud and unconcerned, the noise made by victors who no longer had anything to fear.

For a fleeting instant, Alanna froze in apprehension, not knowing who had emerged triumphant. Then her common sense took over, and she desperately began to work at her bonds once more.

But it was too late, she despaired, as she glimpsed Bravingham's colors coming toward her through the trees. It was all she could do not to cry out in frustrated anguish.

However, in the next instant, it was the Spanish sailors who left the dim shadows and came into view, carrying as part of their booty the garments of the defeated English soldiers.

Enrique appeared first, then Juan, a cruel smile of sated bloodlust twisting his overly moist lips. Next came Pedro, his arms supporting the one they called Luis, who, though not visibly wounded, had sustained an injury of some sort. And then there was silence. Alanna hardly dared to breathe, waiting for the last of them to materialize. Yet no one else appeared to be there.

"Lucas!" she called, his name escaping her lips before she knew what she was doing.

The cry reverberated in the still air, devoid now of even the common twittering of songbirds. A heartbeat seemed a lifetime. Then suddenly he stepped jauntily out of the dim, gray light of approaching dawn, his well-formed body outlined by the sun's first rays even as his ebony hair blended into the fast receding darkness.

"I vowed I would return, Alanna," he said, his tone marked by high good humor. "And it looks as though I did so just in time." He indicated the young widow's unencumbered hands as the leather thong finally gave way.

"Too soon, to my way of thinking," she replied, fighting the urge to fly to his side and gently run her fingers over him in assurance that he was truly all right.

"It is all a matter of viewpoint," Lucas said quietly as the others drifted off to gleefully inspect what they had scavenged from the British camp.

Alanna continued to study the man whose life had suddenly become so important to her. While logically she had understood why Bravingham's men had needed to be eliminated, her heart had cried out from the first that it would have been safer to merely flee, putting them at a distance.

Yet, from what she had learned of Lucas del Fuentes, the rugged nobleman was not the sort to ever run away. Instead, he would confront whatever threatened him, heedless of the peril. And therein, to Alanna's way of thinking, lay the greatest danger of all.

Now he stood before her, like some great grinning idiot, quite obviously expecting her praise and thanks. Well, he could wait until Judgment Day for such a reaction from her, she decided stubbornly. She may have lived with war all of her life, accepting it as the natural order of things, but now, at this moment, she suddenly found it more than she could bear.

"We'll change our rags for the soldiers' clothing," Lucas said at last. His impatience with the Irish wench's silence had set him on edge more than the confrontation with Bravingham's men had done. "'Twill be safer traveling this land wearing their garments. And their weapons, horses and provisions will stand us in good stead"

When Alanna still refused to comment, doing no more than looking at him with solemn accusation in her eyes, Lucas del Fuentes, a man of normally rigid control, all but exploded. Turning to deliver a barrage of orders to his men, he could not help but wonder if his lovely prisoner was not sorry to see him return. Enemies though they might be, such a notion disturbed him almost past endurance, until he remembered the manner in which his name had burst forth from her lips, and he shook his head in bewilderment. Would he ever understand this woman, he mused, even as a voice of caution rose up in his mind, telling him that he had no reason to do so, and admonishing him to keep his distance from her instead.

"Here," he said gruffly and dropped the garb of one of the soldiers at her feet. His steely eyes captured hers. "Those looking for us are searching for a lone woman traveling with men. I would hide you from their view. Put these on at once."

"And do I have my lord's permission to move beyond those trees in order to shed my own clothing?" Alanna asked impassively, unwilling to be goaded by his suddenly aloof and haughty attitude, as she nodded in the direction of a closely knit stand of pines. "I am afraid if I jump to do your bidding and follow your directive here and now, Alvarez would not be able to stand it."

Lucas gritted his teeth at the images her words conjured up. Juan was not the only one who would be unable to control himself at the sight of Alanna's nakedness. Though Lucas had been elated by his victory, he suddenly felt the skirmish to have been of little importance. As he studied this woman returning his stare so defiantly, the urge to conquer sat upon him still.

"Go behind the trees," he said, his voice hoarse and rough. "But do not be overlong."

"Shall I accompany her?" Juan offered. He unstopped a pilfered flask of wine and allowed the ruby liquid to flow into his mouth and down his chin.

"You will stay here," Lucas commanded. Then he turned to Alanna and spoke to her softly in English, an expression clouding his eyes that sent a chill through her body even as it inflamed her. "Be very quick about it, Alanna, or I will come there and see to the task myself. And if you think to run away, know that I will track you down, and when I find you, I will not be responsible for my actions."

Her cheeks burning red, Alanna spun on her heel to swiftly do as she was told. She had not mistaken Lucas's meaning. Nor had he intended her to.

The Spaniards had already transformed themselves into Englishmen by the time Alanna returned. As she emerged into the clearing, Lucas swore softly, cursing himself for a fool. Alanna O'Donnell was a woman who could never be disguised as a man. Though her thick gold tresses had been swept atop her head, their brilliance hidden beneath a helmet, her woman's curves refused to masquerade as hardened, manly lines.

The gentle flare of her hips and swell of her breasts beneath her doublet were enough to stop a man's heart. But her long, shapely limbs, outlined so plainly in masculine hose, released primitive stirrings in Lucas that brought him to instant arousal.

Grateful for the shield he held in his hand, he mounted his horse, snapping out an order for the others to do the same.

Given a fine English steed so old Baibi could rest, Alanna, too, took her place among the riders. She ignored Juan's lecherous glare, conscious, instead, of Lucas del Fuentes's seeming indifference.

"We head northwest," Lucas dictated, using Piobar to nudge Alvarez's horse away from Alanna. "I pray that at least from a distance you will pass as a man," Lucas muttered in her direction before quickly handing Enrique her reins and spurring his own horse forward to lead the line of fugitives on their journey.

His obvious discomfort with her attire and the twisted, begrudging compliment he had paid her inspired a small smile on the Irishwoman's pretty face—indeed, it was the first one she had known in many a day—as she realized that Lucas could cope with her proximity no better than she could with his. Traveling north with his band might yet prove more interesting than she had expected.

It was nearing late afternoon when the riders entered a lush valley, at the bottom of which flowed a crystal brook. The mounts, sensing water and rest were at hand, quickened their pace. Guiding her horse's descent along a steep path took all of Alanna's concentration, so it was not until the first bloodcurdling yell that she feared attack.

Suddenly, trees and boulders lining the road came alive, and the wounded sailor riding directly behind her groaned in agony, toppling from his seat, his hands clutching frantically at the arrow protruding from his throat.

Mother of Christ, these were her own countrymen waging the assault, Alanna realized with horror when she glimpsed their distinctive weaponry and recognized their familiar form of attack. The strategy—men suddenly appearing from the rear or side of the road, stinging swiftly and then vanishing from view—was effective and unknown to her Spanish captors. Why, a company of Irish rebels could cut them down in minutes, and here she was, attired as an English soldier!

But before she could gather her wits and do something, Lucas, astride Piobar, was at her side, shielding her body with his own and slashing at an impudent swordsman who had dropped to the ground from a low overhanging branch.

The glare of sunlight on steel blades slicing through the air, however, pushed her into action.

"We are not English! I am Kevin O'Donnell's own fosterling," she cried out in Gaelic as attackers concealed by a row of brush let fly more arrows. Knocking off her helmet so that her long blond hair might tumble down, she stood in the stirrups of her saddle and addressed them again with a boldness born of fury. "Harm me or these men," she shouted, "and I swear by the saints the O'Donnell will have your hearts!"

At her pronouncement the battle slowed and then dissipated, the attackers moving off from whence they had come, but not before the arm of the swordsman nearest her came crashing down, too caught up in momentum to be stopped by the sight of Alanna's gender or the words she had spoken.

But though the sword's edge had been meant to slash her, it drew not one drop of Alanna's blood as Lucas del Fuentes, instinctively threw himself from his horse directly into the blade's path.

Horrified, she watched as crimson stained Lucas's doublet and the swordsman turned and fled, probably thinking his inability to stay his hand might very well have signaled his own doom.

However, Alanna had no thoughts for him. She instantly scrambled to the ground at the side of the man who had protected her, her gently probing hands seeking to know the extent of his wound.

Abruptly she found herself pushed away as Lucas drew to his feet. Holding his shoulder and swaying slightly, he walked to his men to survey the damage they had sustained.

"Here, let me see to that," Alanna persisted, running after him as he tore a strip of cloth from a blanket atop one of the packhorses and stuffed it inside his doublet.

"There's no need for you to look. Though I am both Spanish and English, my blood is the same color as yours," Lucas grumbled, his eyes riveted to Luis's still form.

"But I wish to help," she explained.

"Alanna," he said, his even white teeth clenched in pain, "yesterday you tried to open my veins. Now you expect me to believe you want to stem the flow of my blood?"

"Yes. I have said as much," Alanna replied simply. She brushed away Lucas's hand so that she could examine his injury.

"It is nothing, only a superficial cut," he growled impatiently. Yet despite his protests, he found himself submitting to her probing all the same, and finding the experience so pleasant that he had little regret the rebel sword had found its mark.

"Have a care, del Fuentes," Juan Felipe cautioned, fixing Alanna with a dark scowl. "She is probably trying to find another way to kill you. Who knows what she said in that barbaric tongue of hers? She called out just before you were wounded, most likely ordering your death and ours, as well."

Lucas regarded Alanna, awaiting her answer.

"I merely told them who I was," Alanna mumbled, "and...and ordered our safety."

"You cannot believe such a tale," Juan said with scorn, his hand coming to rest on the hilt of his English sword. "The woman must be dealt with for her treachery. Since you are unable to do so, leave her to me."

"Stay away from her," Lucas warned. His voice was low and his eyes stormy. "If I ever learn she has tried to betray us, it will be up to me to deal with her. Now see to Luis. Prayers must be said for his soul before we depart, and I have a feeling we should leave this place as soon as possible."

"There's no need to go before you are ready," Alanna stated matter-of-factly, as she reached out to apply pressure to Lucas's shoulder. "My countrymen won't return. They know who we are now, and will fear Kevin's wrath. It might be that this spot is the safest in all Ireland. At least it is one in which we can spend an uneventful night."

"Don't listen to her, del Fuentes," the peacock squawked. "The wench wants us to stay here and be slaughtered at the hands of her savage Irish cohorts. After all, what reason has she to care for our well-being?"

"What reason, indeed, Alanna?" the rugged Spaniard asked, cocking a questioning, raven black eyebrow.

"I did not give you away in the convent, did I?" Alanna exclaimed.

"You had your own safety and that of the nuns to consider," he pronounced quietly. "Didn't you say as much? Had those jackals found me there, you would be spending this night in a bridal bower and St. Bridget's would have been torched. Those Protestants had no love for the Church of Rome."

"Aye, and I have no love for you, but that does not mean I want to see you killed," she retorted.

"Then you have changed your mind about calling for my blood?" Lucas asked with a challenging grin. "Mayhap you will tell me why."

"I will tell you only that those men will not return to-night," Alanna snapped, a crimson flush coloring her face. "Believe it or not as you will."

"Bueno," Lucas said after a moment's silent consideration. "We will camp here. I have pushed the men too hard today already. If we want to have any chance of surviving the morrow, it is best for us to take time to regain our strength."

"Bah! The she-witch has seduced you," a disgruntled Alvarez complained. "If we are slain in our sleep, you half-breed, our blood will be on your head!"

Alanna watched Juan storm over to one of the pack-horses and unlash a small jug. With any luck, it would contain the potent Irish drink the English called whiskey, and the sullen Spaniard would cease to be a problem, at least for the remainder of the night.

Giving Lucas a small smile of thanks, she took his large hand in her own and placed it on his wound to stanch the still-flowing blood. She would have to undo his clothing and stop the bleeding to determine just how badly he had been hurt.

"I'll be back in a trice with supplies to dress that," she promised.

"Not until I see to it that Luis is laid to rest," Lucas replied soberly.

"But your injury!" Alanna objected.

"It can wait," he said brusquely. "This can't."

When the sad task had at last been completed, and the exhausted men had had their fill of food and drink, Alanna approached Lucas once again, bringing with her what she needed to tend his angry gash.

"You can't procrastinate any longer," she whispered, kneeling down before him.

"There are a lot of things I should tend to that I have put off," he grumbled, his deep green eyes probing Alanna's blue ones with an intensity she found disquieting.

"I am talking of your shoulder, del Fuentes, and nothing else," she hissed.

"So am I," he said innocently, his even, white teeth gleaming in the descending darkness. But his smile soon turned to a grimace when Alanna helped him to remove his doublet and then took away the packing he had casually placed against his wound.

"Though it does not demand a needle and thread, it is worse than you led me to believe," she scolded, her fair brow drawing together in disapproval. "And already it has grown hot and red."

Lucas bit back the suggestive reply that sprang to his lips, and instead quietly submitted to Alanna's care. At least he was quiet until she began to swab the cut with a cloth doused in whiskey.

"God's blood, woman, but Juan was right! You are trying to kill me."

"'Tis the fever will steal your life if you don't stop moving long enough for me to do this," Alanna said briskly. She tried to concentrate on her task rather than the bare, broad shoulders and muscular chest exposed to her view. "Now be quiet and don't act the babe. I'm almost through, at any rate. I've simply to apply the moss and then bind it with strips of cloth."

"Moss?" Lucas asked skeptically, eyeing the soggy mess the young widow intended to place atop his torn and tender flesh.

"Aye. We were fortunate. I found the right sort near the stream," she murmured. "It, too, will guard against fever."

Working gently and deftly, Alanna soon completed what she had set out to do. She finished by pressing a cup of whiskey to Lucas's lips and then, to his surprise, gently pushed him to the ground and covered him with a blanket before lying down beside him.

"There's no need to fear Juan tonight," Lucas said softly, nodding in the direction of the Spaniard, who lay snoring, a jug clasped to his rhythmically rising chest.

"I'm not here to seek your protection, but to offer mine," Alanna responded drowsily, fatigued by the demands the day had made upon her. "I want to make certain you do not suffer during the night."

Stay here and I will suffer all the more, Lucas wanted to say. Instead, he settled for asking her a simple question. "Why?"

"Because you took a blade meant for me," Alanna responded in a rush of breath. " 'Tis for that reason and no other."

Then she snuggled down against the muscular body of the wounded commander, making sure not to disturb his injury. A smile crossed her lips when she heard his weary sigh of contentment. And before long, despite their fears to the contrary, the exhausted pair fell swiftly to sleep.

Chapter Eight

Though his shoulder was still stiff, Lucas woke the next morning with a tremendous sense of well-being. He lay contentedly where he was and observed that the sky overhead had never looked so blue, nor the air smelled as sweet. Neither had the ground cradling his head ever been so wonderfully warm and soft. Was it a magic spell that had enchanted him, giving him pause in this rare moment of peace to see a natural, verdant beauty in this land he detested? Or had Ireland perhaps always been so, and his previous perceptions tainted by the hollow visions of war? Spain suddenly seemed so far away, a vague memory compared to the vibrant moment at hand.

He wondered if the others had been similarly transformed, becoming as euphoric as he. Shifting slightly to satisfy his curiosity, he saw the sleeping forms of his men. But even with their eyes closed, their intermittent grunts and fitful movements provided evidence that tranquillity escaped them.

Before he could consider the phenomenon further, the support beneath his head stirred slightly, and a provocative feminine sigh sounded in his ear.

Lucas sat bolt upright, his deep green eyes wide as his sleep-drenched senses struggled to alertness. Looking down cautiously, the Spaniard liked not what he saw.

It had been not a velvety patch of moss that had been his pillow. It had been Alanna's plump bosom, still rising and falling methodically in the throes of slumber. Instantly Lucas became as wary and analytical as his soldier's training had taught him to be in a hazardous situation. Indeed, he thought with irritation, this was perhaps the most perilous he had encountered since setting foot on Ireland's wretched shores.

With swift assessment, Lucas knew that it wasn't this land at all, but Alanna who had cast a spell upon him, lulling him to such a sweet sense of harmony that Spain and his duty had appeared secondary, if only for an instant. It was an error, Lucas swore, that would not be repeated.

What was it about the woman that tempted him so? He sought to identify his weakness so that he might build up his defenses before Alanna opened her blue eyes and the assault on his heart began once more.

Her golden hair, angel's face and alluring feminine form notwithstanding, surely he had seen women more beautiful. And in all likelihood, bedded them, too. She was not meek and demure, as were most females of his acquaintance. And if Alanna's eyes sparked fire, her demeanor could be frostier than winter's ice. Rising quickly to put some distance between them, Lucas realized that, no matter what he told himself, Alanna O'Donnell held an attraction for him as no other woman ever had, speaking to the depths of his soul with no more effort than a telling look or casual gesture. Stepping over Juan's sprawling form, Lucas moved toward the brook, hoping to wash away not only the dust of the road, but the feelings stirred by his pretty prisoner.

Prisoner! Ha! If he was not careful, he would soon be imprisoned by her, he muttered to himself as he splashed the chilling water over chest, shoulders and taut abdomen.

But God in heaven, he could not afford to be affected so by Alanna or any woman who was not of Spanish blood. Hadn't he spent a lifetime trying to prove himself in Spain, demonstrating that his loyalty was with his father's homeland and not his mother's? For this reason, he had always felt the need to be twice as dedicated to Philip's causes,

twice as strong in his service, twice as daring when it came
to furthering his sovereign's ambitions.

In so doing, he had slowly replaced suspicion with acceptance, and had finally gained admiration among the
nobility, with the exception of *El Pavoreal* and those of his
ilk. His actions had brought honor to his father's house.
Could he now cast away the labor of a lifetime for the sake
of a woman? He thought not, no matter how he might
yearn otherwise. Not even for a woman as enticing as
Alanna Desmond O'Donnell.

His mind resolute, Lucas sat on the bank and awkwardly began to remove the bandages hampering his
shoulder's movement.

"I'll do that. Though a little restless last night, you didn't
burn. I think you have managed to avoid the fever,"
sounded a dulcet voice.

Lucas looked up to see Alanna observing him. Standing
as she was, she was the personification of enticement. Her
long, unbound hair, glistening gold in the morning sun's
caress, and her luscious body, as ripe as the berries that
grew along the stream's bed, made her as dangerous to him
as she was beautiful.

Dios, but he thrilled that her gentle smile was for him. He
longed to feel her delicate hands play along his body. But
it was a luxury he could not permit himself, not when he
responded to her as he did, he decided as he fell back on
military discipline. Not when one brush of Alanna's smooth
skin upon his could make him long for the taste of a victory so sweet it could only demand a terrible surrender.

"Do not trouble yourself," he said brusquely, evading
Alanna's attentions as he fought the desire to feel her fingertips soothing away his pains…all his pains. "Pedro will
tend to me." He bellowed the seaman's name so loudly that
the man, still befuddled by sleep, came running.

"I need your assistance, Pedro," the hardened warrior
said in his native tongue, indicating the dressing for his
wound that a confused Alanna still held. Then in a signal
of dismissal, Lucas del Fuentes turned his back on her, and,

he hoped, upon the plaguing problems she presented, as well.

An apologetic Pedro reached out for the materials that would heal Lucas's body but not his heart. Unable to speak with the obviously dismayed lady who had sought to nurse his leader, the sailor wore a look of commiseration, a look that told Alanna Lucas del Fuentes might be a good and honorable man, but he was an arrogant and obstinate one, too. It was a message that simply confirmed what the perplexed Irish beauty knew for herself only too well.

The day's journey saw Lucas's attention absorbed by everything but Alanna. His features were so hardened and his mood so patently foul that not even Juan, still burning with lechery, attempted to fill the void caused by Lucas's absence at Alanna's side.

It was, therefore, no surprise to any member of the tiny party, made smaller by Luis's death, that Lucas drove them hard that morning, hastening their progress toward Blacksod Bay as though the demons of hell were nipping at his heels.

By the time the sun had truly risen and burned off the early mists of day, all the men except Lucas were already showing signs of fatigue. And Alanna, accomplished rider though she was, felt sore and stiff, almost as if she had spent weeks upon the back of her mount rather than a few hours.

But underlying her weariness was something that bothered her to a much greater extent. Lucas's recent attitude toward her forced Alanna to recall just how precarious her position was and emphasized quite clearly that, despite their shaky truce, she was his prisoner and nothing more.

Losing sight of so monumental a fact was galling. Like a spur pricking a horse's flank, it goaded her, prodding her to vow that she would do whatever was necessary to escape her captor, even if it meant falling into the hands of the English. Surely, she persuaded herself, it would be easier to slip through their grasp and return to O'Donnell lands than it would be to free herself from Lucas del Fuentes's steel grip.

Alanna had barely reached this conclusion when it appeared heaven had heard her prayers and decided to render assistance.

Off in the distance, coming toward them from the corner of the field Lucas and his followers were crossing, rode a contingent of Queen Elizabeth's soldiers, her boldly waving banner an affront to the brilliant Irish sky.

"Damn!" Lucas muttered under his breath as their small band drew rein and massed together. He quickly tossed a cloak over Alanna's obviously feminine curves.

"It would seem you have led us from one trap to another," Juan accused in Spanish, to ensure that Alanna could not understand. "It is time I assume command. We might be able to leave this field by holding a knife to the Irish wench's throat, or at the very least trade her in exchange for our lives."

"Do not forget that I am the one who leads, Alvarez," Lucas said forcefully, reverting to Latin for Alanna's benefit. "To try to barter the woman away is a fool's decision. I do not trust these English. And to attempt to avoid them or turn tail and run is fruitless. No, it is better to brazen this out. We wear Bravingham's colors, do we not? I will hail them and ask if they have seen an Irishwoman, our lord's stolen bride, riding in the company of Spaniards."

"And what shall the men and I do?" Juan asked. The boldness of such a plan made him uneasy.

"Nothing. You and the others will sit your horses quietly at my side," Lucas directed before translating his command into his native tongue for the seamen. Then he turned to his lovely captive. "I have told you what is to be done. Have I made myself clear, Alanna?"

Preoccupied by judging the distance still remaining between herself and the horsemen and debating just when she should call out to make her presence known, Alanna was caught unawares by the handsome Spaniard's harsh question. After all, he had barely addressed her all morning.

But now, his attention was fully focused upon her as he impatiently repeated his inquiry.

The sullen, defiant look she sent him in return was a source of both anger and trepidation for the observant Juan, who feared the woman would give them away. But Lucas's calm surface remained unperturbed. He stared at Alanna coldly, insufferably male and arrogant, as though there was no question that she follow his dictates.

"I will have your cooperation, Alanna," he said with little trace of emotion as he gave her back her reins.

"Or I will have your life," Juan added, his hand moving to the handle of his knife after Lucas had once more taken his position at the head of the party.

The tension of the moment built as their steeds started forward, their previous reckless speed restrained. Alanna could hear the singing of birds and the buzzing of insects much louder than before, as was the fall of the horses' hooves, rattling now like thunder through her feverish mind. Every noise had been greatly magnified by the anticipation of what she was about to do. Yet all of the tumult was drowned out by the deafening beat of her own rapid heart.

"Good morrow!" she heard Lucas call, hailing the large, heavily armed detail of soldiers. He stopped his horse abreast of the officer leading the Queen's men.

"We are in the service of Lord Bravingham, out seeking his abducted bride. Have you seen any sign of a woman traveling with Spaniards?" he inquired with such composure that Alanna was more conscious of his actions than she was of Juan's knife discreetly unsheathed and lying atop his saddle.

Despite herself, Alanna could not help but respect Lucas's cool and dispassionate show of courage. Surely no one watching him would think that his life and those of his fellows were perilously close to coming to an end. The man's veins had to be filled with ice, Alanna thought. Then she remembered the battle scar, running like lightning across Lucas's hip, the scar she had glimpsed in the murky light of

Grady's hall. And Alanna knew that Lucas del Fuentes was no stranger to bravery.

"I've seen no lady, but plenty of Spaniards," the captain replied with a hearty laugh. "Of course, they won't be a problem any longer. We've gutted many these last few days. Why, I've heard of at least a dozen Spanish ships that have foundered along these shores during the recent storms. There must have been three thousand survivors, but they don't survive anymore. Though I understand there is a group under siege at Blacksod Bay who have yet to be taken."

"May God be good and grant us victory," Lucas said piously, bowing his head to hide the fury and horror the man's words had prompted.

"I hope your prayers are answered," the Englishman muttered, ignorant of the true meaning behind Lucas's supplication. "We'll be joining the fighting after settling a disturbance at Connaught."

"If you happen to see the woman on your travels, take her," Lucas advised. "My Lord Bravingham would gift you with a hefty reward."

"Abducted, did you say?" the captain asked, his interest now roused.

"That is the story given out," Lucas replied. "But for my part, I believe the bride rode off with the Spaniard quite willingly. From what the ladies tell me, he is considered a very handsome fellow."

Lucas's audacity made Alanna want to trounce him, or at the very least scream. But for some reason, she discovered the air she had taken into her lungs in order to call out and alert the English to her predicament would not find release. In fact, she did little more than shift in her saddle, and even that was accomplished with utmost subtlety.

And so she sat numbly, unable to do aught else. But whether it was the sight of Juan's knife that caused Alanna to hold her tongue, or some other reason, a reason she found much more disquieting, she honestly could not say.

Confounded and uncomfortable with her inability to act, Alanna barely heard Lucas bid the English soldiers farewell. Before she knew it, she and the Spaniards had moved off, their enforced leisurely pace disappearing once the English had moved out of view. Then they resumed riding swiftly and wildly, like a storm-tossed wind roving across the face of the seas.

For Alanna, ignored by Lucas, the remainder of the day was endless. Her endurance was failing so rapidly that she thought surely the next mile would see its dissolution. Yet it was not the result of interminable hours spent in the saddle that made her feel as she did. Nor was it solely her inexplicable behavior in the company of the English soldiers. Rather it was the unbearable sense of loneliness that threatened to overwhelm her.

Indeed, she appeared so forlorn and vulnerable that Pedro sought to cheer her when they finally stopped to give the horses a short but much-needed respite. Where once he had feared her presence and wished her gone, Pedro saw now only a troubled prisoner who had tended Lucas and received but poor treatment in return. He brought a small portion of food, and used gestures to urge her to eat. When she could not bring herself to do so, the sailor cast his rigid, heedless commander a disapproving glance before his own features sympathetically mirrored Alanna's misery.

Curtly directed to return to their saddles by a relentless Lucas, the fugitives pressed on once again. They traveled wordlessly until darkness fell and the rough, unfamiliar terrain would allow them to proceed no more.

Exhausted and dispirited, the mariners tended to the laboring mounts before seeing to their own needs, wiping down the horses' sweat-flecked flanks as Lucas had taught them to do.

When a fire was finally lit, the men gathered around it, too tired to eat. Pedro, however, was not so spent that he could not arrange a blanket at the ring's perimeter to soften in some manner what had obviously been a hard day for the woman. He signaled for Alanna to sit, and saw her settled before moving off to join Enrique, a jug of whiskey their only solace in this strange and dangerous land.

Even Lucas's order that they eat could not bestir the sailors after he apprised them of the fate that had befallen their countrymen along the Irish coastline. They seemed to want only the whiskey and the forgetfulness it bestowed.

Soon, their low, sad songs filled the air, muted by their weariness but passionately melancholy just the same. Perhaps they sang of their dead companion and slaughtered comrades, Alanna pondered, her Celtic heart responding to the odd, haunting melody. Surely theirs was a song of lamentation, and if she had been fluent in their tongue, she would have joined them in their singing, giving voice to the despair plaguing her own soul.

But as it was, she could do no more than sit there alone. Alone as she had been these past eight years.

It was strange, but she had not felt it so strongly until she had met Lucas del Fuentes. She had thought herself satisfied, if not truly happy with her freedom and independence. But the ebony-haired Spaniard had caused her to view her recent life differently, to become aware of just how empty the years had been, how empty they would continue to be.

Yet the man who had brought her to this point was obviously unaware of what he had done. Positioned near the fire as he checked on a set of reins, he kept himself busy long after the others had given themselves over to relaxation.

It was as if he was unmindful of the rest his body needed, Alanna thought, when the soft songs of the intoxicated sailors finally ceased and quiet snores began to puncture the air. Even Juan, who had seen fit to indulge himself with both food and drink, appeared to be settled in for the night, and still Lucas worked on, though whether driven by inordinate energy or desperation concerning the plight of his men, Alanna could not decide.

With a last, sorrowful glance in his direction, Alanna, like the others, decided to seek sleep's numbing solace.

Curling on her side, she adjusted the cloak Lucas had thrown at her that morning and squeezed her eyes shut, hoping to block out all thoughts of her rugged and heartless captor even as her ears strained to listen for his quiet movements.

Shortly, she heard him put the reins aside and rise, his footsteps coming closer before he passed to the other side of the fire. Did he actually pause at her side for an instant, or had she merely imagined it? Alanna mused, conscious of the too-distant location Lucas had chosen for his bed. But, she berated herself, what difference did it make? Apparently he didn't need to have her near as she did him, and with his shoulder mending, she had no excuse to join him. Cursing her feminine weakness, Alanna struggled to lose herself in dreams. Even nightmares would be more comforting than reality, she thought, fitfully drifting off toward blackness.

The rough manner in which her cloak was thrown back screamed to Alanna of danger, and when she opened her eyes to see Juan's leering face above her own, his knife held at her throat, she knew with horror she had been right.

"So now, Irish bitch, we will see who is master," he said with a sneer as he began to fumble with the fastenings of her doublet. "Del Fuentes no longer desires you, and so now you are mine, to do with as I will."

Despite the increasing pressure of the cold steel beside her neck, Alanna began to thrash about, unable to scream when Juan's hand clamped down cruelly across her mouth. Yet for all her efforts, it appeared she was doomed. She could not get free, and no one else in the camp seemed aware of her plight. The drunken pair of sailors snored on, and Lucas, with as much energy as he had expended that day, must have journeyed deep into sleep's realm.

"Had you been cooperative, I might have seen to it that you enjoyed this," *El Pavoreal* whispered fiercely while he straddled her, annoyed at Alanna's frantic struggles. "But as it is, I will simply find my own pleasure. I will—"

Suddenly Juan's crushing weight was lifted from her
chest, his knife gone, as well, and Alanna's lungs gasped for
air. The silent scream that had built within her now came
forth.

Looking up, she saw the identity of her savior. It was
Lucas, a Lucas more fierce and savage than she had ever
beheld him before. Fury blazed in his eyes as he unleashed
a frenzied rage upon Juan Felipe Alvarez.

Alanna watched in stunned silence as Lucas wrapped his
fingers around the peacock's throat, shaking him with such
prolonged violence that Juan's head was pounded against
the earth until finally he was rendered senseless.

Muttering curses in Spanish so vehemently that Alanna
could have no doubt as to their meanings, Lucas dragged
Alvarez away from the fire. He stopped only long enough
to get the reins that had held his attention previously, and
moved off into the brush, where he used the leather to restrain the blackguard should he regain consciousness during the remaining hours of darkness. Then he turned his
back on the king's godson before he could give in to the
still-pulsating urge to kill such a scurrilous example of humanity.

Lucas returned to the now quietly weeping Alanna. He
approached her gently and slowly, as one would a frightened doe.

As she watched him draw near, Alanna could not believe the change in her rescuer. Though still struggling to
steady his breathing, he was no longer the half-crazed
avenger of a few moments before but, startlingly, a man of
extreme tenderness. The transformation was all the more
cherished in that his gentleness was, at this moment, for her
and her alone. It raised a hope in her heart she would have
thought impossible but a short while ago.

Squatting silently before her, Lucas carefully pushed
Alanna's tangled hair away from her face and traced his
forefinger lightly over her throat, as though to reassure
himself that Juan Alvarez had not had a chance to damage
her translucent skin.

"This was my fault. I deprived you of your knife, leaving you no defense, and then failed to protect you as I should. Forgive me," he entreated, his low, raspy voice so unsteady and his face evidencing such remorse that Alanna forgot her own fear and longed to reach out a comforting hand.

"There is no shame in depriving an enemy of a weapon," she replied instead, her whisper lingering in the soft, early-autumn breeze.

"Are you my enemy still?" he asked. His eyes seized hers, burning into them until they seared her very soul.

"No," she said solemnly, breathless in spite of the brevity of the response.

"How badly did he hurt you?" Lucas found it difficult to swallow as he awaited her answer.

"Not at all. But you, did this incident open your wound?" Alanna asked quickly, allowing her fingertips to light softly on his shoulder, like a delicate butterfly upon a hardy flower.

"No, only my heart," Lucas replied when the touch of her skin upon his crumbled his resistance. Even bedraggled as she was by her ordeal, and garbed in men's clothing, Alanna Desmond O'Donnell somehow beckoned to him, whether she knew it or not. She was forbidden fruit, temptation and the glimmering promise of paradise. She was all that a man need be wary of in a woman, and all that he craved, as well.

"I don't understand," she said sincerely.

"God forgive me, Alanna," he uttered in misery, "but I want you—nay, need you with a desperation so great that it has driven me to the edge of insanity. But surely you understand it would be an act of lunacy, the most irrational thing we could do," he finished grimly, as though yet unconvinced himself, but nevertheless reaching the decision for both of them.

"Then let us sink into madness together," Alanna said so softly that Lucas might have thought the words to be a product of his burning desire if she had not held out her arms in welcome. She needed to leave her terror and uncertainty behind, to feel safe and protected in Lucas's embrace.

Cautiously Lucas allowed his lips to seek hers, blaming his inability to reject what she offered on the events of the night. He persuaded himself he would partake of but one kiss, before reality descended upon them once more.

And then, as Alanna's pliant mouth met his and opened submissively to his urgently probing tongue, he stopped thinking altogether. With a groan, Lucas surrendered everything he had, all that he was. He drew Alanna to her feet and to a more secluded spot before he gave himself over to mindless passion, urged on by her joyous whimpers.

"Mi vida, mi corazón," he murmured, unaware of what he said as he buried his hands in Alanna's glorious hair. His mouth traveled downward, seeking to claim every inch of her with his kisses.

Alanna had no care for the future as Lucas's strong hands began to possessively sweep her body, awakening it from a long and deep slumber.

For her, no matter what happened, this moment had to be theirs. Beloved memories of her husband might besiege her later, and indeed there could well exist some woman in Spain who thought of Lucas as her own, Alanna realized with a start as his deep, melodious voice showered her with endearments in his native tongue. But she didn't care. She was beyond caring. Surely, Alanna decided stubbornly, this one night could not be a sin, nor too much to ask. After all, was not this golden man truly hers, a treasure left on the MacWilliams shore by Mananaan MacLir after that terrible storm of a few days before? But then, Lucas's tender mouth captured her own once more, and all thoughts vanished into the sea of sensation that washed over her.

"It has been too long," she whispered so lovingly that it gave Lucas pause before he replied.

" 'Tis not the spirit of your husband returning to you in the body of a mere Spaniard, Alanna," he said softly, in-

sisting she be aware of what she was doing, desiring her to
want him and no one else.

"No," she murmured with a warm and knowing smile.
"You are Lucas del Fuentes, and none other. And I think I
have been awaiting this moment my entire life."

Gladdened by her acceptance, Lucas renewed his attentions with more fervor than before, though always conscious of her needs, her pleasure, her comfort. He treated
her as if she were some delicate treasure to be worshiped
reverently and completely. And though Alanna had known
loving before, it had been as a girl. What she gave now to
her tenderly demanding Spaniard, she gave as a woman.

Gentle as Lucas was with her, undoing the remaining
fastenings of her torn doublet and removing her hose and
the rest of her clothing with utmost care, Alanna could
nevertheless sense a fierceness deep within him. She knew
he held himself in check yet longed to burst free with a force
that could carry them both beyond doubts and obstacles
and into ecstasy.

Seeking to release this masculine force, she moved her
unclad body provocatively under his expert hands, drawing forth a primal growl from the depths of his soul. Bar-
riers began to vanish. And, to assure he withheld nothing
from her, she reached out to slowly and teasingly remove
the garments that he still wore.

But she had driven Lucas to such a point that his impatience would not allow him to wait until she finished love's
game. Instead, he moved her hands away, placed them demurely over the rosy crests of her breasts, a sight inspiring
enough to make him as eager as a stripling lad, and doffed
his clothing more quickly than he had ever done before.

Lucas lay beside her once again, his lips nudging her
fingers aside so that he might take a nipple as booty. The
gentle pressure of his mouth evoked showers of pleasure
that coursed through Alanna's entire being. And she, with
a woman's instinct, sought to please Lucas in turn, to give
back to him what he offered to her.

With their mutual caresses they were transported to an enchanted place where strife and grief did not exist. Yet neither did tranquillity. It was excitement that drove Lucas and Alanna now, making them more and more frantic to know and feel all during this magical time that might never be repeated. And though they had lived their lives in a world torn by war, neither was aware at this minute of either conquering or being conquered. Instead they offered themselves sweetly and completely, lost in the paradox of greedy selflessness that love commanded.

Soon Lucas, urged on by Alanna's whispered pleas, could wait no longer. Running his hands along her inner thighs, he made his intentions clear.

Eagerly, Alanna shifted to receive him, and with one long, slow stroke, he filled her, Alanna's satisfied moan falling upon his ears more sweetly than any melody he had ever heard.

And then passion's dance began, an intricate measure of varying rhythms that brought Alanna to the very brink of ecstasy before leading her back from the precipice once again. But at her small cries of protest, Lucas became so entranced by her responsiveness that he lost all sense of self-discipline. Faster and faster the pace grew, and soon the pair was whirling wildly out of control to the most basic of human rhythms, until finally they crashed against a wall of sensation. Here they shattered in rapture, the boundaries of individuality splintering into minute fragments that could only be made whole again if cemented by the essence of the other.

In the aftermath of love, Lucas and Alanna clung silently together, too overcome to dare put their sentiments into words. There was no recognition at that moment of consequences. They would arise soon enough. Instead, both lovers savored the peaceful sense of well-being that lingered when their passion was spent.

Lucas found their union a balm for his warrior's soul. There was no need to prove his worth here. He was truly accepted for what he was.

As for Alanna, she experienced the healing touch of love for the first time in eight years. It was as though her constant journeying had drawn to an end, and she had finally come home.

Sated though they were, the serenity they enjoyed was shattered by passion's touch when Lucas bent over his lady, pressing a soft kiss to her temple. Then the rhythm of their hearts started to accelerate once more, and the compelling melody of love began all over again.

Chapter Nine

Alanna awakened slowly in the twilight hour before dawn, reluctant to abandon the overwhelming sense of contentment that enveloped her, so unusual these days. In a cozy haze of sensual comfort, she felt deliciously weary, as in the distant past when her body had been sated with the pleasures of lovemaking.

Indeed, wherever this present dream had originated, if she kept her eyes tightly closed and concentrated hard enough, she could almost hear her imaginary lover's heart beating and feel her head resting against his broad muscular chest as he held her wrapped in his arms. Unwilling to deny herself such loving tenderness, Alanna fought valiantly against consciousness, preferring the sweet illusion of resting snugly beside a warm male to the cold reality of her unrelenting loneliness.

If only she had a lover, she would lick his chest playfully, teasing him awake so they could revive their passion with the dawn. Unable to resist the instinctive urge, the drowsy blonde sent her darting tongue forth, and was startled when it encountered warm flesh, tasting of salty perspiration and love.

Withdrawing swiftly to safety, her tongue lingered on her lips, and Alanna was surprised by their tenderness, as though they'd been well used in recent hours. Unbidden memories of a firm, evocative mouth surrounded by a scratchy beard floated just out of range as she came to the realization that, yes, after eight solitary years, she had given herself willingly to a man . . . and enjoyed it.

Afraid to move and awaken the stranger who held her so comfortably, Alanna tried to decipher the lingering sensations of pleasure that haunted her memory, obscuring the identity of the magician who'd loved her so long and so well. Who had sufficiently convinced her of his interest that she would share herself and her life with him—and then block the memory.

Then, with a sudden groan of despair, Alanna knew the truth and wished for death. Tempted to bolt from his arms and run, she forced herself to remain still and tried to calm herself until she could make sense of last night. What ever had possessed her to allow Lucas Rafael del Fuentes, the epitome of all she abhorred, to lie with her? And how could she ever survive the ignominy of waking in his arms? A brief bout of passion might be dismissed as errant lust, but to be content to stay the night with him was folly beyond belief!

All at once he stirred, shifting position in his sleep, throwing a powerful leg across hers, and she froze.

He couldn't—he wouldn't—wake now, she prayed, desperate for time to consider her behavior and what to do about it. But, thankfully, he lay still, the rhythm of his chest's rise and fall beneath her head once more regular and unwavering. It was true his desperate flight from Castle-mount had thwarted the planned kidnapping and marriage to Bravingham, but she couldn't deny that Lucas Rafael del Fuentes was the living model of all that had destroyed her husband, her father and her life. In Lucas, the flashy, empty promises of the Spanish were combined with the heartless efficiency of the English, who let nothing, be it compassion or law, interfere with their domination of the Irish. Hadn't his behavior last night been thus, glittering and domineering, taking her solely to satisfy his urges?

But no, mourned Alanna silently, however reluctant she was to admit it, that was not the truth of it. And her betrayal was therefore all the worse, for she had relished being his, surrendering Sean and everything else she had held dear for the sheer ecstasy of being in his arms.

Fraught with returning memories of the unbridled passion they'd shared, the new heights they'd scaled together, Alanna was filled with as much guilt for her actions as anger for the man beside her. A soldier was expected to behave like an untamed stallion, claiming pleasure where he found it, but *she* had not only suffered his attentions, she'd savored every moment of them, in turn giving as she received.

Had she her knife now, she would use it without hesitation, Alanna decided, though she was not completely certain on which of them she'd turn it first. But what would Lucas expect now? It didn't matter in the least, she determined suddenly. She would not play the fool again. Last night had been a momentary weakness, a regrettable lapse of judgment that should never have happened, but it need not condemn her for the rest of her life. No, memories of her fall from grace were sure to fade, and in a few days he would be gone and she would be thankful to be rid of him. She would concentrate on that inevitability and make it very clear she would tolerate nothing else. If necessary, threats of Kevin O'Donnell's demand for revenge should keep del Fuentes at a healthy distance from her. If he hadn't trapped her under his leg, she would have been long gone already, but it would be better to settle this here, away from his men.

After all, Lucas certainly couldn't love her, Alanna scoffed, struggling to ignore the recollections of how his eyes had studied her so thoroughly at Castlemount, how he had refused to leave her behind at the abbey, how he had taken the sword aimed at her by the Irish rebels and how hoarse with passion his voice had sounded last night when he'd made her his. And then there was the soft black hair that curled so fancifully about the back of his ears, the hair she'd kissed and played with as she lay with him.

Whatever her deluded senses might have accepted last night after Juan's attack, Alanna now saw clearly that Lucas couldn't love her. The episode had been a matter of simple lust. And she, of course, harbored no tender feelings for him. She had already lost one soldier she'd loved. She would never be so foolish as to make the mistake of giving her heart to another. Telling herself firmly that was the end of the matter, Alanna waited, resigned to the inevitable confrontation ahead.

Moments earlier, Lucas had heard her groan, coming awake quickly, ready to meet any challenge that threatened, except for the lovely one whose head rested so temptingly on his chest.

Madre de Dios, he really had possessed her, after all. Unbelievably, he and Alanna had found paradise in a leaf-strewn Irish glen, he realized, dubious as to whether he should rejoice or despair at the occurrence. Like dry kindling, their conflagration had been sudden and all-consuming, destroying their differences and melding them into a temporary union so precious and volatile he knew without question it could never survive the harsh light of day.

Already accepting the separation to come, Lucas recalled the sensual splendor they'd created and mourned its demise. He had sensed Alanna's withdrawal in the sudden tension in her body as it lay against his own. Needing to halt her retreat until he could decide how to handle their unexpected intimacy, he had draped his leg over her and feigned sleep.

Damn it all, what had enticed him to take her? he fumed when she had settled down again. Here he had pronounced himself Alanna's protector, saving her from Juan's attack, only to foolishly claim her charms for himself. What hypocrisy!

It was true he hadn't bedded a woman for months, but he was a soldier, trained in self-denial and discipline. He ought not have turned to Alanna for release, Lucas berated himself.

Yet, argued the military strategist within, he had not chosen Alanna. Any woman would have sufficed after being as close to death as he had been for the last two months. Was last night not but the normal pleasure a man takes in proving himself fully alive?

But what was normal about it? Alanna had been willing to put a knife in his back. She was willful, opinionated, determined and fiercely contrary to all the female traits possessed by a gentlewoman of Spain—and still he had discovered a fulfillment with Alanna Desmond O'Donnell he had never dreamed could exist on earth. It was a situation beyond human comprehension, and it could only end badly. He was first and foremost a soldier who owed his allegiance to Philip of Spain. His duty was to return to his ship and, if need be, wage war against the Irish for the right to survive. In any case, his home was not in these alien lands, but Alanna, loyal to Ireland as she was, would never leave it.

No, the past hours had been madness, a delicious, delirious ascent into a lush paradise of sensual wonder, a world without regard for the consequences. It was but a temporary delusion, Lucas tried to convince himself. Alanna had already given him back his life—he could not destroy hers with a union that had no future. As difficult as it would be, it was only right that he end at once what had just begun to exist between them. Any other path would only lead to their mutual destruction.

"Del Fuentes," came Juan's hoarse voice from the distance.

Even Alanna could understand the fury in the tone.

"Del Fuentes, damn your black heart. You've had your revenge. Free me at once!"

In the space of an instant, Lucas rolled away from Alanna, drawing on the clothes he'd discarded so urgently hours before.

"I must see to him before his screams alert the enemy to our presence," he said curtly. "Juan is fool enough to see that as just repayment for his uncomfortable night."

"About last night—" began Alanna, reaching out for the soldier's uniform she'd worn, anxious to cover herself.

"We'll talk later," the Spaniard answered, his tone formal, his eyes hard and distant. "I shall apologize fully for my conduct, as you deserve."

"No, ah..." Why would he apologize? For the moment, Alanna was thrown. Here she'd been prepared to fight off further advances, and Lucas evidently regretted their coupling as much as she did. Was that possible?

"Del Fuentes, *bastardo, dónde está?*" demanded Juan. "Pedro, Enrique, *ayudame pronto.*"

"I'd better—"

"You'd best—"

"Later," he promised. He walked off without a backward glance, leaving the blue-eyed widow feeling strangely bereft. She hadn't wanted any complications or angry scenes, but couldn't Lucas have acknowledged that what they had shared had been magical, a miraculous experience? Surely he owed her that much, Alanna fumed.

It had meant nothing to him? Fine, she could be just as cold and impersonal as he, Alanna determined, dressing quickly and heading for the horses. The sooner they were moving, the sooner she'd be away from him, and nothing would suit her better... or so she told herself.

Lucas strode quickly over the uneven earth beneath the trees, oddly comforted that his rising temper would shortly find an appropriate target. Looking at Alanna and knowing he could never formally claim her as his own gave birth to a pain sharper than any battle wound. What irony, he mocked himself, that a doomed passion could cripple a man who had withstood the weapons of war. And it was all due to *El Pavoreal*'s misplaced lust!

With every twig that snapped underfoot, the nobleman envisioned one of Juan Alvarez's bones cracking. If it hadn't been for that shallow peacock's pursuit of Alanna from the very beginning, he would never have needed to step in as her protector.

True, Lucas admitted reluctantly, he had admired the woman in the cellars at Castlemount, but the chore of constantly having her so near to him, so very tempting, had finally proven irresistible, much to his intense regret.

"Del Fuentes," cried Juan, his voice breaking and losing its wrath as he watched Lucas advance upon him. The nobleman's cold fury was easily visible in the very purposeful steps he took across the clearing. This was not a soldier to cross, Philip's godson decided, and quickly opted for a display of remorse rather than the rancor that had fueled his earlier shouts for attention.

"Now, remember, I didn't hurt her, I really didn't, and I am sorry if I frightened the woman. I meant her no harm. I simply misunderstood what it was she wanted from me."

Lucas felt somehow cheated of his vengeance by Juan's cowering. Despite his words, Lucas knew without doubt that the peacock would seize any opportunity to approach Alanna again, unless he could be so thoroughly terrorized that he saw his life as the price to be paid for satisfying a momentary urge.

With careful precision, Lucas stopped just short of where Juan had risen to his knees and, without comment, directed a backhanded blow to the peacock's frightened visage. Though its unexpected force knocked the sailor to the ground, Alvarez offered no protest, swallowing deeply and gulping for air.

"Listen, Don Lucas, I am sorry. I swear, it will never happen again," groveled the pathetic figure as Lucas pulled out a knife and bent over to grab him. "No!"

"I am but cutting your bonds, Alvarez...*this* time. If there is another incident, I will gladly cut your filthy heart out and not think of it again."

Juan gulped and succeeded in holding his wrists almost steady while he considered the nobleman who sliced free the leather that had held him. Clearly Lucas had not sampled the woman's pleasures himself last night, or he would have been in better humor. The question was whether she had refused him or he had let his noble conscience control him yet again. What a fool the man could be!

"Why have you made her virtue your personal crusade?" Juan asked as he rolled away from the knife, too curious to recognize the wisdom of silence.

Lucas raised his fist, prepared to slam Juan to the ground once more, but then sanity interfered. It was but a simple question, one he had pondered often enough without resolution.

"The Irish woman assisted in our escape, in effect saving our lives at Castlemount. She helped me get food from the nuns at the abbey and she scattered that band of Irish rebels when we were ambushed," he said quietly. "Other than the Virgin, I know of no other woman who has been as good to us, protecting us from death three times. It is my duty as a nobleman of Spain to grant her safe passage to her home."

"Not as a prisoner any longer, either," leered Juan. The change in her status after their sighting of the English soldiers had irked him since the day before.

"No," murmured Lucas, suddenly realizing how he'd released Alanna's reins when they'd encountered the English party and had never reclaimed them later. Yet she had not fled, much as she professed to want to escape. Nor had she given them away. What did that say about her... and her feelings for him?

Loath to consider the implications of Alanna's lingering, he turned on his heel and moved quickly toward the spot where they'd bedded the horses. The sooner the group was on the road, the sooner Alanna—and these absurd notions of his—would be behind him.

Surprised at Lucas's sudden hurry, Juan struggled to follow after him, slipping on the damp ground as a wet mist began to fall, a mist just as persistent and annoying as that troublesome woman.

Once he'd gotten the group traveling again, Lucas was reluctant to stop, and it was early afternoon before he waved a long arm in the air and pointed to the left, sending them off the muddy path under the shelter of a few trees. He had been riding ahead of them, at a fast pace, scouting the route ahead for possible trouble and then circling back to urge them onward. Unable to stand Alanna's constant glances and unprepared to confront her possible accusations, he had found the endless cycle of surveying the forward trail a welcome escape. Finally, however, their time had come.

The terrain had recently changed. The ground became flatter and at the same time more strewn with rocky patches, and he swore he could almost taste the salt air of the sea. By heading northwesterly for the last two days after their diversionary trek inland, he had expected to reach the coast today, and it appeared that at least those prayers were being answered. Now he must speak gently to Alanna and dispatch her to her family. If there were battles looming ahead of him as the English party had suggested, he would not risk seeing her endangered, and logic told him that the closer they got to the shore, the greater the threat of being taken. No, as dearly as it would cost him, Lucas knew he must release Alanna to meet her destiny and, in so doing, reclaim his own as a son of Spain. There was no reasonable alternative open to him. After addressing Pedro and the others in Spanish, he left them and brought his horse alongside Alanna's.

"Is something wrong?" she asked instantly. After frequent rebuttals that morning, the blonde thought she had become accustomed to his coldness and obvious reluctance to be near her, but she was still pleasurably startled by his abrupt change of tactic. It seemed almost as though he wanted them to be alone.

"It is time we spoke," Lucas replied, his green eyes troubled as he strove to memorize the graceful way her slender neck disappeared into the soldier's uniform she wore open at the collar. His blood recalled the lusciously feminine curves the cloth attempted to hide, however, and the Spaniard found himself rapidly growing warm with desire. This would be more difficult than he'd ever imagined, he realized, stifling a painful groan.

To purge his traitorous body of its unsought urges, Lucas jumped quickly down from Piobar, stumbling in his haste. He pulled the English cloak around him to repel the rain and protect his privacy, and moved to where Alanna still sat on her horse. Holding out a hand, he repeated his suggestion.

"Come walk with me. We can talk."

"What have we to say to each other that matters?" Alanna demanded, irritated that his curt invitation could so easily set her heart to pounding and her blood skimming ever so rapidly through her body. She had promised herself to spurn him. Was that such a formidable task, to repudiate the attentions of a half English, half Spanish cur like Lucas del Fuentes? "You have already made it very clear by your actions this morning that though you wanted my body badly enough last night, you have no use for me today. I'll not trouble you to put that into words."

Urging her mount forward to avoid further discussion, Alanna was unprepared for Lucas's sudden movement when he stepped sharply in front of her and tugged the reins from her small hands. The horse too, sensing her fear, perhaps, was alarmed by Lucas's threatening presence and abruptly shied, rose upward and pawed the air with its great hoofs, sending the Spaniard leaping backward out of range and making Alanna hold on for dear life. Once the animal had settled, Alanna found herself safe and well satisfied with her mount. Not only had she denied del Fuentes his authority, but so had the horse he had stolen for her.

"Alanna, you don't understand," Lucas argued, coming forward to soothe the woman and her beast. He stroked the horse's head and murmured softly, then reclaimed the reins from the mud puddle into which they'd dropped and moved toward a fallen tree. Before Alanna realized his intent, the soldier had used the branches for a foothold and was seated firmly behind her, maneuvering the horse into the forest.

"Now we shall ride a short way and talk," Lucas announced, slipping his arm around her waist to brace himself. Finally, he thought, he had her where she'd have to listen to reason, if only he didn't weaken and cling to her instead of sending her away.

Outraged, Alanna stiffened at his touch, but to her surprise Lucas held her impersonally, as if last night's intimacy had been but a dream.

It was irrational, perhaps. She had been angry when he hadn't wanted to talk to her and now was more furious that he did. If he had truly wished to speak with her, he could have done so in camp. Hadn't his recent actions shown her that Lucas felt nothing for her other than physical attraction? Did he mean to make her his whore? Had he brought her here to take his ease with her before coldly returning to his men and ignoring her once more? Well, she would not acquiesce to his lust so freely, regardless of what he thought.

Ultimately it was Alanna who broke the silence of the misty woods, too impatient to endure any further suspense.

"Well, haven't we come far enough yet?" she snapped angrily, hardening herself to his inevitable blandishments to get his way. "But, I warn you, if you think to ravish me again, you will have to kill me."

"What?" Lucas couldn't believe his ears. *Ravish her?* He had done nothing of the kind, and well she knew it. "What was between us was not like that at all—"

"No, mayhap you are right, del Fuentes. Last night was a choice made by *both* of us, consented to by *each* of us, not like this current expedition to satisfy *you.*"

Abruptly, Lucas reined in the horse, dismounted, tossed Alanna the reins and looked up at her, his livid features barely softened by the falling rain.

"I only wish to talk with you," he said firmly, holding his temper in check as his gaze caught and held her own without wavering. "If you do not believe me, ride away now. I shall not attempt to stop you."

Alanna closed her eyes to block out the pain in his and tried to think. All she had to do was signal the horse, and he would be gone from her life, but still she hesitated. *He may be more your captive than you are his,* Mother Columbine had warned her. Had the old nun been right? Could Lucas be ready to speak of love, ashamed he had nothing to offer her? For a moment, Alanna tasted her own fear of commitment, knowing the frightful price she'd pay for loving one such as he—and then she nodded, slipped from the saddle and held out her hand to him. Whatever her decision as to the workings of her heart, the man deserved a hearing.

Thankful she was still willing to trust him, Lucas accepted her hand and guided her to a small, dry place beneath the sweeping pines after taking but a minute to hobble her horse.

"Alanna, have you noticed the change in scenery?" he began awkwardly, unable to voice his feelings for her. "The land has flattened out but the rocks have increased and the smell of the sea is in the air. It can't be much farther until we reach the shores."

"No," she agreed, more puzzled than ever as to his intent. "I recognized that tree with the three trunks near the stone cross this morning. There is one similar that marks the start of O'Donnell lands near Donegal. Here, though, the sea is about twenty miles straight west, I suppose, and Blacksod Bay is northwest, probably a day and a half away. I think it wiser to stay inland as long as possible to avoid the search parties, though. If we try to travel too far along the coast, it could be dangerous."

"That is what I wanted to talk to you about." He was unable to still the errant hand that had begun stroking her soft curls. "Your safety concerns me greatly. I can no longer guarantee it. What happened with Juan last night, what happened with me should not have..."

Mother of God, she was usually astute when it came to understanding people and their actions. Yet Lucas del Fuentes remained an enigma to her. Perhaps his chilly demeanor toward her had only been for the benefit of his men and now, in the privacy of this moment, he would tell her what was in his heart. At least, Alanna prayed that was the case.

"Lucas, what is past cannot be recalled, so do not regret it. I don't," Alanna confessed, running a soft hand across the coarse hair of his beard, hoping her honesty would spur him to admit his true feelings.

"Perhaps not, but I do regret it," he said harshly, turning from her to stare out into the rain. She was too precious to risk in these perilous times and would be safer home with her family than with him. No matter how much his words cost him, her life depended on his lie being convincing, the Spaniard told himself, deliberately forcing his false words to be especially cruel. "Once in a great while, a soldier loses his self-control, and you just happened to be there to oblige me. I apologize, but I doubt what we did will scar you for the rest of your life. It wasn't all that memorable, after all."

"What?" Alanna was astounded. Even if he thought that were true, he should have had the good grace to be a gentleman. But, this—this was why he needed to see her alone? To cast her off like a used pony? Damn Mother Columbine's meddling! Her own instincts had been correct. The man was a bastard!

"It's not that your performance wasn't adequate," Lucas continued, the words nearly choking him, "but Spain is my home, the place I truly belong. There is nothing I want here in Ireland except my freedom." And you, he thought silently, wishing he could be honest with her.

"I have already granted you that twice—at Castlemount and when the Irish rebels attacked you," she replied furiously. "What more do you want from me?"

"Free me once more," he urged softly, barely able to speak the damning words. "Free me from my responsibility for you. Ride off to your family and let me go to my fate at Blacksod Bay."

Alanna stood unmoving, her worst nightmare come true. She had opened her heart to this man and he was scorning her, sending her off like a child into a world at war. Didn't he realize what was out there?

"A woman alone, traveling in English uniform through northwestern Connaught? If you wish me dead, the only quicker way would be for you to stab me. Why not do that instead?" Alanna challenged bitterly, moving to open her doublet. When he stilled her hand, she laughed bitterly. "Oh, of course, then I wouldn't be available as your little decoy heading in one direction while you and your men take another. I am expedient, am I not? That's quite clear now. And you would have had me believe that you are different from the lying Spaniards who killed Sean?"

"Alanna, it is not like that at all. Despite the perils on the road, you would be safer alone than accompanying me. I do not want to risk your life any more than you would want me to lose mine." Lucas grabbed her in his arms and crushed her to his chest before he could stop himself.

"*Your* life?" The irate female sneered, wrenching herself free from him and spitting on the ground. "That is what your life is worth to me!"

It had not gone at all the way Lucas had hoped. He was deeply tempted to comfort Alanna and declare his undying love for her. After all, what was life in Spain worth if his heart died on these foreign shores?

But before he could move toward her again, voices rang out all about him, calling her name.

"Alanna Desmond O'Donnell, move away from him, woman. We've come to save you," called the loudest as half a dozen men garbed in the clothing of Irish rebels came out of the trees surrounding them, swords at the ready. "Alanna, come to me."

As she ran to the waiting arms of a tall, broad-shouldered redhead, the other men quickly closed in on Lucas, encircling him and leaving him no doubt as to their intention.

"Devlin? Devlin Fitzhugh! Oh, my Lord, it is you," Alanna cried, wiping away her tears as she reached his embrace. "How ever did you—"

"Moira," he said simply, and planted a kiss on her brow. She looked well enough, he supposed, a bit rattled and decidedly peculiar in hose and an English uniform, but he saw no obvious signs of abuse. "We met her as she journeyed with Galen and your retainers from Castlemount, and she told us about the abduction, but that's for later. For now," he growled, glaring at the dark-haired foreigner his men had surrounded, "tell me if this Spanish devil touched you in any way. I aim to kill him one way or the other, but if he's hurt you at all, it'll be a damned sight more gruesome a death that he and his men will suffer than for kidnapping."

"No, I'm fine," responded Alanna, a bit nervous at the repressed excitement in Devlin's voice. She had always known he was a soldier, but he sounded so fiercely protective, she almost thought he relished the task ahead of him. "Really, Devlin."

"My men?" called Lucas. He moved forward to join them until the sharp points of the drawn swords made that unwise.

"Aye, we found them a mile or two back," Devlin replied, surprised at the Spaniard's knowledge of English. But then, after Smerwick, he should have known better than to accept their kind at face value.

"And you've killed them?"

"Not yet, but don't worry. It will happen soon enough." The O'Donnell's gallowglass snorted as he recalled Galen's account of the deception he'd suffered.

"They only obeyed my orders," Lucas announced, his head held high. "Kill me if you choose, but let them go."

"So they can band together with the rest of your countrymen traipsing up and down the coast, nearly a thousand of them, according to reports? Not very likely. With all due apologies to the MacWilliams for my doing his duty, you and yours will meet the devil before nightfall," promised the Irish leader. "You need not watch, Alanna, though it might please you to witness this villain breathe his last."

"No, it wouldn't," began Alanna, her heart quaking at the realization that Lucas's life would be forfeit if she didn't act quickly, the very life she had just claimed not to care about. He might not want her, but that was no reason to let him die. "Lucas del Fuentes is innocent of any crime. He abducted no one."

"What?"

"I—I didn't really object to escaping from Castlemount with him. That is, I pleaded with him to take me."

"What in heaven did you have to escape from that you would willingly go with foreigners? You should have been safe there. Castlemount is your uncle's property." Even though Devlin had grown accustomed to Alanna's wilder escapades, having known her for years, such a claim as hers sounded bizarre even to him.

"And Cordelia's! She had arranged to have me kidnapped by Lord Bravingham's men in order to force a marriage between us."

"Moira said nothing of this," disputed Devlin. He was reluctant to abandon his vision of del Fuentes as the enemy.

"She didn't know. I only heard the guards discussing it early that morning while I was readying the supplies. When I spotted Lucas with our horses," embellished Alanna urgently, "I—I swore I'd alert the guards and see him and the other prisoners recaptured if he didn't take me along with them."

Devlin was silent, weighing Alanna's words against the story the old nurse had told him. Moira had admitted being asleep when Alanna was taken, so it was true that she only knew what Grady and Cordelia had told her. Alanna, however, often possessed too soft a heart for creatures in trouble, be they animals or people. How could he be certain she wasn't lying to save the Spaniards' lives?

"Why didn't you come home to Kevin as soon as you were free of Castlemount?" he demanded.

"You would have wanted me to travel alone in this countryside, with the English, Irish and Spanish roaming wild? If you came to get me because you felt my six guards might not be enough protection, how can you ask that?" She watched Lucas's reaction. Would he accept her version of the truth if it meant saving his life? She couldn't be certain, given his pride, but at least he hadn't yet called her a liar. "Besides, Devlin, you saw with your own eyes when you came upon us, I was not bound or tied in any way. I chose to stay with Lucas del Fuentes because he is a gentleman, albeit one who is half English and half Spanish. I trusted him."

"Is this true, Spaniard?" challenged the Irishman, striding over to where Lucas waited. Motioning his men aside, he stood face-to-face with the prisoner and took his measure, startled at the unusual green eyes that met his without hesitation. Most men flinched beneath Devlin Fitzhugh's stare, but he had to admit this one withstood its implied threat admirably.

Looking over Devlin's shoulder, Lucas studied Alanna's worried eyes, and at her barely perceptible nod, he accepted his fate. For whatever they had shared, she had vouchsafed his life once again.

"Except for neglecting to mention my shame for abusing her kindness by assaulting her priest, Alanna told you the story I would have, if you had asked instead of immediately condemning me," he said, mentally bidding her farewell. "In fact, we were just discussing when Alanna would head out for her foster father's lands, but since you are here, you can accompany her now while my men and I head for the coast."

"No, I can't permit that," said Devlin, and threw a strong arm across Lucas's shoulder, their similar heights making the gesture seem less menacing than perhaps it was intended.

"You can't?" echoed Alanna, fearful her lie had been discovered, though how she couldn't imagine.

"No! Kevin O'Donnell would never forgive me if I let the man who rescued his foster daughter escape...without a proper thank-you, I mean." The gallowglass was pleased with this excuse for keeping an eye on the fellow until Kevin was consulted. If what Alanna said was true, the O'Donnell would be more than pleased to meet the man who'd saved her. If not, he'd want to kill the bastard himself.

"But, Devlin, Kevin's keep is not en route to Blacksod Bay, and that is where Lucas is headed. What if his ship sails in the meantime?" argued Alanna, realizing that Devlin's courtesy might well be but a pretense to hold Lucas.

"We've a temporary camp but a half day from here. I warrant Kevin will see the Spaniard aboard his vessel personally once he's met the lad," assured the Irish commander, his voice brooking no arguments. With one arm about Lucas and the other about Alanna, he started to lead the way back to the main party when he spotted the hobbled horse.

"Wait, Alanna, there's no point in walking when your horse is here. Let me help you mount."

"No, that's an English animal Lucas confiscated," Alanna half-explained with a mischievous look at the Spaniard. She had given him back his life, and for it she'd damn well take her horse, an unequal exchange, to be sure, but better than naught. "Piobar is with the men."

"All right, del Fuentes, mount up, but don't make the mistake of trying to ride off on your own. My men are well armed and nervous in these unfamiliar woods," Devlin warned.

Turning to Alanna, he offered her his arm, and they moved off together, Lucas following slowly, trailed by the Irish guard, most of whom had yet to sheathe their weapons.

Chapter Ten

At the side of the road where he'd left the men, Lucas found that Juan and the others were already resigned to their impending deaths. It took a bit of convincing to make them believe they weren't being led to the slaughter on horseback rather than their own two feet. Briefly explaining Alanna's coloring of her abduction and Fitzhugh's resulting promise of assistance, del Fuentes was able to satisfy all but Juan, and persuade them to mount up and prepare to leave.

"If it's another night in a dungeon and hanging at dawn, I'd sooner die here by the sword," declared *El Pavoreal*.

"Damn you, Alvarez, think. Would they leave you unbound and let you ride alone if they wanted to kill you?" Lucas argued. "You could leave on your own any time, for all they know."

"With more than a dozen of them to the four of us, how far would I get?"

"If you believe that, die here, for all I care!" snapped Lucas, his patience considerably shortened since Devlin appeared. Even now, as he watched Alanna's blond head lean close to the Irishman's incredibly fire-hued locks, the Spaniard felt an unpleasant stirring of anger in his chest. "I for one am taking advantage of the woman's untruth so we may reach Alonso."

"And what if she's recanting those words at this moment?" challenged Juan. "You know better than to trust a female."

"We can only do what we think best," replied Lucas, unwilling to acknowledge the fact that such doubts had already assailed him. "I don't believe Alanna would countenance my death."

"Then you did bed her after all, you lusty devil," chortled Juan, earning a sour look. "All right, then, as poor a risk as it might be, I'll hazard my life on the success you had pleasuring the Irish bitch."

"Watch your filthy mouth!" snarled del Fuentes. He was strongly tempted to throttle his shipmate, but he knew that this was not the time or place. "Alanna is a lady, and I did not pleasure her, as you so crudely put it."

"Well, if you couldn't, then maybe she feels sorry for you, or else she believes life with your inadequacies is a worse punishment than death." *El Pavoreal,* laughed and quickly jumped up into his saddle to avoid Lucas's physical rebuttal.

"Del Fuentes, are you and your men ready?" called Devlin. He was tired of waiting for the Spaniards to settle their differences. If need be, his men could easily subdue the weary sailors and take them along as prisoners, but out of deference to Alanna and her story, he'd prefer to avoid a show of force if possible.

"Right now, Fitzhugh," answered Lucas as he mounted the English stallion and rode up to join Alanna and her Irishman.

Then they were off, a few of the Irish scouts riding ahead, followed by Alanna and Devlin, Lucas with them when the trail permitted three horses to travel abreast, and then the rest of the men, the Spanish first and the Irish behind. From the start, Lucas did not like the pairing, but he saw little he could do about it other than interjecting his comments into the others' conversation whenever possible and glaring at the gallowglass's head when not.

Devlin sat his saddle easily, the vision of a man clearly in control of his steed and his life. In truth, the only thing missing from his existence was the hand of the woman at his side. Part of the O'Donnell's household since he was a lad, Devlin Fitzhugh had been enamored of Alanna since she'd arrived to be fostered to Kevin nearly twelve years ago. A wide-eyed young girl, barely aware of the differences between men and women, she'd been quick to admire the strength, humor and character of the O'Donnell's most trusted gallowglass, and a fast friendship formed between them, despite the few years' difference in their ages. But when Alanna's heart had opened itself to love, she had turned to Sean O'Donnell, Kevin's own son, and, never having revealed his interest, Devlin had gracefully accepted her choice.

Two years later, a few months after she had married, the O'Donnell had returned from following the O'Neill in skirmishes to the north and learned of Sean's death. Immediately Kevin had fetched Alanna from the scene of the slaughter and brought her home to mourn. And, Devlin had hoped, to love again, perhaps him this time.

Despite the ready affection between them and the comfortable fondness she demonstrated toward him, Alanna, however, had yet to acknowledge that she felt anything more. The thought made Devlin frown. He waited patiently, though, his heart taking flight on the occasion of a privately enjoyed laugh or a quiet walk in the meadows as they shared their souls. As long as she was with him at Kevin's keep, he felt there was hope, and they would soon be there once more.

He shifted his weight on the horse to look behind him, content that all were keeping pace. Then he turned to the lovely blonde at his side, a grimace crossing his face as he took note of her alien attire.

"We'll reach the encampment well before sundown, lass, so you can get out of those frightful English rags before Kevin sees you. I fear he'd be horrified otherwise."

"Those *English rags,* as you call them, saved her from being killed once or twice," snapped Lucas, irritated that not only was he indebted to Alanna for her defense of him, but that she so willingly agreed to ride next to the Irishman. Was it because of Devlin's closeness to her foster father, or perhaps a special *personal* relationship they shared? The Spaniard's green eyes were a much deeper hue than usual as he brooded. Though she had whispered otherwise during their night of love, it would be most unusual for a woman to wait eight years—and Devlin had been available. That was easy enough to see.

"Then I shan't decry them again," declared the redheaded soldier with a ready grin as he deliberately ignored the nobleman's tone. "Everyone and everything that kept our lady Alanna safe from harm has earned my gratitude—and Kevin's, as well. He'll probably offer you the world, or at least the Irish half of it, for keeping our lass safe."

"Oh, Devlin, you do go on." Alanna chuckled, momentarily struck by her companion's singular smile, which produced a dimple in one cheek while the other remained smooth. "Your whole face changes when you smile. It's as though the faery folk suddenly stole your somber sense of duty."

"Never that, woman, merely the other hole the Lord had fashioned in my cheek," teased the gallowglass. "They knew with one dimple it would be a terrifying enough task fighting off all the adoring females who clamored for my bed. With two dimples, it would have taken all my strength to pacify the ladies and left none at all for the O'Donnell."

Her blond hair unrestrained by the English helmet, Alanna threw back her head and laughed aloud, her curls billowing in the breeze, her soft voice melodic as the sweetest bird Lucas had ever heard, but still he scowled. Could she not see the Irishman was naught but a rustic flatterer, ready to use her for his own purposes? What was wrong with the woman? he fumed.

"I guess you weren't lying when you said you didn't pleasure her," scoffed Juan, suddenly appearing on his right. "But whatever Fitzhugh is saying certainly amuses the lady. Too bad you don't have his gifts."

Controlling his urge to knock his shipmate to the ground, Lucas instead swallowed the bitter taste of bile and called out to the woman who was once his prisoner.

"Kevin O'Donnell—is he the man you threatened would kill me, Alanna? We know it wasn't Grady Mac-Williams," he shouted, abandoning caution in his illogical desire to attract Alanna's attention to him. "Remember, the man who would delight in my slow and painful death while you watched in delight?"

"Why would Alanna threaten you, the man who brought her to safety out of Castlemount?" challenged Devlin. His eyes narrowed as he turned his horse so he could see Lucas.

Nervous at the mounting tension as the two powerful males confronted each other, Alanna tried to maneuver Piobar between them, desperate for a logical answer to Devlin's observation.

"Of course he brought me to safety," she began. "I was his willing prisoner, just as I said, but—"

"Alanna objected to being bound and gagged," finished Lucas. He abandoned his foolish bid to remind Alanna of the power he'd once held over her.

"But why would you need to do so if she was agreeable?"

"In case we were captured, I didn't want it to seem Alanna had assisted our escape," explained the dark-haired Spanish nobleman. "At least while we were still near to Castlemount's properties, it seemed wiser to make it appear that she was truly my prisoner than to allow her freedom that could cost her life."

"Then he took me to St. Bridget's," interjected Alanna.

"St. Bridget's?" repeated Devlin in disbelief. "That says it all. No wonder she threatened your life, del Fuentes.

From the stories she's told me, Alanna saw that place as hell. All right, then, let's continue on—but Alanna, be nice to the man now. He's served you well.''

Irked by Devlin's condescending tone, Lucas allowed his horse to fall back, preferring a bit of solitude to their cozy prattle, until all at once he realized he could no longer understand what they were saying. The pair had switched to Gaelic, apparently, a tongue he could not decipher.

"I warrant no couple wants their words of love to be overheard by strangers," jeered Juan, quick to take pleasure in the flush coloring his countryman's cheeks. "Still, that's all the better for us."

"What?" Lucas wasn't certain he had heard Juan correctly.

"I surmise if the two of them are busy planning their loving reunion, there will be no one to call for our blood," goaded Juan, "and they do make a fine-looking pair."

"The devil take you and them both," snarled Lucas, unable to hold his anger in check any longer. Needing to escape the peacock's carping and the sight of Fitzhugh courting Alanna, he spurred his mount forward, calling out as he passed Devlin.

"I'll ride ahead with your scouts for a while. This slow pace is putting me to sleep."

"You don't suppose he'd desert his men and go off alone?" Devlin asked Alanna. He was tempted to go after the nobleman and bring him back.

"No, Lucas would never do such a thing," replied Alanna, her eyes fixed thoughtfully on the angry horseman.

Watching him gallop away from her, Alanna felt the same sense of bereavement as when Sean had left her to go into battle. Yet, much as she wanted to call Lucas back, to keep him with her, she realized wanting the man was far different from having him as her own and that was a wish that could never be. Hadn't he been ready to cast her aside before Devlin appeared? Lucas Rafael del Fuentes meant to travel off to Spain and leave her behind. Still, such a voyage would keep him alive—if not by her side forever.

Lucas had not liked the sight of Devlin Fitzhugh's copper brown locks bent close to Alanna's burnished gold ones. It reminded him too strongly of the pleasure he had denied himself. But even when he rode ahead of the pair, the image still danced before him, cruelly nibbling away at his restraint.

He tried telling himself that if he had had the chance to set Alanna free as he had thought to do, he would have been sending her into Fitzhugh's company anyway, a company she obviously found charming if her frequent, delicate laugh was any indication. But damn it, had they already parted he wouldn't have had to *witness* Alanna's meeting him! Neither would he have had to watch Alanna toss her head saucily when responding to one of the gallowglass's comments, nor to hear their shared merriment. He wouldn't have been aware of what was happening between them or been made to feel the outsider by the woman who had responded so sweetly to him the night before. Nor would he be tempted to overlook his duty to de Leiva, to forget his homeland and all that had seemed important to him before Alanna O'Donnell had woven her spell.

Ruefully, he admitted he now understood stories heard and found unfathomable in past years, tales of both Spanish and English soldiers deserting their respective armies after becoming enchanted by Irish women. And could any of those females have been even half as alluring as Alanna? Lucas rejected the possibility instantly, even as he steeled himself against the yearning in his heart. Such longings might erode the resolve of other men, but Lucas could not allow it to happen to him—not when the English blood that flowed in his veins demanded he preserve the honor of his father's family by remaining steadfast in his loyalty to Spain.

A scowl flitted across Lucas's handsome features when he could no longer ignore the urge to glance over his shoulder at the woman who besieged his thoughts. But his surrender to curiosity only set his anger flaming anew, as Fitzhugh had grown more boldly flirtatious and Alanna showed no sign of rebuffing him. The scenario reiterated what Lucas had already acknowledged. He didn't like the sight of them together one jot.

Nor did he enjoy what he saw next. A large band of Irishmen, so scruffy that Fitzhugh seemed the dandy in comparison, suddenly materialized on foot from behind rock and tree along a hilltop. They were a desperate-looking lot, some of their faces forever haunted by the ghosts of battles so gruesome they would never be forgotten.

Instinctively Lucas whirled his mount to return to Alanna's side and protect her, certain that the mirthful Devlin Fitzhugh was not equal to so critical a task, at least surely not as competent as he.

It was after his horse darted forward that Lucas saw the lack of concern Devlin and his men were exhibiting. As for Alanna, her delight was so evident, he easily surmised the identity of this forbidding group. They had to be O'Donnell's men.

Snorting in derision at his willingness to defend such a faithless woman, Lucas pulled his reins hard, stopping just short of Alanna and Fitzhugh.

"No need to worry, Spaniard. No harm will come to you. These are our men," Devlin said calmly. On the surface his words were reassuring, but Lucas could detect the underlying mockery Alanna must surely have noticed.

As del Fuentes's fingers itched to grasp the hilt of his sword, he silently cursed the gallowglass, wanting nothing more than to gift Fitzhugh with a slit across his throat, a slit wider than the grin the Irish bastard wore at present. And well the jackal would deserve it, Lucas inwardly raged, for purposefully making his act of bravery and concern for Alanna look like cowardice before her eyes.

But what could he do about it? Protest that he had come rushing back to guarantee the woman's safety? Would she believe such a thing after their argument and his attempts to send her home before Fitzhugh had come upon them? Probably not. The gallowglass was a clever man, and would have been a worthy adversary in a battle for Alanna's hand if Lucas thought to wage such a private war. But the fact remained that he did not. Much as Fitzhugh's tactics galled him, Lucas would not compete with the Irish devil. He was going to Blacksod Bay and then home to Spain.

Lucas finally looked at Alanna. His masculine pride wanted to determine her reaction toward his unnecessary bolt to her side. He told himself that if she gave no indication of holding him in ridicule, it made no difference what Devlin Fitzhugh said or implied.

But what he saw in her face made Lucas more vexed. She wasn't jeering at him, in fact she was paying him no mind whatsoever. Instead, she was so enrapt by the advance of the Irish rebels that she was ignoring both him and his manly pride, as though they were little more than trifles.

Damnation! He had been willing to once more risk his life for the beautiful wench, and she had the effrontery not to notice. If it wasn't for the savage group now quickly descending from the hillside, Lucas swore he would have given her something to regain her attention, something she couldn't fail to remark.

In spite of the grins some of them wore, the men coming toward them were a hardened lot. Muscular yet lean, their bodies spoke of great toil in a land that often went hungry. Their joy in seeing Alanna was obvious, but tempered by a warrior's glint that lurked within their eyes. They were rough and rugged, coarse soldiers seldom given to emotions, yet miraculously gentled by Alanna's presence.

That they were devoted to her, Lucas had no doubt, nor did he dismiss the observation that they could easily kill to keep her from harm or avenge any hurt she suffered. The threats Alanna had made throughout their journey had not been empty ones. Suddenly, the lie the seductive widow had told O'Donnell's mercenary earned Lucas's gratitude even as it rankled, putting him, as it did, in her debt.

Lucas had little time to sort out his conflicting emotions, however, as a large man dressed in a saffron tunic and cloak separated himself from the group and with gladdened steps approached Alanna.

He was an impressive fellow, tall and solid with shoulders as wide as a doorway. An intelligent face was capped with thick, white hair, his only indication of creeping toward advanced age, and his bearing was noble. But then Lucas mused, watching him swing Alanna from her saddle with ease, among these Irish, being chieftain of a clan probably meant more than any aristocratic rank recognized by the civilized world.

"Where have you been, daughter?" Kevin O'Donnell teasingly scolded in Gaelic, holding the young woman at arm's length after having enfolded her in a bearlike hug. "And what could have induced you to discard modest, womanly garb for cloth woven by our enemies?"

"Oh, Kevin, 'tis good to see you," Alanna responded. Yet as sincere as the greeting was, the Irishwoman was struck by the fact that her foster father's presence did not fill her with the same sense of security and contentment it had always provided. This bewildered her, but she gamely brushed aside the strange disappointment marring her reunion. "I've much to tell you," she added with a smile.

"And so have I," added Devlin, his glance, rife with unspoken meaning, falling upon the Spaniards. All of them except Lucas squirmed uncomfortably in their saddles when the O'Donnell turned to regard them, his cold blue eyes evincing not a speck of compassion.

Seeing Kevin's response, Alanna began to rush ahead with her tale, trying to forestall any possible unpleasantries Devlin's suspicions might spawn, until she noted Lucas regarding her quizzically. Then she realized belatedly that he did not comprehend a word of the conversation.

"This is the man who saved me," Alanna informed her foster father in English. What she said was not exactly a lie. It may have been an unwitting rescue but 'twas one all the same. And then, there had been the matter of the sword wound he had received in her stead. More comfortable now with her falsehood, she continued easily. "Since he understands English, should we not play the gracious hosts and use that language, cursed as it is, for his sake? Though he is a Spaniard, I owe him a debt nevertheless."

"Your savior?" Kevin inquired, an eyebrow lifted in skepticism, after exchanging looks with Devlin Fitzhugh. "According to Moira, 'twas a Spaniard who abducted you. Is this the same scoundrel?"

"'Tis a long story," Alanna replied, "and one better told around your camp fire. But answer me, what are you doing this far inland? I didn't think to see you until I returned to Donegal."

"We were looking for you, of course," the O'Donnell responded, the gruffness in his voice tempered by the tender way in which he took Alanna's hand. He began leading her to his makeshift camp on the other side of the hill, silently signaling to Fitzhugh to follow with the foreigners. "We were out at sea, headed south after a storm, seeking any salvage to be had from floundering vessels, when a fierce tempest forced us to put in to shore. 'Twas while there we began to hear reports of Spanish warships sighted along the coast. You didn't expect me to leave you with Mac-Williams if an invasion was on the horizon, did you? Besides, I wasn't certain you were not already on your way home. After purchasing some horses, I gave my seamen orders to sail for Donegal while the others and I rode to Castlemount to collect you and provide safe escort. On our way there, we encountered Moira and Friar Galen and heard of your kidnapping. We've been turning the countryside top over bottom since then seeking some sign of your whereabouts. And grateful I am to Devlin for finding you, lass. But then I should have known if any man was

capable of ferreting you out it would be he. Sure and no one
else would look so diligently.'' The chieftain gave the smug
Fitzhugh a look of approval while Lucas silently gritted his
teeth, the muscle of his jaw working as though it had a life
of its own.

By this time they had reached the encampment, and more
of O'Donnell's men emerged from threadbare tents, along
with an ancient woman who screeched her thanks to the
Almighty for Alanna's safe return before delivering Lucas
a scathing glance that put him in mind of his austere pater-
nal grandmother, a frightening woman if ever there was
one.

Then, before Alanna could say yea or nay, the aged crone
had spirited her charge off to bathe and refresh herself after the arduous journey, while Lucas and his men were escorted to one of the crude cloth shelters, whether as
honored guests or wretched prisoners, he had yet to decide.

Sitting there, exhibiting a calm he did not entirely feel,
Lucas sought to reassure the others. In muted tones, he told
them of Alanna's continued lie. Though Pedro and Enrique were somewhat comforted, Juan Felipe Alvarez continued to glance nervously at the tent flap, his fear well
deserved. But no matter what their emotions at present,
their future was quite obviously in the hands of the
O'Donnell, and not their own.

"I've your own clothing awaiting you," Moira told
Alanna as she bustled the girl into a tent so threadbare it
offered only simple privacy rather than protection from the
elements. "And when the night is over, you can sleep once
more in Sean's tunic. It was rescued along with your other
things from Castlemount.''

"Nay! I can't," Alanna cried impulsively before she
could restrain herself. Noting the odd look with which the
old woman regarded her, Alanna fabricated another lie, not
willing to tell Moira it was guilt that prohibited her from

donning the garment that had belonged to her husband. "I'm chilled to the bone after my nights on the road," she said. "There's no doubt but that I'll need something much warmer."

"Be that as it may, you'll at least get out of those devil's rags," Moira ordered. "Imagine parading about in masculine garb, and English at that! What in heaven's name could have possessed you to don such apparel? Unless, of course, it was him forced you to it."

"These garments helped save me from becoming Lady Bravingham," Alanna replied with a haughtiness born of the culpability she felt for having slept with the Spaniard. Nevertheless she did as Moira bid. She wasn't in a mood for one of the old woman's scoldings, no more than she was of a mind to think about *him*, much less speak of the heartless, inconsiderate demon. The hurts she had endured at del Fuentes's hands just prior to Devlin's appearance sat upon her still.

"Well, out with it, lass. Did he steal you or did you run off with him?" Moira asked impatiently, unaware of her young charge's reluctance to discuss her escapades, though had she been, it would have made no difference. "Since it's just us women, you can confide in me without having to explain to Kevin or fear his seeking revenge."

"Didn't I already say I went off willingly with the Spaniards?" Alanna exclaimed in exasperation, reaching for the bucket of water and cloth Moira offered her. As she began to wash, the comely blonde told herself she continued in her lie merely because she didn't want to relive her unsettling adventures by recounting them for Moira. Certainly the compelling image of Lucas as he straddled her before they had coupled could have nothing to do with her untruthfulness—not when he had made it so painfully evident today that he didn't really desire her. It was obvious that what she, after years of famine, had considered a feast was naught but simple fare for the highly experienced Lucas.

"I can't say as I blame you," Moira commented non-committally, not yet having made up her mind if the girl was indeed telling the truth. Picking up another cloth, she continued. "Bravingham or no, I daresay that Spaniard is enough to tempt most women into following him anywhere."

"Is he? I hadn't noticed," Alanna fibbed, even though she recalled all too vividly how she had been drawn to Lucas del Fuentes from the first instant she had seen him in Grady's hall, standing boldly despite his nakedness.

"My eyes are decades older than yours, and I can see how much man he is. 'Tis a good thing you're a lass with sense," Moira said with a snort. She walked behind Alanna to scrub the grime of the road from her back. "Still, what does it matter? You're safe, and you don't seem the worse for the trauma you've suffered. Why, your skin is as radiant as— Did that foreigner touch you?" the old woman suddenly demanded.

"What!" Alanna yelped, taken completely by surprise. Did the glow of her body proclaim her as a woman who had been loved last night? "No, of course he didn't!"

"What's that bruise, then, at the base of your neck? And look at your wrists! They've rope burns on them as if you had been bound. That dirty devil! I've heard about the indecent and abnormal sports some men demand when bedding a woman. And from the virile look of that Spaniard, I'd put nothing past him."

"So that's the sort of thing you dream of when you sit nodding before the fire," Alanna said with a gentle laugh, trying to dismiss the topic.

"Nay, Alanna, 'twon't be so simple to shift the direction of our discourse. We were speaking of you and that Spaniard, not me. Now I want to know exactly what happened. There's no shame in taking a man to your bed if that's what you want, but there's no need to allow him to abuse you, either."

"Del Fuentes did not abuse me," the young widow protested. Unless, she thought, his ungallant behavior after possessing her counted as such. But the man was such an enigma. Having saved her from a rebel sword, taking an injury in her stead, he had nevertheless been ready to send her on her way after their loving. Had any man she had ever known been so unfathomable? Or for that matter, so irritating?

"Say what you will, Alanna," Moira muttered as she unpacked a soft Irish tunic that had been among the things the older woman had refused to leave behind at Castlemount, "but one day, the story will out in its entirety."

"There is no more to say," Alanna insisted. She slipped the garment over her head, glad that her perfidious body was now hidden from the sharp-eyed, skeptical woman who had known her since birth. "Del Fuentes wants me no more than I do him."

"We'll see just who wants what when we join the men after sundown," the servant promised, beginning the task of taming Alanna's long tresses with a comb. "I know longing in a man's eyes when I see it, and in a woman's, too."

Alanna prayed she would not be so readily transparent that evening. She couldn't let del Fuentes know, after he had said he did not want her, that the womanly desire he had but recently reawakened had become so urgent and demanding that she craved him still. Only God alone knew why, though, when he was the most abominable man she had ever known!

It was long after they had entered the camp that Lucas and the others were summoned and taken before the O'Donnell as he sat near his fire. Alanna was at his right hand, dressed in finery that made her appear an Irish princess. Her thick blond hair was tamed into a single braid that traveled halfway down the back of her long, saffron-colored tunic, with errant curls escaping to frame her lovely face. A flowing, carefully woven cloak was anchored to her right shoulder by a large, silver brooch worked in a Celtic design, while hammered bracelets were worn at intervals along her bare arms. To Lucas's appreciative eyes, she was barbaric beauty, primitive enough to make a man forget all he knew about civilization, yet so refined she would outshine any noblewoman in Christendom.

While Lucas's men did not understand Irish customs, the solemnity of the occasion was evident. Frightened by the hawklike profiles of the rebels in the flickering shadows cast by the campfire, they hung back. To the seamen and Alvarez, it was a scene straight from the depths of hell, the blackness of the night and the red glow of the flames turning the Irish into minions of the Prince of Evil.

Lucas del Fuentes, however, walked boldly forward, seeing among those gathered the irate prelate he had overpowered in Grady's dungeon. The priest's presence did not bode well. But if death was imminent, Lucas wanted to face it nobly. Standing before the seated O'Donnell, his feet planted firmly on foreign soil and his head unbowed, the young Spanish aristocrat met the steely gaze of Alanna's foster father.

The two men silently took each other's measure, assessing what they had previously heard from others in the light of what they now saw for themselves.

"I like not your raiment, del Fuentes," Kevin drawled, referring to the English uniform Lucas still wore. "It should have been removed."

Immediately Lucas recalled the Irish tradition he and his men had already suffered in Grady MacWilliams's keep, that of stripping prisoners naked. Was that what he and the others were, prisoners? But surely, Alanna would not look so calm and serene if her foster father meant to take either the freedom or the life of the man who had been her lover, no matter how briefly, would she? Lucas meant to find out, daring words that would either bring him swift death or inform him of his liberty.

"This garb is not to my liking, either," he began, indicating his scorn for the cloth that marked him as Elizabeth's man. "As I have no other clothing, 'twas this or nothing. I thought it better manners not to put your men to shame." His eyes swept the line of Irish before coming to rest on Devlin Fitzhugh, who bristled at the Spaniard's insinuation.

As Alanna's cheek became suffused with red not of the campfire's making, the O'Donnell threw back his head and roared with laughter.

"A thoughtful guest, indeed. I thank you on behalf of my men, though as for myself, there is no need. Your concern, sincere as it is, was misplaced."

"As you say," Lucas replied, the devilment in his smile an indication he was agreeing merely to be polite and nothing more.

Kevin regarded the young foreigner with keen eyes. He believed neither Devlin's suppositions nor the story Alanna had told him. He knew the source of Fitzhugh's sentiments but not, however, why Alanna would twist the truth. The Irish lord was only certain that the man before him must mean something to his son's widow. For that reason alone, he was ready to offer friendship.

Looking at the Spanish nobleman, Kevin O'Donnell was well satisfied with his decision. Here was a strong man, one who could well protect any woman placed in his care. As for del Fuentes's nationality, it mattered not to the O'Donnell. True, Sean had been his son as well as Alanna's husband, and Curran Desmond his friend. But the chieftain did not share his foster daughter's deep-seated hatred of Philip's nation. Kevin was a seasoned warrior. He had lived with battle his entire life, and most probably would end his days in combat. As a soldier, he possessed a pragmatism born of experience, unlike his emotional Alanna. He knew that promised troops did not always arrive on time, if they appeared at all. Circumstances often dictated otherwise, and so he did not blame Spain for the tragedy at Smerwick. No, his hatred was for the English, bloody butchers that they were. And for that reason, Kevin welcomed these Spanish around his campfire, adhering to a basic premise—the foes of his enemy were his allies. Besides, he mused with a chuckle, any man who could put up with Alanna's tirade after having untied her was one worthy of admiration.

With a nod of his shaggy, prematurely white head, Kevin O'Donnell signaled for food and drink to be brought forth. The aged female Lucas had observed when they had first arrived in the camp came scuttling to her chieftain bearing a huge silver cup and muttering indistinctly under her breath. Before retreating again, she stopped to unabashedly study the Spanish nobleman, and without further comment disappeared from view.

Odd as they were, Kevin paid no mind to the woman's antics. Instead, he raised the chalice and drank deeply. Then he held it out to Lucas and commanded him to drink, as well.

The handsome foreigner took the vessel with steady fingers, but nevertheless breathed an unheard sigh of relief into the cup when he brought it to his lips. It would appear he and his men were not prisoners, after all.

As Lucas partook of the fiery liquid, a cheer went up among the Irish, and those fierce-looking demons were suddenly transformed into laughing, congenial men. All, that was, except the priest and Devlin Fitzhugh. The others, however, moved among the Spanish, slapping them on their backs and freely offering drink as Lucas del Fuentes was given the seat at Kevin's left hand, and a full cup of whiskey was pressed upon him.

"We feast tonight," the O'Donnell's voice boomed over the noise, "to celebrate Alanna's return to us. I thank you, del Fuentes, and the others for keeping her from harm. In turn, I offer you my protection. You are our honored guests, and whatever is in my power to grant you is yours."

Alanna's delicate eyebrow rose in surprise at her foster father's generosity. Her lie had been told to save Lucas's life, not turn him into a hero. How dare that bastard ac-

cept honors and tribute not due him? she thought with
mounting ire. Though memories of his willingness to cast
her aside heightened her anger, she was more annoyed by
the impulsive fabrication she had told when Devlin had
appeared.

As the pretty blonde watched her people demonstrate
their appreciation, she wanted to scream out that the foreigners' behavior had not warranted such gratitude. What
they truly deserved, however, she could not give them under Kevin's observant eye, at least not without sentencing
them to death.

Most disturbing of all, though, was something else entirely, and that was the easy acceptance by the Irish of these
Spaniards into their midst. The thought of it made her
seethe. Yet whom did she have to blame for this present
travesty other than herself and the foolish woman's heart
that had caused her to alter the truth?

Unable to do anything to rectify the situation, Sean
O'Donnell's widow remained quietly where she was. Aside
from Moira, who looked at her in puzzlement now and then
as she went about serving the men, no one noticed Alanna's reluctance to participate fully in the festivities. In fact,
none of those gathered, either Irish or foreign, heeded her
at all. Friar Galen sent del Fuentes an occasional glower, yet
the clergyman continued to raise his cup all the same. As
for Kevin and Lucas, they were engaged in serious drinking and light banter as if they were friends of long standing.

Bringing her goblet to her lips and delicately sipping at
its contents, Alanna allowed her eyes to survey the ludi-
crous scene over the vessel's ornamented rim. Almost everyone, with the exception of a wary Juan, was enjoying
himself. At least, that was what Alanna thought until she
spied Devlin Fitzhugh, his face a study in misery.

Curious, Alanna conjectured what could have caused his
dismay. Then she happened to meet his eyes. With sudden
clarity, she understood. Within their depths she saw the

hunger of a man for a woman. Devlin loved her, and had for a long time.

Startled, the comely widow wondered why she had never recognized his devotion for what it was. Might it be that she had forgotten what could exist between male and female until she had seen the expression reflected in Lucas's deep, green eyes? But what was she thinking? Lucas did not love her! He had merely enjoyed a quick tumble. His subsequent behavior had proven as much.

After giving Devlin a quick, tight smile, Alanna looked away, not able to bear the sight of his poorly disguised longing. Everything was wrong, all wrong, she told herself, her unhappiness a match for that of the gallowglass. Her newly acquired knowledge had cost her a dear friendship. Surely she could never again think of him as she had before. But worst of all, Devlin, a fine, decent man, loved with no hope of having those feelings returned, while she, Alanna admitted bitterly, harbored feelings for an unsuitable foreigner who, once he had bedded her, had forgotten her existence. God help her. God help them all.

As she sat deep in thought, providing spiritless monosyllabic answers to Moira's infrequent questions, Alanna's misery grew. The men, however, went on with their celebrating, their voices growing friendlier and more boisterous with each sip they took. A drinking contest was declared, and cup after cup drained. Watching in distaste as inhibitions among the soldiers vanished, Alanna saw Lucas, on his way to replenish his whiskey, pass Friar Galen. Suddenly the nobleman was facedown in the dirt. Alanna almost swore her very proper clergyman had tripped him.

"Pardon my clumsiness, Friar," Lucas said, his demeanor friendly as he extended a hand for assistance in rising.

Helping del Fuentes regain his feet, the cleric delivered a sharp thrust of his knee to the sensitive area above the Spaniard's groin. "All is forgiven, my son... finally," the churchman intoned piously.

Alanna could not believe what she had witnessed, nor
was Lucas's eventual good-natured laughter at Galen's all-
too-human wish for revenge what she would have expected. But with old scores settled to the prelate's satisfaction, the two men shared a drink together, talking,
laughing, stopping short only of singing a bawdy duet. Men
were nothing more than lads, Alanna thought, even those
who had taken the cloth, and she had no patience for them
and their incomprehensible behavior, steeped as it was in
masculine pride.

Still, the high spirits of the night did not end there. The
drinking competition continued until only Kevin and Lucas remained, matching each other gulp for gulp as though
the ability to withstand the whiskey's potent clutch was a
true test of manhood. Meanwhile, good-humored scuffles
erupted around the campfire, relieved by snatches of song
and the solitary sound of a lute. And Alanna was part of
none of it, the happiness surrounding her only emphasizing her own lonely state.

Finally, she could deal with it no more, and stood to take
her leave. But Kevin's large hand at her wrist stayed her.

"'Twould be discourteous, Alanna, to retire before I
have bestowed gifts upon your rescuers as a sign of my
thanks," the O'Donnell stated simply.

"You have already given them the gift of life," Alanna
said, horrified at the prospect of these charlatans having the
impudence to accept anything more.

"Hush, daughter. That was theirs already," Kevin
slurred slightly in gentle rebuke. "Now do not shame me
here before both our men and these foreigners to our
shores. Surely you would not have them think me less than
magnanimous."

Reluctantly acquiescing to his demands, Alanna sank to
the mossy ground and lowered her eyes so that none might
see the angry sparks glinting there. She had never thought
to put Kevin in such a position with her lie. And yet to
speak out now would only shame him further.

"Lucas del Fuentes," the O'Donnell pronounced, unmindful of Alanna's inner turmoil, "now is the time for me to hold true to my word. I have said I would give you whatever is in my power to grant. But before you make your request, know that I am willing to part with that which is most precious to me. I offer you my foster daughter, Alanna, in marriage."

Alanna's body went rigid, her emotions an unbridled vortex of shock and rage. Love Kevin O'Donnell she might, but the comely blonde detested him at this moment for having the insensitivity and audacity to give her as wife to Lucas del Fuentes simply because he and the Spaniard had shared a few too many cups and fallen into easy camaraderie.

Well, she would have none of it, she swore! Del Fuentes was everything she abhorred, half English, half Spanish, traitorous races, both! He was a man whose kisses had caused her to betray her principles, to forget them as if they were straw before the wind. What else was he but a foreigner who had used her and been ready to desert her? Well, he would use her no more to get whatever it was he wanted from Kevin O'Donnell.

She relished the idea of rejecting the perfidious Lucas in front of this assembly, of making him realize once and for all that though his kisses might eat at her very soul, her beliefs were intact. She desired him to know that she had overcome her physical cravings, that she no longer wanted him, would never want him again despite the hard, lean lines of his body and the soft fullness of his lips.

With this thought in mind, Alanna opened her mouth to speak. But before her intended rejection could be spoken, another voice sounded.

"No!"

The word, delivered swiftly and sharply, hung heavily in the air, buoyed up by the surprise of those gathered.

"I appreciate the extent of your generosity," Lucas said slowly, intent on repeating his refusal, while seeking with a whiskey-numbed brain the reason he must say nay to so delightful a prospect. Then, painfully, he remembered. "Before I am anything, I am a soldier in the service of the King of Spain. If you wish to grant me something, help me fulfill my duty to rejoin my captain. I am free to do nothing else."

"Spoken like a man of honor," Kevin murmured, impressed yet marveling with a father's love that any male could decline the pleasure Alanna would give a husband. "If that is what you truly want, I will do my best to satisfy your wish."

"He says no, and wants to be taken to his captain," guffawed one Irishman, his mood quickly becoming contagious among the besotted group.

"To cross the seas to Spain," added another.

"Well, what difference does it make? A ship or Alanna, the ride would be just as stormy," called someone else.

"You're drunk, all of you!" Alanna accused before turning to her foster father. "And you—you're no better than Grady MacWilliams!" Then she ran off, the echoes of laughter ringing in her ears. Oh, how she hated del Fuentes! How dare he decline her hand before she could reject him!

Watching Alanna's sudden departure sobered Kevin O'Donnell for a moment, until the cup of liquid fire in his hand and the merriment of the men around him called the chieftain to revelry once more. He couldn't blame the girl, he thought with a shrug of his massive shoulders, for being disappointed when a near-snared husband as fine as del Fuentes managed to wriggle free. Yet there was nothing he could do about it other than respect the man all the more for adherence to duty.

Clapping Lucas soundly on his wounded shoulder, Kevin re-filled the Spaniard's cup, oblivious to the younger man's slight wince. The pain was centered not in the physical injury, but in the memories of Alanna's sweet nursing and the road upon which it had set them.

Drink heartily though he might, Lucas found himself unable to regain the good humor that had previously been his. The lines of his handsome face hardened, and he gazed off into the darkness along the path Alanna had taken, wishing he could have walked beside her. Moira, settled near the fire, ready to assume her role as *pisoque,* teller of tales, looked from Lucas to Devlin to the tent where Alanna most likely spent her time tossing and turning.

"What fools the young are," she muttered in disgust. Searching her memory for an ancient story that would substantiate her opinion, she poured herself a hefty measure of good Irish drink, *her* only recourse for warming a chilled but aged body. "The fire in their blood is wasted on such dolts!"

Chapter Eleven

When Alanna, still considerably nettled, left her quarters the next morning, she immediately encountered a sheepish Kevin O'Donnell. The coincidence made her suspect that he had been lying in wait for her.

"Good day to you, daughter," he called, his manner hesitant and his voice soft. He was unsure of Alanna's mood and loath to encourage the pounding in his head with loud speech. He knew, however, he had to speak with her alone before she encountered del Fuentes. "I'm that sorry things did not end as I planned last night."

"You *should* be contrite," she retorted. "Drink or no, imagine offering me to a Spaniard!"

"Now don't be shrewish because so fine a prospect turned down the chance to wed you. A sharp-tongued woman will never find a man willing to go before a priest."

"That's not what has me undone," Alanna protested vehemently. "It is your behavior. I was going to refuse to marry him anyway."

"Aye, lass, of course you were," Kevin agreed. His excessively soothing tones grated on Alanna's already raw nerves.

"Well, 'tis true!"

"You don't hear me saying otherwise, do you?" the O'Donnell asked with an injured expression.

"And I'd better not," the feisty blonde warned peevishly before anger turned to hope. Perhaps the foreigners were already gone and her problems at an end. "Have they left then?"

"The Spaniards? No, I've received reports their shipmates have moved on to Elly Cove where they have joined the crew of another Spanish ship cast on our shores, their own vessel no longer being seaworthy. I'll escort del Fuentes and the others there myself, but at present we are readying them for the journey. You know those born in this land have no compassion for men wearing the uniform of England. For precaution's sake, I've decided to dress your Spaniard as one of us. His men, too, of course."

"He's not my Spaniard!" Alanna objected heatedly.

"And more's the pity," interjected Moira, passing by with a basin of water.

"Quiet, old one," Kevin ordered sternly. He could see that the servant's words had further upset Alanna, and he wished to present her this morning in her best light. After all, who was to say that any man, even one as dedicated to his cause as del Fuentes, could not be made to change his mind if the woman was alluring?

"I only speak the truth, Kevin O'Donnell, and well you know it," the old woman replied, "and if Alanna had any sense, she'd acknowledge it, too. Hasn't she learned anything from this Bravingham business? She needs a husband to protect her. If not the Spaniard, then let her take Devlin Fitzhugh to her bed."

"I require no man," Alanna avowed, resentful of being reminded of yet another dilemma. What was she going to do about Devlin?

"Perhaps, but there are times a man can use a woman's touch," Kevin said slowly, hoping to orchestrate a situation that would force Alanna and Lucas together before the Spaniard sailed out of her life. "Even dressed as one of us, Philip's men will stand out with those beards of theirs. Moira was on her way to divest them of their whiskers. I think it meet that you lend your assistance to the task."

"Is this a jest? You'd suffer me near the heroic del Fuentes with a razor in my hand? If so, you can't seriously mean to safeguard his life."

"And I had always deemed you a brave woman," Kevin said with a disapproving shake of his white-thatched head. "But if you are afraid to perform so intimate a task, I understand—especially in light of his rejection last evening, though you claim not to care. 'Twould seem del Fuentes has more effect upon you than you wish to admit."

"Give me the damnable razor, then! I'll show you who's afraid!" Alanna snapped. She snatched the implement from Kevin's hands and followed a smirking Moira across the compound to where the man in question sat upon an outcropping of rock.

Despite her current distaste for Lucas and the embarrassment he had heaped upon her the previous night, Alanna had to admit she found the sight of him attired as one of her countrymen nothing short of splendid.

His broad shoulders strained against the tunic, as did his expansive chest, its fine mat of hair barely visible beneath the loosened laces of the garment's neckline. Bronzed legs and muscular thighs were bare, and the sight of them was so compelling that Alanna shivered slightly when she recalled what was atop their juncture.

But she told herself she wouldn't think of that as she brushed aside Lucas's muffled greeting.

"Save the salutations, del Fuentes," she said. "I am here only as a courtesy to Kevin and to save Moira an odious task, from which her advanced age alone should protect her. And if you object to my involvement, as your scowl indicates, you shouldn't. Count yourself fortunate I am here, as Moira's hand is none too steady."

In spite of his throbbing brow and his dry mouth, remnants of the previous evening's overindulgence, Lucas chuckled and translated for Juan, whose eyes turned wide with horror as he fought to sit still beneath the blade Moira was running under his chin.

"But your hands, as I recall, are capable of trembling, as well," Lucas said softly, his eyes locked to Alanna's slender fingers.

"Only when they have cause," the golden-haired beauty muttered. "I can assure you that this morning, they will be steady, which is more than I can say for you after the amount of *poitin* you drank."

"About last night," Lucas began tentatively, unsure of what to say. How could he voice his regrets, knowing they might only fuel her hatred further? He had already told her he didn't want her, but he needed to explain why.

"It is of no importance. You mean no more to me than I do to you," Alanna replied. "Now be silent, or mayhap we will discover my hand can slip, after all. You wouldn't want to die such an ignoble death, would you? Not when you are so close to reaching your captain."

"*Bueno,* then begin the transformation," Lucas commanded irritably. Though he had wanted to leave Ireland thinking Alanna unscarred by their brief union, her cold words did not sit well with him all the same.

"To my way of thinking, a few swipes of a razor and a change of clothing can never make a Spaniard into an Irishman."

"Praise God Almighty for that," Lucas muttered. He was about to say more until the razor scraping none too gently along his upper lip silenced him.

Soon the task was done, and when Lucas lifted his head from the square of linen he had used to wipe his face, Alanna's breath caught in her throat. Always handsome, Lucas was now devilishly so. Like some magnificent fallen angel, he could tempt any woman to follow him to hell. Any woman but herself, Alanna amended quickly. She would not fall prey to the beauty of that strong, square, masculine chin now so clearly revealed, or to the clean lines of Lucas's fine jaw. It mattered not that his lips were more enticing and his smooth cheeks begged for the touch of her fingertips. She would not oblige. He'd be gone quickly enough, and she needed no more burning memories to plague her than she already had.

"You could almost be one of us," Moira said, looking up from her still uncompleted task to admire Alanna's handiwork. "Except, of course, no Irishman would be as anxious as you are to depart our shores. I even heard you ask the O'Donnell to lend you one of his boats. Of course you didn't know at the time how small and unsuitable they are and that the craft are not here at all, but anchored home at Tur Muir. Your eagerness to leave Ireland almost suggests you are afraid to stay, a fine brave man like you! Whatever could be here to frighten you so?"

"You are being absurd, old woman," Lucas protested gruffly. "There is nothing here to send me scampering off like some timorous hare."

"And are you so sure of that?" Moira asked, her eyes settling meaningfully upon Alanna, who had already turned her attentions to Pedro.

Lucas's only reply was a scowl as he stomped off to confer with Kevin. At his reaction, the old woman cackled, terrorizing Juan when the razor passed over his exposed throat. But Moira was oblivious to the squirming form beneath her hands as she watched Lucas cross the encampment. Perhaps, she thought gleefully, the rabbit could be ensnared yet.

It was nearly midnight when Don Alonso de Leiva, lieutenant-general of the Spanish fleet, stared out over the scarred battlements of the Irish castle his men had taken, his attention caught not by anything he saw, but by the constant sound of the pounding surf. The merciless waves echoed in his ears, the rhythm he'd once found exhilarating now haunting not only his dreams but his waking hours, as well.

Without interruption, hour after hour, the ocean continued to remind him of the lives she had claimed, the relentless battering of the coast but a demonstration of her fury at the mortal men who dared to challenge her moods,

believing they could best her might. Already she had taken
La Rata, tossing its eight hundred and twenty tons brutally
against the shore, barely permitting him and his men to escape before the ship foundered, torn free from its anchor
and heaved onto the sandy bar beneath the deceptive water.

"You have won again, mistress," the commander murmured, finally coming to terms with the recent loss he had
refused to acknowledge until now. A man of great personal wealth and inestimable political influence, as well as
a valued member of Philip's court, the twenty-four-year-old
Don Alonso had attracted the strongest and finest of
Spain's young nobles to sail with him against the power of
England. Now, reluctantly, he would admit responsibility
for losing another of them, Lucas Rafael del Fuentes, a
nobleman who probably would have headed the expedition but for the fault of being half English.

Alonso turned to a waiting servant.

"Tell the bishop and Don Diego I wish to see them."

It had been de Leiva's decision, his alone, to permit del
Fuentes to lead the shore party in search of fresh water and
whatever food they could scavenge. Alvarez could have
handled the task well enough, but Lucas had been anxious
to be ashore. Thus, despite his misgivings, de Leiva had
yielded and awarded command of the small group to del
Fuentes, unwittingly consigning him to death.

Now, six days later and nearly a hundred miles north of
where *La Rata* had sent them ashore, he had to concede
that Lucas del Fuentes and his men must indeed have perished in the wilds of Ireland. Only after such an admission
could de Leiva set his mind to his desperate attempt to reach
home on the *Duquesa Santa Ana,* another Spanish ship,
which had suffered less damage at nature's hand than his
own. As was expected, her captain had relinquished command to Philip's lieutenant-general, and her sailing would
soon be upon them.

"You sent for us, Don Alonso?" asked the Bishop of Killahoe, entering with Diego Martinez y Goya. Each hoped that, for a change, the news would be good.

"Yes, my friends, the repairs on the *Santa Ana* will be completed within two days, and Captain Mores and I have decided we shall sail at the first high tide thereafter."

"And Lucas?" asked Diego, who had known the nobleman since his birth and considered him the son he never had. "What of him?"

"As painful as it may be, Diego, I must regretfully accept what God decrees. Since we have had no word of him, I fear we must accept the demise of Lucas and his party." Having already seen so many human lives sacrificed during this campaign, he had not anticipated the sudden grief that clutched at his heart as he admitted Lucas's loss, but he withstood the pain stoically, accepting it as his punishment for approving the mission. "Your grace, please arrange the appropriate memorial service for Don Lucas and his crew."

"Alonso, you can't be certain he and the others are dead," protested Diego.

"It is nearly a week since we set them ashore. If Lucas has not made his way to us in that time," declared de Leiva harshly, "he cannot. He is either dead or captured, and we can do nothing about either. We will pray for his soul and those of his men. They served us well."

Diego was silent, afraid in his heart that Alonso was right, but loath to accept the finality of declaring del Fuentes gone.

"Lucas is very resourceful—and he knows English."

"From what our Irish allies report, the English along the southern coast have slaughtered more than a thousand of our people in the last fortnight without giving them the opportunity to say a word," argued the bishop. "Surely those Spanish souls, if not del Fuentes, deserve our prayers. Indeed, should he still be alive, our litany may help him, as well."

"Not before tomorrow evening—or the following day. Do not surrender your hope until then," urged Diego. Somehow he simply knew that Lucas del Fuentes, possessing the inordinate amount of determination he did, would appear before the final prayers were said for his soul.

"Very well," conceded de Leiva, smiling at his adviser's stalwart faith. "Arrange the service for the morning following tomorrow, your grace."

Their pace the next morning was much swifter than when they had traveled alone and uncertain of the terrain. Lucas was thankful for Kevin's supportive company, if not Devlin's, whose constant presence was a thorn, reminding him acutely of the woman he could never claim as his.

The Irishmen had insisted it was their obligation to see Lucas's party to Elly Cove, where de Leiva was camped, claiming it was on their way north to Donegal. Since O'Donnell had sent most of his men off in another direction, and the land here narrowed and became more of a headland between rushing waters, such a route hardly seemed likely to the Spaniard. However, Lucas had come too close to death to question the goodwill of Kevin O'Donnell, and he had accepted his assistance gratefully. Clearly Alanna was precious enough to be worth their trouble, and he was not about to argue with such a judgment. All too soon, though, he would be aboard ship, he told himself, and she would be left behind.

Unbidden, his eyes searched for the woman who unknowingly held his heart, and when he caught sight of her graceful body astride her horse, the dark-haired soldier once again tasted the bitterness of regret.

He had been wrong to be so cavalier toward Kevin's offer last night, but he'd had too much to drink, and besides, hadn't Kevin been joking? No man would surrender such a gift so casually. Lucas imagined for a brief minute that he had been free to accept Alanna's hand in marriage. Then he chuckled, realizing full well that the fiery widow would have probably taken as much umbrage at his assent to the proposal as she had at his rejection of it.

Since then, however, Alanna had been awfully curt. Maybe he ought to make his peace with her before they reached Alonso's camp and they had to part. Yes, it would be easier that way. Besides, on horseback she couldn't kick him, he reminded himself with amusement, remembering with a grimace the passionate nature she'd displayed on the few occasions he had held her against her will...and the one when she had been willing indeed.

Alanna had certainly proven him wrong about the coldness of Irish women, he acknowledged, his taunting words at Castlemount echoing in his ears. No, Alanna Desmond O'Donnell would never be the angel he had first thought her to be, for him or any other man. She was too physical an entity for that, but he hoped with all his heart that she'd find a paradise of her own and the everlasting love she so richly deserved, the love he was not at liberty to give her.

Intent on speaking with her, Lucas signaled his horse to overtake hers, and was startled when she dug in her heels and spurred Piobar into a quick pace away from him.

"Alanna! Alanna, you know I can't keep up with you when you take off like that," complained her old nurse. How could she be a proper chaperone if Alanna chose to escape her watchful eye? Moira's worry eased as she saw the Spaniard she admired ride after her charge. "Go quickly, lad, and don't let her fire make you back off! I warrant she's passionate in most things."

Lucas could not understand the old woman's muttering, but he suspected she found it as frustrating as he had to try to control Alanna, and he sympathized. Perhaps he could persuade her to rejoin Moira, once he caught up with her.

Riding hard in pursuit of the Irish widow, the golden-skinned nobleman found unexpected pleasure in the way the damp salt air caressed his now-smooth cheeks and the moist breeze tousled his hair in the morning mist. The chill climate, rather than irritating him as it did Juan and the others, challenged Lucas's instinct for survival, causing his blood to race and his heart to pump with an energy he hadn't enjoyed in months. Unless it wasn't the air, he considered suddenly, but Alanna, the woman who had returned his life to him.

There, ahead of him, on a small hilltop she waited, facing him, her expression cold and forbidding like that of a warrior about to do battle. Yet could he truly blame her? He had given her so little and taken so much. Could he ever make amends?

"Alanna," he began, his voice soft and his smile broad, "I needed to explain about last night."

"I already told you I have no wish to hear your pretty words. You said all that mattered to Kevin," she replied, her pride still smarting, and she lifted her arm to point to the water below. "There is the only thing you crave, Spaniard, your way home."

For a moment Lucas was silent, weighing the acerbity of her words with the grief displayed on her face. She would not meet his eyes, he noted, preferring instead to gaze out on the angry waters as though they held more interest for her.

"I am a soldier, Alanna, a man sworn to the service of his king," he said quietly. "It is my life...if not my choice."

With a start, she looked at him and found his deep green eyes fixed on her, not on the ocean as she had expected. The absence of his beard made him more youthful, more vulnerable, she observed, wishing to run her hand over his newly shaved face and caress him with the same gentleness he'd shown her. Did he mean he would stay if the decision were his to make? Her heart yearned to pose the question, but her pride refused. Once a soldier's wife, still an Irish rebel's foster daughter, she knew she could not voice the demanding words that would wring such an admission from him. Dismissing her errant thoughts as an aberration of her exhaustion, she forced herself to look away from his face and once more at the bay below.

"I would it were otherwise," he whispered to himself. His utterance was carried away by the wind and the pounding seas, so Alanna took no notice of it. Still, he felt better for saying it. Raising his voice to counter the ocean's rhythmic roar, Lucas spoke again. "I am sorry if I've hurt you, Alanna. Nothing could be further from my intent. I owe you my life."

"You need not apologize," she replied coldly, stung by his reference to debts. Was that all their night together had been, an obligation, payment of a debt? "I am well acquainted with the ways of warring men—"

"No, no matter whatever I may have said in the past, it wasn't." Lucas interrupted, horrified that she still believed what he had told her earlier.

"Perhaps not, but we both realize it *cannot* be anything more," Alanna insisted fiercely. While part of her wished she could reach out to this dark-haired stranger and keep him safe with her, she knew that if he ever allowed such a thing, he would only grow to hate her. No, Mananaan MacLir had ordained their brief encounter, casting his treasure temptingly on the shore for her to find, but just as surely the sea god took back his gifts, and she would not interfere. "But, look here, these are the remains of your ship. The other one, the one that will take you back to Spain, waits in a small inlet not far from here."

Unhappily accepting the wisdom of her words, Lucas stared in the direction Alanna pointed. At the sight of the still-smoldering carrack, its three decks barely discernible through the smoke as it lay in the shifting sand, he felt the loss of a friend. *La Rata* had served them admirably, he reflected, withstanding Lord Howard's brutal attack off Plymouth as well as the countless battles through the length of the English Channel, even the fierce storms as they had rounded Ireland.

According to the sketchy reports O'Donnell had received, the valiant lady had finally been brought down by a combination of the heaving winds, a surging incoming tide and an insecure anchor. As was custom, Alonso had probably set her ablaze.

"Kevin said your captain and his men are camped in Torane Castle, around the bay," said Alanna, turning her horse northward. "Shall we go find him?"

"Aye," agreed Lucas. He tore his eyes from the plundered carrack only to confront the womanly temptation he had to force himself to ignore. He was first and foremost a noble officer, he reminded himself, whose duty lay with Spain. "Come then, Alonso awaits."

Spurring their horses forward, they set a quick pace toward their destiny, deliberately discounting the message of their hearts.

As Kevin halted his men on the narrow strip of land separating Blacksod Bay from Broad Haven, he had to admire the military strategy of whoever had selected the Spanish encampments. By occupying both Torane and Elly castles, the men of the Great Enterprise had neatly eliminated any possibility of a surprise attack, their location such that all entrance onto the Mullet Peninsula required passage through the exposed land before the castles.

Displaying his Irish colors, the O'Donnell was about to call out to the sentries when they surprised him by speaking first.

"Have you come to barter food and water for weapons and horses, or for some other purpose?" challenged an unseen guard, his words proclaiming him a Spaniard.

"He brings some of Don Alonso's men back to him," called Lucas as he and Alanna cantered up to join Kevin. "Del Fuentes, Alvarez and a few more from *La Rata*."

"De Leiva is settled straight through at Torane," replied the guard. He could afford to accept the nobleman at his word, as there were nearly a thousand Spanish gathered here on the Mullet. Nothing short of English cannon and an accompanying militia would take them.

Alanna looked about in surprise as they entered the foreign stronghold. She had never seen so many soldiers, let alone foreigners, in one place in her life. Everywhere she looked there were men cleaning weapons, rubbing down horses, eating, cooking over open fires, drinking from tankards, playing at dice and sorting goods from large trunks, yet there was not a single woman. Still, that didn't amaze her. Battle, after all, was viewed as a man's occupation. Waiting for him to return was a woman's duty.

"Kevin," she shouted over the din, suddenly anxious to be away, "couldn't we leave Lucas here? Donegal is still quite a piece from here."

"Surely you will spend the night?" protested Lucas. His aristocracy was showing itself. He sat taller in his saddle, more visibly confident among his own than he had been earlier at the Irish encampment. "You might be able to give Alonso some advice on sailing the waters around here, if you can spare the time."

"Of course we shall stay," agreed Kevin, pleased that the Spaniard considered his knowledge useful.

"If it is not too much trouble, I'd like to see the muskets those men are refurbishing," interjected Devlin, ever the efficient gallowglass, "and maybe watch some of your swordsmen at practice."

"Certainly," concurred Lucas, though he still wondered at Alanna's sudden eagerness to depart. Did she hate him so?

"Lucas!" called an urgent voice as an older man, white-haired and resplendent in a fine brocade doublet, rushed out onto the road. "Lucas, I knew you'd find your way back to us, though, of course, I prayed for it daily."

"I am not only certain you did, Don Diego, but that your prayers, as those of any saintly man, were well heard." Lucas chuckled and jumped down to embrace his parents' good friend and his own. Diego Martinez y Goya had always been like a second father to him, advancing his cause with Alonso and even Philip. It was only fitting that this man should be the first in the camp to know he was alive. "But I forget myself, sir. This is Alanna Desmond O'Donnell, her foster father, Kevin O'Donnell, and Devlin Fitzhugh. This, my friends," he said, switching back to English, "is Diego Martinez y Goya."

"They are welcome, of course, but what of Alvarez and the rest?" asked Diego as he nodded at the Irish. Clearly unwilling to relinquish his hold on Lucas, the nobleman stood with one arm stretched up to rest on the younger man's shoulder.

"Coming up behind you," said the soldier.

"I suppose *he's* been taking all the credit for our escape and telling you I led the scouting party too far inland after a wild boar so we were captured," started Juan in Spanish as he dismounted beside Lucas. "It's not true, not a word of it."

"Actually, Lucas has said nothing of his adventures," corrected Diego, already tiring of the ever-complaining Alvarez. "Why not refresh yourselves now, and you can share the whole story with Don Alonso and the rest of us at dinner? I will gladly tell him you have returned."

"As usual, you will undoubtedly believe Lucas's account and doubt mine," muttered *El Pavoreal* while Lucas mounted and translated Diego's suggestion for the Irish. "When I tell Alonso how Lucas almost killed me out of jealousy because the woman wanted me rather than him, then you will see him as he is."

"I already do," retorted Diego. He hurried off to find de Leiva and give him the good news, adding to himself, "And I would trust him any day I can still draw a breath, while you, you mongrel, are not even worth my disdain."

Left alone in the dust, Juan scowled at the soldiers who stood watching and shook his hand at the heavens. He would have his justice yet. There would be no rest until he did, even if it took a while.

With the grime of their ride washed away and her hair bound up again at Moira's worried urging, Alanna waited for Lucas to fetch them for dinner. Her first instinct had been to remain with Moira and leave the men to their talk of tides and war, but when Kevin chided her about showing proper courtesy to their hosts, she had relented. Now, oddly enough, she was looking forward to the evening and seeing Lucas in his natural setting, as it were.

"That foreign devil is here," complained the old nurse suddenly. Her scowl clearly conveyed the disapproval Lucas had earned when he had not changed his mind about wedding Alanna. "Now, don't you leave Kevin's side, not for an instant, or they'll steal you off to Spain with them, see if they don't. The way that one looks at you is positively scandalous."

"You've said the same about the English and the Irish," laughed Kevin, thoroughly amused by Moira's mothering.

"But they aren't savages who would refuse marriage," snapped the old woman. She fell silent at the sight of Lucas's changed appearance. Then, in the space of an instant, she was gone from the room.

With her first glance at Lucas, Alanna found herself sorely tempted to heed Moira's example and disappear. No longer a hunted man, Lucas had resumed his life as a Spanish lord and was dressed accordingly in an onyx black velvet jacket and pantaloons with a stiff ruff at his neck and dark-colored hose, emphasizing the lines of his well-shaped legs. Unable to tear her eyes from the elegant man who stood before her, the young widow felt dowdy and ill-costumed in her road-weary Irish tunic, but she had never possessed such finery as his, let alone traveled with it. Retreating slightly, she started to make her excuses when he held up his hand to stop her.

"How lovely you look, Alanna, now that you have rested. You have the face of an angel when you smile, and your eyes are like periwinkles in spring," he said winningly, somehow attuned to her hesitation. "Alonso will be entranced by your beauty."

"Thank you," she murmured, holding her head high. She allowed Lucas to take her arm as Kevin and Devlin fell into step behind them. His courtly behavior had earned him her forgiveness, as had the memories of the one magical night they had shared. For this evening, at least, she would put her hurts aside and enjoy his company.

"I shall have to translate for you," Lucas explained, guiding them to the makeshift dining hall. "Most Spanish nobleman frown on all languages other than their own, but Alonso sincerely wishes to meet with you, and Diego has some English."

"Then we shall manage," said Kevin. "I've found soldiers can communicate no matter what the difficulties."

And so began the strangest evening in Alanna's memory, a grand celebration of Lucas's rebirth in which everyone but she, Kevin, and Devlin were attired as if they were about to be presented to the monarch. Doublets of satins, damasks, silks and brocades, all of darkest black, exquisitely trimmed with exceptional bits of lace, colorful embroidery, braid and even jewels, decorated the room, though those wearing the regalia of court seemed uniformly unimpressed by the spectacle. Candlelight danced from emeralds to rubies with the dexterity of moonbeams, making the entire room a fantasy land.

Plates of gold and silver adorned the ancient wooden table, and gem-encrusted goblets waited beside each place, refilled after every joyous toast by the numerous sailors who loitered everywhere, prepared to honor any request for service. The wondrous grandeur so astounded Alanna that she wondered if anyone had told these men they were still in foreign lands, in danger of losing their lives, if not to the English then to the ravenous seas awaiting their passage.

The young widow now understood Lucas's disdain for Castlemount. What she couldn't fathom, however, was how the Spanish nobles could appear so carefree in the face of their uncertain future.

"Lucas," she whispered finally when the men ceased their conversation to partake of the surprisingly humble meal.

"Yes," he said to her, amazed as ever by the gentle beauty that resided in her. "I apologize for having ignored you, Alanna."

"Your work for Alonso is important," she replied. "But, tell me, how can they live like this? What I mean is, do they always—'' she began, uncertain how to phrase her question without sounding offensive. ''They could die.''

''All the more reason to live life fully while it's yours,'' the dark-haired nobleman explained carefully. He realized immediately the stark contrast between Kevin's ragtag camp and the opulence of this display. ''Every man here has sworn his life to the service of Spain, and our ships have been outfitted with all the luxuries of home to remind us of what we have to lose. When *La Rata* foundered so close to shore, most of the valuables were recovered by the servants before they set her aflame.''

''Servants?'' Alanna wasn't certain she had heard correctly.

''Of course. Don Alonso has a staff of thirty-six, but most of us only brought one or two men.''

''Do they fight for you, as well?''

''Of course not. They cook and serve the meals, see to our wardrobes and perhaps clean our weapons, but soldiers are the men who are trained to fight.''

''And kill,'' she said quietly, angry at the memories of Sean and Curran, living off the land on what they could forage, waiting hopelessly for the Spanish reinforcements that never arrived. Had trouble with the servants detained them? She fumed, unable to understand the decadence that had turned war into an experience surrounded by luxury. No wonder the Spaniards had lost against the English in the Channel. Philip's men didn't know how to suffer.

''When it is a choice of dying or killing, yes, soldiers do kill—and I have done so, as you well know,'' Lucas answered solemnly, wanting to erase the tears threatening her eyes. ''But your husband and father faced those same choices, as do Kevin and Devlin. Alanna, you have every right to hate war and even Spain, but I am not your enemy. Please, do not hate me.''

Without warning, his strong fingers caught her hand where it rested on the table. As her mind accepted what her heart already knew, releasing the last remnants of blame she had harbored, Lucas slowly bent his head to her hand, delivering a gentle kiss, an unplanned gesture of solicitude that caught Juan's attention. Before Alanna could reply to Lucas, Juan responded with a vicious tirade.

"See—there, I told you he had designs on her from the moment he saw her in that place. Del Fuentes was more concerned with pleasuring himself with the woman than seeing to the welfare of his men," charged *El Pavoreal* loudly. "It wouldn't surprise me if he arranged the whole Irish ambush so he could look like a hero saving her from attack. Yes, he was wounded, but Luis died, he didn't. He never even killed one of those Englishman who attacked us. Given his mother's blood, he had no stomach for it, I warrant."

"Lucas, have you anything to say in response to such charges?" Alonso de Leiva inquired while his Irish guests looked on in confusion, not comprehending the words Juan spoke but clearly concerned by the escalating tension in the room.

"Lucas," said Alanna, worry visible in her eyes.

He merely patted her hand and turned to look at de Leiva, saying nothing.

For a moment the commander was silent, considering his options. Just as he accepted that most of what Alvarez said was worthless, so, too, he realized he must demand an answer to the charges. Whatever the outcome, de Leiva knew Lucas could be trusted to speak with the utmost accuracy, no matter who was hurt by it.

"Lucas, I must ask you to reply to Juan's claims. Have you enjoyed Alanna O'Donnell's charms at the expense of your men?"

"How can you even entertain such absurd thoughts?" protested Diego Martinez y Goya, jumping to his feet in indignation. "Though Lucas is a man like any other, the urges that fire his blood come not from lust but loyalty to Philip and Spain."

"I appreciate your fine words, Diego, but I willingly admit to having desired Alanna," the dark-haired noble stated calmly. His glance caressed her even as he spoke.

"See, I told you he was irresponsible," Juan rejoined, too drunk to expect there to be more to Lucas's words.

"If appreciating the beauty and charm of the Irish woman who saved our lives makes my fealty to Spain suspect, so be it. Unlike Juan Alvarez, however, I have learned to control my baser instincts," asserted Lucas, unflinching under de Leiva's close scrutiny. "As for his words, they are, as usual, half truths. While it is true that I killed no Englishman who attacked our party, that is because none did. It was my decision, though, to lead my men into the English camp before daybreak, and mine alone. Pedro or Enrique will substantiate the fact that I, not *El Pavoreal*, took the lives of three men there. Is that not true, Señor Alvarez?"

"I—I was struggling to save my own life, not watching what you did," muttered Juan, avoiding Alonso's angry glance by dropping his chin like a cowed dog. "I cannot be certain of your every move."

"As for my mother's blood, yes, it flows through my veins, but just as surely does my father's, Esteban Cortez del Fuentes, and it is to Philip II of Spain that I've pledged my allegiance, not Elizabeth," concluded Lucas, his voice harsh with emotion. "I would have thought by now there was no doubt of that."

Knowing only that this man who had accompanied her on the trail for days was upset, Alanna reached out her hand to his and squeezed it under the table, pleased at the light pressure with which he responded.

Devlin noticed her covert gesture and scowled in annoyance. She was too innocent and inexperienced to recognize the devilment of the man, he fumed, suddenly pleased at the thought of their early departure in the morning. Donegal had never called to him so sweetly as now, when it promised escape from these foreigners.

"Instead of suspicions cast in his direction," Diego suggested, "Lucas deserves our thanks and commendation for eluding capture and death and returning his men safely to our bosom. Don't you agree, Alonso?"

"Yes, most certainly, and I shall inform Philip of it upon our return," concurred de Leiva, his displeasure at Juan's troublemaking clearly evident. "Alvarez, I will speak with you later, alone. For now, Lucas, you started to say that the O'Donnell urges we go north rather than south to reach home?"

As Lucas resumed his task of translating, Alanna felt herself relax. Whatever Juan had charged regarding her and Lucas, and well she could imagine, had been dismissed. Still, she sensed the peacock's continued hatred and, turning her head, she found Juan staring straight at her, his beady eyes cold and hard even as he licked his lips and sneered. She would be certain to avoid him for the rest of the evening, Alanna decided, glad he could not see her hand still nestled in Lucas's. For that matter, Devlin, too, was looking irritated. Perhaps it was the frustration of not understanding Spanish and having to await the translations, she mused, even as she feared she fathomed only too well what had caused the gallowglass's atypical scowl.

"Tell Alonso and Captain Mores that between them, they have too many men to risk the journey to Spain in these rough waters. In May or June, your ship might possibly survive it, but not in the heavy winds and high tides of September on such an overloaded, battle-weary hulk as the *Santa Ana*. She was not designed to carry nearly a thousand men and their supplies," argued Kevin. As an experienced seaman, he was well-accustomed to navigating the treacherous seas off Ireland, but he would not have ventured forth on such a mission as these men proposed. "It might sound bizarre to travel back the way you've already come, but I know, too, that a direct route south will doom your expedition even before it passes through Blacksod Bay."

As soon as Lucas finished conveying Kevin's advice, Devlin added his own comments.

"Scotland is only two hundred miles by sea and you could avoid the worst of the headlands by hugging the coast, while Spain is at least four times that distance in

much more insidious waters. The Scots will see you home
safely, have no doubt of that. They've no love of Elizabeth, either."

And so the decision was made. Captains Pedro Mores
and Alonso de Leiva accepted the Irishmen's advice, their
navigators carefully noting the dangerous shoals off Annagh Head, Erris Head and the successive rocky outcroppings up the coast as Lucas continued to translate well into
the night. Only Juan Felipe Alvarez counseled against the
journey, and his eagerly voiced suspicions of an Irish plot
to destroy their ship were quickly discounted by the others.

Finally, after detaining Juan, Alonso wished the Irish a
safe journey on the morrow, and the bishop bestowed his
blessing on them. Then Lucas escorted the trio from the
hall.

"My thanks to you once more for returning Alanna to
us," said Kevin formally, grasping the Spaniard's hand in
a hearty shake. "I will see Alanna safely to Donegal and
then head for Castlemount to deal with that peculiar matter of Bravingham and the MacWilliams, so I will take my
leave of you now. I wish you well in the life you choose to
lead, though it takes you from us. I have no doubt you will
succeed."

"Would you mind if I walked on the beach a bit,
Kevin?" asked Alanna, knowing that her body was too
restless for sleep.

"I will accompany you if you like," volunteered Lucas.

"Thank you," Alanna agreed readily, anxious to ask him
about what Juan had said.

"Go ahead," said Kevin. He smiled as the blonde moved
swiftly to the nobleman's side, only to hesitate at Devlin's
angry bark.

"I question whether it would be wise, Alanna, or, for
that matter, safe for you to go off alone with him," objected Devlin as he moved to block her path.

"Devlin, you sound just like Moira." Alanna laughed, stepping lightly around the gallowglass. "I assure you, Lucas will protect me from any danger that arises."

"Of course," agreed Lucas. He took her arm and led her off into the moonlight.

"But the question is, who will protect her from him?" muttered Devlin as Kevin chuckled.

"Alanna's no lovesick young girl, Fitzhugh. My foster daughter is a wise woman who knows what is best," counseled O'Donnell. "Besides, whatever the Spaniard is to her, he will be gone from her life when she heads to Donegal with you tomorrow. Indeed, it was his choice not to take her in marriage, if you recall."

"Aye, a choice you never offered me," scowled Alanna's longtime admirer, reaching for the flask of *poitin* he always carried. "But suppose he didn't have to go to Spain, what then?"

"Why worry about what is not the case? Be useful and pour us a drink instead," advised Kevin, glad when his friend complied without further comment. He had enough on his mind, deciding how to approach Grady and Cordelia MacWilliams, without having to fret about Alanna and Devlin, as well.

As she and Lucas walked slowly through the camp, Alanna smiled at Devlin's absurd worry that she would be alone with the Spaniard. After the eighth man had come forward to slap her companion on the back and congratulate him on his safe return, she lost count of the numerous welcoming sailors, each anxious to share a few words with Lucas. Even though she could not understand their language, the blonde was still aware of the deep regard they had for the nobleman as a friend as well as their superior officer.

"They care about you," Alanna said softly when they had finally escaped the men's attention and reached the beach.

"You find that surprising? It seems to me that even you were concerned when I didn't return immediately from the attack on Bravingham's men," Lucas replied, turning her to face him and unable to keep himself from drawing her into his arms. "Remember calling my name?"

"Yes ... no ... that is, I feared what Juan might do."

"And not what I might?" Lucas pressed, running his large hand across her velvety smooth cheek. As wrong as he knew it to be, he wanted this Irish rebel, craving once more the sweet taste of her passion. Helpless to still his roving fingers, he permitted them to trace the heartlike outline of her lips, hesitating only briefly when she opened her mouth to speak, then stroking her lower lip.

"No, I never feared you," murmured Alanna, surprised at the truth of her words, even as her blood began to roar in her ears at his touch. Tentatively she extended her tongue and delicately licked his exploring fingertip, unprepared for his sudden shudder of excitement. "No. I have hated you, I have cursed you and I have even prayed for your death on occasion, but fear was never a part of it."

"I did not think it was," her golden Spaniard admitted. He lowered his dark head, and his lips laid siege to her mouth. While Lucas knew he could never have her, that she'd be lost to him by morning, tonight he would sear her soul with his kisses, creating memories that would stay with them to the grave. It was all he would have, but he would make certain it was enough for both of them.

Without a moment's hesitation, Alanna welcomed his efforts, crushing her body tightly against his. All her previous anger dissipated as her arms embraced him with complete abandon, her soft hands slipping beneath his doublet to explore the well-muscled planes of his back. The costume made him different, she mused, but it was more than the matter of his clothes. Lucas now was a free man, not haunted by the specters of warfare, and his kisses reflected his impunity, devouring her soul and then returning it to her, tantalizing her and, when she thought she could stand no more, artfully fulfilling her.

Aflutter with the whirling sensations of delight that infected her, accepting gratification before she realized the need, Alanna never questioned their sudden collapse to the damp sand of the beach nor the demanding mouth that so readily found and pleasured her questing nipples. Deep within her heat-filled body, there was a sense that this moment was the one for which she had been created, the ultimate epiphany of her human journey.

Moaning with joy, Alanna curled her slender fingers in Lucas's dark hair, lifted his head and urged his mouth to return to hers so that she might share the tumultuous excitement he had awakened in her.

"Lucas, you are all I want," she whispered hoarsely. "Make love to me again. Be mine and make me yours."

But they were the wrong words, Alanna realized suddenly as he halted his tender ministrations only to roll away from her on the sand.

"Lucas?"

"*Madre de Dios!*"

The simple syllables reverberated between them in the silence. There was only the pounding of the ocean where moments before had been shimmers of paradise. How could he explain his sudden overwhelming guilt, the knowledge that this was a terrible mistake he could not commit, a wrong he would not do to her? She with her abhorrence of the Spanish would never be happy in his homeland. As for him, who knew where his duty to his king would take him next?

"I am sorry, my dear Alanna, but this cannot happen," he announced firmly, getting to his feet and extending a hand to help her up. "Hate me again if you must, I would not blame you, but I cannot use you this way, cowering together in the darkness, listening for the footsteps of strangers who might discover us. You deserve to be loved boldly in moonlit fields and sun-drenched meadows sweet with the smell of fresh-cut hay, Alanna, loved by a man who will stay by your side forever. And that man will never be me."

"But..." she began, silent tears trailing down her flushed cheeks as he led her across the sandy expanse toward the castle.

In her heart, Alanna didn't care for anything but that very moment, the brilliant beauty he had selfishly denied her, and she would have argued with him, but his tone was the imperious one men used when there was no hope of changing their minds. No, it was clear that for Lucas the price of loving her was too high.

"Well, then," the widow proclaimed, her voice tight and pain-filled, her pride keeping her from telling him what was in her heart, "I suppose I should express my gratitude to you, but you will excuse me if I simply say farewell instead."

"Alanna, you are a very special woman, too precious for one such as me," Lucas whispered as they stopped before her quarters. "But I will pray Our Lady keep you safe and show you the love you truly deserve. I can wish you no greater good than this."

Then he was gone from her life, and Alanna felt completely forsaken. She knew sleep would never come this night. Lucas del Fuentes had just had the audacity to reject her for the second time in two successive nights, and by all that was holy, she somehow understood and forgave him. The man was a sorcerer!

Chapter Twelve

Alanna and Lucas had said their goodbyes last night on the beach. There would be no seeing him this morning. And still, as she helped Moira settle on her beloved Baibi, the young widow surrendered to the urge to scan the water's edge, teeming with men and littered with cargo, for the handsome aristocrat's impressive form. Yet search as she might among those frantically loading the *Duquesa Santa Ana* so they could catch the tide, she could seize no last glimpse of him, no final memory to press to her heart.

Alanna had once hated Lucas Rafael del Fuentes, and in truth, a part of her detested Spaniards and Englishmen still. But Lucas, the man of golden skin, gentle hands and full-blooded passion owned a piece of her heart, and probably always would. She had been his captive from the first.

"Come along, lass," Devlin said kindly, his strong hands at her waist as he lifted Alanna to her horse. "Kevin is in a hurry to reach Tur Muir and reclaim his ship. Then he'll sail south."

"To pay your uncle a small *social call*," the older man clarified dryly. "It should be a grand visit, though I promise I'll attempt to tame my anger sufficiently to leave him breathing when I turn my ship for home."

"But don't think about that, Alanna, or anything else that distresses you. Within a short time, you'll be able to feast your eyes on Donegal. You'll be home, Alanna, and safe," Devlin said, his fingertips still lingering at her sides.

Though his touch was sure and firm, it did not set the pretty traveler afire as Lucas's hands upon her would have done. But even as she rued the comparison, Alanna was thankful for Devlin's efforts in trying to ease this difficult time for her. Calling upon her inner resources, she rewarded him with a small, tremulous smile before he mounted his steed and they set off.

While she followed her protectors out of the camp, Alanna looked wistfully over her shoulder, wishing she had told Lucas all that was in her heart as they had stood under the starlit sky, that she had admitted to him, as well as to herself, what he had come to mean to her.

In a few days' time, he had battered down the walls of the invisible tomb in which she had buried her soul after Sean had died. It had been a painful process as well as a joyous one, and there had been no turning back.

She had felt that every slow measure she had taken toward her handsome captor had been a betrayal of her husband. And still, she had been drawn, stumbling forward with confused and resistant steps. On and on she had gone, until she had reached this moment when she wanted to jump from her horse and run to his side, throw herself against his broad, muscular chest and feel his welcoming arms enfold her. She wanted to beg him to return to her one day.

But it was too late. Her eyes fell on the rock-embedded road ahead of her, a lonely one despite the company of the servants and Kevin and Devlin, two men who loved her. Pride and bitterness had caused her to forfeit all that was really important. The destructive forces had held her hostage as surely as Lucas had kept her prisoner when they had escaped Castlemount. And now possibilities had crumbled. Her golden-skinned Spaniard was lost to her forever at the very instant she had at last truly found him.

However, even as the realization came to her, Alanna wondered what Lucas's reaction would have been if she had openly declared her love for him and had asked him to stay. Would he have remained in Ireland or have been all the more anxious to leave? Would he have invited her to go with him? She would never know. He would be a beloved ghost, haunting her always, a poignant, bittersweet promise of what could have been.

"I've never seen you so quiet and withdrawn," Devlin said, riding alongside Piobar and working, for Alanna's sake, to keep the frown that threatened to overtake his mouth at bay.

"I was merely giving free rein to my thoughts," Alanna said quietly.

"And would you like to share them?" Devlin tried to coax a smile from her with one of his own, his manner more solicitous than usual as he silently acknowledged the probable cause of her upset. He feared she was already missing the Spaniard.

"Ah, but they are too many and too varied," Alanna replied in confusion, dropping her eyes. Certainly she couldn't share with this man who loved her all her feelings for Lucas.

"Aye, and you've been through a lot this past week. I suppose you've plenty to think about," the gallowglass commented kindly. An unusual trace of melancholy barely tinged his voice before he could banish it. "But once we get you home to Tur Muir, you can put this whole episode behind you and be yourself once again."

Alanna appreciated Devlin's intent and the effort he made on her behalf, even if she recognized the falsity of his words. As Piobar carried her farther and farther from the man who held her heart, the pain of separation grew, and she knew she would never again be the person she had been. But in spite of her current misery, given the choice, the young Irish woman would rather have possessed Lucas del Fuentes for the brief time that had been theirs. Lucas had given her new life, and even though his departure had saddened her, she was richer for having known him.

Aristocrats and servants, soldiers and sailors, men of war and men of God, all had been loaded onto the small *Du-*

quesa Santa Ana along with provisions, arms, powder, shot, gold plate and bejeweled artifacts. The vessel was now packed as tightly as a miser's strongbox.

Trying to make his way starboard, Lucas stepped over the bodies of those huddled on deck. They were exhausted men, oblivious to the noise around them, preferring the pelting rain and the heavy winds to the stench-filled area below, which was overflowing with humanity, each person as miserable as the next.

Lucas finally approached the rail, hoping to deceive his senses into capturing an image of spaciousness by gazing at the open expanse of ocean. Not that he could blame de Leiva for the unspeakably vile state of the heavily laden ship. It had been necessary to board the entire crews of both ships on this one small craft, noblemen and peasant alike, elbow to elbow. What else could Alonso have done? Leave loyal retainers and soldiers behind? Such a thing was unthinkable in so hostile and primitive a land as Ireland, where English as well as Irish hunted down Spaniards stranded on shore, robbed them and killed them in the most horrible manner.

Hadn't he almost lost his own life in that godforsaken nation? Yet for all that, Lucas had been filled with sadness at having to leave Ireland behind. Alanna was there, and so was his heart.

For every mile that they traveled along its deadly, rocky coast, Lucas Rafael del Fuentes had grown more wretched, just barely managing to hide his feelings behind attention to duty.

The others may have been jubilant when the top-heavy *Santa Ana* had moved safely out of Elly Cove, but his heart had been filled with longing even as it was constrained by his damnable sense of honor. Later, his companions had cheered after the ship had sailed past the shoals of Erris Head and what must have been the outskirts of Donegal Bay, yet he had spent his free time gazing wistfully at the coast, wondering how his Alanna fared. Still later, when the straining vessel had unexpectedly withstood the gales of two northwesterly squalls, the ship's complement had offered prayers of thanksgiving. Yet Lucas, plagued with visions of Devlin Fitzhugh courting Alanna, had been able to find little reason for gratitude.

And now another major storm was brewing, and the *Duquesa Santa Ana* had sought refuge from the weather in a rocky bay. The ship twisted and turned at anchor, the groan of straining boards all but lost in the howl of increasing winds.

As the waters rose and fell beneath the tempest's cruel caress, the *Santa Ana* shuddered like a living thing that feared the beating it was about to take. Lucas, his usually full lips set in a thin line, wondered if any damage would be sustained, and if so, how much time would be needed for repairs. Though at first he had hated departing this land, the constant sight of Ireland's forbidding shores was becoming unbearable, and in some perverse way, despite his yearning to jump ship and go ashore, he needed to see Scotland's coast.

Such thoughts were unexpectedly banished by a tremendous snapping sound and a sudden lurch as the *Santa Ana* danced free of its mooring. Although he was no sailor, Lucas nevertheless knew that the chain connecting the ship to its lone anchor had broken. Nature had conquered the order man had attempted to impose, and upheaval reigned as wave after wave sent the wildly pitching vessel into the deadly rocks lining the bay.

Grabbing the railing, Lucas survived the initial impact only to be shaken again as the ship was once more rammed against kelp-covered boulders. Over and over the waves and the lethal coastline played with the wooden vessel, tossing it back and forth, battering it until finally, with a splintering of timber and a great rush of water, the weary craft surrendered to the angry seas. Then men and cargo were afloat everywhere, spilled out of the broken ship like grain from a sack that had burst.

Managing to find the surface of the water after having been dragged down, Lucas looked about him. Many of those who had been aboard were swimming desperately for shore, but the sick and injured did not have the stamina for so arduous a task, even if they could escape the hold. Lucas struck out in the direction of the disabled *Duquesa Santa Ana*, heaved himself up on to the deck and went below. There he began hauling those unable to walk up into the salty air. Others who saw his efforts came to his aid, while practical souls started to gather whatever provisions they could salvage in hopes that they could be brought ashore. But there were men to whom other things were more important, and valuables were snatched up before they could be gobbled by the sea by those who held them as dear as their own lives. Everywhere, as the ship slowly sank lower and lower into the cold waters, chaos dominated amid the shouted prayers and imprecations of men and the savage force of the storm.

In a final sweep of the deck, Lucas saw Alonso expending efforts as great as his own. He hailed his commander and was on his way to help him when the ship listed violently and a mast came crashing down, pinning de Leiva's leg.

Swiftly Lucas was at his side, water washing over them both as he struggled to lift the mast and release Alonso. But it seemed a superhuman endeavor, more than a match for any mere mortal, no matter how strong.

"Go, my friend," Alonso ordered between clenched teeth. "Leave me here."

"I'm not going anywhere," Lucas shouted over the roar of wind and water.

"You disobey my command?" de Leiva asked angrily.

"What did you say, Alonso? I can't hear you," Lucas replied, working feverishly to shift the mighty weight that condemned his young captain to death. Still he could not budge it. Just when he thought he and his friend were doomed to perish together, the *Santa Ana* tilted wildly. The sudden movement tossed the mast aside as though it were no more than a twig, and Alonso, though seriously injured and barely conscious, was at liberty.

Lucas dragged de Leiva to the rail, now no more than a few feet from the lapping waves, and managed to get him overboard without losing him. Then, one muscular arm clutching his commander, Lucas started for land, battling wave, rock, wind and debris. After a prolonged battle with Ireland's waters, he pulled himself and de Leiva up on the rocky shore. There he lay gasping for breath while others tended to the captain.

It would seem he was back in Ireland, at least for the time being.

In the three days since her return to Tur Muir, Alanna had resumed her management of Kevin's household. But while she tended to her responsibilities, her actions were mechanical. In her foster father's absence, she undertook some of his tasks, appointing a tenant to take charge of the harvest and another to monitor the mending of sails. She dutifully listened to the supplications and complaints of the keep's inhabitants, but in this, as in all things, her mind was elsewhere. And though she worried about Kevin's well-being during his confrontation with Grady, it was not Castlemount that drew her thoughts, but rather the rough-planked deck of the *Duquesa Santa Ana* and its proposed route through the treacherous North Sea.

So caught up was she with fear for Lucas, her own regrets and impossible daydreams of what might have been, that her conversation was often listless and distracted, and her infrequent smiles were wan.

Seeing her go on in this manner, Devlin was tortured. He wished he was at Kevin's side rather than watching the woman he loved mourn the departure of that bloody Spaniard. What he wouldn't have given to be the recipient of her devotion! But he was not, and there was little he could do about it other than wait for the wounds of Alanna's heart to heal and pray that in time she would turn to him, her eyes smoldering for Devlin Fitzhugh even if her desire burned for Lucas del Fuentes.

Devlin's pity, however, was only for Alanna and never for himself. Simply put, he had already proved he could play a waiting game, and after all, del Fuentes *was* gone.

These were the gallowglass's thoughts one morning as he mounted the steps to the solar to invite Alanna on a short outing. The miller's cat had but recently delivered a litter of kittens, and the lovely widow's loyal if undeclared suitor thought the tiny mewling bundles of life might bring her some diversion from her misery.

Seated at her loom in the company of Moira, Alanna looked up at the sound of a heavy masculine tread disturbing the freshly strewn rushes on the large chamber's floor. The wild, improbable hope in her eyes died instantly when she saw the visitor was Devlin Fitzhugh, but she tried to smile all the same.

In Alanna's heart, forlorn as she was, there still existed room for compassion where Devlin was concerned. Looking at him with his handsome features, masculine strength and irreverent smile, she knew that any woman he took to wife would be fortunate. And indeed, many a female had tried to catch his notice. But he would have none of them.

Her poor, blue-eyed Devlin! Alanna thought. How she wished she could respond as he wanted and offer him what he so patiently and tenderly sought. But she could not. Her brief encounter with Lucas del Fuentes had irrevocably marked her, and she feared no man but he could still the cravings he had initiated in both her body and her soul.

And to think, when she had first encountered Lucas in Grady's keep, she had thought to hold him for ransom so the honor price for the deaths of Sean and her father could finally be satisfied. But things had not proceeded as she had planned. Her handsome Spaniard had sailed free, his honor intact, while it was her heart that was held for a ransom which could never be paid. How ironic life was, she thought sadly, turning aside from her loom and rising to greet her guest.

If Devlin noted Alanna's disappointment, he wisely hid the fact. He might silently rail against the Spanish nobleman who had won her love, but the thoughtful Fitzhugh shielded her from such feelings in order to spare her additional pain.

"Good morrow, milady!" he said lightly, executing a playful, courtly bow. "I have just come from the mill and have discovered something that needs your attention. Get your cloak and come at once."

"A problem?" Alanna asked, fretfully brushing back a golden curl. She was in no mood to deal with anything of consequence.

"Not at all, lass," replied Devlin, his blue eyes sparkling merrily, "that is, unless you count an increase in the village's feline population a terrible dilemma. There's a litter of newborn kittens that I hoped we could take pleasure in together."

"Oh, that's kind of you," Alanna said, " but—but I've my weaving to attend and a host of other things that clamor for my time."

"And they can all wait," Moira pronounced from her seat before the hearth. "You can't ignore the joys of everyday life as you have been wont to do lately. Now wait a moment while I fetch that cloak to keep out the rain."

"You don't have to accompany me if you really have no inclination to do so," Devlin stated after the old woman had gone, his engaging half grin not quite reaching his sea blue eyes but emphasizing his one roguish dimple all the same. "I simply thought 'twould be something you'd enjoy."

"On reconsidering, I think I might," Alanna rejoined with a tentative smile. Her heart nevertheless wrenched at the hopelessness of Devlin's cause.

"Good," he said, laying a fingertip briefly atop her pert nose. "Who can tell, there may be a champion ratter in the lot, though knowing you, you'll be taken with the smallest and weakest, and then be fiercely determined to see that it reaches maturity."

"Devlin! Devlin Fitzhugh!" called one of Kevin's lieutenants from the courtyard beneath the solar. "Come quickly, man! There's something you should know."

"Stay here," Alanna's companion ordered, suddenly serious. Then he was outside in an instant.

Running to the small window cut into the gray stone wall, Alanna strained to see the cause of the commotion. But there was nothing in sight, no clue as to what had precipitated such an unusual intrusion.

After a bit, however, she did hear Devlin loudly barking orders for horses to be saddled and provisions gathered. Her heart quickened at the possible causes for such activity. Had Kevin been attacked and taken prisoner on his journey to the south? Or was Tur Muir soon to fall under siege?

"Here be your cloak," Moira announced, as she held out the large, heavy piece of wool. "And if you follow my advice, you'll try to find some cheer in Devlin's company."

"I fear I won't be using this, after all," Alanna replied, her tongue darting forward to nervously moisten her upper lip as she ran her hand across the fabric's soft nap. "I think something of dreadful import has arisen to claim Devlin's attention."

"Don't be a ninny! What could have happened in the space of but a few moments to keep that man from your side?" Moira clucked.

"Take the cloak, Alanna," the young woman heard her rugged gallowglass command grimly from the doorway, his face somber and drawn. "You'll have need of it."

"I don't understand," Alanna whispered. "Is it Kevin or Tur Muir that demands I go forth today?"

"I've just had a report from your uncle's seamen, returned from a salvage run. The *Duquesa Santa Ana* has gone down, dashed against the rocks of Loughros Mor Bay. There are survivors, and I surmise you'll want to hasten to the site. But I won't have you crossing such dangerous terrain alone. I'll take you." The effort the words had cost Devlin was etched across his handsome features. As much as he had thought briefly of withholding the news from her, that had not been an option. He had never lied to Alanna and would not do so now, no matter how tempting it might have been.

"Dear God!" Alanna cried. Then she bit her lip, wanting desperately to ask for news of Lucas. But she found herself afraid to do so, as well as unwilling to subject her unselfish Devlin to such cruelty by inquiring after the fate of his rival.

"I don't know if he's alive, sweetling," Devlin said simply. He was aware of the raging anxiety that was in Alanna's heart without her having to utter a word. Then he heaved a heavy sigh. "Now collect your things and hurry along, woman, before I change my mind."

Riding along the crests of the rugged cliffs guarding Ulster's coastline, Devlin was grateful they had come overland rather than taking one of Kevin's remaining small boats. The seas had been too unpredictable of late with far too many storms, and he had no wish to expose Alanna to unnecessary danger. As to what they would discover when they reached their destination, he had no idea, but he sincerely hoped they would find the Spaniard alive. His reasons, however, were far different from Alanna's.

On its own, Lucas del Fuentes's life held no meaning for him, yet the devoted gallowglass could not bear to see Alanna suffer the grief of the man's demise. More importantly, though, Devlin realized how much easier it would be to contend with a rival who had chosen to desert Alanna O'Donnell than with a ghost taken by death from her arms. That was a lesson he had gleaned from his experience these last eight years.

As they traveled along, the wind whipped at their faces, as if issuing a chilling warning to turn back. But neither Devlin nor Alanna had any intention of doing so. Each of them knew that the outcome of this journey would color the rest of their lives.

Finally their path brought them to the heights above the
bay where the Spaniards' ship had gone down. From the
narrow trail cutting along the top of the cliffs, the broken
carcass of the mostly submerged *Duquesa Santa Ana* and
the deserted, rocky shore behind it presented a morbid sight
in the rain-ravaged, early-morning light. Far more hopeful
was the lazy swirl of smoke coming from Kiltoorish Castle, a long-abandoned ruin situated just north on O'Boyle
Island in the middle of a lake.

"There'd be no better place to quarter so many men,"
Devlin commented.

"If many men survived," the young woman answered
grimly. She longed to rush across the narrow approach of
land leading to the castle's gates in order to learn of Lucas's fate.

But she sat frozen, unable to urge Piobar onward. Until
she actually knew what had happened, hope could exist that
the man she loved had escaped a watery grave. Once she
reached Kiltoorish, even that slender comfort might be
ripped from her grasp.

"'Tis a fine, brave lass you are, Alanna," Devlin said,
reaching for her hand as if he could read her thoughts. "I'll
be right beside you if 'twill make it any easier."

"You've been so good to me, dear Devlin," Alanna
whispered, gently withdrawing her fingertips from his
compassionate hold. Then she picked up her reins once
more. Straightening her slender back, she took a deep
breath and signaled her horse to continue its descent.

When Piobar cantered past the water-covered wreck of
the ship that had carried her beloved, Alanna averted her
eyes. But even with the dashed hulk hidden from sight, the
thunderous pounding of the surf against the rocks reminded her of the peril her handsome Spaniard had faced.
Would his shoulder, not quite healed, have allowed him to
arrive safely on the rocky shore? The question tore at
Alanna's heart as they continued on their way, Devlin's silent presence providing a comfort of a sort, as it had done
throughout their entire journey.

Soon they crossed the distance between the bay and Kiltoorish Lake, and followed it around to the narrow strip of land that served as a natural bridge to the island. Its disintegrating keep was a toppling pile of huge slabs of stone. It was guarded now, Alanna saw, by a Spanish cannon that could only have come from the *Duquesa Santa Ana*. Her spirits soared, though she reminded herself that this was no indication that Lucas had not perished.

Drawing abreast of the entrance to the path that divided the lake's waters, Alanna spied a sentry standing tiredly beside the deadly weapon, a scraggly, weak-looking man who regarded her and Devlin curiously.

Having no knowledge of his native tongue, she called out nevertheless, giving voice to the only thing she was capable of uttering. "Lucas del Fuentes?" she asked, her tone high and strained with anxiety as she gestured toward Kiltoorish Castle.

The guard granted them wordless permission to proceed with a sweep of his hand, his solemn expression giving Alanna no reason for either hope or fear.

Leaving their horses outside the walls of the keep, they entered the compound, Devlin's steadying hand at Alanna's elbow.

As she looked around her, Alanna was overwhelmed by the change circumstances had wrought in the Spanish forces. All of them were leaner, their eyes more wary, their high-spirited hopes for reaching the land of their birth reduced to weary prayers for survival wherever fate took them.

Even those few Spaniards she recognized as noblemen, those who had been present at the banquet shared with Alonso de Leiva, were quite different. In fact their reversal was perhaps greatest of all. No longer were they haughty, well-fed men richly bedecked in plush velvets and precious gold. Now their clothing, though of the same fine cloth, was bedraggled, stained with sea water, sweat and in some cases blood. Their hair was unkempt and their formerly precise beards untrimmed. Where once they sipped fine wine from jeweled chalices, they were now grateful to lap water from their own cupped hands.

Alanna's heart cried out as she envisioned the hardships that had toppled such grand men. For surely their suffering was Lucas's, too...if he was still alive. Yet no matter where she looked, no matter how carefully her eyes scanned the multitude congregated in the keep's courtyard, she found no trace of the beloved figure she sought.

Finally, the increasingly desperate woman saw Diego Martinez y Goya, the older man who had held Lucas in such esteem, descending from an outer staircase on the other side of the bailey. The moment of truth was at hand. If anyone knew the fate of the young aristocrat, it would be he, and Alanna found herself shivering in apprehension as she took a faltering step in his direction. But before she could collect herself and continue on her way, with Devlin's strength to sustain her, the unwelcome figure of Juan Alvarez appeared before her, proving that it was not only the worthy who survived.

"So, it is the Irish wench come to plague us once more," he said in stilted Latin. His eyes glittered maliciously as he dipped into a courtly bow meant to deceive the vigilant Devlin Fitzhugh. "But what can you want here? You will not find Lucas del Fuentes among us. You may as well return to your barbaric family and pray for his salvation. That is, unless you have finally come to your senses and decided you want a real man."

"You lie!" Alanna whispered, her face turning ashen. Devlin's brow drew together in concern and he stepped to her side to place a solicitous arm around her waist.

But Alanna knew Alvarez for a mean-spirited man, one who hated both Lucas and her. Surely the swine was capable of telling a heinous untruth to take his revenge for the grievous wrongs he imagined he had suffered at both Lucas's hands and hers. Alanna clutched at hope while her emotions began to plummet as she considered the dreaded possibility Juan was telling the truth.

But she swore the now tattered *El Pavoreal* was not going to witness the tears building at the corners of her eyes. Nor would she run off from Kiltoorish to grieve in private until she heard from a reliable source that Lucas had met his doom.

Turning a rigid back on Alvarez and his cruel smile, Alanna intended to seek out Don Diego when she saw a party of Spaniards returning to the protective walls of the keep. And there, at their head, strode the man she cherished above all else. His clothes were as ragged as those of the others. Fatigue showed in his face, and hunger had left its mark on cheeks more gaunt than she had known, covered though they were in a week's growth of coarse beard. Yet his stride, as he led his men across the compound, was as firm and determined as it had ever been.

"Lucas!" she cried, disentangling herself from Devlin's grasp and running toward the man she loved. She no longer cared what blood it was that ran through his veins, but only that his valiant, loving heart still beat.

"Alanna?" he murmured in surprise. His arms reached out to enfold her even as she threw herself into his embrace. And then his lips were on hers, searching and demanding, selfless yet possessive, as he silently praised God for this miracle. He had thought to never see her again, but she was here, and all the reasons for his former reserve were dissolved as he reveled in the feel of her, the fragrance and touch of her. If this was a dream, it was one from which he never wanted to awaken.

Lucas raised his dark head to look at her, to feast on the loveliness he had supposed lost to him forever. But as he did so, his eyes fell upon the imposing form of Devlin Fitzhugh standing in Alanna's shadow, and his unbridled joy came quickly to an end. Reason warred with passion, concern for Alanna's welfare with his raging desires.

Muttering a curse, he berated himself for giving way to impulse and putting his own needs before those of his beloved. Though he had survived a shipwreck, his circumstances had not changed. He was a stranger to this land who would soon be gone, perhaps never to return again. How could he ply this woman with kisses only to leave her unchampioned in a war-torn land? How could he distract her from Fitzhugh, a man who would care for her and keep her safe? The sad truth was, he could not. Yet, he loved her, he admitted to himself. He loved her fiercely.

Calling on every ounce of resolve he possessed, Lucas firmly set her from him and inclined his head stiffly in formal greeting, fighting to ignore the pain mirrored in Alanna's eyes, caused by his abrupt actions.

"What are you doing here?" he asked softly. "This is too dangerous a territory for a woman. Devlin should never have brought you to this place."

"Do you think I could have kept her away?" the Irishman asked.

"I would have come alone if I had to," Alanna said. "I needed to know if you were alive."

"It might have been best for all of us if you had never been sure," Lucas responded, including Devlin in his glance. "Things have not altered, Alanna."

"Is that why Juan told me you had not survived? Did you instruct him to say such a thing, should I come looking for you?" Alanna asked. The tears that had been glistening in her eyes were beginning to flow freely.

"By the Virgin, I would never deceive you! Juan!" Lucas called angrily. He demanded in Latin, "Why did you inform the Lady Alanna I had perished when the *Santa Ana* foundered?"

"If she thought I did, it was merely a matter of misunderstanding," the aristocrat said unctuously, beginning to back away to avoid del Fuentes's wrath. "My Latin is not as fine as yours. I simply told her you were not here. How she chose to misinterpret what I said is not my concern."

"At the moment, I don't care about Alvarez or what he said," Alanna insisted in English to exclude Juan. "There are things I want to say to you."

"I've no time for conversation now," Lucas replied brusquely. He knew that if he remained in her presence his determination would fail him and he would give in to temptation. "I must see to the fortification of the keep. We have been here seven days already. Surely the English will find us soon."

"Then there will be war that will tear this country asunder, and 'tis the Irish who will suffer," Devlin accused.

"There is nothing else we can do. But before that happens, I want you to take Alanna far from here, and see to her safety," Lucas ordered.

"I'm not going anywhere," Alanna declared obstinately. Lucas del Fuentes was her treasure, her gift from Mananaan MacLir, left not once but twice on Ireland's shores for her to find. She would not be such a fool as to ignore this second chance for happiness.

"There's not much I can do with her once she's determined. Nor can anyone else," Devlin said, to emphasize to the Spaniard that he knew Alanna much better than Lucas did. "However, if she will not come away with me, perhaps it is you who should depart."

"Would that we could," Lucas muttered, glaring at the woman who returned his stare so defiantly.

"A chance exists for you to do so. When Kevin's men brought me word of your disaster, they told me of three ships run aground in Killybegs. Two are beyond repair, but the third might be made seaworthy by salvaging parts from the others. The place is not that far from here, no more than twenty miles south through the mountains."

"A ship!" Lucas exclaimed softly. "Come along with me to Don Alonso. This is something he should hear." Then with an exasperated sigh, he turned to regard Alanna, the one person above all others whom he wanted to ignore. However, having seen the hungry look of those around them, Lucas knew she would have to come with them, as well. He couldn't leave her on her own amidst eight hundred men and expect her to remain untouched.

"Tell your captain I will take you there if he so desires," Devlin offered as the trio crossed the bailey.

Though her heart cried out, Alanna knew she could not protest Devlin's suggestion. Without a ship, the Spanish forces would stay, but only to be found by the English, and cut down, taking many of her own people with them. As much as she would like to keep Lucas by her side, she did not want to see him and his men endure the same fate suffered by her father and Sean. A solitary Lucas remaining behind was one thing, but the entire body of Don Alonso's men was something else altogether.

"I know Alonso will be grateful for your help," Lucas said, leading them through the inner passages of the crumbling Kiltoorish Castle until they came to the remnants of its great hall. "But I fear that at the moment he is incapable of granting you much of a reward for your services."

"The reward I have in mind is not his to give me," Devlin said. His eyes settled upon Alanna's slender back as she preceded them through the archway and into the great chamber.

Lucas looked hard at Devlin. What he saw before him was a man of great strength, with a sense of honor and loyalty enough to rival any nobleman of Spain. Fitzhugh cared for Alanna, and he would keep her from harm. Her future would be assured, at least as much as anyone's safety could be guaranteed in the tumultuous world in which they lived.

Lucas knew he had no choice but to entrust the woman he loved into the care of this other man. With a grimace, he nodded silent assent. And though he considered that he had done the right thing, that his motives had been noble and true, Lucas del Fuentes had never felt so empty and cheated.

When they entered the large, decaying hall, Alanna saw Alonso de Leiva half reclining upon a makeshift bed, his face a study in unrelenting pain, a leg, bound in bloodied bandages, propped up before him. Yet even at this disadvantage, courtesy did not fail him. Rising up slightly upon his elbows, he inclined his head and greeted his visitors graciously. Lucas translated his warm words of welcome.

At de Leiva's side sat an Irish chieftain, introduced as the MacSweeney, who was obviously at an impasse in trying to communicate with the Spanish captain. The chieftain's reputation was known to both Alanna and Devlin. A crude individual of middle years, he was an Irishman who, above all others, hated the English. His entire life had been spent at war with them, and their destruction was the flame that consumed him. From the outset, Alanna did not like him. Though he had come bearing food for Alonso's men, it was obvious to her that the vermin had done so only to serve his own purposes. Certainly, MacSweeney wanted to keep the starving foreigners from ravaging his countryside in search of something to fill their empty bellies, but he was the sort of man to make his insincere largess seem an act of charity rather than one of self-preservation.

Having lived for so many years in a chieftain's household, Alanna was no stranger to the manipulations and strategies one man employed against another. She assumed MacSweeney thought to put the Spaniards in his debt so that he would not come away empty-handed. It was likely that at the very least he wanted to trade his food for de Leiva's firearms. Or else he had more pernicious plans, desiring the Spanish commander to join forces with him in a campaign against the English.

Alanna did not have to wait very long to have her worst suspicions confirmed. Upon learning her identity, the war-like chieftain addressed her in a rush of Gaelic. "As Curran Desmond's daughter and the fierce O'Donnell's foster daughter, add your voice to mine. If we can find a way to make this fellow understand, help persuade de Leiva to join forces with me, so that we may wage war on the devils who have implanted themselves on Irish soil."

"Speak in English, in order that Don Lucas may translate for Don Alonso," Alanna ordered MacSweeney, her voice cold and regal. "I will have no conversation with you to which they are not privy."

"Then tell Alonso that when he decides to combine his eight hundred men with mine, your foster father will lend support and send more troops and supplies," the man said in English, annoyed at Alanna's dictate but complying nonetheless.

"It makes no difference what is pledged to me," de Leiva replied through Lucas after MacSweeney's words were translated. "My answer is the same."

"I would think that after so recently tasting defeat at the hands of the English upon the high seas, you would grasp at any opportunity to take your revenge. Or have you lost your stomach for war?" the chieftain asked disdainfully.

"That is the only thing I have not lost along the way. But I will not take weary, hungry men, many of them injured and all of them now poorly equipped, into battle against a well-fed force. There will be other times for attacking England. Right now, I only want to bring my men home."

"But that's the point," MacSweeney argued. "Join with me and after we defeat the English, there will be ships aplenty for your journey to Spain. At this moment, you have no way of getting there."

"That is not true," Devlin said solemnly, speaking up for the first time as he turned to Alonso de Leiva. "There are three Spanish ships run aground in Killybegs. Two are beyond repair but one of them can take you and your men home."

As Lucas rapidly conveyed this information, Alonso's pain-filled face was transformed by joy, and a prayer of thanksgiving fell from his lips, signaling to the MacSweeney that his scheme would come to naught.

"But I have had no news of this," the MacSweeney bellowed, "though I have as many men who run the coast to salvage as Kevin O'Donnell does."

"Then either they are not adept at the job you set them, or they do not tell you of everything they find," Alanna interjected, earning a baleful glare.

"The ships are there. You have my word on it," Devlin declared with quiet contempt for the MacSweeney while Lucas communicated the entire exchange for Alonso's benefit.

Silence fell upon the room, disturbed only by the sounds of nature wafting through the partially missing roof, as those gathered awaited de Leiva's decision. Even wracked by physical agony, he was a leader of clear and decisive thought as well as a fine judge of character. He believed Devlin Fitzhugh and the beautiful woman who had already saved the lives of some of his men. Swiftly he informed his second in command of his plans.

"Lucas, you will lead the men to this ship tomorrow. As I can neither walk nor ride, I will remain behind."

"Do you think I could do that to you, Alonso? Abandon you to this merciless barbarian?" Lucas asked quietly, not caring that the others did not understand what he said. This was a time for privacy. He was already being forced to forsake the woman he loved. He would not relinquish his friend and captain, as well. "You, above all men, deserve to see our native land again."

"I will not have the others condemned to death on foreign shores to satisfy my own desires," Alonso pronounced obstinately. "You will depart with the men at sunrise tomorrow."

"Aye, that I will," Lucas agreed, "and you will be coming with us. There are ways around every obstacle. Hasn't that always been your philosophy?" Then he turned to the others and addressed them, his face sterner and more grim than Alanna had ever seen it. "We leave for Killybegs at dawn tomorrow. Fitzhugh, we will rely upon you to be our guide."

"And I your escort," the MacSweeney said, without a trace of charity in his voice. He would not permit eight hundred Spaniards to march through his lands taking what they would. Besides, there was always the possibility he could still change de Leiva's mind.

"As you will," Lucas replied for Don Alonso. After all, they abided in this man's territory. It would serve them well to appease him if they could. "But for now, there is much to be done. The men must be readied."

"And things chosen to be left behind," Alanna said. Her eyes searched Lucas's face so poignantly that he was forced to shift his gaze.

"Aye, that cannon for one thing. You'll never be able to get it through the mountains," Devlin said, pretending he did not see what was going on before him.

Immediately Lucas seized the excuse of the ship's gun to commence a new discussion with his commanding officer, a ploy that would allow him to ignore the issue Alanna had just raised. Soon it was decided that the weapon would, of necessity, be abandoned. MacSweeney, meanwhile, was dispatched, somewhat mollified, to gather food in exchange for other firearms. His departure left Devlin, Alanna, Lucas and Alonso to discuss the logistics of their forthcoming trek.

Yet every time Alanna asked a question or made a comment, Lucas directed his response to Devlin Fitzhugh, until the pretty widow began to question whether this was the same man who had swept her into his arms so passionately upon his return to Kiltoorish Castle.

Indeed, if it had been up to Lucas, he would have ignored the enchanting siren altogether. Yet it was impossible for him to do so when he was constantly called upon to translate the always-gracious remarks Alonso made to the lovely woman whose companion had brought him such welcome news.

"To show his appreciation," Lucas stated on his captain's behalf, "Don Alonso will do what he can to make you comfortable. He says that is, unfortunately, very little. However, he is ordering the displacement of some of his men so that you might have a room in which to spend the night, but—" Lucas paused almost imperceptibly, his face suddenly carved in alabaster, so devoid was it of emotion "—he regrets that so many men in so little space makes it necessary to assign both you and Fitzhugh to one chamber."

"One room for the two of us? 'Tis a pity, but something I'm sure that can't be helped," Devlin said innocently.

"In addition," Lucas went on, ignoring the roaring urge to throttle the beaming Irishman, "given that Alanna is one woman among so many men, Alonso deems it best to have her protector constantly at her side."

"A brilliant man, your captain," Devlin said.

"And a kind one, as well," Alanna added, unaware of Lucas's rising anger. "Please convey my thanks to him."

"And now, Fitzhugh, seeing as you have received your reward, mayhap we can set about our work. There is much to be done," Lucas said gruffly. Though he had decided Alanna and Fitzhugh belonged together, he had thought to be long gone before ever such a thing occurred. Now, however, he found that the idea of their spending a night together, while he tossed restlessly alone, had him seething in rage. He unconsciously rubbed his shoulder, still tender from the sword wound he had received.

"Lucas, wait," Alanna called, reaching out to lay her hand upon his injury. "It might be best for me to see how you heal."

"There is no need, and I have no time to be coddled," the handsome Spanish nobleman said brusquely, firmly grabbing her wrist before he had to endure her gentle touch. Such intimacy, he felt, would drive him to madness.

"But—"

"If you have to see to someone, your efforts would be better spent on Alonso." His voice betrayed nothing of the burning desire he felt for her. "See if you can do something to alleviate his pain. In the meantime I will send Don Diego to tend to your welfare. When you are done here, he can take you to others who are sick and injured. There are men who would appreciate your care."

With that, he turned and left the room, Devlin at his heels. A bewildered Alanna stood watching him go. Surely she had not imagined the joy he had expressed at finding her at Kiltoorish. Had she?

Chapter Thirteen

Dinner was over, though the sky still held the echo of the sun's last rays when Alanna concluded that she would have to take the initiative with Lucas. Since her enthusiastic greeting that morning, he had done his best to avoid being alone with her. Even when they had been together after she had finished her nursing chores, his eyes had been sternly focused elsewhere, his attention given wholeheartedly to Alonso, MacSweeney or even Devlin. Anyone but her.

Puzzled by Lucas's clear reluctance to approach her and too anxious to remain still, Alanna paced the stone battlements of the old castle as she pondered the situation. She had not crossed Malin Mor at breakneck speed to have del Fuentes treat her like a casual acquaintance, for heaven's sake! She wanted Lucas. It was that simple. She had let him leave her once, accepting his attack of conscience on the beach at Elly Cove, but after realizing how close she had come to losing him to the whims of the sea god, Manannaan MacLir, Alanna would be denied no longer.

Lucas would have to understand that no one could control tomorrow, but today, or rather tonight, was theirs for the taking. If she wanted him and he wanted her, who was to condemn their joining? Besides, she thought suddenly, Lucas had justified all the pomp and splendor of life on board the Spanish warships as well-deserved amenities the soldiers enjoyed on the premise they might never return home. How logical was it then that he refuse himself the few glorious days they might share?

She would ask for no more than that, no promises, just the time until he sailed, Alanna swore to herself. Then she would relinquish him to Spain. Her mind made up, the widow called out to one of MacSweeney's retainers, stationed as a guard.

"Would you find Lucas del Fuentes for me and tell him I must see him at once in my quarters? The matter concerns breaking camp tomorrow and our journey to Killybegs," Alanna said.

"For a glimpse of your smile, anything, milady," grinned her compatriot. "And if he won't come, I will."

Rewarding her messenger's sauciness with a mischievous grin, Alanna scurried off to the room Alonso had given her and Devlin. Devlin! Oh, Mother of Mercy, she had forgotten all about him. The gallowglass had aired the room, gathered wood for a fire to keep her warm, helped her arrange a comfortable pallet on the floor and then informed her of his intention to sleep outside the door to protect her. That would never do now! Damnation, she should have known that when she had need of privacy, she would have an alert chaperon, though of course Devlin would not define his role as such. And how could she tell the Irishman what she had planned for that night, knowing how he felt about her?

With a groan of annoyance at the complications of having two men in her life, one of whom she desired, the other who desired her, Alanna released her hair from its single braid. Vigorously, she began to brush her tresses, seeking inspiration in the repetitious activity. As much as she cared for Devlin, he could never set her heart on fire the way a simple look from Lucas could. No, unfair as it might be, Alanna knew she must keep her old friend from her door that night so she could welcome Lucas. Her body would settle for none other than the Spaniard.

All too quickly a knock interrupted her thoughts, and she jumped from the stool. It had to be Lucas, her pounding heart acknowledged, but she had not spoken to Devlin. Yet, come what would, she would not send Alonso's lieutenant away.

"Yes, Lucas, come in," Alanna invited as she opened the door. She was startled to see the man she had sent as her messenger rather than the raven haired nobleman for whom the message had been intended.

"I am sorry, milady, but del Fuentes said he is busy organizing Alonso's troops into traveling contingents for the journey tomorrow. He said to express his regrets, but to tell you now was no time for him to shirk his duty to his men for a bit of conversation."

"Where is he?" demanded Alanna, more angry than she would have believed possible. Indeed, the burning rage that flared in her soul was far hotter than when she had learned of Grady's duplicity. The devil take duty, she fumed. Lucas would be hers tonight in one place or another. "Right now, I mean, where can I find him?"

"On the south side of the castle gate, talking with the sailors from *La Rata*," MacSweeney's servant answered, feeling sorry for the man who would soon know her wrath. This del Fuentes would be lucky if he escaped with his head still attached to his shoulders.

Moving abruptly past her messenger into the corridor, Alanna strode rapidly down the hall, her sandals' staccato rhythm echoing her irritation. His men always came first, she bristled. Very well then, she would not dispute that, but sometime this evening, be it at eleven, or twelve or one or two, it would be her turn to receive his attention, and she would tell him so in no uncertain terms. Lucas del Fuentes would not ignore her any longer.

As she hastened through the main hall, intent only on the words with which she would castigate Lucas, she turned a corner too quickly, and collided solidly with Devlin.

"Alanna, are you all right?" he asked in concern, taking in her unbound curls, flushed cheeks and bright eyes as he grabbed her arm to steady her.

"Oh, yes, Devlin, I'm fine. I wasn't paying heed to where I was walking, that's all."

"Where are you going? That is, may I accompany you?"

"No, I don't think so," she declined nervously, avoiding his eyes. "In fact, weren't you supposed to consult Mac-Sweeney about tomorrow's route through the mountains? You said something about being sure to avoid the peat bogs going south."

"Yes, I was off to see him now, but that can wait. I would be more than happy to escort you, Alanna. You know—"

"I know that I take up too much of your time as it is, Devlin. You pamper me so, but there is really no need for you to be concerned. I am perfectly fine. You go talk to MacSweeney, share some *poitín*, maybe throw the dice a while or exchange war stories. Enjoy what is left of the evening as you like, for I won't need you to guard my door," she said hurriedly, hoping to escape questions.

"I don't mind at all—"

"No, I will not have you inconvenienced like that. The soldiers know I am Alonso's guest, so there is no reason to protect me."

"Really, Alanna, it would be no trouble—"

"Actually, Devlin, your presence might cause trouble," she admitted, straightening her shoulders and raising her head to look him directly in the eyes. "Now, I do not wish any further discussion of the situation. Please respect my privacy, Devlin."

"As you choose, Alanna." He nodded, his usually open face shuttered, his emotions hidden from her. She was his mistress in name, if not deed. How could he not abide her wishes, no matter what it cost him? "I will say good-night, then."

"Good night, my friend," Alanna called softly.

It is only for tonight, Devlin told himself, forcing his feet to carry him from her side, or at the very worst, until the ship sailed for Spain. Certainly he could withstand the pain that long. He had no choice. But once del Fuentes was gone for good, he would console Alanna and teach her to laugh again. The gallowglass tried hard not to imagine what would occupy her until then. His time would come yet.

Watching Devlin stride away from her, Alanna was struck by the poignancy of it. There could be no doubt he understood her intention to have company that night, yet, faithful and loving as he was, the Irishman had accepted her decision. For a fleeting instant, she almost wished he hadn't, but that was sheer and utter lunacy. Lucas, not Devlin, was the man she cried for in the darkness before dawn, the reason she had come here. Lucas was the man she needed to see now.

Quickly the widow shook her head, sweeping her loose blond tresses over her shoulders. She was sorry she had not taken her cloak, but she was unwilling to return for it. Then she took a deep breath, gathered her arguments and hurried down the steps out of the main keep. A brief walk brought her to the area MacSweeney's man had mentioned, and she stood still a moment, her eyes adjusting to the falling dusk as she scanned the huddled groups of men for Lucas, not realizing how inviting a sight she presented until their raucous shouts reached her ears.

"*Una mujer hermosa—*"

"*La belleza—*"

"*Señorita muy bonita—*"

"*Ven acá, muchacha—*"

"*Un regalo imprevisto, no?*"

"*Alto!*" Lucas's voice roared suddenly from the shadows of the castle wall as he hurried toward her, speaking to the men in furious Spanish, cuffing those he could reach as he passed them, apparently caring not in the least who had actually spoken.

The fury in his tone was nothing compared to the unholy wrath that contorted his features. Alanna tried to quiet her quaking heart as he neared her. No stranger to his anger, she was still startled by the way his display of temper engulfed her, setting her blood aflame with desire for this vengeful male stalking her way. Then he was upon her.

"Are you completely demented, wandering out here alone?" he demanded heatedly, grabbing her elbow and whirling her around to position himself between her and the men. That redheaded Irishman was the one responsible, he fumed. Fitzhugh should have been here to guard her from such foolishness. Was this the way the lovesick fool fulfilled his obligation? If so, the man didn't deserve her! "Where is Devlin? Alonso said he was to remain by your side."

"I have no idea where he is," Alanna lied. She dug in her heels and refused to take another step as Lucas tried to urge her back to the castle entrance. "It is you I want to see, not Fitzhugh."

"I sent word I have no time—"

"And that is why I came to you." Alanna raised her eyes to stare defiantly at his flushed face. Her small chin, set firmly, gave evidence to her determination. He was worried about her, she realized joyfully, a small frisson of satisfaction coursing down her spine. Whether he would admit it or not, Lucas did care about her, and that made the rest so much easier. Deciding abruptly to change tactics, she smiled beguilingly at the poor man who had yet to acknowledge he was lost.

"Since you refused to come to my room, I knew I had to see you to change your mind. I want you there, Lucas."

To his credit, Lucas didn't bluster angrily, but hesitated, temporarily undone by the promise in her softly spoken words and the desire in his heart. Weighing the fierce resolution visible in her independent stance against his nearly overwhelming urge to crush her in his arms right where they stood, the Spaniard swallowed deeply.

If Alanna remained here in view of the sailors, they would be hard put to contain their lewd remarks despite his angry threats. Yet, if he accompanied her to her quarters, Lucas sincerely questioned whether he could trust himself to resist the primal urges already battling to destroy his composure. After all, despite his most earnest resolve, he was still a man.

"Lucas," she murmured deliciously. Her delicate tongue licked her upper lip. Her large blue eyes were so alluring that he felt himself drowning in their depths. "We do have unfinished business."

"Alanna..."

"If you need a bit more time here, I understand, but I must speak with you," she continued, her partly open mouth a subtle invitation.

"I hardly think that would be a good idea," he said, the words so untrue, they cut him to the quick.

"On the contrary," she disputed, "it is the only way we can settle the debt you still owe me."

"Debt?" Lucas repeated. He was so entranced by the unspoken messages her body was sending that he could barely concentrate. Despite the audience surrounding them, he had eyes only for her mouth. He remembered the power it had to enthrall him, the way it took him to the brink of ecstasy, then tumbled him over with a mere flicker of her tongue.

"All right, then," he agreed. He cursed himself for yielding to her enticement even as he vowed not to touch the alluring vixen, no matter how much he craved her. He was a soldier first, he reminded himself, a man second.

"Thank you," Alanna replied formally, nodding her head as regally as if she were an Irish Queen of old. Without a backward glance, she moved quickly toward the entrance to the keep. "I shall await your coming."

Alanna returned to the room Alonso had given her, intent on making it a soothing haven to welcome her unwilling guest. The more at ease she could make him, the simpler it would be to seduce him, she concluded. Quickly, she lit the torches set into the wall, drew her pallet before the hearth and set fire to the kindling Devlin had gathered, hoping the intimacy of the small area before the fireplace would make the large, drafty room less imposing. Since the castle had been empty for years, its furnishings were almost nonexistent, yet she was thankful for the privacy the room afforded her. If Lucas allowed himself to cooperate, the night would indeed be magical.

Recalling his gallant refusal to *use* her that night at Elly Cove, however, the Irish woman shook her head in dismay. How could such a clever man be so frightfully stupid? she wondered, marshalling arguments to counter his should the issue arise.

When his knock came, sooner than she expected, all was in readiness. With a pinch to her cheeks to assure their color, the widow gathered her cloak around her, opened the door and stepped back for Lucas to enter.

"Will you share a drink with me?" she invited, motioning toward the stool on which the *poitín* waited.

"No," he replied curtly, determined not to fall prey to the temptation Alanna represented. If he did not look at her, he told himself, she would not be able to bewitch him, and he'd not fall victim to her charms. Difficult as it was, he trained his eyes on the rushes that covered the floor rather than the delicate curve of Alanna's cheek and the soft hollow of her ear. "I am here to settle the matter between us. Then I must leave. A debt, you said?"

Alanna frowned, setting tiny lines fluttering across her brow. Though he appeared the same as he had outdoors, his broad shoulders straining provocatively at the once-splendid shirt, now open at the front, his hose clinging to muscular thighs, Lucas refused to even meet her eyes. Before she could reason with him, Alanna realized, she would have to shock him into seeing her.

"A debt of sorts," she murmured, wetting her lips and moving to stand by his side. She was thoroughly confounded when he backed away, almost as though he was afraid of her.

"Because you lied to O'Donnell?" he asked, still refusing to look in her direction.

"No, because you would not lie with me at Elly Cove," she challenged, tired of his games. If shock was the only thing he would respond to, she would oblige him.

"Alanna, I told you I cannot—"

"Cannot *take advantage of* me? Is that what you were going to say, Lucas?" she cried angrily, surrendering to frustration. She unfastened her cloak and tossed it onto the pallet behind her. Beneath it she wore nothing. Her flesh danced in the flickering light of the fire, her nipples already taut and yearning for his touch. "Don't I look like a woman longing to be loved?"

"It is not right—"

"Lucas, listen to me. I said *loved*, not *used*. You are too giving and caring a man to ever demean a woman that way. I want you to make love to me, no promises, no commitments, just you and me tonight."

"Alanna, you don't know how hard it is to refuse you—"

"Then don't," she whispered seductively, unwilling to be so close to success and see it fade. He was alive after she had supposed him dead. He had come to her when she had feared he would not. She couldn't let him deny her this. "Besides, as I recall our one night together, your desire was as great as mine. Has that changed?"

"*Was* is the key word, Alanna. I, er, I find I no longer have any interest in bedding you," claimed Lucas, barely able to breathe as he struggled to keep from feasting his eyes on the fetching woman before him. The test was nearly too great. He measured the distance from where he stood to the door. He wanted her so much, he could taste it, but Devlin was the man who should have her. Where was he, anyway? "What have you done with Fitzhugh?"

"Damn you, del Fuentes, stop being so *noble* and remember that you're a *man* first. Forget about Devlin. I don't care about him. Let yourself make love to me!"

He said nothing, but at least he had turned back from contemplating the door to study her, Alanna noted. His face was awash with the agony of his indecision. If she reassured him...

"Lucas, I know we have no future together and I can accept that, but we do have a here and now, if you'll only let it happen. As immoral as living for today may be, I will settle for that, if that today includes you," she confessed shakily, her eyes piercing his as she crossed the room to him. Tentatively, she reached forward and splayed her slender fingers against his chest. Stroking the thick mat of his dark hair, she found herself tingling, her body was so aflame with need. "I can't promise I won't weep for you once you have set sail for Spain, but I swear I shall never regret sharing myself with you."

Without warning, her soft hands pushed aside his tattered shirt and her teasing mouth danced across his chest, making him tremble.

Then, with a wild growl of acceptance, he fell to his knees, wrapped his arms about her waist and buried his head between her breasts, content to hear her pounding heart, knowing his own must be echoing with the same fervor.

"Alanna, I dreamed of you, called your name to the winds and wished you were beside me, but I never thought..." he murmured against her silken flesh, his slowly expelled breath further tantalizing her.

"This is not a time for thinking," chided his Irish temptress. She caught her fingers in his dark hair and turned his head slightly, positioning his mouth within reach of a questing nipple. "You have more rewarding chores to concern you."

Lucas needed no further encouragement. He was eager to atone for the hours he had wasted in refusing her. With a hunger he feared might devour them both, he teased one thrusting peak with eager fingers while his rough tongue laved the rosy sweetness of the other until she gasped aloud with the pleasure of it.

Resting her hands on his broad shoulders, she gave herself up to the flames eating at her soul, uncaring who might hear as she called his name, the only name that existed for her at that moment.

"Lucas! Oh, Lucas, don't stop!"

In the ever shifting light thrown by the fire, he couldn't miss the burgeoning flush coloring her, its intense pink hue arousing him till he found her even more desirable. He cursed the qualms of conscience that had kept them apart. No caring God could deny them this act of loving, he decided, gratified by the way Alanna quivered in his arms.

Realizing how completely his caresses enthralled the lovely vixen who'd captured his heart at Castlemount made him all the bolder, and he was determined to pleasure the beauty as no man ever had.

Slowly Lucas eased back on his heels, trailing featherlight kisses down her stomach and across her abdomen. His strong hands grasped Alanna's buttocks as sudden tremors coursed the length of her. Then, as she cried out his name again in wonder, he raised his mouth to sample the sweetness of her core, his tongue gentle at first, then plummeting wildly within, tasting her honey.

"Oh, Lucas!" Alanna screamed. A frenzy of incredible sensations blinded her to all but the jagged bursts of violent lightning animating her being even as Lucas lowered her to the pallet and held her close. Fighting to catch her breath, she found she could only pant uncontrollably, yet, still in the throes of passion, she struggled to speak of her joy. "Lucas, you are a miracle."

"No, *querida,* it is you who are," he whispered hoarsely, nearly as overcome as she by what they had already shared. And the night was still young.

Moments later, while Alanna floated down from the clouds of euphoria that had borne her up to the heavens, she became aware that Lucas had undressed and lay beside her, his body a wondrous testament to divine workmanship. Anxious to reward him with the same glory he had bestowed on her, the blonde moved toward him, moistening her lips in delirious anticipation.

"Alanna," he welcomed her, opening his arms. Without further preamble, his mouth covered hers, his tongue seeking entry into the warm cavern that instantly claimed him. He wanted her so badly that he felt as though he would burst with desire. He clutched her slender form tightly to him and rolled over, taking her with him.

For her part, Alanna knew she could deny this man nothing and shifted position willingly, delighted by the rough expanse of his length against her heated flesh as her hands grasped the corded muscles in his back, urging him closer. This was as it should be, Alanna exulted, feeling him slide into her female chamber, already moist and clamoring for him. Her muscles tightened about him instinctively, welcoming the intimate intrusion. His presence made her whole and filled the void she had never recognized until she had met Lucas del Fuentes.

Then, relishing the heat that pulsed within her, Alanna began to writhe beneath him, echoing the rapidly escalating rhythm he set. A fierce tempo of rocking desire spurred them on, each sensing the same feverish urgency as they rode the building storm to its heady pinnacle. Unable to withstand his need any longer, Lucas suddenly shuddered in her arms and found fruition. Alanna crested within seconds, her body quivering in mindless ecstasy as the universe around her exploded into tiny diamonds of sparkling light, each brighter than the one before.

"Amante de mi vida," Lucas cried aloud, tearing his lips from hers, only to seize them once more in a demanding kiss, driven by the inexpressible passion that filled his being. *Love of his life.* Alanna was all that and more!

"You were right," he whispered a few minutes later as his breathing slowed, "all that matters is here and now. This and you are absolutely perfect."

"It is, isn't it?" she murmured, unwilling to relinquish the warmth of the sensations still enveloping her. Content to be in the arms of the man who had loved her so completely, she closed her eyes again, savoring the wonder of the experience.

Later, she awoke at the sound of her name, but it was Lucas, calling her in his sleep. Smiling at being part of whatever dream had put such a seductive look on his face, Alanna leaned over to kiss him. Her fingers gently traced the ragged scar on his hip. Wondering at its origin, she was intrigued by the starkness of the irregular line that traveled across his otherwise dusky golden skin. Yet, oddly enough, rather than destroying her interest, the sight of the old injury sparked her fire once more. Slowly she eased herself free of Lucas's embrace and bent her head to kiss the uneven flesh, her mouth lingering over the salty taste of him, her long hair caressing his manhood as she moved.

"Come here, my Irish waif," he invited, suddenly pulling her up to lie against his chest. "Don't you know you could drive a man wild with desire, wriggling about on him like that?"

"I rather hoped that might be the case." Alanna giggled. She felt for all the world like a starving woman who, having sampled her first taste of food, yearned for further sustenance.

"Oh, greedy, are you?" chuckled Lucas, as he kissed the hollow of her throat. "I will just have to do something about that, I suppose."

And then he did.

Morning came all too soon to suit the Spaniard. He groaned, throwing his arms across his eyes to obscure the sun's rude light. Alanna's room was on the east side of the castle, he recalled, so he was probably among the first awakened, but still, it wouldn't be long before it was time to leave. Sighing, he reached out his hand to touch her. There were things that must be said before they parted.

"Alanna," Lucas called softly, "we have to talk."

"No," she murmured drowsily, "that was only an excuse to get you into my bed, and I did that. Go back to sleep."

"Come," he urged. "Wake up and look at me."

"That might be more tempting if you didn't appear so frighteningly serious," she complained, opening her eyes. "For heaven's sake, Lucas, smile. Last night we tasted paradise."

"But now it is today, this morning, and I must return to my duties," he explained quietly, reluctant to pierce the glow of happiness that surrounded Alanna. Still, she had known the joy they shared was but a temporary aberration. He had made no promises to her. "Alonso made me responsible for the transfer to Killybegs."

"Do whatever you must," she agreed. "I'll be waiting for you in camp tonight."

Startled by her ready acceptance of his terms, Lucas fell silent. He had expected an argument from the female who had been so fiercely possessive in the darkness of night and couldn't quite believe Alanna was willing to compromise.

"You don't mind?"

"Naturally I would prefer it if we could spend day and night together, Lucas."

"That's impossible."

"Of course it is, but I told you last night I am yours until you sail for Spain. That is all you need to remember," she said. She kissed him lightly as she stood up and began to dress. "When you can come to me, I'll be there."

"With a reward as splendid as you, I won't forget," he murmured, his green eyes shimmering with desire at the thought of the evening to come. "The day already drags on too long."

More than two hours later, the camp had just been struck and the long trail of men began snaking its way toward the mountains that separated them from Killybegs and the *Girona*. Devlin and MacSweeney had worked out the route between them, hoping to minimize the distance to the pass through the mountains while at the same time avoiding the deceptive peat bogs that all too quickly swallowed any man foolish enough to venture onto them. But, as always, despite the most careful planning, there were aggravating delays, each of which fell to Lucas to resolve.

First, there was that odd meeting with Devlin as he left Alanna's room that morning. As if he had been waiting in the hall, the gallowglass had straightened up, looked him over carefully and scowled before proceeding to knock on Alanna's door, speaking not a word to him. For a moment, Lucas had been half tempted to apologize to the

Irishman, but then, realizing the idiocy of such an admission, he had turned on his heel and left. Still, the encounter had left him ill at ease.

Then there was Alonso, fretting at the effort that would be needed to convey him over the arduous trail and asking to be left behind.

"I am not so precious a commodity that the stamina of four of our men should be wasted to transport me to a ship I might not be hale enough to command," he had raged at Lucas. "Those four should never have been so foolish as to volunteer—"

"You are wrong about that, Captain. There were not four men who volunteered to shoulder your weight for twenty miles," Lucas corrected, "but more than six hundred!" He lifted de Leiva from his pallet, despite his protests, and carried him down the castle steps to where the improvised litter waited.

As he brought Alonso outside, the waiting men rose to their feet and yelled their support, cheering and clapping for the leader who had seen them through the English Channel and two shipwrecks and now felt himself unworthy of their assistance.

"*Alonso, viene con nosotros,*" they roared. *Come with us.*

For a brief moment, it seemed to Lucas that he saw tears in the lieutenant-general's eyes, but then de Leiva waved vigorously at his sailors, a broad smile on his face.

"Well, then, del Fuentes, what are you waiting for? Put me on that blasted litter of yours and let us get started," he commanded sharply. "My men want to get home to Spain, and it seems Killybegs is our next port of call en route."

The dark-haired Spaniard quickly obliged, settling his captain as comfortably as he could before motioning three sailors forward from the crowd.

"Esteban, Guillermo, Pedro and I will take the first stretch," he explained to de Leiva, preparing to hoist the pallet.

Juan Alvarez burst forward. "Naturally, there you are, Lucas, grabbing at the honors again. Did you bother to ask if I, godson to Philip II, wished to be among the first laborers for our good captain? No, of course not, you stole the place for yourself though you know you do not deserve it," Juan spouted, his vitriolic temper clearly at full pitch. "Just because you are not fully Spanish—"

"My mother has nothing to do with this," snapped Lucas.

"Then, too, probably you figured to be less tired this morning than later in the day. I imagine the road now is flatter than it will be when we cross the mountains, but you thought of none of those things, did you?" asked *El Pavoreal* with a sneer.

"Fine, take my place if you wish," offered Lucas, anxious to avoid another debate and finally get the contingent moving. MacSweeney had traded him a horse to simplify his overseeing the men once they were underway.

Making a mental note to relieve the first group of litter bearers earlier than he had intended, Lucas stepped away from the foursome and signaled them to lift de Leiva.

For the others, the task seemed an easy one, but Juan struggled a bit, growing red in the face at the exertion. Shorter than the other sailors, he would be hard-pressed to keep pace with them but, observed Lucas, that was not his problem. Juan had demanded the assignment and, for at least a little while, he would have to contend with it. Nodding at de Leiva as he passed, Lucas went to check on the rest of the sailors.

Devlin and MacSweeney were already on horseback with the chieftain's retainers. The two would alternate monitoring the front and rear of the assembly, to watch for stragglers and any unforeseen problems that might arise.

While it was improbable the English would attack a force of more than eight hundred men, some of the nobles were wounded and might make easy prey since many of them had salvaged their personal valuables and carried them for safekeeping. Though some had bartered with MacSweeney.

for horses, the vast majority of men would be traveling on foot, in the small bands of six or eight Lucas had grouped together for mutual protection.

Nodding at the gathering of waiting sailors, Lucas directed them out of the castle behind de Leiva, watching carefully to be certain Alanna was not left behind. She was the cause of his next headache, for she objected to riding Piobar when so many of the wounded were forced to drag themselves on foot.

"Alanna, be reasonable," Lucas argued. "If you insist on walking, only one man or maybe two will benefit. In the meantime, someone will have to walk with you for your own protection."

"Don't be ridiculous. None of these men would hurt me."

"You heard them last night! Each one of them wants you for himself—and a few of them might not hesitate to take you if the opportunity arose," he chided, his green eyes suddenly hard and bright with emotion. "I don't want to have to worry about that happening."

"Is that jealousy I hear in your voice?" Alanna teased.

"No, damn it! It's irritation. I've no time to watch out for you now, Alanna, and it's unfair of you to expect me to do so."

"You are being rude and insufferable!"

"Fine, then get on your horse and ride," Lucas demanded, praying she would do just that so he could be certain of her safety. "If you hurry, you can probably catch up with Devlin, who treats you as if you were a royal princess."

Alanna, flushed with indignation, raised her hand to slap the arrogant male, only to be caught by the intense expression in his eyes. Suddenly, she realized his purpose. With a bright laugh of understanding, she lowered her hand and leaned toward him.

"I would kiss you in appreciation of your concern, but your men are watching. Consider that kiss one I owe you tonight," she whispered, turning to her horse and accepting Lucas's hand to boost her up. Without a backward glance, she gave Piobar his head and moved quickly past the column of observant seamen.

"All right. Onward to Killybegs," Lucas called, thankful that, for the moment at least, all was well.

Four hours later, riding quickly alongside some of his shipmates from *La Rata*, Lucas cursed the steady downfall that had turned the uneven dirt path into a morass of mud, sucking at their feet and making the trek even more difficult. He and Diego had managed to rig a makeshift covering for Alonso's litter, but the captain was suffering a good deal of pain from the constant jostling, and the day's journey was not yet half over.

As for the sailors, the early exhilaration of actually taking a hand in their own survival had dissipated by now. Stretched out in a line more than three miles long, they followed the plodding men in front of them, trying not to splash through the puddles that formed everywhere. Tempers, shortened by teeming skies and unseen holes in the road, flared quickly and arguments broke out for no purpose. Even the most composed among the men had begun to bemoan their circumstances, fearing the change in weather was a bad sign for the future.

"Our souls are doomed."

"We shall die in this accursed land."

"Why did God not let us drown at sea instead of on land?"

"Del Fuentes, can we not take shelter from this water?"

But it was a futile query. There were no trees or natural growth nearby, nothing but the irregular stretches of peat bogs, seductive but deadly, from what Devlin and Mac-Sweeney had said.

"Once we reach the mountains, there won't be so much mud," Lucas assured the grumblers, taking care not to promise the way would be any easier. From what the Irish had told him, the pass was narrow, cutting between heights that seemed to resent man's intrusion, often tossing boulders down their slopes, making progress hazardous under the best of conditions.

Still, the Spanish were stalwart fighters, accustomed to hardship and unflagging in their efforts to achieve victory. They might have lost against the English forces in the Channel but, Lucas realized, having come this far, few of them would be vanquished by Ireland's foul weather and rough terrain, no matter how disheartened they sounded at the moment.

About to head farther back in the line of men, he was startled by frightened shouts from the troops forward of his position. The dark-haired leader urged the animal he rode toward the source of the commotion, half-expecting the problem that awaited him.

Two of the men, exasperated by strict orders to stay on the circuitous route around the bogs, had chosen instead to cut across the soggy turf. All of a sudden, perhaps twenty feet onto the greedy morass, they had begun to sink into the insatiable marsh. Flailing their arms and furiously trying to extricate themselves only made the spongy muck more receptive to their weight, however, and both had sunk rapidly, now almost up to their waists in the treacherous mire. One fellow, Lucas observed, had his arm in a sling wrapped tight against his body, clearly at a disadvantage.

"Why are you sitting there so calmly?" del Fuentes challenged MacSweeney, who was watching the drama as though it were staged purely for his enjoyment. "Can't we do something?"

"Nothing. They wanted to shorten their path. Well, it's quicker than that they'll be done with this life." The chieftain scowled, clearly annoyed with the Spaniard's criticism.

"I can't stand here and watch two men die."

"If you go out there, you'll only make it three," advised the Irishman. "It is said more men lie unshriven under the peat than blessed beneath all the churchyards of Ireland. I'll not add to their number."

"You won't help me?" Lucas asked. His scorn for the Irishman's lack of bravery was evident in his voice.

"I agreed to help lead you through the mountains, del Fuentes, not endanger my life for the sake of two fools—or three. If you want to reach safe terrain for camp tonight, we had better move on before this storm worsens," counseled MacSweeney as Devlin rode up, quietly observing the exchange. "As for them, have the priest say a few prayers for their souls and forget about it. They're getting what they deserve."

"We should keep moving, you know," intruded Juan from the group of spectators, surmising the topic of conversation. "Those two are only common sailors, not even from *La Rata*'s crew, but the *Santa Ana*. They are not worth jeopardizing another life, even if it is yours!"

"Well, Alvarez, that is the difference between us," snapped Lucas. "I would gladly trade your miserable life for theirs."

Ignoring the royal peacock's shout of rage, Lucas called out to the struggling seamen, urging them to stop moving and, difficult as it might be, to stay still.

"We will have you out in just a bit," he said encouragingly.

"How can you lie to them, you dishonorable half-breed?" reproached Juan, looking to the others for sympathy but finding none.

"Pedro, gather as much rope as you can find," Lucas instructed, dismounting and looking for a means to attach the rope. But like all Irish saddles, this one had neither horn nor stirrups. The lines would have to be tied around the horses' necks. Then, turning to Kevin's gallowglass, the Spaniard minced no words. "MacSweeney says I am risking my life to attempt a rescue. I know it wouldn't pain you to see me lose a gamble such as that, but are you man enough to help me win it, Fitzhugh?"

His hard green eyes challenged Devlin's cold blue ones. Neither man blinked as each took the other's measure. Slowly Devlin shook his head in puzzlement.

"I can understand that you would hazard your life for those men, and even respect you for such an action," he admitted quietly, his eyes not leaving Lucas's. "But why would you take a chance depending on my assistance?"

"Alanna trusts you implicitly, and her judgment is sufficient reason for me," replied his rival.

"I suppose it is for me, as well," agreed the gallowglass reluctantly. For, as much as it disturbed him to recognize the fact, except for the friction between them over Alanna, he and del Fuentes might have been good friends, their values and instincts were so similar. As the Spaniard must have suspected before he asked, not only would Devlin lend support, but he would do his damnedest to keep Lucas alive. "All right, tell me what you want me to do."

"If we use three horses, looping a rope around each of their necks, it should be enough to counter the sucking of the bog. I will go out with a rope tied around my waist and secure one around each of our unfortunate friends out there. Then you can haul us out, but be careful not to let the bond slip or loosen."

"Lucas, Devlin, be careful," urged Alanna, appearing out of the crowd, her cloak obscuring her blond hair.

"We will," Devlin assured her, "but you can help by following MacSweeney and moving the other sailors out of our way and then lending us your horse. We'll need room to maneuver these three animals, and we don't want anyone else injured."

Lucas watched in amazement as she docilely accepted Devlin's instructions and began using her mount to herd the watching seamen back on the trail before she turned Piobar over to the gallowglass. She would have argued with him, Lucas knew, yet she took Fitzhugh's orders without complaint. Who could explain the actions of a woman? He directed his attention to the task at hand.

Soon he was ready to venture across the bog and with only the slightest trepidation he stepped forth. The sensation of sinking farther with each step was an uncomfortable one, and it was only his iron resolve that kept his limbs from struggling. But he knew such action would only see him disappear into the peat all the quicker. Slowly he inched his way forward, paying no heed to the shouts from the watching sailors, concerned only with completing the task he had set for himself. When he had successfully reached the two men, he made sure their lines were secure and signaled Devlin to urge the horses backward. The muck was reluctant to give up its victims, but ever so slowly it released its grip with a groaning sigh.

Then, before he imagined it possible, the rescue was over. Though covered with wet peat, Lucas found himself so warmly embraced by his Irish vixen, he didn't even mind that she had hugged the gallowglass first.

"Don't forget tonight," Alanna murmured softly in his ear, while she brushed a clump of mud from his hair. "And try to stay out of trouble in the meantime."

From Fitzhugh he received a grudging handshake and even a few words of praise.

"As much as I hate to admit it, del Fuentes, under any other circumstances, you are a man I would be proud to know," the Irishman confessed. "As it is, you'll understand if I continue to pray daily for your speedy departure from Ireland and Alanna."

"You'd be less of a man if you didn't." Lucas chuckled, oddly pleased to have earned even that much of a concession from Devlin. He doubted he would be so magnanimous in a similar situation.

After the excitement of the morning's unexpected adventure, the rest of the day's journey seemed almost anticlimactic. The men, the route and even the weather cooperated until it was finally time to make camp for the night. Gone was the dissension and grousing among the sailors, and even the sullen skies lifted to provide some weak sun.

To Lucas's surprise, by the time he had herded the last of the trailing men to the chosen site, cooking fires were already burning and tents had sprung up as if by magic, leaving him little to do but look for Alanna.

"You could do with a bath, del Fuentes," observed Alonso as he lay outside the shelter arranged for him. "I must say, what you did today was the act of a true leader. Not only did you save two lives, but you reassured all the other men that they were just as important to us as those two. I have already asked Diego to make note of it in his report to Philip, as will I, of course. I suspect it will earn you a royal commendation, perhaps even a knighthood."

"That is not why I did it," protested Lucas, embarrassed by the captain's words of praise. He had seen an emergency and acted upon it, not to unite the men as Alonso intimated, but merely to save two lives.

"It does not matter," said de Leiva. "However, wash before you go to your woman. She deserves as much."

"An order I will be pleased to obey," the green-eyed Spaniard admitted. He wondered how Alonso had come to be so well-informed. That, however, was a matter to be pondered at another time. Lucas wanted nothing more now than to find peace in Alanna's arms.

And he did, but first they sampled the feverish excitement inherent in a reunion after danger and fear had threatened. They clung to one another, desperately seeking the reassurance each needed that the other was indeed real.

Again, for Lucas and Alanna, the night passed all too quickly as dawn and Killybegs beckoned.

Chapter Fourteen

From the moment of their arrival, the hours that Alanna spent with Lucas at Killybegs were among the most joyous of her life. Though he worked hard to prepare the *Girona* for sailing, and they both knew that its completion would mean their separation, they did not refer to it, never spoke of the dreaded future looming before them. Instead, they continued to dedicate themselves only to reveling in the moment at hand.

Since the first night they had occupied a small, crude shelter together, but to Alanna, it was a more wondrous place than any chamber a castle could boast. In the coolness of early October, Lucas was there to enfold Alanna in his loving arms and share his warmth, staving off the chill of both the mists and the years to come. And at night, after they had made love, she rested her head upon his broad chest, living a dream rather than waiting for sleep to bring her one.

The meager meals they enjoyed in each other's company, a bit of bread, a cup of the *Girona*'s wine, the occasional portion of meat, were more satisfying than a banquet set upon a groaning table. They found in each other all they needed to make even their dark circumstances seem the best of all possible lives.

From the first, Alonso's men, along with those who had been aboard the *Girona* and the other crippled ships, left the young lovers in peace, glad that at least one of their number had found a measure of tranquillity and happiness.

Only Devlin, always at a distance now, cast a shadow over Alanna's flagrant joy. She wanted to speak with him, to tell him how very dear he was to her. In fact, she longed for him to know that she would give her life for his, even if she could not give her heart. But the handsome gallowglass presented her with no opportunity to make her pretty speech. And in reality, if he had, Alanna would have felt unsure doing so. Attempting to soothe a suitor who had never actually declared his feelings might only serve as insult.

At least that is what she told herself one noontime, not long after Alonso's forces had reached Killybegs. It was something the tenderhearted beauty tried to make herself believe, too, as she walked down the rocky beach to bring Lucas and his men bread, water and some thick slabs of MacSweeney ham, had for the price of an arquebus and some rounds of shot.

Though the day was cool and Alanna glad of the cloak she had wrapped around her, the men were warm and uncomfortable from their exertions, removing spars and timbers from one of the ruined hulks to fortify the *Girona*.

The toiling sailors were glad to see her, especially Pedro and Enrique, who were among the crew that day under Lucas's direction. After waiting quietly and respectfully for Alanna to distribute the stores that comprised their meal, the sailors quickly fell to devouring the victuals once they had them in their possession.

Lucas came to join the woman he considered his own, if only for a short while.

"The men have a mighty hunger today," Alanna commented to him daintily, sitting on a boulder at the water's edge and drawing her bare feet up under her.

"Aye." His sea green eyes took hers hostage and spoke of another type of hunger entirely.

Alanna blushed, recalling their sweet lovemaking of the night before. "They're tired, too," she said in an attempt to change the subject before her memories of the pleasure he gave tempted her into throwing herself at Lucas then and there.

"And hot," he said provocatively, running a finger lightly over her skin, "as am I."

"Think you I should do something to alleviate your heat?" Alanna asked, minxlike, when she noted the devilish delight Lucas was taking in her rising discomfort.

"'Twould be a prayer answered," he declared. He rose and followed Alanna as she left her perch to saunter along the tide line.

"I wouldn't want to distract you from your work. Are you certain?" she inquired seductively, running her palm along the hard, strong lines of his jaw, her voice husky and low.

"Aye," he replied. A virile, predatory glint of anticipation lit his eyes so that he appeared more hunter than soldier.

"Very well, then." Alanna swiftly bent down, scooped up water in the tightly woven basket she had carried and boldly threw the icy liquid in his direction. Seeing her aim had been true, she gave a peal of laughter that rang out melodically over his surprised roar, dropped her basket, then turned and ran off down the beach, away from the ships and Alonso's camp.

"I'll teach you how to behave, wench," he yelled in mock severity as he gave chase.

Once or twice he nearly caught her, but at the last moment, with squeals of merriment, Alanna feinted and managed to elude his grasp.

Most of the work crew were shocked that a mere woman would dare to tease the grand and powerful Lucas Rafael del Fuentes in such a brash and frivolous manner. And more than a few of them worried for the likable girl's safety when del Fuentes should finally catch her. But Pedro and Enrique, used to Alanna's antics, assured the others that Lucas had come to expect the unexpected from this alluring Irish woman, that in fact he rather enjoyed it. Their

apprehensions assuaged, even the most seasoned and taci
turn of the mariners soon found themselves grinning a
they witnessed the lovers' frolicking play, some calling en
couragement to Alanna and others to Lucas.

In short order, however, the couple was out of sight
running around the bend where Lucas's patient manipula
tions had directed them. Once hidden from view, Luca:
lengthened his stride and easily overtook Alanna. Throw
ing himself at her, he toppled them both to the ground.

"Yield," he said, his face flushed and more boyish thar
Alanna had ever seen. He loomed over her, lightly holding
her prisoner.

"Gladly," she whispered, closing her eyes in rapture a:
he besieged her with urgent kisses that truly taught Alanna
just how her handsome Spaniard wanted her to behave.

Though the midday episode on the beach had been de
lightful, it had also been rare. Most days saw Lucas gone
for long hours, overseeing the refitting of the galleass that
represented the Spaniards' only hope of returning home.
Still, Alanna was content, knowing that her handsome
lover would be ever so attentive each night when he re
turned to their shelter and again in the morning before the
first light took him from her side.

When they were apart, Alanna kept busy in order to dis
tract herself from the speed with which the days at Killybegs dwindled. She spent many hours tending to the sick,
pleased that Alonso's wound remained clean and he free
from fever, even though the aristocrat was not yet able to
walk or sit a horse. Still, he was dedicated to his men, and
declined the offer of shelter from a local lord, a vassal of
the O'Neill, in order to oversee repairs to the *Girona*. To do
so, however, de Leiva had to be carried about in the chair
Lucas del Fuentes, his second in command, had ordered
fashioned for him. Yet, incapacitated as he was, he managed to lift some of the burden he had placed on Lucas's
shoulders all the same.

Sometimes, Alanna found herself in Diego's company, and the elderly warrior treated her as he would a daughter. Their communication was stilted, at best, but she soon developed a surprising fondness for him. Occasionally, too, she would see Devlin, always spying him in the midst of a crowd. But when she did, he would merely wave in her direction and send her a lopsided grin that made her heart lurch with guilt before he rushed off to involve himself in one task or another, clearly determined to spare no effort to speed the Spanish on their way.

And there were always many chores that needed completion. They were seemingly unending. Yet, for the number of men now living on the beach, the camp was run smoothly and efficiently. Besides Alonso's forces, there were those who had been aboard the *Girona* when she had run aground, as well as the men from the two zabras that had sunk in the area, bringing the number of Spaniards to over thirteen hundred. Then, too, MacSweeney and his men were encamped in Killybegs, and oftentimes the local lord could be found there with his soldiers, as well. It was no wonder that, according to the rebels' spies, the English were growing wildly concerned and amassing a huge army in order to destroy the large Spanish contingent.

And well Elizabeth's subjects had reason to fear this force, Alanna thought as she looked about her one afternoon. In spite of their numbers, the primitive conditions under which they lived and the hardships they had endured, there were few outbreaks of temper, and insubordination was almost nonexistent. The men remained cohesive and disciplined, a credit to any nation.

In fact, Alanna felt that now it was known she was under Lucas's protection, she could go anywhere in the camp and fear harm from no one, with the possible exception of Juan Alvarez. But surely, he would not be so foolish as to bother her again, though she did notice him sporadically skulking about, regarding her with a malicious sneer. However, for the most part, his presence was ignored if not forgotten, eclipsed as it was by Alanna's happiness and her determination not to allow anything to mar her precious time with Lucas. Not even the work on the *Girona*, which was proceeding at a rapid pace, dispelled her joy.

One afternoon, as Alanna was seeing to Don Alonso's injury, she heard the MacSweeney's raucous voice demanding an audience with de Leiva.

"Ah, so here you are, Alonso. There's something we must discuss. I've already given you barrels of pitch for one of the *Girona*'s cannons, and with fifty such weapons, you have plenty to spare. But I've received no powder, though I thought I would," MacSweeney carped, coming into the commander's makeshift quarters and setting his large bulk down heavily. "Now what do you want, you thief, for the gunpowder I need to make the bloody thing useful?"

"There's no one here who can translate," Alanna said quietly. She had to work hard to contain the laughter that threatened to bubble up inside her. Hadn't Lucas already told her most all of the galleass's guns were to be left behind anyway, as their added weight made the cannons more a hazard than a source of protection? But Alonso had not thought it necessary to so inform the MacSweeney, trading an occasional weapon for what he needed and thus besting the Irishman at his own game.

"Then don't stand about gawking, lass. Go and fetch del Fuentes," the angry chieftain ordered, "before there's an explosion here that needs no cannon shell."

"Aye, MacSweeney," she said, "I'll be back as soon as I find him, though with so many men milling about it may take a while." Then she scampered off, her laughter erupting as soon as she was out of earshot.

No matter what she had told the belligerent Irishman, the pretty blonde knew exactly where to find Lucas. Each morning before he kissed her goodbye, he informed her of his expected whereabouts should she have need of him. This day, which saw Alonso's men so much closer to sailing away, had been set aside for waterproofing the interior of the *Girona*'s hull with the very pitch MacSweeney had contributed to the Spanish cause. It had been Lucas, be-

cause of his attention to detail, who had been entrusted
with supervising such an important task.

But as Alanna made her way to the fire needed to melt
the thick black substance, she saw that her beloved Lucas
had not been content to merely bark orders. Instead, he had
thrown himself into the job at hand. From what reserve he
drew his energy after last night's prolonged and exquisite
passion, she had no idea.

Although the usual autumn chill pervaded the air, the fire
that kept the pitch slowly simmering was so huge and blaz-
ing that the men tending it had removed their shirts. Even
from afar, Alanna could see that Lucas was one of them,
standing, as he did, taller than the others.

Drawing near, Alanna saw that the common sailor's
breeches that were his only article of clothing rode low on
his slender hips so the jagged scar he bore peeped out in
what she considered a most provocative fashion. As he
stirred the heated tar, his powerful arms and thighs bulged
with iron-hard muscles, while his exquisite chest and back
glistened with a thin sheen of perspiration that made him
appear as though he had been lovingly sculpted from the
finest bronze. He was so beautifully male, so remarkably
hers, that it was all Alanna could do to remember why she
had come to fetch him.

"Hello, Alanna," he said without looking in her direction, making it seem he had just then sensed her presence,
when in reality his hungry eyes had devoured her movements ever since she had begun her trek along the water's
edge.

"MacSweeney is here and yells for your services so he can
communicate with Alonso."

"He can wait," said Lucas, peering down at her. The fire
dancing in his eyes was fiercer than the one beneath the
pitch. "I can't."

He handed a seaman the oar he had been using to stir the
thick, bubbling substance, and took Alanna's hand in his,
leading her behind one of the large outcroppings of rock
ringing the stony beach. Then Lucas bent his head to hers

and claimed her lips as his own. The heat his body emanated was more a result of her proximity than the fire at which he had been standing.

"Mi corazón," he murmured softly. His heavy arousal was evident when he pressed her against the tall rock, his large frame dominating her small one. "There are things I would rather tell you that need no translation, that use no words."

"But what about MacSweeney?" she asked breathlessly, arching her neck to give him access.

"I have already said he can wait," Lucas whispered between the tender kisses he planted along Alanna's alabaster throat.

"And Alonso? Will you have him bide his time, as well, until you are ready to see him?" she asked in a breathy, preoccupied whisper.

"Damn! Alonso never did like to be kept waiting," Lucas swore as his mouth found her eyes and nose.

"Are you so vexed because we must stop?" she asked, entwining her arms around him and allowing her hands free play along his unclad, well-muscled back.

"No, only because Alonso will not be in the best of humors when I finish what I am about to start and finally do go to him." Lucas's fingertips expertly tormented Alanna's rigid nipples, telling her that he had no intentions of calling a halt to their present intimacy.

"You can't mean to ignore his summons," Alanna murmured. Her voice was more a moan than anything else, and she had difficulty concentrating under Lucas's ardent ministrations. "Not when I have left him with the MacSweeney. Attend him. I will be waiting for you later, and our need, grown all the greater, will make our loving most cherished, indeed."

"I suppose you are right," Lucas said with an exasperated sigh, reluctantly putting some space between them. "Alonso does not deserve to be left with such a boor. But I warn you, Alanna, if I delay my pleasure and my desire escalates any more than it is now, our loving will be most fierce. Will you be able to keep pace with my ravaging demands?'' He made the question more of a tantalizing promise than an inquiry.

''The issue, Lucas, is whether or not you will be able to keep apace of me,'' Alanna replied with a saucy swish of her skirt to induce him into concluding his business with all haste.

''All right, minx, for now we will rescue Alonso, and leave it to later to see if it is you or I who surrenders first,'' he said with a seductive laugh. And then they walked back to de Leiva's quarters together, discussing what might be obtained from the MacSweeney for goods the Spanish had already intended to abandon.

That evening, their lovemaking *was* more tempestuous than any they had previously enjoyed. Passions ran unchecked and inhibitions ceased to exist. But in the aftermath, both Alanna and Lucas silently wondered whether their unbridled fire was the result of their provocative play that afternoon or their mounting desperation, aware that every sunrise brought them closer to the hour that would see them torn apart.

It was a fate they had as yet to discuss, trying, instead, to cling to each minute that was theirs, absorbing and committing to memory every jot of happiness found in each other's company.

Incredibly, with each day that passed, the urgency of their lovemaking continued to grow. But as time became dearer, more demands were placed upon Lucas so that even the few hours remaining to the loving couple were not theirs to dispose of as they would. Every completed task aboard the ship became a triumph that drove Lucas closer to despair. Alanna, too, fought to keep her heart from breaking, struggling against allowing the thoughts of a bleak future to tarnish the reality of her present rapture. But she had, she decided, the rest of her life in which to mourn, and refused to do so now when happiness might still be hers.

Lucas and his Alanna had managed to reap much joy until the instant when the days they had to share had waned to merely two. Then their love became a bittersweet thing.

Watching the sun slip toward the horizon when only one such evening remained, the two lovers stood upon the shore, his strong, sure fingers positioned possessively at her waist.

With her head resting against her lover's chest, Alanna could hear the mighty thump of his heart, each beat marking the passage of time and bringing them closer to misery. Once again, she wished she had the power to make the hours stand still. But she was no enchantress and Lucas no sorcerer. Though what they had created between them was magic of the most potent sort, they were still only mortals, and completely at the mercy of fate.

"I'll be back tonight as soon as possible," he murmured, dipping his head to hers. "If I could avoid Alonso's summons and this council meeting, I would. But surely things will be settled quickly, and then what remains of the evening will be ours."

"Each time we couple, it is as if all eternity belongs to us. I can wait a few hours for paradise," said Alanna earnestly. "Go now, that you may return all the sooner."

As he made his way to the now-readied captain's quarters aboard the *Girona,* the site chosen for the gathering of Alonso's officers, Lucas was struck yet again by the force of his feelings for Alanna. He loved her more vehemently than life itself. Yet the one thing he craved to lay at her feet, the pledge of a future together, was not his to give. And she, in her loving wisdom, had not asked him for such.

Even now, when he was on his way to meet with de Leiva and the others to plan for the *Girona's* departure and plot her course to Scotland, Alanna had not sought to stop him. Instead, she had put aside her pain in order to ease his, and sent him on his way with a smile upon her lips if not in her heart. Her actions had endeared her to him all the more, though but a mere hour ago, he would have thought such a thing impossible.

Heaving a heartfelt sigh, Lucas arrived at Alonso's meeting and took his appointed seat. Though he had been a man of honor all his life, never had he found its price as costly as he did at that moment.

For Juan, neither the days nor the nights at Killybegs had offered anything but growing resentment as he watched del Fuentes's star rise to a fiery heat, commanding increased admiration from the common sailors and elite noblemen alike. Where some of them had once scorned Lucas's parentage and questioned his loyalties, just as Juan had encouraged, the simpering fools had now turned to Lucas as if for deliverance. Though Devlin Fitzhugh had brought the news of the *Girona* to camp, it had been del Fuentes who translated the message of apparent salvation, del Fuentes who, by de Leiva's appointment, had organized the trek to reach her, and in the eyes of his countrymen, it was Lucas del Fuentes who would see them safely back to Spain.

While before only a handful of *La Rata*'s crew could be expected to countenance the half Spaniard's notions, now nearly thirteen hundred men willingly followed his orders, lining up at dawn to obey him and to take on the chores he assigned. And when Juan, godson to Philip II, had tried to see Alonso the first week to protest such an absurd apportioning of power, he had been put off. Alonso, victim that he was, sent word he was not up to a meeting, but said that Alvarez might want to consult with del Fuentes about whatever the problem was!

Gritting his teeth at the continued injustice of the situation, *El Pavoreal* had bided his time, waiting for his opportunity to tear down the false idol circumstances had created. He had endured the scornful glances of the woman Lucas had paraded through camp, boldly indifferent to common decency. He had stomached the taunts of his compatriots who had once respected and feared him, and he had even swallowed his pride sufficiently to occasionally assist on the *Girona* for a few hours to hasten their departure from this cursed land.

All the while, though, the stocky nobleman had nursed his hatred for Lucas, storing up the petty insults, the off-hand remarks, the blatant disregard for courtly convention and the numerous incidents of improper behavior in which the man indulged. Through all of this, Juan had counted the days until he could stand before Philip and charge Lucas del Fuentes with treason. Daily the industrious peacock had catalogued Lucas's actual sins and those others of which he considered it possible to accuse him: consorting with an enemy, even one so attractive as Alanna O'Donnell, providing information about Spain's naval secrets to the Irish, deliberately delaying repairs on the ship. Surely such crimes would see Lucas hanged.

And if he charged that the *Duquesa Santa Ana* had been sunk through del Fuentes's actions, a desperate bid to return to shore and reclaim the Irish woman, rather than as an accident of tides and winds, who could prove him wrong?

After all, he had calculated in the dark of night, how could Philip choose to publicly discredit de Leiva's leadership and hold the captain up to condemnation for using poor judgment in overloading his ship or selecting an unsafe anchorage for the *Santa Ana* when Juan would offer him a much less costly scapegoat in the person of Lucas del Fuentes? Surely the loyal, if insipid, de Leiva, the man Philip had granted so much authority over his Great Enterprise, was worth a thousand half-breeds like del Fuentes. Besides, wouldn't censure of de Leiva amount to Philip's admission that he had chosen wrongly in giving Alonso such a responsible position?

No, Juan thought gleefully, del Fuentes might exist as a demigod on these heathen shores of Ireland, but once back in the royal courts of Spain, he would be seen for what he was, a glory-hungry traitor and exploiter of misfortune, disloyal to his father's Spain, all for the transitory pleasures he found under the skirts of the Irish woman.

Indeed, Juan, concerned only with his plans for vengeance, had not realized how badly his position in Alon-

so's entourage had slipped until he had heard from a few
of the sailors there was to be a council meeting that night.
Irritated that he had not been informed of the impending
parley, he set out to correct the oversight.

Approaching Diego Martinez y Goya, he had asked after Alonso, hoping to see him privately to register his displeasure.

"The captain's injury is healing, though rather slowly, as
you would be aware if you bothered to spend any time on
the *Girona,*" de Leiva's adviser had snapped, impatient to
be about his chores. "Alonso is there most days for a few
hours."

"Oh, ah, he is well aware I am busy seeing to affairs in
the camp, making certain all here is in order," Juan blus-
tered, hearing the derision in Diego's tone. He ought to
have recalled that the old fool was Lucas's champion and
avoided him, Juan realized too late. "In fact, that is why I
wished to see him."

"He is resting. What, specifically, did you want from
him now?" the nobleman had challenged.

"Merely to know when he expects me this evening."

"This evening?"

"For the advisory meeting concerning the *Girona*'s departure. Everyone knows that de Leiva is conferring with
his closest advisers to coordinate plans."

"That is so, but Lucas, Fitzhugh and everyone else whose
opinion the captain values has already been apprised of the
details. Your name was not mentioned," the white-haired
noble had retorted, perversely satisfied at the sudden flush
coloring Alvarez's face. "I imagine that they will manage
without you."

As Juan had stomped angrily away, his small figure
contorted with fury, Diego had frowned. He was naught
but a scheming weasel, the aristocrat had reflected, pleased
he would soon be able to apprise Philip of the true nature
of his godson's character and let him deal with Alvarez. So
many things would be easier once they were home again,
Diego had sighed. He was anxious to feel the sun's wel-

come heat on his skin, its brightness coloring his days with warmth. Ireland, he had found, was too dark and chilled for old bones such as his.

"There is the pious blackguard and his panting dame," scowled Juan toward sunset as he spied Lucas and Alanna near their quarters on the beach. As always, he had been intent only on disappearing from the work detail, and he had come up the hill to contemplate his vengeance once more. Now, watching Lucas embrace the lithesome blonde, the scurrilous noble recalled the half-breed's irrational fury any time he had dared to approach the woman. Suddenly, Juan's small black eyes gleamed with inspiration.

"It is only fair," *El Pavoreal* told himself, holding back a laugh. Del Fuentes had usurped de Leiva's role, along with the power and glory inherent in refitting the *Girona*, even going so far as to displace him from Alonso's regard. It was only through Lucas's interference, Juan was certain, that the name Juan Alvarez would not be associated with the recognition and praise due the nobles of the Great Enterprise. Therefore, as Lucas was a thief, Juan would steal from him, and Alanna O'Donnell would be his plunder. If he could not claim her affections, then her body would nonetheless be his!

There were many ways to enjoy a woman, the Spaniard leered, especially if she could not talk when he was through with her. All he need do was follow her when she left Lucas, make certain there were no witnesses and kill her when he had taken his pleasure. For all del Fuentes might suspect him, he would never be able to prove a thing, not with over thirteen hundred men who could be suspects and only a day and a half until they sailed. Of course, if he could somehow make it appear that Alanna disappeared by choice to avoid a grand farewell, it would be neater, Juan schemed, unless he could perhaps make it appear Lucas had killed her in a jealous rage.... Well, he would resolve that later. First, to get the woman alone.

Lingering near the path down to the beach, he tried his best to be inconspicuous when a group of seamen passed heading toward the ship with more supplies to be loaded and a cask of wine for Alonso's cabin.

"Alvarez," called one, "what are you doing in the bushes? Isn't it time you were headed to de Leiva's strategy session? I have heard that most of the nobles have been invited."

"Aye, but some of us have better things to do." Juan chortled mindlessly, grasping for an excuse to make himself envied rather than pitied. "Me, I'm off to enjoy the womanly charms of a local Irish wench, sort of a last memory of this damned place, you might say."

"Give her one for me, but have a care, *amigo*. Mac-Sweeney near killed one lad he caught fiddling with a maid of his."

"This woman is more than willing, and believe me, she won't have anything to complain about to MacSweeney when I'm done with her." *El Pavoreal* chuckled.

The sailors moved on, guffawing at Juan's crude remarks, doubting the truth of them but all the same wishing they might be so lucky.

Once again, Alvarez resumed his vigil. He sneered when he saw Lucas kiss his woman goodbye before heading to the *Girona*. For Juan, there was great satisfaction to be found in knowing that Lucas and Alanna would never again be together. The nobleman reveled as well in the thought that for every minute of gratification Alanna had provided Lucas, her disappearance and death would cost him a hundredfold the grief.

Suddenly, the young blonde was coming up the hill toward him, her ugly saffron smock a bright beacon against the shrubbery, while Lucas continued across the sand toward the *Girona*. Juan ducked back out of sight, determined not to take her within the camp where her shouts might be heard and too many curious Samaritans would interfere. It would be better to watch to see where she headed, Juan plotted, squatting low in the undergrowth.

Alanna passed quite close to him without noticing anything amiss, too restless to be concerned with anyone or anything other than her thoughts. She had known all along that the time would come for parting, but she had never anticipated its approach would be so wrenching. Each day her heart contracted a bit more and she had to work even harder to appear cheerful, to concentrate on living the here-and-now she had promised Lucas. Sending him to Alonso had been almost unbearable when they had so few hours left together.

Losing Sean had been far different, she mused, for it was at once final and absolute. While she had grieved passionately, the deep sorrow had been a mourning without hope. Now, however, for all the futility of dreaming of a future with Lucas, a small part of her soul still envisioned the impossible, and that made each passing day more bittersweet. Had he proven an inconsiderate, selfish bastard, using her for his own pleasure, she might have survived their encounter without scars, but Lucas was her dearest friend as well as a remarkably sensitive lover. To her unending despair, Alanna knew she would never find another man whose soul so complemented her own.

Following the footpath without conscious effort, the weary woman faced the truth. Although she had not said the words aloud for fear of distressing her golden Spaniard, she loved Lucas with every ounce of her being. And, as she hesitated at the turn in the hill to watch the ebb and flow of the waves in the harbor, there was little doubt in her mind that Lucas loved her, too.

The tender way in which he stroked her cheek, the manner in which his long fingers caressed her palm, his habit of following her with his eyes even when others were about, the peculiar way in which he interspersed Spanish and the little Gaelic he had learned until she couldn't withhold her laughter and they collapsed in one another's arms. These and many more were the actions of a man who valued her life as much as his own, who cherished her smile, her laugh, her existence, a man who loved her deeply, though he had not spoken the words, either. Still, Alanna knew, at dawn the day following the next, regardless of their hearts' desires, the *Girona* would set sail with Lucas aboard, and she would ride home to Donegal with Devlin.

She had yearned for Lucas's touch and then frolicked in both its gentleness and its exuberant passion, but when the time came to leave, she would be true to her vow. There would be no pleading, no apologies, only a deep thanksgiving for all Lucas had given her. Indeed, if God were good, she might even be able to hold off the tears until after Lucas boarded—but that was not to be thought of tonight, or she would surrender to her melancholy and weep right now.

Seeking a distraction from her worries, Alanna decided to walk a while. There was still an hour or two of daylight left, she estimated, plenty of time to ease her mind by stretching her muscles without the danger of worrying Lucas with her absence. He would be occupied at least that long with Alonso. That way, by the time she returned to camp, Lucas would be ready to begin their night together, always something splendid to anticipate. She smiled and turned onto the path that headed east to the pine woods. The brisk smell of nature's greenery and the salty air had never failed to brighten Alanna's heavy moods before. Hopefully this evening would be no different, the young woman thought, lengthening her stride as she proceeded up the trail.

Juan, too, smiled as he slipped from his hiding place to track Alanna, his stubby fingers stroking the knife in his pocket. Though his upturned lips should have lightened the expression on his face, somehow his smile had the opposite effect. With his intense black eyes half-closed, his mouth half-open and his beard scraggly and unkempt, Juan appeared, as he concentrated on his quarry, more one who would follow Satan than a pretty woman.

Quickly he moved after her, artfully avoiding the occasional branch or rock in his path, as stealthy as the growing shadows of evening as he strove to keep Alanna in his sight without alerting her to his presence. The farther into the forest she went of her own accord, the simpler she would make his vengeful pleasure. And with del Fuentes busy with Alonso, there would be no one to interfere.

Chapter Fifteen

On board the *Girona* Lucas sat, impatiently drumming his fingers on the arm of his chair, his attention far from the florid speeches being made around the table. It was centered instead on the woman who became more precious every day he knew her. Each minute he was away from Alanna seemed like an eternity, and since he knew their time apart would be forever, these wasted hours were particularly aggravating.

Alonso had started the conference well over an hour ago and, in honor of the occasion, had arranged a sumptuous meal more in keeping with their earlier standards though the goldplate was rather the worse for wear. Soup, fish, beef, mutton, potatoes, cabbage, breads, and sweets along with vast quantities of wine salvaged from the three ships here in the harbor, had graced the table. But, in that expanse of time, despite the hearty appetites for food, no one had made any substantial reference to their plans for the sailing, a much more vital issue than their stomachs, Lucas fumed.

Restlessly the golden Spaniard fretted, disapproving of the flamboyant tones of the other captains present, each trying to curry favor with de Leiva, more concerned with how his exploits would be recorded in the ship's log than when the *Girona* might leave Killybegs. About to interrupt Captain Spinola's third toast to "the unflagging example of bravery displayed by Alonso," Lucas started at the sudden pressure Devlin exerted on his arm.

"Relax, del Fuentes, they will finish soon. It is much the same at gatherings of the clans. The chieftains of all the individual families dither about, eating, drinking and telling grand stories until they pass out. Once that formality is accomplished, the gallowglasses of each house resolve the various questions of territory or whatever and in the morning compliment their respective lords on the great decisions they made the night before. Though the chiefs cannot remember anything, they dare not admit it and so the agreements stand." The Irishman chuckled. "From the way your fellows have been lifting their cups, I figure things can't be too different with them, even if the language is."

"No, I suppose not," agreed Lucas, settling back in his seat, oddly grateful to Fitzhugh for soothing his temper. "I had hoped we could dispense with the preliminaries tonight and get to the meat of the evening. First I wanted you to review the route we must set for Scotland, and then it has to be decided how the duties will be dispersed on board the *Girona*. We can't have her usual crew work the whole voyage while the men from the zabras, the *Santa Ana* and *La Rata*, don't."

"True, but isn't that usually the case, even getting your repairs done here in Killybegs? Some men toiled like slaves, yourself included, and others avoided labor at all cost."

"I wasn't really aware of anyone shirking his duty, though I did keep myself busy, as you say," admitted Lucas. "I'm surprised you know the men well enough to notice."

"Well, Alvarez, the one who had been with you since Castlemount, sticks in my craw, but that may be because I never liked his attitude toward Alanna. I saw he was rarely present when there was work to be done, though he would appear readily enough near the supper hour."

"Actually, we should be thankful he wasn't around more of the time, complaining as usual. I've had enough encounters with him to know he can be an irritable specimen when his back is up.''

"You said Alvarez, Don Lucas?" interrupted one of the sailors in Spanish as he cleared the remains of the meal.

"*Sí.*"

"You won't have to worry about him tonight. He was busy bragging about the Irish woman he was going to pleasure, his final souvenir of this wretched land, he called her," said the serving man. "To my way of thinking, though, the only way he could make a female happy is to leave her alone. I tell you I pity the woman he is with."

"And what woman is that?" Lucas demanded harshly. A horrible suspicion formed in his mind as he abruptly rose from the table and grabbed the man by the shirt while the other nobles looked on, aghast.

"Lucas?" called Diego in alarm.

"I—I do not know. He just told us he would not be at this dinner because of her, but you know Alvarez. He is always spouting off," the crew member mumbled, suddenly realizing why the officer was so perturbed. "It does not mean he was going after your lady. Surely it was one of MacSweeney's women he was after, or maybe it was just talk."

"And maybe it wasn't," Lucas growled. He released the sailor and turned to address Devlin in English. "Fitzhugh, Alvarez may be intending to harm Alanna. Will you come with me?"

"Need you ask?" The gallowglass was on his feet instantly, following Lucas to the door.

"I will check our tent while you examine Juan's. If neither of them are there, we will separate once more and search until we find them."

"Del Fuentes? Fitzhugh?" questioned Alonso, but Lucas was too concerned about Alanna to worry about his captain's problems. If there was trouble over his leaving, he would settle it with de Leiva tomorrow, but now Alanna might need him... desperately.

* * *

Momentarily winded, Alanna stopped to look about her and realized she had come much farther than she had intended, having reached a small clearing near the end of the path only twenty yards from the towering walls of a sheer cliff. The whispering of the pines in the evening breeze, their distinctive scent and the peaceful solitude had soothed the frenzy in her heart to the point that she had actually enjoyed her stroll. It felt good to know that she could now return to Lucas, at peace with his duty to Spain and freshly committed to her own vow not to burden him with her tears.

Nature had been generous to her, as always. Alanna smiled, her spirits buoyed by the elements about her. In the distance she heard the tumbling waves of the ocean as she turned back the way she had come. Just then, a flock of birds took flight, their discordant song indicating some disturbance they had sensed.

It was odd that something should bother them at this time of night, she thought. But before she could ponder the matter further, she saw him leering at her from the shadows, not ten feet away. All at once, her blood chilled and she felt strangely uneasy.

Why would she encounter Juan Alvarez here in the woods at this hour?

"What do you want?" she asked, striving to keep her voice calm as she realized he was blocking her way. Moving backward as he came silently toward her in the small clearing, she remembered one of the Spanish phrases Lucas had taught her in their lovemaking. *"Que quiere, Juan?"*

"Solamente tu, Alanna." He leered. Step by slow step, he herded the woman backward, gradually inching closer to her as her eyes darted anxiously left and right, seeking an escape.

In desperation, Alanna decided to stand her ground. She realized a sightless flight through the trees to the side of the path would serve no purpose. Glancing down toward the ground, she grabbed a rock and boldly flung it at him, but to no avail. Again, she stooped low, afraid to look away from him as he crept closer. Her hands felt for anything she might use as a weapon to deter him long enough for her to get around him and run.

Touching a fallen branch, the young woman grasped it tightly and swung the uneven weight at Juan, praying it would strike him hard. But the limb was too short and he laughed at her efforts. In a moment of panic, Alanna took aim, let the bough fly through the air and rejoiced when it hit his ugly face. As blood spurted suddenly from his nose, however, Juan's brow darkened with rage, and he leaped toward her, ignoring his wound. She had to flee, but where? Once more, Alanna could only move awkwardly backward.

Then it happened. Unable to see where she put her feet, Alanna tripped over an exposed tree root, losing not only her balance but precious moments as she lay sprawled in the dirt, unable to regain her feet. That was all the advantage Alvarez needed.

With a warrior's cry of conquest, the stocky Spaniard towered over the widow, delivering a punishing kick in retaliation for her attack as he loosened his clothing and prepared to mount her.

Not yet ready to concede, however, Alanna unleashed her legs, jerking her knees viciously upward, and was delighted to see Juan topple to the ground in amazement. To her immense dismay, though, his recovery was all too rapid.

As the widow scampered to her feet, *El Pavoreal* reached out, grabbed her skirt and yanked her down, the force of her landing momentarily stunning her. Even as she threw up her hands, spitefully raking her nails down his cheeks, Juan was already imprisoning her between his body and the damp earth.

"Puta," he screamed, rising up on his knees to unleash a backhanded crack at her face. The whore had freely given herself to del Fuentes and yet she dared fight him off, he raged. He would teach her how to respect Juan Felipe Al-

varez, at least for as long as he allowed her to breathe. He knew now he would enjoy killing her before he abandoned her. He found a curious gratification in watching her blue eyes widen in disbelief as his fist descended, a satisfaction that only deepened at the actual impact of his blow. Striking her again for good measure, Juan relished the surge of power he felt. Del Fuentes might have gotten his reward in bowing to Alonso, but Juan would have his tonight, right here.

A gleeful howl escaped the jackal's lips as he knelt over Alanna, straddling her hips. One hand captured her arms and the other tore her Irish gown down the length of her body. For a moment the Spaniard's breath caught in his throat, so arresting was the sight of her fair skin against the shadowy darkness around them.

"Magnifico," he murmured hoarsely in anticipation. Her creamy breasts were perfect.

Bounding toward the stand of trees that clustered at the far end of Killybegs's harbor after finding neither Alanna nor Juan in their tents, the frantic Lucas was like a wolf running down its prey.

Alanna was his to protect, and the idea that he may have failed her tore at his heart. If Alvarez or anyone else had harmed her while he had sat ready to plan the *Girona*'s departure, he swore before God that he would have vengeance so swift and terrible even Ireland's barbarous shores had never seen its like.

The light of the full moon shining overhead cast an eerie glow through the treetops as Lucas entered the forest, and long, grotesque shadows painted twisted and deceptive images along the ground. But he dashed onward, never seeing the spectral quality of his surroundings, its effect not so terrifying as the landscape of his own heart as he worried for Alanna's safety. Anxiously his eyes sought some sign of his beloved, and his ears strained for the sound of her voice. From patch to patch of darkness he ran, his overworked lungs near to bursting and his throat raw from screaming her name.

"Alanna," he yelled, the agony in his soul pouring forth and reverberating in the night air. But no reply came rippling back through the darkness.

On and on he searched, until he began to question if possibly he was on a fool's errand. He was almost ready to turn back, to see if Fitzhugh, who had gone off in the other direction, had had better luck, when something arrested his attention.

Lucas heard the muffled moan before he sensed any movement from behind the inordinately large clump of pines. Wondering, at first, if it was perhaps only the harbor winds taunting him, he nonetheless altered his path and charged through the gorse in that direction.

The view he encountered horrified him. There, on the pine-needle floor, was Alanna struggling wildly with Juan Alvarez.

Juan's face, distorted by a malefic sneer, was a field of scratches, red furrows plowed by Alanna's desperately clawing fingernails. A demonic luster glowed in his dark eyes, making him the most unholy being Lucas had ever encountered.

But more horrifying was the sight his angelic Alanna presented. Her mouth was bloodied and her hair in wild disarray. The saffron-colored tunic she wore was ripped from neckline to waist, and her breasts were exposed to Juan's noxious lust, while the hem of her garment was drawn up to her thighs, making her appear all the more vulnerable despite her obvious, valiant efforts at self-preservation.

With a savage roar of rage, Lucas rushed forward to protect the woman who had so thoroughly overpowered his heart. Taking hold of Alvarez, he wrenched him off Alanna, yanking him to his feet in the process. When his searching eyes assured him that Alanna was relatively unharmed, Lucas turned his full attention to her assailant, the ominous power of a thousand storms clouding his vision to all but revenge.

Lifted into the air only to be roughly thrown to the ground some distance from Alanna, the villainous Juan looked up at the furious figure standing over him like some ferocious beast.

"Del Fuentes, there is no reason for your outrage. What you see is what she wanted. The woman is but a whore, and one you mean to abandon anyway. How many more men less noble than we will claim her after the *Girona* has sailed?"

El Pavoreal's attempts at strutting even as he lay prone did not exculpate him from blame, as he had hoped. Rather, they drove Lucas into a frenzy. All rational thought disappeared as he threw himself on top of Alvarez like a primitive animal with only one instinct—to protect his mate.

The violent struggle between the two men, once begun, could only be ended by the death of one or the other. Fierce blows flew unchecked, and hands gripped at throats as the merciless battle escalated. But Juan, whose strength originated only in hatred and fear for his own safety, was no match for the relentless Lucas, driven onward by the desire to end the threat to his beloved posed by this vile creature and to wreak destruction for any harm Alvarez many have done her.

Terror replaced the normal insolence in Juan's eyes as he clutched at the steel-like vise now tightening around his throat. In a last attempt to stave off death, he reached down and managed to loose his knife from his belt. He was about to plunge the blade into his opponent's side when Lucas tightened his hold. Unable to breathe, Juan felt his grip grow feeble, and the lethal weapon fell to the ground. In another moment it was over. Juan Felipe Alvarez, godson to Philip of Spain, lay dead, his corpse sprawled ignobly on a forest floor far from home.

Rising upright on his knees, Lucas threw back his black-maned head and allowed his lungs the huge quantities of air they craved. Then he got to his feet, knowing that the worst was yet to come. He may have put an end to *El Pavoreal*, but now he had to see to his precious Alanna, and the handsome nobleman tasted fear as to what she might have suffered.

Cursing himself for not having killed Juan the first time the bastard attacked Alanna, Lucas ran toward the quietly weeping woman, blaming himself for any harm she had suffered this night. He wondered if she hated him for his failings, but as he dropped down to one knee and opened his arms to her, she readily burrowed into his embrace and laid her head atop his chest as if there was no more natural place for it to be.

"My life, my soul," he whispered while he knelt there tenderly stroking her hair. His endearments were spoken for the first time in English because he wanted her to know exactly what was in his heart. "How could I have not protected you from so vicious a beast?"

"'Tis not your fault, Lucas," she said with a shudder, clutching the shredded front of her tunic closed against the chill of the night. "Men as wicked as Juan always find a way to work their evil. You could not have stopped him."

"Did he hurt you badly?" Lucas asked in a soft voice, though he gritted his teeth imperceptibly as he braced himself for her response.

"He did nothing I won't survive," Alanna murmured, unable to look at the corpse of her attacker, preferring to concentrate on the rugged planes of Lucas's face instead. "But all the while I fought him off, I somehow knew you would arrive to save me. It is as if you are the other part of myself, and where I am, so are you."

The handsome Spaniard was touched by Alanna's trust, but her words, as conciliatory as they were meant to be, only served to remind him of their impending separation, a parting that was likely to become all the more cruel as a result of Juan's death.

Lucas del Fuentes was a soldier in a time of war, and he had killed a fellow officer and nobleman, one who was also godson to his sovereign. Even as he had meted out justice, Lucas knew that there would be penalties, yet that knowledge hadn't deterred him. Juan had earned his death. But what lay ahead of Lucas as a result was not a subject he could broach with Alanna now, not when she sat shivering and weeping softly within his arms. As for himself, he had no regrets for what he had done.

Pressing his lips reverently to the top of Alanna's golden head, Lucas heard footsteps sound along the forest path. It was the solitary tread of one man, and he knew instinctively that it was Devlin Fitzhugh. Was the gallowglass, too, so attuned to Alanna that he would always find her no matter where she might be? The idea was as bitter as it was comforting. In order to cast it from his mind, Lucas called out to him, hoping the Irishman's presence would bring Alanna some measure of peace and distract him from the anguish that clawed at his soul.

Devlin appeared quickly, sword drawn and ready to do battle. The scene he saw before him was not to his liking.

"Sweet Jesus," he whispered, his fierce gaze going from the still body of Juan Alvarez to the distraught and disheveled Alanna, wrapped tenderly now in Lucas's protective embrace. "I wish it had been I who had put an end to that miserable bastard's life."

"That act was my pleasure," admitted Lucas, "though I warrant he deserved to suffer longer than I permitted."

"Then let me finish his punishment. I will see to it that his head is placed on a pike while his body is left to rot. He deserves no more."

"Leave him, Devlin," Alanna said wearily, raising her head from Lucas's chest. "It is over. All I want now is to go back to camp where I can find the comfort of my own pallet, where Lucas and I can put this in the past and savor the time left to us," she added, apologetic yet loath to be less than truthful with this man whose continued kindness demanded her honesty.

But Devlin, like Lucas, knew that this terrible business was not finished, in fact it had only just begun.

"Have you told her what this means?" Devlin asked Lucas quietly.

The aristocrat was unflinching as he gravely returned Fitzhugh's stare. The only reaction Lucas allowed himself was the tightening of the embrace with which he tried to shelter Alanna from the night's terrible memories. Yet Fitzhugh was right, there were things that had to be said. Tilting her chin upward, he looked into her beloved face, wondering if this was the last time they would share such intimacy.

" 'Tis best we all return to camp, *mi corazón*. But as this incident must be reported to Alonso, it is Fitzhugh who will take you to our quarters." Lucas resisted the urge to kiss her with all the passion and longing that was in his heart. "I may be gone a long while. He will stay with you until you hear from me."

"Or about you," Devlin corrected with brutal honesty. "Shielding Alanna now will only make things difficult for her should matters turn out for the worst. She is not a child to be coddled, del Fuentes, but a strong woman who has lived a hard life in a harder land. She has always managed to deal with the tragedies fate has sent her way, to survive and turn hardship into inner strength, much like the tempered steel of the finest sword. I know it is as much a part of her beauty as the golden hair or comely features you admire. Don't leave it to me to tell her what may lie ahead."

"Lucas?" Alanna questioned anxiously.

"I have killed one of de Leiva's men and there will be questions asked. It is that simple. But do not weep, *querida*. I do not regret my action, and I would do it again. As to the future, what will be will be."

"Surely when Alonso finds out Juan attacked me—"

"I cannot be confident of anything, Alanna. But you, you can rely upon one thing with certainty. Always know that I hold you dear, that I would consider it an honor to give my life in your defense.''

"Nay! Do not speak to me, *leannan,* of surrendering your life for mine. A separation of distance I found hard enough. But to think of death coming between us is more than I can bear," she cried, her tears flooding anew.

Watching her, Devlin Fitzhugh considered Alanna's speech so moving, her appearance so fragile, that he felt as if his own heart had been cleaved in two.

Damnation, he swore silently, but it looked as though he might be forced to compete with a ghost rather than an absent lover, after all. That was, unless he took fate into his own hands. But his decision to do so sprang from purely selfish reasons, he assured himself... and nothing else.

"There may be a way around this dilemma," he began gruffly, before he could analyze his motives further. "You have merely to say that it was I who found that swine and throttled him."

"No, friend," Lucas said firmly. "I alone will take the credit... and the blame."

"Oh, Devlin!" Alanna exclaimed. Her eyes still glistened with tears while her heart spilled over with gratitude. "You are among the best of men. But to offer your life for—"

"Do not make me into a hero when I am none," the normally patient Devlin flared. "I am not offering to surrender myself in del Fuentes's place. What I'm suggesting is that the blame be affixed to my name while I disappear, melt into our Irish landscape. Then no one will unjustly suffer for the death of that ignoble bastard, who is, I hope, already rotting in the flames of hell for his misdeeds."

"I appreciate that you would think to proffer such an alternative," Lucas said, "but—"

"Don't deceive yourself, Spaniard," Devlin growled. "I would do this not for you, but for Alanna and myself, as well."

"Whatever your reasons, it is a noble gesture, and I tender thanks. Still, I must decline," Lucas continued, the trace of a rueful smile haunting his lips. "My honor and that of my family insist that I accept responsibility for what I did. I will not hide from the consequences of my actions behind your buckler."

"Honor be damned, you proud, doltish Spaniard. What about your life?" Exasperation tinged Devlin's deep, melodic voice. "Doesn't that count for aught? Though I care not what befalls you, Alanna does, and I would think you might."

"Of course I do. However, Alanna's life is more precious to me than my own."

"But, Lucas," the distressed woman began to argue, her troubled eyes searching his.

"Hush, *niña*," he said with gentle firmness. "If I *were* to be so unscrupulous as to assign the blame to Fitzhugh, and he was caught before he escaped the area, who would tend to you after I sailed away to Spain?"

"If that is your fear, rest assured that no one will take me," Devlin asserted scornfully. "This is my land, and I know it better than any of you foreigners."

"I cannot take that risk where Alanna's welfare is concerned," Lucas pronounced with finality. "Nor can I compromise my own sense of integrity."

"You are a great fool, del Fuentes," Devlin growled.

"Perhaps," Lucas replied, rising and bringing Alanna to her feet. "But tell me you would do any differently were you in my place."

"Nay, in truth I can't. But you . . ." The gallowglass hesitated, trying unsuccessfully to marshal further argument.

"Don't expect me to be any less a man than you are," Lucas said with a detached lift of one raven eyebrow as he slipped his arm solicitously around Alanna. "Now we will return to camp and trust in God to watch over us. He will not allow any of us to suffer unduly."

Though the handsome aristocrat's deep voice was rife with confidence, both Devlin and Alanna silently questioned the veracity of his words.

"I hope you are right," the beautiful widow said at last, reluctantly beginning the walk back to the Spanish encampment under Lucas's patient direction, his hand still possessively at her waist. "Yet there are times when I fear God has forgotten our very existence."

Proceeding along the rock-strewn beach in the direction that only a few moments before had promised a heaven but now threatened a hell, Alanna fervently prayed that this would not be one such instance.

Chapter Sixteen

Hugging herself tightly, Alanna paced the ground in front of the shelter she shared with Lucas. The rest of the beach within her view was ominously deserted, and she, too, would have been gone, standing in the fore of the assembled Spaniards, if she had had her way. But Devlin Fitzhugh had halted her, keeping the anxious young woman from answering the summons that had called the Spanish seamen and soldiers together, some from their tasks undertaken even at this late hour and others from exhausted slumber.

The gallowglass's actions had surprised her. Never before had Devlin forbidden her anything. But with a stern face, he had prohibited Alanna from following her heart in this.

"Don't be a fool, lass," he had said harshly. "Even disciplined soldiers can turn into an unruly mob very quickly when something incites them. I will not have you caught in the midst of a sudden rebellion, nor would your Spaniard like it overmuch. Besides, del Fuentes will likely be no more inclined to hide behind your skirts than he was to accept my offer. Stay here and allow the man some peace to do what he must."

"But what if Lucas needs me?" she had countered to no avail.

"Your presence might be more detrimental than comforting for him. What would happen if the men, hungry for the arms of a beautiful woman, look at you and decide Alvarez was guilty of nothing more than being unable to resist temptation? The sight of you could easily arouse understanding and sympathy for a soldier far from home, slain simply for following the urges of his heart.''

"His loins, you mean," Alanna had rejoined hotly.

"Call it what you will. All I am saying is that if you want to help del Fuentes, you will stay where you are."

And so Alanna had reluctantly remained in front of the shelter that had brought her so much joy but had become in the last hour her prison. And time, which had sped by all too swiftly these last few days, now dragged on interminably.

Without success, she tried to take comfort in reliving the touch of Lucas's lips upon hers just before he had turned away, entrusting her to Devlin's care. But every time her mind was close to capturing that moment, it vanished, so that she experienced no solace at all, only tremendous longing for another kiss to take its place.

Alanna continued to walk restlessly back and forth before the tent, straining her eyes along the beach for some sign of her beloved Lucas, listening intently for the sound of his approach. Nothing greeted her, however, other than the mocking calls of seabirds, and the taunting whisper of Mananaan MacLir as the harbor's waters lapped rhythmically at the shore.

Alonso de Leiva sat upon his improvised litter surrounded by his officers. His injured leg throbbed mightily, but he suffered a hurt that ran deeper. Before him and the majority of his forces stood Lucas del Fuentes, self-confessed murderer of a fellow nobleman.

The crime was one that demanded swift punishment. But Lucas del Fuentes, as he faced his captain, did not cower or plead for mercy. Instead, despite his ruined and tattered garments, the man was possessed of a fierce and proud demeanor. His ebony head held high, the rugged Spaniard gave no sign of remorse. He was a man who, having done what he felt he had to do, was defiantly ready to pay the consequences.

And the consequences were grave ones, as every man there knew. There was no question that the killing of another officer under any circumstances was an offense punishable by death. Even Juan's despicable nature and the vulnerability of the young woman involved could not alter that.

Yet Alonso found himself repulsed and terribly saddened at the thought of ordering Lucas del Fuentes's immediate execution, no matter what justice demanded. Still, his private regrets could not alleviate his public obligation. Discipline had to be strictly maintained among soldiers at war and was especially essential given the situation in which the remnants of the Spanish fleet now found themselves.

If he followed his heart rather than his duty, de Leiva knew he would never be able to lead the vast number of men under his command on one questionable ship with any realistic hope of having them reach their homeland. Though the men of *La Rata,* having known both del Fuentes and Alvarez, might have understood a pardon, the combined crews of the zabras, the *Santa Ana* and the *Girona* would not. They would expect the punishment prescribed by a strict military code. Anything less would confuse them, signaling the demise of all regulations under his command. De Leiva could not sacrifice the good of so many for the welfare of one individual, regardless of how worthy the man might be. Should he falter in his responsibilities now, the lieutenant-general knew all would be lost.

He might have considered his decision inevitable, but Alonso was also determined to give Lucas his due and allow his case to be heard. And so the young captain sat quietly, patiently listening to Don Diego's impassioned arguments on Lucas's behalf.

During the course of his speech, the older man pleaded eloquently and passionately for the life of his valiant protégé, recounting del Fuentes's dedication and his invaluable contributions to Spain's cause. He gave voice, also, to an account of the base behavior of Juan Alvarez. But nothing the man said could sway Alonso's sense of duty. And powerful though he was, de Leiva knew that his personal feelings counted for naught—especially when one considered Juan's connections with the man who ruled the Spanish Empire, the sovereign to whom they all owed their first allegiance.

After all, before he could be any man's friend, Alonso was a soldier in Philip's service. So was Lucas del Fuentes. The two of them understood that it mattered not that Lucas was the man who had saved de Leiva's life when the *Duquesa Santa Ana* went down, the man who had seen to it that his commander had not been left behind in Loughros Mor Bay. They both knew what had to be done.

With a heartrending sigh, Alonso was about to pronounce Lucas's death sentence when his desperately churning mind presented a possible avenue of escape—at least for the time being. Impossible though it might seem, *El Pavoreal*'s being godson to Philip might be Lucas's temporary salvation rather than his condemnation.

"Lucas Rafael del Fuentes," Alonso intoned. A hush fell over the crowd as he began to speak. "What you have done calls for your death here and now."

"God have mercy," Pedro shouted out, while the crestfallen Don Diego's weathered face began to crumble into sadness, his whole body speaking of his despondency. Yet among all of the men present, Lucas, his eyes fixed on those of his captain, remained stoic. He had known there was every chance it might come to this, and at least he had the comfort of having seen Alanna safe in Devlin Fitzhugh's care.

"However, as a loyal subject of our sovereign, I cannot deprive him of the opportunity to witness your execution," Alonso continued solemnly. "You have slain His Majesty's own godson. Therefore, del Fuentes, I decree that you be held under guard and brought back to Spain, where you will be given over into our gracious King's custody."

"*Gracias,* Alonso," Don Diego whispered, realizing despite de Leiva's harsh words what miracle the captain had just performed. Though the commander of the Spanish force had not felt he could grant Lucas del Fuentes liberty, he had postponed his death. And for Diego, a reprieve of any sort was a victory.

"Don Diego, see to securing del Fuentes on the *Girona,* and be sure to set a guard over him," de Leiva ordered before motioning for his litter to be carried to his quarters aboard ship. He never once looked at the man to whom he owed his own life, the man whom he had just repaid as best he could.

"I feared this night would see the end of you," a relieved Diego said affectionately to the prisoner placed in his custody as most of the others began to disperse. "When you came marching back into our meeting and told us what had occurred, I did not think that even Alonso could save you."

"As it is, he has but postponed the inevitable. The Alvarez family holds much sway at court," Lucas said, trying to prepare his mentor as well as himself for what lay ahead. "But still, 'twill spare Alanna the sight of my death and perhaps give me an opportunity to see my family once more. For that I am grateful."

"How much more thankful would you have been, if you had stayed aboard the *Girona* and learned of Alonso's plans for the embarkation," Diego said slowly, uncertain of how to break this news to his old friend's only son. "It was decided that, given the numbers of men assembled here and the size of the ship, Alonso will ask for volunteers to remain in this accursed land. Had you but waited, boy, you could have stayed here, a free man, a hero who gave up his place aboard ship to others, and you would have the woman, too."

There was silence for a moment while Lucas, his face shuttered dangerously, digested what Diego had said. Then he responded, his voice sure and his dark green eyes ablaze with righteousness. "If I had not left when I had, Don Diego, it is Alanna who would be dead, and then I would have had no wish to stay in Ireland. Things have happened as they should have. She is safe, and that means more to me than anything else."

"You are a man in love, Lucas," the old man muttered sympathetically. "Could any creature be more foolish?"

"Perhaps not, but allow this fool to ask a further favor of you, Don Diego," Lucas said while the guards began herding him up the gangplank to the ship and the small cabin that would serve as his cell. "Go to Fitzhugh and make him understand that he must take Alanna away from here tonight. It would be for the best, as I can no longer guarantee her safety."

"And should I try to tell the woman you love her?" Diego asked, feeling pity for the young couple fate had torn apart.

"There's no need," Lucas said somberly. "Though I have never said the words, I think she knows. And if she doesn't, her grief will be all the less. Go now, and do as I have requested."

Don Diego coughed nervously as he stood outside the shelter, talking earnestly to the gallowglass. His meager English and Devlin's sparse Spanish made communication difficult at best, but the nobleman felt that at last he had made himself plain. He was glad it would be left to Fitzhugh to deal with Lucas's woman, who could be docile one moment and fiery the next. And he had no doubt but that she would not take kindly to leaving, as Lucas had ordered her to do. It was with rapid steps that he made his retreat, going to join Alonso once more. Perhaps between them, they would find some method of persuading Philip to spare the young nobleman's life.

When Diego had first approached, Devlin had thrust Alanna inside the confines of the shelter and ordered her to remain within, his tones brooking no argument. Yet even as he spoke to Diego, the gallowglass had monitored the tent, prepared to block her path of escape. Now, after watching the old man depart, he turned to face both her wrath and her feverish curiosity, though in which order, he couldn't be certain.

"Well," Alanna asked, her face pinched with anxiety, "why didn't Lucas come himself? Is Don Alonso keeping him busy with preparations for the sailing?" she added hopefully.

"Though I found it the devil's own task to understand Diego, I think I've finally made some sense of the matter," Devlin said. He took Alanna's hand within his own. "Lucas won't be coming back to the shelter."

"They didn't—"

"No, Alanna, your Spaniard is alive, but under guard," Devlin replied, trying to make this as easy as possible, though he wished Alanna's melodic voice would soften when she said his name as it did whenever she spoke of del Fuentes. "He'll be in custody until he returns to Spain. As for us, we are to leave the camp immediately."

"By Alonso's command?" Her voice was trembling now, and the sheen of unshed tears glistened in her deep blue eyes.

"Nay, 'tis Lucas who says we are to go without delay."

"Well, I won't!" Alanna yelled as she snatched her hand from Devlin and stepped away from him. "I'm not going anywhere until de Leiva and his men sail."

"Now, lass. This is for the best. You knew when you started this it would not end happily. 'Tis time to relinquish him, Alanna, time to go home to Tur Muir."

"But it's not," she argued. "We've still another day and night ahead of us, precious hours Lucas and I were supposed to have spent together."

"You forget Alvarez," Devlin said patiently. His soul raged nonetheless at Alanna's determination to stay with her lover. For the love of God, he thought, the man was imprisoned. When would she let go? And when, oh, when, would this whole damnable mess be at an end?

"I only wish I could," responded Alanna grimly, seeing once more the demonic contortions of her assailant's face. "But by all that's holy, Devlin, I won't allow that bastard to take his revenge from the grave. I must talk to Alonso. He has to set Lucas free!" With that, she darted past him and ran off.

"Mother of God, Alanna, but you're enough to drive a man insane," Devlin muttered as he watched her go. He did not even attempt to stop her. He knew that if he did, she would hate him for all time, blaming him for whatever fate eventually befell del Fuentes. No, trying to save him was something she had to do, but Devlin would be damned if he would accompany her. He couldn't bear watching her grovel for the Spaniard's sake. It would rip his heart in two. As it was, he would have trouble dismissing this painful interlude and helping the woman he loved above all else to forget it, as well.

Still, Devlin knew he could not allow her to run about unescorted, and so he followed at a distance to see that she arrived safely aboard the *Girona*. Once she had set foot on the gangplank, he would take a seat on the shore, prepared to keep guard until she disembarked, when in all likelihood she would need him as she never had before.

While Alanna ran swiftly along the shore, she had eyes only for the ship moored in the harbor. But even that hulk had been obscured from view by her blinding tears as she skimmed along the water's edge, barely feeling her feet touch the ground.

Arriving at the *Girona*, she found it was the crew of *La Rata* that was standing watch that night. These were men who knew and liked Lucas, and so Alanna had passed on unimpeded, none of the guards having the heart to keep her away.

Up the gangplank she went, and on to the main deck, knowing from time spent aboard while Lucas was directing the reconstruction of the ship where the captain's quarters lay. Immediately, the *Girona* struck her as being much different than when she had last seen it. The vessel had lost its desolate look now that it was made seaworthy and provisioned for the voyage ahead. Its new appearance only caused Alanna to be more conscious of the little time left to her as she had hurried onward, forging her way with determination to Alonso's cabin.

When she reached her destination, she threw open the portal and rushed inside without so much as a knock upon his door, startling the man who had been lost in memories of campaigns shared with Lucas del Fuentes.

As she threw herself beseechingly before him, Alonso saw her tear-stained face, and though he understood nothing of what she said, he knew why Alanna had come. There were some things for which no words were needed.

Though he had not thought he could feel worse than he did when he had ordered Lucas taken away under guard, Alonso discovered he had been wrong. The sight of this delicate creature, who had tended his wound so carefully and gently and now endured such misery after already suffering at the hands of Juan Alvarez, made even his hardened soldier's heart constrict with regret. He, too, would have killed to keep her safe. But still, Alanna's visit could do nothing to change things. Alonso had already rendered all that was in his power to give Lucas del Fuentes. With one possible exception, he thought, inspiration coming to him. Perhaps he could ease his friend's plight and repay this woman for her past kindness by arranging for both Lucas and Alanna to have one last taste of paradise.

Loudly he summoned the guards in the passageway, and barked instructions to them. One of the men who appeared at his command was Pedro, and Alanna could not believe it when, though gentle about it, he and his companion put their hands upon her and began to lead her away.

"No!" she screamed. She escaped their grasp and fell before Don Alonso again, trying once more to plead her cause in a tongue that was not hers.

But no sooner had she sunk to her knees than Pedro and the other guard seized her, conducting her mercilessly from the cabin. Though Pedro uttered words obviously meant to soothe, Alanna would have none of it. She continued to struggle, kicking and screaming, as she called piteously upon Don Alonso, begging him to show Lucas mercy.

But Alanna soon found herself removed from the cabin despite making it so difficult for the men that they finally had to resort to dragging her behind them. Soon, Alanna thought, she would be escorted from the ship and her pleas relegated to a place where they would no longer disturb de Leiva. But to her surprise, the men forced her below, along a narrower passage so that, furious as she was, Alanna began to worry for her own safety. She wondered if she, too, was being placed under arrest. Before she could decide what to do, the men stopped outside a small cabin and unlocked the door, then Pedro shyly but insistently ushered her in.

She was about to whirl around and give vent to her fury, when she saw him, and her face became suffused with joy. She was with Lucas, and nothing else mattered anymore.

He, however, was instantly on his feet, demanding to know from Pedro the meaning behind Alanna's sudden appearance. He would not permit her to suffer further for *El Pavoreal*'s death.

Apprehensively, the seaman began a halting explanation, visibly embarrassed at having taken part in Alanna's expulsion from Alonso's quarters. But after a few words passed between them, Lucas's attractive mouth broke into a smile of sorts, and he quietly signaled the men to leave.

"When they grabbed me, I thought I would never see you again," Alanna cried, running to Lucas and burying her head in his broad chest the instant the door closed. "But I don't care that I have been arrested as long as it means we can be with each other."

"You are quite free, Alanna. Your being here is not a punishment, but rather Alonso's gift to us," Lucas murmured, his heart filled with gratitude for his captain's kindness, "one last night spent together before you leave camp tomorrow morning."

Alanna raised her face to his, her fingertips lightly tracing the planes of his cherished features as if her ability to see and touch them were the result of one of God's greatest miracles.

Lucas, too, was filled with awe, drinking in the sight of this woman he had thought forever beyond him. Hurriedly, his questing lips fell to lightly besieging Alanna's golden hair, her temple, her eyes and nose. His long, sure fingers settled upon her cheeks. His tenderness touched Alanna as deeply as the grandest, most frenzied passion they had ever shared. Suddenly their relationship seemed new, and she felt as shy as any maiden beneath his soft caress.

Wordlessly, Lucas enfolded her in his powerful arms and led her to the narrow bunk where he had been lying when she had materialized in his cabin, as if his desperate longings had conjured her presence.

Sitting beside his beloved Irish vixen, Lucas bent his head until his lips met hers, exulting in the taste and feel of the woman he loved. Having her with him had driven all thoughts of the future into merciful oblivion. But such was not the case for Alanna, who seemed distracted.

"Lucas, what will happen to you?" she asked, finally finding the courage to put the question plaguing her into words.

"Imprisonment," he said lightly. "Mayhap I will even be released when we arrive in Spain."

"I don't believe you," she accused, pulling away from him.

"*Querida,* it's true," he replied. He reached for her hand to bring her back to his side, needing to revel in the warmth and fragrance of her, trying to commit such sensations to memory so they could bring him solace when he would require it most.

"You're lying," she whispered, her body stiffening with fear. "It is there in your voice. You told me once before you would never deceive me. Don't do so now."

"'Twill be but a few years in prison at the most," he insisted, to keep her from unnecessary pain.

"If so, I will wait for you," she said softly. She knew his assurances were false and was baiting him into telling her the truth. She could not allow him to bear his pain in solitude, but wanted to share it with him, needing him to tell her his fate as much as she dreaded the prospect of hearing it.

"No! Go on with your life, don't wait for me to return," he exclaimed. He had thought that his deception would spare her, not condemn her to a life of wretchedness.

"They are going to execute you once you reach Spain," she said dully, his outburst telling her what his words would not. "That is the truth of it, isn't it?"

"What does it matter, Alanna?" He lovingly brushed a golden strand back from her face. "We still have here and now. Isn't that all we have ever had?"

"But it does matter," she cried. "How can I live without you? Without knowing that the sun that warms me kisses your skin as well, without believing that the breeze into which I whisper your name will carry my endearments to you? Dearest God above, Lucas, how can I lose you? It would have been torture enough knowing you were alive, but for you not to be—"

"Hush, *querida*," he said gently. "We have enjoyed a rare thing, and I do not regret any of it. But if you leave me thinking you will be inconsolable, I will repent ever having made you mine. I will fall down on my knees before God and beg His forgiveness for the dolor I have brought you."

"But you have given me such happiness," she said, looking up into his compelling green eyes, her slim hand stroking his strong jaw.

"Then allow us to be happy," he urged tenderly. "We yet have the night before us. We dare not spoil it by grieving before we must over the things we cannot change. Let us give each other this one last, perfect night."

Alanna bravely nodded. Though her heart felt as though it had broken, she could do no less than grant Lucas what he had asked of her. Snuggling against him, she worked at banishing the misery and tension that bedeviled her. Soon, the simple gratification of feeling her lover beside her made other, more dire thoughts recede.

They sat contentedly for quite some time, fingers entwined, Alanna's fair head resting on Lucas's broad shoulder, until yearning, bittersweet though it was, they started to stir, and their contentment gave way to something much more, something that swiftly engulfed them and became fiercely demanding.

Lucas's hands began to sweep possessively over Alanna's lithe form, seeking and finding her woman's curves, then celebrating them with his touch. The heat of his body penetrated Alanna's, and she threw back her head, a small moan escaping her barely parted lips.

It was all the encouragement Lucas needed. Capturing his lover's lush mouth with his, the bold warrior demanded entrance to its inner recesses. She acceded readily, yielding to the urgency of his quest, allowing his tongue the exploration it sought as it danced seductively with hers before caressing the tender skin lining her cheeks.

"Lucas," she murmured. The sound of his name was a cry of surrender as she allowed her slender fingertips to burrow within the thick, black strands of his hair.

"*La amor de mi vida,*" he answered, his hands working slowly but deftly to remove her clothing. "I hunger for you with an appetite that is never satisfied. Each time I think that I can want you no more than I do at that moment, a greater craving arises to drive me wild with desire."

"You awaken the same feelings in me, my beloved," she said. "Come and love me, Lucas, make me your own once again."

After rising only long enough to remove his clothing, Lucas returned to her, his desire clearly evident. Lovingly,

Alanna ran her hand across his chest. Then her touch moved across his hip, her fingertip seductively following the scar she had noted the first time she had seen Lucas del Fuentes in Grady's hall. Even then, when she had told herself she hated him, she had been drawn to him. And now, in the space of a few weeks, he had come to mean more to her than life itself.

Her hand idly traveled farther, until it found itself stroking the proof of Lucas's throbbing need. Her light touch evoked a groan in him so primitive and filled with such craving that it incited her more, bringing her a yearning that seemed to threaten her very existence.

Languidly, Lucas guided her down toward the bed, towering over her like some proud stallion. Straddling her hips, he bent to place a kiss upon her throat, his lips dawdling when they came to her delicately formed collarbone.

"I want to sample you, *querida*." His voice was hoarse with wanting her, with longing to make her his if just for this one more night. "I want to savor all of you, to have the taste of you linger on my lips long after our lovemaking is through." Without waiting for her consent he began to turn his wishes into reality. His mouth seared her flesh as he moved downward, teasing and further exciting her already swollen nipples before his mouth descended farther yet.

Urged on by her whimpers of pleasure, Lucas explored each sensitive inch, every delicate fold of the woman he was worshiping. And then he lifted his head and brought his lips back to hers before starting all over again.

He loved her slowly and exquisitely, as if time had no constraints. Each moment of their prolonged, enravishing play was one of mutual joy and sweet, shared torment. When he finally suckled at her breast, his hand stroking the core of her femininity, Alanna began to writhe so violently beneath him that Lucas smiled, certain she had ascended to new levels of pleasure.

As she brushed her palms across his back and called his name in a broken whisper, he knew their moment had come. With an incendiary touch, he reverently parted her quivering thighs and lay between them, knowing that in an instant she would be his, totally and completely.

He entered her moist, secret center, the essence of her womanhood, filling her with his own unbridled masculine energy. Slowly, he began to stroke her with the most intimate part of his being, causing her to toss beneath him like a petal before the wind.

Now, he thought, beginning to increase the tempo that would call them to shared ecstasy, now was the moment to rectify his one regret, to set to rights the one thing their union had lacked, to shed his last inhibition. "I love you, Alanna," he gasped, his voice heavy and rasping with passion. "I have always loved you, *mi amor,* enough for a thousand lifetimes, enough to last me through all eternity."

"Oh, Lucas," she responded. The words caught in her throat as she rose, reaching for the sensual heights to which he beckoned her. "I love you, too, my dearest heart. Never have I loved anyone more, nor will I."

The words they uttered released not only the emotions they had hidden in the recesses of their souls, but their passion, as well. It spilled over, cascading around them like a fountain of life, eternal and potent, buoying them up and carrying them away to a distant shore where nothing existed but the rapture of their union. There they lingered in a mindless euphoria, experiencing pure sensation, no longer able to voice what they felt for each other but knowing it all the same.

Afterward, more sated than they had ever been, they lay in each other's arms, their limbs entangled every bit as much as their hearts.

"You will forever be a part of me, Alanna," Lucas said softly, stroking her long, pale hair, "the best part of me, *mi corazón.* And now that I have said it, let me tell you again. I love you, my sweet, wild Irish witch, now and always."

"And I you, Lucas." Alanna gave herself over to the elation of hearing those words tumble once more from his lips, the words she had seemingly waited a lifetime to hear.

"Then life is perfect," he whispered against the sensitive flesh of her neck. "Could any man ask for more?"

"Why didn't you ever tell me how you felt before?" Alanna asked, her voice saturated with all the contentment of a woman who has been well and recently loved.

"Did I have to say it for you to know how I feel?" Lucas chided gently.

"No, but—"

"How could I have told you what was in my heart, Alanna? How could I give voice to my emotions when the fates had decreed I would be going away, leaving you far behind? How could I speak to you of love when I could not give you commitment?"

"Yet you do so now," she said, sadness creeping into her voice, "when things have only become the worse."

"Perhaps I am being selfish, disclosing the secrets of my heart," he stated as his fingertips glided along the surface of Alanna's sleek leg. "Forgive me if I am, but I find I could not go away, never to return, leaving you in doubt. I want you to know how much I cared for you . . . how very much I loved you."

"Oh, Lucas," Alanna said. Tears brimmed along her thick lashes. "It is not fair that my life has cost yours, that I will go on while you will not! Each breath I take will be one you gave me, one of which I deprived you. I cannot bear the thought of it, my dearest love."

"You must understand something," Lucas whispered fervently. "While you live so do I, while your heart beats so does mine. The price I pay is but a small one, *mi corazón,* but if you wish to assure that any sacrifice I have made is worthwhile, you will do one thing for me, Alanna."

"What?" she asked, brushing away her tears.

"You will put this grief behind you and enjoy the life you say I have given you. You will not pine for me, Alanna. I would not like to think I saved you from Juan only to condemn you to everlasting despair. Do not do that to me, *mi vida,* or else I will never find paradise."

"You ask the impossible," she cried, clinging to him with all the desperation that was destroying her very essence.

"No," he responded gently, "I have seen your strength. Fitzhugh has told me of it, as well. If you want my soul to find peace, Alanna, you will do as I have asked. Remember this time, remember me, but do not allow it to interfere with your happiness. Your future smiles will be mine, *querida*. Do not be miserly with them."

"How could I have found my heart only to lose it again?" Alanna asked as tears rolled down her cheeks.

"You have not lost it, yet, *niña*," he said. He tenderly kissed the palms of her hands, setting her skin ablaze all over again. "Let us celebrate our love once more."

At her nod, he came to her, loving her with all the depth of his being. And amid whispered pledges of love, they found Eden again... and yet once again. Each time was more consuming than the last, more desperate, as well. But they no longer spoke of that. Instead, they immersed themselves in what they felt, one for the other, eventually finding renewal rather than an ending.

With the intensity of their enraptured lovemaking, Lucas and Alanna tried to hold back the dawn. But as the first gray mists of morning gathered outside, there was a movement in the passageway. They looked at each other and knew. It was time for her to go. Numbly, Alanna and Lucas donned their clothing. Then, in their last few seconds of privacy, Alanna threw herself into Lucas's arms, telling him by the way she held him that she never wanted to leave. In response, Lucas crushed her to his chest, his lips tracing patterns through her sunny locks until Alanna raised her head and her lips sought his.

With a groan, Lucas responded, and the two of them stood, pouring their souls one into the other. Caught up in the fever of the moment, they did not hear the cabin door open, until finally an embarrassed seaman coughed to alert them of his presence.

"*Diego espera,*" he said awkwardly. *Diego awaits.*

At his words, Alanna's pretty face fell, and Lucas stepped back from his love.

"Smile for me, Alanna, *mi amor*," Lucas said, his rich, deep voice as soft as the finest silk. "The last sight I have of you is the one I will carry in my heart for all time. I would not have it marred by your tears. Smile because we have enjoyed, if but for a brief time, what others never find. There is no reason to feel sorry for ourselves, merely to pity the rest."

Alanna looked at her beloved, her lips valiantly turning up ever so slightly. It was a tenuous smile at best, but her effort was for him, this man who loved her, and whom she loved so utterly in return.

"*Vaya con Dios, mi corazón*," he called softly as the guard escorted her to the door.

At the threshold, Alanna stopped and looked over her shoulder at him, her smile as brilliant as that of any angel. Then she was gone, and the door shut and locked behind her.

"*Vaya con Dios*," Lucas whispered again to the emptiness of his cabin. And then he began to wonder if, as Alanna had so recently suggested, God did not sometimes forget the existence of those who needed Him the most.

Chapter Seventeen

As the Spanish nobleman led her out on deck, Alanna glanced up at the sky. She could not believe the night had passed so quickly. Deep gray clouds hung low over the horizon, blocking the light of sunrise and making the dawn as heavy as her own heart, burdened as it was with painful regrets. No matter what she had promised Lucas, sorrow was foremost in her thoughts. Though the murky day seemed to echo her distress, Alanna found no comfort in it.

At the foot of the gangplank, she saw Devlin waiting with their horses. Yet as glad as Alanna was that she would not be alone on her journey, another part of her resented the gallowglass's presence. She could not help but think, had Devlin been the first to find her, he would have dealt with Juan's perfidy, not Lucas. If it had been Devlin, Lucas would not be returning to Spain under a death sentence! Still, there was no point in brooding, and she had no right to blame Devlin, however much she needed to share the guilt she bore. Slowly she descended the wooden platform to the dock, hating each successive step, knowing it took her farther from Lucas and closer to a future filled with desperate emptiness.

"I tried to reach you last night," explained Devlin, coming forward to drape Alanna's cloak over her shoulders, "but the guards would not let me aboard."

"There was no need," she said.

"So Diego finally told me, but I was worried—"

"There was no need," she repeated, her blue eyes wide, her voice strained. "It was useless to plead with Alonso, Devlin."

Perusing her features carefully, the Irishman nodded. Though Alanna appeared physically unharmed, her eyes were bright and her body tense with emotion. The sooner he got her away from the camp, the sooner she would recover, he decided. Abruptly, he drew Alanna toward Piobar, intending to help her to mount, but she stayed his effort and turned back to Lucas's mentor, who yet stood on the gangplank.

"Diego, I want you to know how sorry I am," she confessed. Her soft voice was awash with emotion, despite her vow to be strong. Although she was uncertain how much the nobleman would understand, Alanna nonetheless felt the need to explain. "I only wanted to have him for a little while, to love him as no one else could, but now I cost him everything."

Realizing how insignificant her words sounded, how futile her regrets were, Alanna fell silent, her eyes downcast, unable to meet the accusations she expected to see in Diego's eyes. But suddenly she felt the Spaniard gently pat her arm.

"It is God's will, child. I shall do what I can for him," the old aristocrat awkwardly assured her. Sorrow deepened the lines of his face as he struggled to make himself understood in this unfamiliar tongue. "But you must go."

Fighting back her tears, Alanna called on the courage of the bloodlines deep within her, raised her head, squared her shoulders and proceeded to where Devlin waited. She placed her small hand firmly in his, accepted his assistance and soon sat astride her horse, her back straight and chin held high. Then, for the first time, Alanna allowed herself to focus on the hundreds of sailors standing all about the ship, watching.

Small clusters of three or four, bunches of six or eight, larger groups of a dozen or more, single men isolated within the crowd, they waited silent and without expression, their eyes trained on her. She did not know what they had been told or if mere instinct had drawn them here this morning to watch her depart in disgrace, but their mute presence was singularly unnerving. Alanna recognized some of the faces from *La Rata*'s crew, others from the march to Killybegs and still more from their time here in camp, but none of the stony countenances acknowledged her. Each man refused to meet her eyes, each completely impassive as if withholding judgment.

Did they blame her? Alanna wondered, chilled by their silent scrutiny. It was not my fault, she wanted to scream aloud, yearning to defend herself against the unspoken charges until she looked deeper and saw the sorrow in their eyes, sorrow that originated in the selfsame pain that pierced her heart.

Lucas had been her lover for barely three weeks, but he was their friend, their leader, their compatriot. Just as he was lost to her forever, so, too, would these men be deprived of Lucas del Fuentes.

"Alanna?" called Devlin, noting her hesitation. He had promised Diego he would have her away early before there could be any trouble when the sailors brought Juan's body back to camp, but she seemed almost in shock, staring at the gathered crews. "Alanna, it is time to go."

Hearing her name amid the deafening quiet, Alanna turned to see Devlin's concerned eyes, and she nodded, yielding to his command. Slowly she urged Piobar forward. The anguished faces of the sailors imprinted themselves on her mind as she rode past them, refusing to look away, though she seemed to shrink within herself a bit more with every accusing glance.

When she was nearly out of camp, Alanna saw Pedro standing apart from the others, his visage clearly beset by misery. It was the final catalyst to release her sorrow. Without sound, she surrendered to the salty grief pouring from her eyes, making no effort now to stem the tide of tears. At least the veil of water obscured the path she and

Lucas had gamboled on with such carefree hearts as her horse followed Devlin's from the camp.

At the crest of the hill where the roads divided, Alanna stopped, however, and looked back. From this height, the *Girona* seemed smaller, almost too diminutive to survive the sea's power, certainly too fragile to carry her love away from her.

She could not leave Killybegs, she decided suddenly, wiping her tears with new determination, until she had witnessed the *Girona*'s departure for Spain. Until that happened, there could be hope for a miracle. Until that happened, her life would not be over.

"Devlin," she called, "we shall take this trail."

"Alanna, that way curves around the harbor close to the rocks along the hilltop. It is a longer route home. This road is the better one to Donegal," he protested, noticing sadly how exhausted she looked. As exasperated as he had been with her last night, he had loved Alanna for years and could not help but react to her pain. Even the way in which Alanna sat the saddle suggested the young woman would not have the stamina to travel long hours that day. Still, the more distance he could put between Alanna and Killybegs before they stopped for the night, the better he would like it. "Come on, let us go this way."

"No, Devlin. I cannot leave until they sail," she announced, turning Piobar in the direction she had chosen.

"Alanna, you promised that you would go this morning."

"I said I would depart the camp, and we have," she corrected icily. "I said nothing about leaving Killybegs."

For a moment the gallowglass saw red. Despite all he had put up with, all the sacrifices he had made to give her time with Lucas, Alanna still was not satisfied? The Spaniard was sailing off to a death sentence tomorrow and she wanted to watch him go? Damn it, at this instant Devlin half-wished he had killed del Fuentes himself. It was not that he had wished the man harm, but he wanted him out of Alanna's life once and for ever. Perhaps Alonso should have ordered his immediate execution, after all.

Forcing himself to remain calm, Devlin weighed his words carefully, finally deciding to be frank with his charge.

"You know I care deeply for you, Alanna, and would do almost anything to make you happy, but this idea is utter foolishness. We raced to Loughros More Bay when I heard the *Santa Ana* had been wrecked, because I knew you had to see for yourself. Then I went with you to Killybegs and stayed out of sight, allowing you and Lucas as much time together as possible, not interfering when I might have. Now, however, it is over. You cannot expect to see him again—even from the top of a hill. Why, the *Girona* will not be visible, where she is anchored now, no matter which road we take," the gallowglass said harshly, hoping his blunt words would bring her back to reality. "Accept the fact that del Fuentes is lost to you, Alanna, and the sooner you get on with your life, the better you will feel. To linger here will only deepen your misery."

"Perhaps you are right, but it does not matter, Devlin. My mind is made up. While I swear to you I shall not go down to the camp or try to interfere with the sailing, I cannot leave until the *Girona* departs these waters. From here, I will see her sail past after she takes to the seas," she stated. Her usually melodic voice was hard and uncompromising. "If you wish to return to Kevin's keep today, then go ahead. I assure you I can find my way back without your help."

Then she was gone, cantering down the dirt lane that ringed the harbor, leaving Devlin muttering angrily at the obstinacy of the female sex. He scowled. Why did they always have to persist in following their hearts when such a path only led to grief?

Truly, Alanna did not care one way or the other what Devlin chose to do. Her focus was totally inward as she rode away, the gallowglass forgotten amid her roiling thoughts.

The day seemed eternal to her, as she found herself beset by tender memories of the man who had shielded her body with his own long before they had admitted their love. Even when she had been naught but a prisoner sparking his fury, his concern for her welfare had made Lucas different, mused Alanna, recalling his ire in Grady's stable when he protected her from Juan's suggested cruelty.

During their days together Lucas had come to share himself with her without reserve, so that he had become far removed from the arrogant foreigner she had first encountered at Castlemount, unyielding before those who held his life in their hands. Images of his lean, muscled body, naked as when she had first seen him, haunted her as she went through the motions of setting up a small camp. Initially resisting the reminders of the past month, the young woman soon yielded to the bittersweet pain they brought, as she sat huddled on the hilltop, welcoming the vivid portraits of the past as a means of shielding her from the hurtful present. Lucas del Fuentes had attracted her at her uncle's keep, she acknowledged, delving into the recesses of her mind to picture him so golden and majestic. Even then his disdainful glances had set her on fire.

Fetching water from a stream swollen with the rains, she remembered the Spaniard's sympathy when he had tended her bruised wrist, and then his reaction when their roles were reversed, when she saw to his shoulder after the rebel attack. His deep, green eyes had held hers, sending unspoken messages, but she had not been attuned to them yet, and condemned him for his ancestry rather than accept him for the man he was. How foolish she had been. Alanna wished she could reclaim those days on the trail when distrust and hatred had so colored her reaction to him.

Later, gathering pine boughs for a pallet beneath the trees, she recalled Lucas coming to her after he had hauled Juan off her the first time. Quickly the anxiety in his emerald eyes had become passion, his comforting flesh firm and unyielding, transporting her to a world of desire she had never expected.

And what had she done? She had turned away from him the very next morning, rejecting all that he had offered, so afraid of his love that she had been unwilling to admit her own. Maybe she should have followed her instincts then and woken him with a kiss that morning. Her heart wept, aggrieved by what had transpired since, yet knowing she could not have sacrificed the joys they had experienced.

How could one balance the agony of loss with the splendor they had created? Alanna wondered, watching the sky darken at the approach of evening, but she heard no answer to her query. Then, as she sat before the small fire, the memories of the meals they had eaten together intruded. Mother Columbine's look of concern formed a poignant backdrop to the vision of Lucas in friar's robes, eagerly supping on bread and soup, though worry for his men had quickly suppressed his ravenous appetite. And then the night at Kevin's camp thrust itself to the forefront of her mind, and Alanna found herself ruing Lucas's demand to return to Alonso, spurred by a sense of honor that was so much a part of him that he refused to take her to wife. If only he had accepted Kevin's offer that night, her heart cried, ravaged by despair, but the past could not be changed any more than an imperfect world could be made new. Both had to be accepted as they were.

In the darkness before dawn, Alanna mourned alone, assuming the mantle of guilt that wove itself about her as her due. Indeed, had she not attracted Juan's attention from the first, albeit unconsciously, would Lucas not be a free man? Had she not selfishly traveled to Loughros Mor Bay to seek him out, would Juan not yet live? It was, in the end, her lustful appetites that had led her to confront Lucas, challenging him to take her, demanding that he abandon his scruples, promising no harm would come of it, only pleasure.

Briefly in the cold despondency of the blackest hours, Alanna knew there was no way she could possibly reach Spain to argue before Philip for Lucas's life but, even could she do so, she was all too aware that the ignominy of such an action on her part would shame her golden Spaniard. Offered such a reprieve, he would choose death over a life spared by her fervent importuning. No, there was nothing she could do.

And now, as the first rays of the pale sun rose, Alanna acknowledged the tragic consequences of her behavior, shouldering a loathsome weight she knew she would carry to her death. Lucas's life was forfeit for loving her. No one and nothing could change that. Theirs had been a love she had fought against, fearing its outcome from the start, and yet eventually it had been she who had called him like a moth to flame.

Yet their passions had flared so hot, there had been no tempering the fire, and now she must suffer, Alanna admitted. She watched the *Girona* glide by, her sails filled with the same cold wind that chilled Alanna's heart. She mourned the departure, knowing only that she had lost Lucas, and what was left of her life was insignificant.

Suddenly Devlin could no longer wait in the shadows. He had stayed close by, watching Alanna from a distance, unwilling to leave her alone yet wary of intruding on her mourning. Now, however, the damned ship had finally put to sea, and she needed him.

Riding toward her, he was aghast at her pale face and her languid air of resignation. Had he done wrong, permitting her this time apart? he wondered. But then, she had left him little choice. The Irishman dismounted and picked up Alanna's cloak from where it lay on the ground.

She observed his movements without reaction, permitting him to wrap the garment about her and lead her to her horse. This time, there was no argument about which way to travel. She followed the gallowglass without objection, her face turned firmly away from the harbor below, her eyes dry and unreadable.

"Once I get you back to Donegal, you will feel better," the Irishman promised as he shepherded their mounts onto the road to Donegal. At least he would do his damnedest to make her so, vowed Devlin silently, now that that Spaniard was at last out of her life.

Their return to Kevin's keep had been without incident, but Devlin's promise had not proven true. Sitting on the edge of her bed at Tur Muir, feet dangling listlessly from its side, Alanna Desmond O'Donnell had never felt more wretched. A piteous expression and unbraided hair hanging in disarray made her look small and fragile, like some forlorn fairy queen pining for past gaiety that would never be again.

"You've had naught of the posset I made you," chided Moira, bustling into the chamber to check on her faded charge.

"I wasn't of a mind for it," Alanna said. Her words were barely audibly and her once-bright eyes had lost their sheen.

"This can't go on," the elderly servant said, her tone made sharp by her concern. "Shall I tell you a tale?" Moira asked, seeking to soothe the woman, as she had the girl so many years ago, with one of Ireland's compelling legends.

"No," Alanna replied. "The sad ones would only make me feel worse, and those with happy endings are lies. They have nothing to do with the way of the world."

"This earth is magical only if magic already lives in our hearts. Deny that part of you, and you deny your very essence. You'll waste away until only a puddle of your tears remains if you continue as you are."

"What does it matter? I would almost prefer it," Alanna murmured.

"See here, Alanna, you were morose before you went north with Devlin, and you've come back to the keep in a worse state. 'Tis a fine man del Fuentes was, but you've always known, living at the water's edge as we do, that Mananaan MacLir gives us things only to snatch them away again. You should have remembered that and expected no more where your Spaniard was concerned. Now look at you. 'Tis as if the *sid* have cast a spell upon you, poor mortal child, making you yearn for joys no human can ever know. I'm about at my wits' end, lass.'' The older woman fetched Alanna's comb and began to run it through the uncharacteristically tangled gold tresses, hoping the act would put the girl in a better state of mind.

"You are well aware, Moira, that the *sid* have nothing to do with it. Things are worse than you have just painted them. Lucas didn't merely go home to Spain. The man I love is going to die because he saved my life. If I had known what it would have cost him, I would rather have died myself.''

"But you didn't," the faithful retainer insisted. "'Tis more often than not a woman's lot in life to go on when her man's been lost to her. You should have learned that lesson when Sean—"

"They are two different men," Alanna protested mildly. "And forfeiting a second love to death isn't made any easier for having sustained a like loss before."

"Aye, you've had it hard in your few years, but there can be happiness ahead.''

"Never!"

"Never is a long time, Alanna. When you thought you'd not ever allow another man in your bed, your Spaniard came along to make you smile. That can happen again, my lamb. There can be some man exists who will give you love. Why, right now, Devlin is waiting below in the solar to attend you.''

"Send him away. I've no wish to see anyone.''

"He's come morning, noon and evening since your return, and you've yet to receive him. The man is so concerned about you that he has brought some fine honey with him today, hoping to sweeten your life, or at least tempt you into eating. Imagine a fighting man out foraging honey for love of a lass. Surely you'll have some. We could mix it with milk or spread it on bread. Shall I fix a bit for you while you go below?'' Moira asked soothingly, finishing her task and replacing the comb in the chest at the foot of Alanna's bed.

"I have no desire to eat or drink. I don't want the honey and I don't want to see Devlin Fitzhugh!"

"Well, you're going to do so anyway," came a rumbling voice from the doorway. But unlike the Devlin of old, who had kept her regaled with funny, improbable tales, this man's face was haggard and drawn, his mouth set into a grim line. "Good morrow, Alanna," he said somberly.

"Devlin," she acknowledged reluctantly. Her eyes remained downcast so that she would not have to look at the change her circumstances had wrought in him.

"We have much to discuss," he announced, his voice ringing with determination. He motioned for Moira to leave the room, then quietly shut the door behind her hurriedly retreating form.

With a purposeful tread, he stalked over to Alanna and towered over her like an angry giant. Reaching out, he took her jaw in his large, viselike hand and tilted her face upward, forcing her gaze to meet his own. "It's going to stop, Alanna, and it's going to do so now."

"Then tell the pain within my heart to subside," she whispered, a tear cascading down the contours of her face, more angular now for her lack of appetite. "You don't understand what it is to feel as I do."

"Don't I?" he asked. His calm response was nevertheless laced with harshness. "When you hurt, Alanna, so do I. When your tears flow, I must brush aside my own. When you sigh pitifully, the sound reverberates deep within my heart. I know what you have suffered, lass. I've been at your side throughout the entire ordeal. But I know, too, that 'tis time to put your misery behind you. If you don't, you'll wither as surely as a summer flower during a drought. You can survive this, Alanna."

"Mayhap I don't care to," she uttered with quiet defiance. She was immediately sorry for her impulsive words when she saw the hurt flash through Devlin's clear, blue eyes. But despite his anguish, she meant what she had said all the same.

"I'll make you live," he said ominously.

"You can't," she stated.

"I won't allow you to starve yourself to death," he all but bellowed, reaching for the already scorned posset. "You're going to eat something, starting right now."

"It won't stay down," Alanna told him.

Her words gave him pause, and he studied her intensely, his hand immediately loosening its hold so that it became more a caress than a grip.

"You have to at least attempt it, Alanna," he said, the tone of his words almost tender now.

"I tell you I don't want to," she replied obstinately, regarding him with a wary eye.

"Have you ever thought," he asked softly, falling to his knees before her, taking her cold, limp hands, "that you could be carrying del Fuentes's child? You might think to starve yourself to death, Alanna, but would you deny life to the babe, as well?"

"A babe?" she echoed. Her eyes filled with wonder at the idea, and her demeanor became animated for the first time since she had left Killybegs three days before.

"Aye. Eat, Alanna," he urged, his handsome face wistful as he pressed a spoonful of nourishment to her lips. "If you will do it for neither yourself nor me, do it for your Spaniard and his child."

The next day, Alanna forced herself to at least nibble at every dish set before her, much to Moira's relief. Though the young woman was no longer given to bursts of spontaneous laughter or even sporadic smiles, a dim gleam appeared occasionally to dance in the recesses of Alanna's once-sparkling eyes whenever she thought of the possibility Devlin had raised. Should she be carrying Lucas's baby, something might be salvaged from this disaster. Perhaps her body could give her beloved the gift of immortality by allowing him to live on through his son. While he would never have any knowledge of their triumph over death, it would be a victory of sorts all the same.

In desperation, Alanna clung to the notion, praying to the Virgin and even St. Bridget to grant her this one small solace in the midst of her grief. In light of all that had occurred, she had a suspicion that Mother Columbine would understand, and perhaps even approve of such supplication. As for Friar Galen, he, too, would come to accept such a miracle. Dreaming of a child was the one thing that sustained Alanna's will to go on, the one thing that gave her hope.

For the most part, however, she continued to keep to her chambers, unmindful of the looks exchanged between the other inhabitants of Tur Muir at her unnatural behavior. She did not notice if the day became sunny and pleasant with the smell of harvest hanging in the cool, crisp air, because even that could not displace the gray mist shrouding her heart. Her emotional state was more akin to the storms that had battered the Irish coastline of late, forceful winds and dark, crashing waves drowning out the sounds of life and human existence.

Finally, his heart rubbed raw by Alanna's behavior, Devlin could bear it no more. Taking the advice of Moira and the friar, he went to her in a prodigious attempt to regain the woman who had been lost to them all.

"It pains me to see you continue in this fashion, Alanna," he said gently after he had gained begrudging admittance to her room. Placing his hands on her shoulders, he wished that, like some warlock of old, he could transfer his strength to her as he mumbled some ancient incantation. But he was only a man, and she was not even aware of that, he thought in frustration. Still, he would try to help her. Perhaps the magic of the human heart was more potent than the forgotten black arts of centuries gone by.

"I know you are overtaxed," he began tentatively, "any woman would be. But I want to pledge something to you that may alleviate some of the burden you carry. I swear, Alanna, that should you have this child, it will never want for protection and affection. I would treat it as my own."

"Why would you do such a thing?" the wraithlike blonde asked, fearing the answer he would give. Though Devlin's words had obviously been meant to comfort, they had only added to Alanna's dilemma by unleashing the guilt she felt where he was concerned.

"You know well that fostering is a common practice, sweetling," he replied. "In a land as harsh as this one, it often takes the resources of many to raise a child."

"Aye, so it does," the relieved Alanna commented, satisfied with his answer and grateful he had not declared himself as she had feared he would. That was an additional problem and one with which she was not yet capable of dealing. Wanting to see him gone before he could say anything further, she slipped out from beneath his hands. "I thank you for your offer of assistance. Should it become necessary, I will bear it in mind."

"Wait," Devlin ordered softly, capturing her fingers in his own. Suddenly he wanted her to know what was in his heart. "There is a far more important reason for the proposal I make. I would help raise and love this child because it would be your babe, Alanna. That's what would make it dear to me. Surely you realize that by now."

"Devlin," she protested, flustered by his acclamations of affection. "'Tis not meet to talk of such things just yet."

"When will we speak of them?" he persisted. He longed to comfort this woman, to hold her in his arms and assure her that together they would overcome all the obstacles that fate put in their way. His gravest mistake in the past had been waiting patiently, and he was unwilling to do so any longer.

"I don't know. Mayhap we never will," Alanna whispered. She did not want to hurt him, but was unable to lie to this man who had always held her happiness above his own.

"Don't say that, Alanna. I have to believe that time can change your mind," he said, relinquishing her hand. Then, heaving a sigh when she turned away from him, he went out of the room, leaving Alanna glad her solitude had been restored to her, but sorrier for the hopelessness of their conversation.

Despite Devlin's continued efforts to lighten Alanna's sorrow, to avow that he could make her know joy once more if she would but allow him to do so, it soon became apparent to him that his attempts were futile. In fact, he began to suspect his presence did little more than add to her unsettlement. Upon drawing such an unwelcome conclusion, Devlin discovered his tolerance for pain had reached a level that would allow him to absorb no more. He couldn't deal with Alanna's unhappiness and his own, as well, so he decided to take his leave of Tur Muir for a few days.

Outfitting one of Kevin's small boats, he thought to busy himself along the coast. He knew that the recent storms must have seen ships founder, and he had no doubt the seas had left riches scattered among the dross on the shore. A bit of salvaging would stand him in good stead, he decided. The chance existed that such an expedition would increase his wealth and enable him to have more to offer his blue-eyed beauty. At the very least, the exhausting work would occupy his body if not his mind.

As Devlin put out to sea, his handsome features grim while Kevin's keep faded in the distance, he was aware that he would carry visions of Alanna with him no matter where he went or what he did. And if fate was kind, his absence for a few days might teach the reluctant object of his love that she did indeed miss him, and she would be all the happier for his return.

Devlin's departure, however, did not leave Alanna in peace. Her self-imposed banishment from the daily goings-on at the keep came to an abrupt end when a clamor arose in the bailey early one afternoon two days later, signaling Kevin O'Donnell's return to his home. Normally his foster daughter would have left whatever task claimed her attention and gone running out to greet him, this large, gruff Irish rebel who had taken her into his heart as well as his home. But at that moment, she couldn't face him, couldn't recount the heartbreak that had been hers since last they had seen each other. Not when nature had made it plain that very morning that there would be no child, throwing an already grieving Alanna into further despair.

In her disconsolate state, Kevin's presence made her suddenly ashamed of her inability to cope with her tragedy. Hadn't the lord of Tur Muir always taught her to be strong? She didn't want to shame him with her weakness, yet with her crushing disappointment that morning, how could she be anything else but weak? If she could but wait a day or so before they talked, she might be able to do so with calm reserve. Hearing his booming voice in the great hall below, she prayed he would honor her wish to be left alone, out of love for her if not out of understanding.

Chapter Eighteen

"Devlin? Alanna?" Kevin's call echoed through the courtyard, but neither of those he sought answered, though the appearance of his two favorite wolfhounds, barking and throwing themselves at him, temporarily distracted Kevin from the oddness of it. Here he had returned, having neatly bested not only the MacWilliams but Bravingham, as well, and his loved ones weren't about to applaud his exploits! What sort of homecoming welcome was that? "Devlin? Alanna? Moira? By all that's holy, where are you hiding? Hallo!"

"For the love of sweet Mary, will you quit your cater-wauling, you demented old fool? No one with half a mind would come near you with that racket you're making," scolded Moira as she scurried to calm the lord of Tur Muir. "I heard you outside in the kitchens!"

"And why not give voice to my good humor, woman? 'Tis glad I am to be home after being so long away," bellowed Kevin all the more loudly. "Though if truth be told, I would have expected Alanna to be quick to greet me and hear the concessions I've wrung from Cordelia and that weasel Grady. How he could have been sired by the same man that fathered Alanna's mother is beyond comprehension. But never mind that, where are she and Devlin?"

"Devlin is out scavenging with your crew in the north, and Alanna is not available at the moment, but come inside and I'll pour you some *poitin*," urged the old nurse.

Deciding the fastest way to assuage the man's wounded pride was to give him the attention he desired, she determined to let him enjoy a bit of pleasurable bragging before she revealed Alanna's sorrow. The girl was upset enough without having to deal with the O'Donnell ranting at her right now. "I dearly want to hear every detail of that English witch's humiliation, though I still believe death would not have been too great a sentence for betraying Alanna as she did."

"Nay, why kill the woman when I was able to make her live in dread, cowering not only at the idea of Spanish invaders, but Irish and English, as well?" Kevin guffawed as he followed Moira into the hall. "I tell you, one would barely recognize the new Cordelia, so thoroughly changed is her behavior."

"Oh, get on with you, milord. Unless you've turned sorcerer, you will not make me believe that." The nurse poured liberal drams of the Irish drink for each of them. "She's too mean to be affected by another's opinion."

"True, I used some sleight of hand and misdirection, as well as a bit of force, but how else could I have convinced Castlemount's Anglo neighbors that the MacWilliams's loyalties were not as pro-English as Cordelia had led them to believe?"

"I don't understand your fancy phrases. Speak plainly."

"All right. The lads and I were a trifle weary, missing the excitement of scavenging, so we decided to claim some booty from the English landholders in Connaught, after hiding our small boat in a cove. We started with Bravingham, carrying away most all of his horses, sheep and cattle and hiding them on MacWilliams land in the days before I visited Bravingham himself," explained the O'Donnell. A broad grin split his weathered face at the memory of that encounter. "I must confess, considering that I called on him after midnight one evening, he was quite hospitable. Indeed, after a bit of conversation, he was ever so ready to forswear any claim on Alanna and to vow to remain a bachelor till death."

"He swore that?"

"Aye, though to be truthful, the only other choice I offered him was losing those body parts that are most essential to the married state," admitted the white-haired Irishman, quaffing his *poitín*. "I imagine he would rather live as a man and dally with the maids than marry as a eunuch."

"And what about Grady and Cordelia?"

"Oh, I let the MacWilliams stew for two weeks, raiding most of the other estates allied with the English crown, always letting it be known that Cordelia's kin were the ones responsible."

"Didn't the English soldiers bother you?"

"No, they were too busy riding hither and yon slaughtering Spaniards to worry about a few Irish rebels. We helped a few of those poor devils escape, but I expect that most of them hid from us just as urgently as from the English."

"The MacWilliams?" reminded Moira, her impatience growing. Any minute Alanna might choose to appear, and Kevin shouldn't see her without knowing about her and del Fuentes.

"Well, by this point, Cordelia and Grady were convinced that Alanna had died and I was after their lives in revenge. I permitted them to quake a while, occasionally stealing from them, but mostly freeing their neighbors' cattle to be found with the MacWilliams's mark newly burned into their rumps. That was finally what gave me the idea."

"What?"

"How better to haunt Grady for the rest of his life with his heinous betrayal of Alanna than to make him face it daily?" asked Kevin, his pride at his cleverness clear in his tone. "My men waylaid the spineless weasel when he was riding his lands and brought him to our camp in the woods where I put the O'Donnell brand on his ugly hide."

"My lord, you branded him?" Moira didn't know whether to be horrified or to applaud. While it was com-

mon for some landowners to brand slaves and criminals
Kevin had never been known to engage in the barbari
practice.

"And what better way to make certain the contemptible
blackguard never forgets that he owes me his life and I ca
claim it any time I choose?" demanded Kevin, angered tha
Moira didn't appreciate the subtle justice of his judgment
"The man is disfigured but still alive, and now Cordeli:
believes not only that I am as much of a barbarian as she
has always suspected, but that I could easily return and
brand her, as well. None of her neighbors or relatives wil
have anything to do with her, since I made sure to visit then
and lead them to the rest of their missing herds on the land
of Castlemount."

"Then your time was well spent."

"Indeed, Cordelia was so accommodating when she
woke to find me in her chamber, she offered me anything
desired, including herself, but I merely had her sign Cas
tlemount over to Alanna and rename it *Radharc Alainn*.
Naturally I left a complement of men there to protec
Alanna's interests, and the MacWilliams now know better
than to do anything but cooperate with them."

"I commend your efforts. I doubt anyone else could have
achieved so much," praised Moira, "though I must tell you
I fear that Alanna will not care about any of it."

"Why? What's wrong? Is she ill? Why didn't you tell me
before?" raged Kevin, bolting to his feet in exasperation
Sean's widow was the sole reason he had lingered in Con
naught, spreading fear and extracting vengeance for her
mistreatment, but now it appeared he would have done
better to have come home sooner. "Where is Alanna? I
would see her at once."

"Not until I explain." Moira blocked the lord's path to
the stairs. "She is well enough in body, but her spirit is an
other matter, and I won't have you sending her off into
tears again, blundering about without knowing what has
happened to her. Now sit down there and listen for a
change."

Openmouthed at the nurse's forceful manner, the O'Donnell nodded curtly and settled himself once more, clearly on edge. "Very well, but be brief," he instructed. His heart was suddenly chilled with a fearful apprehension that grew as Moira spoke quietly, telling him all she knew. By the time the old woman had finished, his white head was sunk low in his hands, his excitement forgotten.

"I won't let her give up now, no matter how much she hurts. When you weaken in Ireland, you invite Death to take you. With all Tur Muir has already lost, I will not lose Alanna, too," he said, finally looking at Moira as he rose to his feet. "I will go to her."

But his tread on the stone steps was heavy, his pace slow as he climbed upward, worried how Alanna's grief had affected her. He would not let the vagaries of fate prevent her from grasping the very fiber of life and wringing from it all that she could, be it the sweetest of wines or the most bitter. Only Alanna could determine her portion, but determine it she must. She could not give up living merely because it was hard work. That was not the way of a Desmond or an O'Donnell.

"What's this I hear about you doing so poorly?" boomed a thunderous though not unkind voice as the door to Alanna's chamber crashed forcibly inward to admit the indomitable Kevin O'Donnell. Her recent hopes of putting her foster father off now fruitless, Alanna rose quietly to greet him.

"Well?" he asked when no explanation was forthcoming.

"Aye, Kevin, 'tis true. I've not been myself of late," Alanna said, stretching on tiptoe to plant a dutiful kiss on his weathered, smooth-shaven cheek.

"You don't look much like yourself, either," the middle-aged warrior said with a disapproving snort. "I've never known you to surrender to misfortune, Alanna. Such behavior is not seemly when you consider the blood that flows through your veins. What are you about, girl? Ire-

land is a nation beleaguered by misery. To submit meekl
to suffering, to wish for death, is tantamount to treason, t
betraying the rest of us who struggle mightily to go on in th
face of unkind fate."

"I hurt, Kevin," Alanna protested. She wanted him t
understand yet she was reluctant for him to see that she wa
grieving more for Lucas and the child that would not b
than she had mourned for Sean and her father.

"Aye, I know it, lass," the gentle rebel said, taking he
hand in his own and leading her to the bench runnin
alongside one wall. "Could I have raised you since you wer
young, loved you as my own daughter, my own flesh an
blood, and not comprehend your pain? When you firs
came here, didn't I observe for myself that you were wear
of the war the English waged on Curran? Yet didn't I als
realize how much you pined for your parents, feeling guilt
that you enjoyed peace while they were tormented by dev
astation? I knew all that and more, Alanna. But, more im
portant, I saw a spark of survival burning within your sou
so brilliant that it touched me and made me respect a mer
lass for the courage she displayed. Do not allow presen
circumstances to douse that spark, Alanna. I grant you, a
man as admirable as your Spaniard deserves to b
mourned. But not here, daughter, and not now, not in a
country that is merciless to those who lack strength. Her
a hint of frailty does not evoke clemency. Instead, it call
forth more destructive forces to stamp out those among u
who are already half-spent."

"Aye, Kevin. What you say is true," Alanna mur
mured, resting her tired head against the man's broad
shoulder, willing, after the effort he had made, to say
something that would appease him. "But I am trying, truly
I am."

"Then you must do so all the more." He awkwardly
patted her hand and recollected with sorrow the events tha
had precipitated the last time he had been called upon to
give her solace. Squeezing his eyes shut for an instant, he
brushed the past and memories of Sean's death aside, hop-

ing that Alanna would be able to do the same with her grief in the months to come.

"There's a good, brave lass," he said at last. "Now come along with me! 'Tis a rare, fine day, and a walk in the sunshine will do you some good. Besides, I've yet to tell you of my sojourn with your mother's brother and that harridan he has taken to wife."

With that, he guided her through the doorway and down the steps to the solar, descending to the Great Hall and finally out into the bailey, where he hoped the golden rays of the sun would alchemize her leaden spirit into a glittering gold.

Tucking her hand in the crook of his elbow, Kevin led Alanna forward, slowly circling the perimeter of the keep's courtyard. Kevin did not hurry her, but let his foster daughter set their pace. That she was still deeply troubled was obvious, and he sought for a way to assure her of her value in their lives, his, Moira's and Devlin's. Perhaps it was time he spoke of the gallowglass, he mused as Alanna turned toward him.

"You were going to tell me about Grady," the dispirited lass prompted. She wanted the tale over and done with so she could retreat to her quarters once more.

"Aye, so I was. But before I do that, I've a mind to discuss something else," Kevin replied, worried by Alanna's extreme pallor, exposed to him by the sunlight. He couldn't let her fade away without trying to open her heart to the love that had been waiting all along. "There's been a thought clawing at my peace of mind ever since Moira mentioned it before we set out for Elly Cove."

"What is that?" Alanna asked, snapping her head around to scrutinize Kevin's face, searching for some clue as to the subject he was about to broach.

"We should have learned something from that incident with Bravingham. 'Tis time you chose a man and wed," the chieftain said. He ignored the shock and hurt that descended upon Alanna's delicate features and steeled himself to continue. He'd left her alone too long after Sean's death. It would be better if he addressed the future now, before she became too accustomed to mourning again. "You need someone to look out for you, lass. I won't be around forever, and I'd like to see you settled."

"Kevin, don't speak of this now," Alanna pleaded, trying unsuccessfully to wriggle her hand from his grasp.

"This might be the best time," he pronounced with as much determination as sympathy. "You can't go on like this. You require something to ease your heart. I understand that while I was gone, Devlin Fitzhugh took good care of you, Alanna. 'Tis obvious to all but you that you own a piece of the man's heart. And he could make you content, and protect you against misfortune, both now and long after I have gone in search of my eternal reward. Devlin has been your friend, daughter, but have you ever thought of him as a man?"

"No!" she exclaimed in a rush of breath, needing desperately to put an end to this conversation. She would not talk of such things, not today when she was mourning not only Lucas but the possibility of ever bearing his child. Under such circumstances, she considered the notion profane, indeed a sacrilege. She had to get away from it at all costs. But with Moira, then Devlin himself, and now Kevin besieging her, urging her to betray Lucas while he might yet live, there was nowhere in the keep that promised her peace. Not even her bedchamber, the burrow in which she had recently immured herself, provided any slender hope of solace.

"Then I suggest you do so, dearling," Kevin was saying, unaware of the turmoil he had created within her already-fragile soul.

"Mayhap I will," Alanna lied with deceptive tranquillity. She was willing to say or do anything in order to remove herself from Kevin and the suffocating atmosphere of Tur Muir. "But not just yet. I hadn't realized how much I missed the sun's cheerful, warming rays. At present, I find I only want to enjoy them, savor them and store them up against the darkness of impending winter. And now that I am out and about, I've a mind to see the ocean, as well. That, too, is something of which I have deprived myself, a foolish thing when you consider how the O'Donnells have always derived so much from the sea. Would you mind if I left you to walk down to the water's edge?''

"Not at all," Kevin replied kindly, releasing her hand. As he watched his foster daughter pass through Tur Muir's gate, her step as stately as that of any queen, he congratulated himself on the manner in which he had handled the girl and her grief. Moira had told him that ever since her return from Killybegs, Alanna had been dispirited, exhibiting no interest in anything or anyone around her. The serving woman, Devlin, even Friar Galen had spoken to her, and all to no avail. But now, after his talk, she had yearned to see the ocean. Surely that was a positive thing! A strong-headed lass, Alanna had merely needed a firm hand, an observation he'd pass on to Devlin Fitzhugh, as well. The O'Donnell had no doubts, as he mounted the steps to the Great Hall, that he had just set his foster daughter upon the road to healing.

It was not the path to the beach Alanna took, however, when she left the keep behind. Rather, she had followed the rocky trail that wound up the precipitously steep cliff that formed Tur Muir's natural western defense.

She had thought this place, with its broad view of the waters that traveled in swift currents to mingle with those of Lucas's route to Scotland, would bring her a measure of tranquillity, would somehow give her a sense of closeness to the man who had kidnapped her heart.

But Alanna found no such peace as she stood at the edge of the sheer stone bluff rising out of the frothing surf below. The seeming endlessness of the seas and the unceasing line of the horizon made her feel the vast distance that separated her from her beloved all the more acutely.

She had expected the rhythmic lapping of the waves to remind her of the steady beat of Lucas's heart when she had laid her head atop his powerful chest in the aftermath of

love. Instead, the churning waters beneath her did little
more than reflect her own turbulent emotions. And the
brutality of the sea, as it slapped at the jagged rocks ringing the sharp, uneven base of the cliff, put her in mind of
nothing more than her own buffeting at the hands of fate.
And fate it must have been, she decided, for surely God
would never have been so cruel as to deliver Lucas to her
arms only to abruptly take him away again.

Even the air surrounding her conspired to keep Alanna
from finding comfort. When she tried to whisper Lucas's
name into the breeze, foolishly trying to deceive herself into
believing that the invisible current would bring the murmur to him, a gust of wind arose to throw it back in her
face, the keening sound it made echoing the bereavement
she felt. Nor did the sea breeze carry Lucas's soft caress
across the waters to her. Instead, cold fingers tugged dis-
respectfully at her hair and clothing, making them flap
harshly against her in the most punishing fashion, pushing
her insistently forward.

No, this place brought her no respite. It merely renewed
her agony as she calculated where Lucas might be now. Had
de Leiva's force left Scotland and landed in Spain yet? And
if it had, was this the moment Lucas was facing his doom,
the unjust destiny he had called down upon his own head
as a result of his devotion to her?

From experience, Alanna knew that when one grieved,
each day that passed made things seem a bit better than the
last. It was a slow process, yet progress was made all the
same. But in this instance, she realized, her uncertainty
would not allow that to occur. Each morning when she
arose, she would ask herself if this was the day that would
see her golden lover's death. And not getting an answer, she
would raise the same question upon the morrow, existing
in fresh, lingering torment, as though she was being forced
to face his execution again and again each time the sun
peered over the eastern mountains.

No, time would not cause her to feel better. Hadn't each
succeeding dawn already only made things worse until to-

day when it was not Lucas alone who caused Alanna's eyes to brim with stinging tears as the wind howled about her, mocking the desperation that had sent her climbing to this isolated perch? No, today she had been confronted with the reality forced upon her that morning. Her beloved would not live on in his child. The finality of death had emerged victorious. And perhaps the black horse of ancient lore had grown so powerful that it sought to claim another victim, as well, Alanna thought, studying the seething, writhing waters beneath her.

How easy it would be. A brief step was all it would take. As for the pain of landing on the cruel rocks below, it could not be any worse than her present anguish. She could give herself to the ancient god who had brought Lucas to her, only to bear him away again. It would be over in an instant, and then sweet oblivion would be hers.

Or would it? she wondered suddenly, fighting the temptation that threatened to overwhelm her. Friar Galen and the church had taught her about the fires of hell. Yet when she considered it, could damnation's everlasting suffering compete with the agony of existence without Lucas?

But taking her own life would mean an eternity without him, Alanna realized with a shaky start. She quickly placed the foot she hadn't been aware of lifting back on solid ground as she recoiled from the abrupt precipice's rim. Such an infinite duration would be a hell, indeed. She loved Lucas too much to chance such a thing. Her desire to put an end to her life was nothing more than selfishness, she decided. It had been ordained as her lot to endure, just as it was his to die. Could she throw away an eternity together because she was not strong enough to bear a transitory hurt, searing though it was?

Kevin had been right. To give in to the ocean's seductive enticement to put an end to her mortal existence would have been a betrayal of all those who had struggled to preserve her life. Her father, mother, Kevin, Sean, Moira, Devlin and, of course, Lucas had all prized her safety. Who was she to judge them wrong? Above the wind whipping around her head and the chaos of her own confused thoughts, she heard Lucas's last words to her, exhorting her to go on and to be happy, demanding that she not make his death a vain sacrifice. Loving him as she did, Alanna had no choice but to comply with his wishes.

"I will do as you asked, my dearest heart," she affirmed softly against the discordant breeze and the pounding of the surf. And then, despite the ferment around her, Alanna Desmond O'Donnell finally knew the beginning of peace.

Sinking to her knees, she gratefully recognized her newly sprung tears were those of relief and not of sorrow. She had survived the crisis, proved her mettle, passed the test that had been ordained for her. Not only had she accepted the earthly purgatory set for her, she had demonstrated that the effort others had made on her behalf had not been foolish and groundless. It would not be for naught that Lucas had given his life for hers.

"I will not come to you, Mananaan MacLir," Alanna shouted defiantly, her voice competing with the demanding roar of the still beckoning waves. Throwing back her head, she braved the wind as she continued her denial of death and grief and surrender. "Look for another bride, I will not be yours. I am faithful to Lucas del Fuentes and the vow I made him. You may have carried him from me, and there is to be no infant. But as long as I exist, he lives, drawing a breath with each beat of my heart."

Although she welcomed the briskness of the winds that hurried her back to Kevin's keep, Alanna could not deny the chill that still pervaded her soul, despite her intention to look forward and not back. She knew she was more fortunate than many, having been deeply loved twice in her life, but that splendid part of her existence was now over. From this moment on, Kevin, Castlemount and, within the boundaries of a friendship, Devlin would be her only concerns. She had promised Lucas she would go on and she would, but she'd not expect happiness.

At dinner that evening, the young widow struggled hard to be attentive to Moira and Kevin, a less difficult task than she had imagined, since the O'Donnell worked tirelessly to make her smile, recounting his adventures in Connaught with deliberate whimsy. Yet the image of Lord Bravingham on his knees, pleading for permission to wrap a blanket about his scrawny nakedness, while initially amusing, only led to memories of the Spaniards' attack on the English camp and her remembered dread that Lucas had been killed.

When she saw Kevin's concerned eyes upon her, Alanna decided abruptly that he deserved to know more about the man who had replaced his son in her heart. He and Lucas had liked each other on meeting, she recalled, but now Kevin would learn how good a man Lucas truly was.

With simple words and an easy grace, Alanna shared the tale of her journey with Devlin to Loughros Mor Bay and the love she had encountered there. Strangely enough, in a way she would never have thought possible, the airing of her most precious memories of Lucas made them vibrant, giving them a new texture, revitalizing her golden Spaniard in her mind. By the time she excused herself to retire, Alanna was filled with a blessed peace, living once more in the joy she and Lucas had created. For the first time since that awful night in Killybegs, her sleep was not a fitful one. Even her dreams were gentle as she reclaimed from her memory the featherlike kisses Lucas had oft used to tease her.

She slept undisturbed until the weak rays of the November sun peeped into her solar, causing Alanna to snuggle deeper into the downy warmth that caressed her. Slowly she wondered at the peculiar absence of the heavy heart to which she had become accustomed, until she remembered her debate upon the cliff. She had decided to go forward with her life!

Yet reluctant to swing her feet from out of her warm cocoon to confront a cold floor, Alanna drifted pleasantly amid thoughts of the weeks in which she had awakened

beside Lucas. He, too, had loved to cuddle beneath the
blankets, she recalled, her body warming at the bittersweet
memories of the heat that flamed at their couplings.

But he didn't share her bed this morning, except in her
thoughts. She might as well rise and break her fast with
Kevin before he went out to inspect his lands. Descending
the stairs half an hour later, she heard Devlin's voice.

The sound of it gave her pause. He was back, and she
would have to apologize to him, Alanna realized. He had
only wanted to help her through her grief, not hurt her
further, she knew. He was the kindest of men, and with all
he had done for her, how could she deny his suit? But she
knew as she wavered on the threshold of the Great Hall that
was what she must do. Perhaps, Alanna decided, she
should leave Kevin and Devlin to talk between themselves
and come back later.

"You can't *not* tell her," Devlin was arguing.

"She expected him to die anyway once he reached Spain.
So, if he was drowned instead of executed, what difference
does it make?" disputed Kevin, his voice hoarse with tension. "Del Fuentes is lost to Alanna either way, but by not
telling her of the *Girona*'s wreck, I'll let him live a little
longer in her mind instead of her memory. Is that so
wrong?"

"Until she knows he *is* dead and feels that pain, Alanna
won't heal. That is what happened with Sean. Like the rest
of us, she was so certain of a victory at Smerwick, it took
her months to accept Sean's death there and years to get
beyond it. It is not fair to deceive her."

"Devlin is right, Kevin," announced Alanna, entering
the hall. Her eyes were filled with tears, her voice barely
audible. "I overheard enough to guess—Lucas is dead, isn't
he? Tell me the truth."

The gallowglass looked at Kevin for orders, but receiv-
ing no sign, he turned to Alanna and nodded.

"I am sorry, but the *Girona* did not make Scotland. She
sank off the Giant's Causeway in Antrim. There were no
survivors."

"None? Alonso, Pedro, Lucas, all gone? Have you been there to see for yourself?" It was a question she hadn't meant to ask, but still it had come unbidden, a desperate appeal for hope.

"No, I knew most of those men, some as friends. They had lost everything already. How could I take anything else from them?" Devlin asked, referring to the practice of scavenging from wrecks and the dead they left ashore. "I met up with Daugherty and MacLaughlin at Sligo, though, and they had been up there. Near thirteen hundred men, washed up on the beach, not a sign of life except for those picking over the bodies. The ship was gone."

"But maybe a few survived. You've both told me stories of strange tides that can carry a man far up or down the coast from a wreck," Alanna protested, clinging to a dream she knew was hopeless. "Why can't I go up there and be certain?"

"No, Alanna. He is gone along with all the others," said Kevin softly. Rising slowly, he came toward her and opened his arms. "Cry if you will, rant and rave, curse the skies and the seas, Alanna, but you must let Lucas go."

"I'm not ready." She wept softly.

"Would you have him linger, unhappily bound to an earthly existence by your selfishness, Alanna?" asked her foster father, alluding to the old legend that a soul could not soar to heaven until those whom it loved gave their leave.

"No, of course not, but—"

"Del Fuentes loved you unconditionally. From what you've told me, he also saved your life, protecting you from Alvarez and surrendering his own life because of that love. Maybe he died off Ireland because God couldn't bear to take him so far away from you, but for whatever reason, you have to accept the fact that he is dead."

"I had him so briefly," protested Alanna, "but he will always be a part of me."

"Release his soul, child," soothed Kevin.

"All right," whispered the young woman. "Lucas, I relinquish you, though I'll never stop loving you, and one day

we'll meet again. But, for now, my dearest heart, be on
your way. I know I can't come with you.''

Closing her eyes tightly, she flew into Kevin's embrace
and made no protest when he caught her up and moved to
his chair, cradling her gently. For a moment, Devlin
watched foster father and daughter, torn by the grief they
represented, the love they shared. Then he shook his head
at the injustice of it all, an injustice that prevented him
from giving Alanna the comfort she needed, an injustice
that rent at his soul far deeper than the untimely death of
Lucas del Fuentes.

Chapter Nineteen

"You sent for me, Kevin?" asked Devlin as he strode into the Great Hall the next morning. Standing strong and virile as ever, the steadfast gallowglass nevertheless gave evidence to the strain these last few weeks had brought him, yesterday, perhaps, being the worst of all. His face was meant to be an impassive mask but it betrayed him, evincing hints of weary disappointment in the lines about his eyes and mouth. Yet for all that, Devlin Fitzhugh was a warrior, and therefore ready to obey his chieftain's command.

"Aye, there's a task to be undertaken and very few to whom I would entrust it," responded the O'Donnell. His hand moved from the arm of his chair to absently stroke the head of one of the massive wolfhounds always underfoot.

"You can't mean to tell me that you want me to go to Antrim and search for the Spaniard's body!" exclaimed Devlin. Surely someone in the north country would see the corpses had a decent burial if only out of pragmatism and not charity. As for himself, he had had enough of del Fuentes. While alive, the man had played havoc with his life, and his memory was sure to linger, haunting Devlin's future for some time to come.

"I would not ask that of you," Kevin replied quickly, seeking to alleviate Fitzhugh's anxiety as he signaled for the man to take a seat. "Nay, not even to appease Alanna would I order such a thing. You have suffered enough on her account already."

"Has she begged it of you, then?" Devlin inquired. Curiosity baited him so, that he could do little else but ask the question despite the dreaded answer he might receive.

"She has not spoken of the matter," the O'Donnell replied, "though I fear she dwells silently upon it. Still, it is not Alanna, dear to me as she is, who concerns me at the moment. We've another problem before us, one that could destroy the lives of all who call Tur Muir their home."

"What is that?" demanded Devlin, a soldier's territorial glint illuminating his blue eyes. His hand unconsciously moved to the hilt of his sword. At present, he welcomed the idea of action of some sort, longing to wield a weapon rather than merely nurse the injuries he had sustained in his recent battle of the heart.

"Word has reached me that there are still Spaniards abroad along the coastline," Kevin began, "although the number already slaughtered is beyond belief."

"What has that to do with Tur Muir?" Devlin asked, taking the mug of ale a serving girl placed in front of him, completely oblivious to the interest shining in the wench's speculative eyes.

"A few of the poor bastards have been found by the English on Irish lands," Kevin announced grimly. "And though the lords of the estates in question had no idea as to the Spaniards' presence, Elizabeth's men have seized the happenstance as an excuse to take punitive action.

"The Irish nobles have been accused of aiding enemies of the English crown. Some have been arrested. One was slain as he protested his innocence. Nearby villages were set to the torch, women raped, men and lads killed. Fields heavy with harvest were so thoroughly destroyed that there is nothing left to fill the bellies of those remaining when winter's deathly cold descends. The brutality was swift and unwarranted. I will not give the English a reason to attack Tur Muir. I want you to scour the northern areas of O'Donnell lands for stranded Spanish. Seamus will be sent south and Dermott to the eastern borders."

"And what are we to do if we discover such foreigners?" Devlin asked, ready to perform any deed required of him to protect his home and Alanna, as well.

"I want no innocent blood on my hands if it can be avoided," Kevin pronounced with a heavy sigh. "Bring anyone you uncover back to the keep, and we will hide him until we can find a way to get the pitiful devil to his homeland."

"Concealing Spaniards here at Tur Muir puts us as much at risk as allowing them to roam our soil," Devlin commented. His tone was pragmatic, but his emotions were roiling. Hadn't the sons of Spain already caused damage enough? Devlin had no tolerance left for Spaniards after what they had wrought in his life. And yet, Kevin was willing to take another grave risk on their behalf. "Why would you do such a thing?" he demanded.

"For the most part, these are brave souls who have already suffered overmuch. I would not be the cause of additional pain."

The younger man was about to protest, but then he thought of those he had known at Killybegs and the grudging admiration they had earned, Lucas foremost among them. He had to concede that Kevin was not wrong in what he intended to do. Still, the gallowglass could not honestly say that he liked Kevin's dictate.

"When do you want me to leave?" he asked quietly, raising his cup to hide his frown of dissatisfaction.

"As soon as you summon the others and explain the situation," Kevin replied. "When de Leiva departed, the large English force amassed to engage him in battle was dissolved. Now there are numerous small bands of men who feel they have been cheated of war traveling the coastline. The sooner this thing is attended to, the better we will be."

"Aye," Devlin stated with a somber nod of his head. "I'll see to it as quickly as possible."

He was on his way out of the cavernous chamber when Kevin halted him.

"Godspeed, Devlin Fitzhugh," the rebel chief called out with more understanding of Devlin's emotional situation than he had allowed his friend and second in command to see. "And take cheer, man. There may be no one but our own on O'Donnell lands."

A short while later, provisions gathered and Dermott and Seamus already dispatched, Devlin crossed the bailey on his way to the stables. His graceful, catlike step and his concentration upon the mission ahead made him look like some predator. However, a slender form in saffron, glimpsed from the corner of his eye, gave him immediate pause and banished all other thoughts.

There stood Alanna, the sleeves of her smock rolled up and the top lacing of her overlying tunic undone as she saw to the cleaning of Tur Muir's courtyard. Not content to merely issue orders, she had taken up a broom herself and was employing it with such vigor that it appeared as if she were seeking to sweep away not just the debris scattered about, but her own demons, as well.

Despite the reasons she might have for throwing herself so energetically into such a mundane task, the sight of the Irish beauty once more taking part in the daily goings-on of the keep warmed Devlin's heart. Without even thinking about it, he approached her, drawn to her like a lodestone to the North Star.

Only when his shadow crossed the path of her broom did the industrious blonde become aware of him. Raising her head, she greeted him, trying to strike a balance between warmth and reserve. She owed this man much, but Alanna was painfully aware that her obligation to Devlin Fitzhugh included being careful not to inadvertently raise hopes in his breast that could never be fulfilled.

"Good day to you, Devlin," she said, fighting the urge to look away from him out of guilt over being unable to return his love.

"'Tis a good day now, lass, coming unexpectedly upon you as I have," the handsome gallowglass responded with a smile that, despite the light flirtation of his words, was so small his one dimple remained hidden from view.

"Aye, well, there are matters that beg my attention, and I can put them off no more," Alanna replied with a hapless shrug, sad at no longer feeling comfortable in the company of the man who had been such a dear friend. "However, I suppose I should be grateful for something to keep me busy."

Inspired by Alanna's realization that there were things she could no longer ignore, Devlin yearned to tell this lovely female that he would be only too grateful for the chance to distract her in another manner entirely. But instead, he merely shook his head and drove the wistfulness from his heart before he answered her. "I would think 'tis best to keep yourself occupied," he said. He was hesitant to pressure Kevin's foster daughter when she still appeared so fragile and was only just beginning to make her way back to them.

"Mayhap you should try it, as well," Alanna suggested softly, wishing it was within her power to give Devlin the happiness he sought, the joy he so richly deserved.

"That's just what I'm about to do," he retorted. His manner was almost curt, stung as he was by the not-so-hidden message of Alanna's words. But then, he knew she had spoken only out of concern for his well-being and would never willingly set out to hurt him. His half smile returned, and he continued in a gentler tone. "I'm off to ride the northern border for a bit at Kevin's request. Will you be all right while I'm away?"

"Aye, I'll be fine," she assured him. She wondered if Kevin was sending Devlin from the keep only to give her a respite from the self-reproach that plagued her each time the gallowglass looked her way. But the reason behind her foster father's order didn't matter, she decided practically. The result would be the same, and Alanna was thankful for it. "Now then, I don't want to detain you with my prattle. I'll be here when you return."

"Aye, I know you will, lass. Without you, Tur Muir would not be home for me," he said, no longer able to suppress what was in his heart. Conscious of the wary expression that arose in her eyes, Devlin turned on his heel and continued toward the stables before every feeling that he had for this lovely woman found voice and came pouring forth.

Alanna's delicate brow wrinkled as she watched him go. Lord in heaven, what *was* she going to do about Devlin Fitzhugh? She shouldn't be glad that he was leaving the keep for a while, because she truly liked him and was in his debt. But that was exactly how she felt, and the thought disturbed her until she decided that perhaps relief was a better word to describe her reaction to his departure. Somehow, this idea brought her a degree of solace as she returned to her work, striving with each jot of energy she expended to keep other, more mournful thoughts from her mind.

The sky was dark, though streaks of a paler blue gray hovered near the horizon when the man awoke, uncertain whether he had slept through until dawn again or if it was just after twilight. The truth was that he had lost track of not only the number of hours that had passed recently, but the number of days that had gone by since the *Girona* sailed from Killybegs.

Had it been six days or eight since the damp, brisk winds off the coast had filled her towering sails, billowing the tattered canvas and driving her out to sea, spurring her homeward while he watched from the shore, his heart shattered yet joyous? Torn by conflicting emotions at the sight, wanting it, yet fearing what was to be ahead, he had been forced to admit that the ship's departure had made him solely responsible for his tomorrows. No longer would he be able to blame duty or honor for keeping his love at bay.

Yet, to his continued disappointment, each successive sunrise saw him weaker, his struggle for simple survival more crucial than timekeeping. The calendar might indeed show two weeks' passage rather than eight days, but all that mattered to him now was that, by some miracle of grace, he was still alive and, he hoped, growing closer to Alanna with every hour.

Suddenly, hearing an unfamiliar sound, Lucas del Fuentes tensed and wondered whether it was the imminent threat of discovery that had called him from sleep, or his untreated injury. He had a vague memory of constant pain gnawing at his wounded leg, dragging him from faraway dreams, but no awareness of anything else. Usually his military discipline was able to keep the pulsing ache at a sufficient distance to permit him a few hours' rest. If he had sensed danger lurking nearby, however, his soldier's instinct might have alerted him, even as exhausted as he was. Deciding his only choice was to wait for further warning, Lucas settled himself quietly, listening for the odd noise that didn't belong in the green meadows, damp with the most recent rain. A lone bird called its mate, reassuring the Spaniard somewhat, but he would have been more confident if the mate had replied, signaling all was safe.

Then there it was again, but this time he recognized the sound as the muffled bark of dogs in the distance. Hunters, the raven-haired male supposed, but that was not necessarily comforting. He had no way of knowing whether the men with dogs were hunting Nature's largess or stranded Spaniards. Since Lucas had escaped MacSweeney's slaughter, he had managed to avoid discovery, it was true, but each day saw him less capable of mounting a defense or eluding pursuit. Still, he couldn't be taken now, not when he must be so near O'Donnell lands.

The three-trunked tree Alanna had mentioned stood on a hill not far from where he had collapsed earlier. And from the way Alanna had described Kevin's domain, just beyond the hill there was a wide stream, forded by some scattered stones that had escaped a rocky outcropping she enjoyed on sunny days. In his dreams of late, Lucas would finally reach the crest of the hill and see her below him, her luxurious blond hair loose about her shoulders to catch the sun.

Alanna would glance up in disbelief, her lush lips slightly parted, her breath coming in quick pants as she realized it was truly he. And then she would fly up the grassy hillside into his arms, too excited for explanations, interested only in embracing him and knowing he had come back to her. For all he knew, she might be there waiting this morning as the sky brightened.

Impatient to make his dreams come true, Lucas could not wait any longer and so raised his head slightly to peer from behind the uneven hedge of stones and briars that had afforded him shelter through the now-ending night. In the distance, back the way he had come, he spotted two dogs and a lone poacher, bending to claim some small game the dogs had routed. If God was truly good, the nobleman prayed, He would send the fellow back in that same direction, away from where he hid.

For some minutes, Lucas waited anxiously, his injured leg throbbing unmercifully as his awkward position put undue pressure on the weakened muscles. Then, barely believing his good fortune, he watched exactly the disappearance he had hoped for. Evidently satisfied with their success, the hunter and his dogs headed back the way they'd come, leaving the meadows peaceful once more.

He, too, would have to move on soon, Lucas realized. He drew a deep breath and reached down to massage his knee, testing its maneuverability even as he took care not to strain it. The shot had probably splintered the bone, and infection had distinctly established its red claim both above and below the site of the wound. But there was nothing he could do about it but press onward to find Alanna. She would care for him.

De Leiva had spared his life, Lucas acknowledged, remembering that fateful day the men of the Great Enterprise were to have sailed, and he was not about to squander such a precious gift by lying around waiting to die.

On that now-distant morning, he recalled, without warning, a guard of unfamiliar sailors had appeared in the tiny cabin and hauled him roughly to his feet, giving no explanation but the name de Leiva. Bound as a common prisoner, he had been dragged up on deck of the *Girona* to find the entire company of Spaniards from all the ships assembled, some aboard ship, some on shore, and Alonso on his litter before them.

Any minute Lucas had expected to feel the bite of the lash on his back as an example to the joint crews, or to hear that his sentence of death had been reconsidered and pronounced immediately. Aware of the need for discipline aboard any ship, especially one carrying over a thousand men, at the very least Lucas had anticipated being chained to one of the galleon's oars and made a slave for the journey home, but whatever was to be, he had determined not to fight it.

"Lucas del Fuentes," the lieutenant-general of the Armada had intoned solemnly, his deep voice silencing the gathering. "Tell me true, do you yearn to once more see the shores of Spain, your beloved homeland?"

"Of course, Don Alonso. My life is in Spain. Though returning to her will mean my death, I wish to see her once before I die," he had replied, startled by the question. For as much as Lucas dreaded the outcome of his meeting with Philip, he could not deny the justice of it. Spain had given him birth. It was only right that she claim his death, a price he would pay willingly, knowing he had kept Alanna safe.

"Then hear me well," de Leiva had instructed, his dark eyes unreadable, his mouth set in a grim line. "The *Girona* is a noble ship, filled to capacity with brave and loyal servants of Spain, aristocrats and commoners alike who have fought hard and behaved admirably despite the temptations to do otherwise, temptation to which you succumbed."

Remaining silent, Lucas studied the captain's unusually stiff posture, wondering what new grief had upset him so.

"Lucas del Fuentes, it is my judgment that, as a com mon criminal and a blight on the honor of my officers, I d hereby declare you unworthy to occupy valuable space o this vessel. I therefore command you to remain behin while we take others, more deserving, in your stead. Yo are condemned to be left ashore to make your way in Ir land alone, to die one day in this accursed land without th comfort of your family, unmourned and unmissed, a pa riah to all honorable Spaniards." De Leiva refused to mea Lucas's eyes. "You shall be escorted from the *Girona* an my sight at once. Diego?"

His punishment was to be exiled in Ireland rather tha transported as a murderer to Spain? Lucas had not trul believed Alonso's edict until Diego led him to the gang plank, tears running down his cheeks, and cut Lucas' ropes.

"My near-son, I am sorry to lose you, but I know tha had I not argued for this, Philip would only have claime your life. Please God and perhaps He will spare it," the ol man had whispered. He handed him a small parcel of sup plies and embraced Lucas tightly. *"Adios, mi amigo."*

"Gracias, Diego," he had murmured, incredulous at th old man's artful scheming. Thanks to Diego and Alonso he was not only free, but he could find Alanna and love he as long as they both lived. Lucas had marveled at the quix otic hand that fate had dealt him. Could life be sweeter? b had rejoiced, unprepared at the time for what lay ahead.

Frowning ruefully at his once-naive presumption tha dreams could be so easily accomplished, Lucas gritted hi teeth and put his memories aside. He forced himself to gra the crude crutch he had fashioned and used it to stagger t his feet.

The worst was always the first few steps, the Spaniar reminded himself, his green eyes burning with effort Within a half mile or so, the swollen knee joint woul loosen and ease its protest for perhaps an hour, if the ter rain was not too rugged. After that, he had but a brief spel in which the agony became so fierce that he could block i out for only a short interval and stumble awkwardly forward until he all but collapsed in the mud, dragging himself along until he had no choice but to rest again, exhausted and discouraged.

But he had survived thus far and he was not about to die at this point. Lucas forced one foot to move a few inches and dragged the other along to meet it. Having evaded the English and the Irish until now, there was no way he would surrender to mere human weakness when the O'Donnell lands were close at hand. Neither MacWilliams nor MacSweeney had conquered him, despite their best efforts, and he was not about to give them the satisfaction of doing himself what they had failed to accomplish, not with visions of his beautiful Alanna awaiting him over the very next hill.

Still, it took him until midafternoon to reach the tree with three trunks, and by the time he dropped to the ground beneath its branches, Lucas was thoroughly disheartened. The sky had opened shortly before, pouring down its wrath on the earth, drenching him and turning the dirt path beneath his stumbling feet into a greedy morass that had menaced his crutch and him, as well. Only stubborn, pigheaded determination kept him moving, that and the memory of his honey-haired Irish vixen. Inch by inch Lucas had taken the hill on sheer nerve, his strength ebbing though he promised himself a well-deserved respite when he reached its pinnacle.

In his heart, the Spaniard had known Alanna would not be waiting for him in sight of the landmark tree. But nonetheless, the disappointment at seeing only more green meadows and jagged streams meandering in the distance had disheartened him. How much farther could he drag himself before the infection invading his leg took over? From the increasing heat in the wound and the growing stiffness of the leg, he suspected healing would not be easily accomplished even once he found safety. But each time he weighed the delight of seeing Alanna against the pain of going on, there was no choice to be made.

For the moment, though, his body demanded rest. He had learned the hard way if he did not surrender to its complaints periodically, the chills and the fever would claim him, and he could not afford that. Settling himself against the rough bark of the tree trunk, he listened to the far-off rumble of thunder, unable to keep from thinking once more of the day the *Girona* had sailed, the day his life had been spared not once, but twice.

The air about the ship had been charged with sudden tension as he had descended the gangplank that morning, passing through the markedly silent assembly of men. Sailors waiting ashore for his appearance moved out of his way quickly, avoiding his eyes as they hastened to step aboard. Their attitude clearly conveyed the scorn they held for him even while they jockeyed to claim the space his vacating the small cabin that had been his prison would provide. Forty or fifty others, nobles who had volunteered to make a future in Ireland rather than risk the perilous sea again, were gathered in small groups to witness the sailing, anxious yet fearful of this new chapter in their lives that was about to begin.

Still amazed at the abrupt reversal of Alonso's judgment, Lucas moved toward one of *La Rata*'s noblemen whom he recognized, intending to share the happy prospect of their tomorrows on these foreign shores. Noting Lucas's approach, however, the aristocrat pointedly turned his back and walked in the opposite direction. A second man caught Lucas's eye and spit on the ground.

"Now, murderer," he taunted, "will you kill me, too?"

Others, witnessing the blatant insult to del Fuentes, imitated their countryman's example and completely ostracized the Spaniard who had been exiled with them. They had chosen Ireland freely, while Lucas del Fuentes had been deprived of the opportunity to return to his home, and for them that made all the difference. For them, he was now an outcast and would be treated as such.

All too quickly, Lucas found himself isolated on the rocky quay, alone but for MacSweeney and his men. The

Spanish had all moved back from him and the *Girona*, distancing themselves from the criminal who stood near the gangway.

That he did not deserve to return to Spain was clearly a judgment with which they agreed, and they, as loyal, honorable citizens of that country, would not deign to associate with him, Lucas realized, saddened by their rejection. Many of these men had known both Alanna and Juan, he mused. How could they not understand that he had only done what was necessary?

Unforeseen bitterness coursed through his veins until Lucas wanted to damn each and every one of the hypocrites who condemned him. They had once accepted his protection and friendship yet now they had no memory of anything but Juan's death. His only fault was that he had defended a woman under attack. He wanted to bellow aloud, but he realized all at once the futility of his anger.

It was unlike him to react so, Lucas acknowledged as the gangplank disappeared aboard Alonso's ship. Yet as he looked forward to a new existence, he would have hoped that his men could wish him well, not curse him. But then common sense returned, and Lucas cast aside his brief melancholy.

It didn't matter what they thought. He had no cause to be ashamed of his actions. If the other Spanish condemned him, he would pay them no mind, for truly he had won. Lucas del Fuentes had been relieved of his duty to Spain, a lifelong responsibility he could never have abandoned, and for that unexpected release, provided by Alonso, he thanked God. Once the *Girona* sailed, he had but to find Kevin's lands, and he and Alanna would share paradise, a dream these men could never comprehend.

He waited for Alonso, Diego and those others he had once loved to disappear from view, finally freeing him from his bonds. The ship had begun to move slowly as oarsmen settled into their rhythmic strokes, and Lucas wanted to experience the farewell with someone.

"MacSweeney," Lucas called to the Irish chieftain, who sat astride his large white stallion, watching the gradual motion turning the Spanish vessel seaward. "Tell me, which is the quickest road to O'Donnell's holdings from here?"

"That road there, due west, probably two or three days' journey," the rebel chief replied, wondering why he bothered to lie. He had already decided that del Fuentes wouldn't leave Killybegs alive, any more than would the other Spaniards left behind. The greedy foreigners had cheated him out of too much not to pay, ostensibly trading in good faith for the supplies they needed, while actually surrendering only materials they had intended to abandon on Irish shores anyway. The very memory of Alonso smiling as he engineered the various exchanges while del Fuentes negotiated for him in English galled MacSweeney even now, coloring his face with fury and causing him to tighten his grip on the harquebus in his hand. It would be most fitting, the Irishman noted, for these Spanish scum to die by their own weapons.

"Say, two days' ride from here, if you don't encounter trouble," MacSweeney added, his voice harsh with anticipation of his revenge.

Lucas looked at the chieftain oddly for a moment and wondered at his words. As he recalled their approach to Killybegs, it seemed to him they had come through the mountains from the northwest. Surely Alanna's home was in the opposite direction, nowhere near Loughros Mor Bay. Indeed, hadn't she told him that she and Devlin had traveled with the sun at their backs on the journey from Tur Muir? Yet what cause had MacSweeney to lie?

Watching the rebel chieftain stroke the gun he held, Lucas had a sudden sense of foreboding. Neither he nor Alonso had ever trusted the fellow, and surely his ominous countenance said he was up to something now.

"Thanks, then," he replied, his deep, green eyes continuing to measure MacSweeney's mood. "Is there a chance, however faint, that you might spare me a horse? I assure you I'd see it returned promptly."

Lucas could not have chosen a more telling question, for immediately the rage he had sensed smoldering flared hot in MacSweeney's face, narrowing his beady eyes and contorting his brow as he scowled in anger.

"Haven't you treacherous Spaniards stolen enough from us? You took our food, our shelter and our protection, and gave us what in return? Guns for which we'll soon have no ammunition, cannons too weighty to transport, butts of wine poisoned with the brine of the ocean and salt-drenched cloth too fine for use in our lands!"

"We gave you what we could spare," Lucas answered. Glancing toward MacSweeney's men, he realized that each of them had a weapon at the ready, just as their leader did. At first sight, the relaxed Irish guard posed no evident threat, but on closer observation Lucas noticed they had clearly not stationed themselves at random, but were artfully positioned to surround the Spaniards.

"And what of your gold ducats and jewels?" challenged MacSweeney angrily. "We saw none of that."

"I had none."

"But there were those who did, including your Alonso de Leiva."

Lucas made no reply. He looked toward the huge sails now filled to capacity with the gusting winds. A loud cheer echoed from the hundreds aboard the ship, and those ashore responded, waving frantically and calling out in Spanish as the heavily laden vessel sped quickly across the waves, leaving Killybegs far behind. The men on shore shouted, knowing their words could no longer be heard, but still caught up in the excitement.

"Vaya con Dios."

"Maria, ayudarle."

"Adios, amigos."

Even as the jubilant farewells echoed in the cold light of the misty dawn, Lucas kept one eye on MacSweeney, concerned that the man would somehow extract vengeance against the Spanish. He could not have sabotaged the *Girona*—there had always been too many sailors and work-

ers aboard—but what about those left behind? Would the
rebel leader claim their fortunes and betray them to the
English for whatever price he could obtain? While
the thought was yet a glimmer in Lucas's mind, he saw the
chieftain raise his arm and call out to his men.

"Now!" he bellowed in Gaelic, dismounting from his
horse and raising his weapon. "Kill them."

Uncertain of the words, Lucas still grasped the intent,
but before he could issue warning, it was already too late.
The slaughter had begun. The Spanish guns flamed hot in
Irish hands as his unsuspecting countrymen fell to the
ground, unable to defend themselves. The sharp retort of
the harquebuses, the acrid smell of powder, the wretched
screams hung in the air, making the scene one he could
barely believe. Men ran for shelter, huddled behind their
fallen shipmates, dashed toward the dirt paths away from
camp, but none of it helped. One by one they were slain
while MacSweeney watched, a wicked grin on his face.

"Why?" Lucas asked. He inched toward the water as the
leader turned his attention to him, loading his gun and
taking careful aim. "They asked nothing of you."

"You filthy foreigners have already asked too much,
bleeding Ireland dry. I won't have you traipsing across her
bosom, stealing our meager resources and giving the English more reason to do us harm. Better you die than us, del
Fuentes, much better," proclaimed the rebel, firing at his
target. At the same instant Lucas jumped backward into the
water.

Unfortunately, he realized as the shot embedded itself in
his knee, he had made his escape a few seconds too late.
Holding his breath, Lucas forced himself to float with the
tide and prayed MacSweeney would prefer to safeguard his
stash of powder and shot and not shoot again. When
nothing further happened, the dark-haired nobleman
carefully turned his head away from the beach and let it loll
to one side, rocking with the waves as he filled his lungs
again and took stock of the situation.

The shooting had stopped, he noted, risking a glance at the shore. What he saw sickened him. MacSweeney's men were bent low over the corpses they had created, checking for signs of life and stifling them before they stripped the bodies and claimed what booty they could. Occasionally a shout went up as a well-loaded purse was discovered, but gradually even that activity ceased, and he heard the horses snorting anxiously in the presence of so much blood. Hoofbeats sounded among rebel yells. Finally, there was only silence, the ominous quiet that accompanied the departure of men's souls, and then Lucas swam in to the beach.

Cautious in case the chieftain had left guards behind, Lucas stayed in the water as long as he could, only to collapse on the shore when he tried to stand. The salt water had soothed his wound sufficiently that he had not realized its extent, but on land there was no denying the agony it afforded him. Still, he had survived.

Unable to desert the men he had once led without being certain he could not help any of them, Lucas spent precious minutes inspecting the mangled bodies strewn with such wantonness along the beach. But his effort was in vain. None but he had survived MacSweeney's petty vengeance. He, Lucas del Fuentes, would be the only Spaniard off the *Girona* to live in Ireland, he reflected, too weak now from the exertion and loss of blood to even consider the awesome task of burying the dead. If the English found him before he finished, he, too, would forfeit his life. Not about to permit that, he had set out for Donegal and Alanna Desmond O'Donnell.

The days since then had comprised an arduous journey. Still, Lucas reminded himself as lightning split the sky, he was not yet out of danger. He had managed to get this far, starving and wounded as he was, but safety was not yet his. He could not imagine dying before he reached Alanna's arms, though once or twice, as he lay shaking with the fever in the darkness of the night, the possibility had occurred to him. Yet the appearance of each dawn had argued that surely no God, even an Irish one, could be so cruel as to deprive him of his earthly reward after expending so much in its pursuit.

Now, Lucas decided, before the chills and weakness descended upon him again, he would press onward. Perhaps he could make another mile or two before he succumbed to the more frequent bouts of delirium that seized his mind and rendered his body helpless. It couldn't be that much farther to Tur Muir, he told himself, staggering to his feet.

Biting his lip to keep from crying out, Lucas rested his weight on the crutch and stepped slowly from the shelter of the tree as lighting struck again in the distance, brightening his path and his hope.

Devlin had been away from the keep for days now, and as he rode along in his stirrupless Irish saddle, his eyes scanning the surrounding landscape for any sign of stranded Spanish, he castigated himself yet again for his procrastination. He should have spoken openly of his love for Alanna before he left Kevin's stronghold. The lass had led him a merry chase long enough, and he would no longer allow any circumstances to hinder his suit.

Though propriety said he should bide his time, give Alanna a few months to conquer her grief, Devlin Fitzhugh, who had once possessed the self-control of a saint, had become restless and impetuous where his blue-eyed beauty was concerned. His present state was understandable, however. It arose from his past mistake of being overly hesitant in speaking his mind and declaring himself to the woman he loved.

And a mistake it had been, the rugged gallowglass acknowledged, so caught up in his seething emotions that he was unmindful of the natural beauty surrounding him, the lush green of the grass and conifers in sharp contrast to the brilliant hues of the autumn foliage. In his life, love had come to mean longing, and he was unwilling to settle for that anymore.

However, he blamed no one but himself for what had come to pass. If he had only prodded Alanna, he would have possessed her long ago. Then they would have all been happier, and she would never have had the opportunity to fall in love with Lucas del Fuentes.

Del Fuentes! How he had grown to detest that name. The Irishman guided his horse through a glen toward the northern-most ridge of hills signaling the beginning of O'Donnell property. He had not liked the man's relationship to Alanna when he had first met him, and even less when del Fuentes and the girl had gone walking in Elly Cove. In Loughros Mor Bay and Killybegs, it had been all Devlin could do not to engage the foreigner in mortal combat. By all that was holy, he had truly hated Lucas, Alanna's lover, yet oddly enough had come to respect the man.

And how had the bastard repaid him for his forbearance? Devlin answered himself with a snort, giving his mount its head as if racing through the glen would permit him to leave regrets far behind. The damnable foreigner had had the audacity to go to an early death, leaving Alanna to mourn his passing to a greater degree than she ever would have grieved over his departure for his homeland. But whether executed in Spain or lost at sea, what difference did it make? For Devlin Fitzhugh, the result was that he had been left once more to battle a ghost for the woman he loved. However, this time he would not be so foolish. He would not wait contentedly for Alanna to notice him. He would claim her attention!

At least this quest of his, riding the lands with no one in sight, had given him a chance to sort things out. He had never before realized how soothing solitude could be, and he silently thanked Kevin for sending him forth on what had so far been a fruitless search.

As for missing Alanna while he was away from Tur Muir, he had only to close his eyes to see her in all her moods. But the image that was the most precious to him was the one of her smiling, her spirits carefree as she had once been. He would see to it that she smiled again, and the gentle upward curve of her lips would be for him, he thought, his mouth set in a determined line.

But first, before he could do anything about that, he had to conclude this business upon which Kevin had sent him. The sooner he ascertained that there were no Spaniards roaming O'Donnell lands, the sooner he could return to Tur Muir and Alanna.

Yet, unfortunately, more riding would have to wait until the dawn, Devlin decided, as the sun had begun to set and the wind that ruffled his copper hair carried the scent of approaching rain. Right now he would have to find shelter for the night, and tomorrow he could continue his sweep of the northern coast with renewed vigor.

With the damp chill of the air creeping beneath his cloak, Devlin turned his horse toward the slight bulge in the otherwise flat field, a rise that the crofters called a *sid* mound or fairy fort. Intending to settle on the other side of it, and thus be protected from the worst of the wind, Devlin Fitzhugh had no superstitions concerning the mound's danger to mortals. In his experience, man had more to fear from himself than he did from legendary creatures. Besides, he had already been enchanted for years, having long ago fallen under the spell cast by Alanna Desmond O'Donnell. Therefore, what harm or mischief could the fairies, if they did exist, work upon him?

Reaching his destination, Fitzhugh pulled at his reins, ready to dismount, when he discerned in the deep purple shadow cast by the fairy fort the outline of a human form lying facedown at the base of the earthwork.

Immediately Devlin's hand was upon his sword, and he cast about him for signs of any others in the vicinity. But he neither saw nor heard indications of another presence.

"You!" he called harshly, still sitting astride his steed, his sword drawn. "Get to your feet and make yourself known."

When the intruder stirred not at all, Devlin repeated his command in English, his voice louder and more demanding. But still he elicited no response. He slid cautiously from his horse and approached the motionless figure, swearing furiously under his breath. The black thatch of hair exposed to his view proclaimed this huddled trespasser could very well be one of Philip's men taking refuge on O'Donnell land. It could also be that the wretch was dead, Devlin thought, and there would be no need to cart him back to Tur Muir. But if the stranger did live, Devlin vowed he would make certain this was one Spaniard Alanna would not come to love.

Standing over the still shape, Devlin heard the difficulty the fellow had in breathing, his sides shuddering with each sporadic breath he took. And yet the man stubbornly gasped for air.

Curiously, Devlin poked lightly at the man's back with the tip of his sword and noted with a grunt of satisfaction that the interloper remained unmoving. Having retired that weapon, the gallowglass unsheathed his dagger, knowing it would stand him in better stead if the stranger's apparent unconsciousness was a ruse and he was unexpectedly engaged in conflict at such close quarters.

Shifting the hilt of the knife gracefully within his nimble hand, Devlin hunkered down to further inspect his find, poised to hurl himself into combat should it become necessary. But even as he reached out his free hand to shake the man by the shoulders, Devlin could feel the intense heat of fever emanating from the poor devil's body.

When he turned the Spaniard on his back to search for injuries, Devlin was unprepared for the sight that met his disbelieving eyes.

"Sweet Jesus!" he whispered. His face went white and then turned red with rage. The refugee was none other than Alanna's Spaniard, Lucas del Fuentes!

Devlin knew this was no cold, unearthly being, but the man himself returned to haunt him. Just when he had thought himself finally rid of the bastard, here del Fuentes was again, turned up to ruin his future once more.

What was he to do now? the gallowglass wondered with rising anger. To follow Kevin's dictates and bring the Spaniard to the keep would only mean destroying his own hopes for happiness with Alanna, hopes he had but recently thought might be brought to fruition. Running a hand through his fiery hair in frustration, Devlin tried to determine his course of action.

But a soft groan escaped the Spanish aristocrat's lips, parched as they were by fever, which caused Devlin to consider that perhaps death was going to claim del Fuentes soon anyway. If that was the case, why bother to haul him to the keep at all? Certainly, leaving him here to die would make things easier for all concerned. A thoughtful gleam came into the Irishman's eyes. Alanna already thought the Spaniard dead. Why return him to her only to have the lass suffer his loss all over again? And, after all, there were no witnesses to say that he had ever survived the *Girona* and made his way to O'Donnell holdings.

But del Fuentes had already proved himself to be indomitable. In all likelihood the foreigner was too tough to be carried off by fever. The man had made it this far, hadn't he? And from the looks of him, with his bloodied, swollen leg and his muddy, bedraggled clothing, it couldn't have been an easy journey. Damnation! The Spaniard had no business coming back now, not when his shade had only lately been laid to rest.

Devlin realized with a start that there was another option as the forgotten dagger in his hand began to set his palm atingle. He could see to it that del Fuentes became a ghost once more, this time permanently. Then the gallowglass could claim Alanna as his own, with no fear of interference from Lucas del Fuentes. Who would ever know? Ever suspect? No one. It was almost too easy a solution to so mighty a problem.

The vision of seeing Alanna once more in del Fuentes's arms blinded Devlin Fitzhugh to all other considerations, moral or otherwise, and the hilt of his weapon seared his skin like some enchanted thing demanding to be used.

Slowly Devlin raised his knife, ready to strike. Blood lust sang in his veins as his narrowed blue eyes regarded the unconscious form beneath his blade. Lucas del Fuentes was all that stood between him and his long-awaited happiness. One quick thrust would be all it would take to put an end to his problems, and Devlin Fitzhugh, hardened warrior that he was, told himself it was a temptation he could not afford to ignore.

Chapter Twenty

Uttering a quiet prayer for courage, Devlin assured himself that he had done the only thing that made sense. Now, please God, he would have the strength to see the matter through. Still, he hesitated outside Alanna's solar, marshaling his emotions before he knocked. As always, his first glimpse of the attractive blonde would undoubtedly drive all rational thought from his mind, and this night especially he would need full command of his senses. One small misstep would see a quick end to what he had hoped, exposing his frightful vulnerability and earning him only Alanna's pity. That above all else he would not tolerate, he decided. The last week had been far from easy, and the strain of it had left him not adequately prepared to confront the only woman he had ever loved.

Sadly aware that his regrets might never subside no matter how long he waited, the gallowglass rapped solidly on the wooden door even as he glanced into the gray shadows of the corridor, trusting no one would disturb them at such a late hour. It would be better if he could speak with Alanna alone, at least at first.

There was a brief rustling sound and then the door opened and Alanna stood before him, a splendid vision of feminine allure, framed by the candlelight from within her rooms. Evidently she had been prepared to retire, since her pale blond hair hung loose about her shoulders and only a brief nightdress covered her, exposing her graceful legs to his admiring glance.

"Devlin? Welcome home," Alanna murmured, startled by his late appearance and the distress clearly displayed in his face. Deep furrows crossed his brow, his cheeks were unshaven and, most unusual, his once-easy smile had not appeared at the sight of her. "What brings you to my rooms so late at night? Is everything not all right?"

"Only that the sun cannot warm my bones nor the rain cool my ardor when I am apart from you," he replied. He crossed the threshold to embrace her warmly. "It has been all of ten days since I've beheld you, but I am pleased to see that despite my absence, you are looking better. I was quite concerned."

"Oh, Devlin," Alanna sighed sadly, troubled by his tender words. Escaping his arms to stand before the fire, the weary woman considered how best to deal with Devlin. She had hoped he would have realized the futility of his pursuit of her while he was gone, but clearly that was not the case. As exhausted as she was, she would have to discourage him before he went further. "I do wish you wouldn't—"

"Wouldn't what?" he asked brusquely, following her across the room. On leaving Tur Muir, he had promised himself to address his love for her in no uncertain terms, and his encounter with del Fuentes hadn't changed his determination to speak his heart. Yea or nay, he would know their future tonight. "Wouldn't love you? That is like asking me to stop breathing or the tides to stop their eternal ebb and flow, deeds that cannot be accomplished by the mere will of mortal man. Since before Sean declared for you, I have loved you, Alanna."

"And I you, Devlin, as my dearest and most loyal companion," admitted the young woman. She placed a delicate finger across his lips to halt the sentiments she was incapable of echoing. "Loath as I am to dash your dreams, I pray you to accept my love for you as that of a cherished sister, for it will never be anything more."

When Devlin said nothing, Alanna searched her hear
again, trying to find the words to make him understand
She wouldn't hurt him for all the world, but lying about her
feelings, giving him false hope, would be the cruelest deed
of all.

"Believe me, my friend, I know such a love is not wha
you want from me, but what you desire can never be. I am
sorry," she whispered, her voice filled with pain.

Devlin's eyes flickered from her face to the open door as
he drew a deep breath and released it, nodding slowly. In
truth, he had expected nothing else, and his mind accepted
what she told him, however reluctantly. His heart, though,
was not so obliging, and he knew many a sleepless night lay
ahead.

"I could not but tender my suit one last time," the gallowglass said softly, certain now that he had made the right
decision that night in the darkness. "Lucas?"

"Yes, I still love him, Devlin. I suppose I always will, but
even before Lucas, you and I weren't— Oh, merciful
God!" Alanna cried, gasping for breath as she looked to
the door only to witness an apparition of the man she
cherished. Tur Muir had never been reputed to be haunted,
but how else could she account for the gaunt presence
leaning against the doorjamb, her own golden Spaniard?
"Lucas?"

Not believing her eyes, Alanna glanced quickly at the
gallowglass. She needed only his sad nod of agreement before she flew across the room into the arms already extended to embrace her.

"Easy, woman," cautioned the Irishman, a grudging
smile gracing his face at her unbridled excitement. "I've
had the devil's own time keeping del Fuentes from death's
door this past week. I don't need you knocking him over
the threshold."

"Oh, Lucas, you heard me tell Devlin my heart," Alanna
cried. She ran urgent fingers across the Spaniard's haggard face and pulled him closer to shower him with kisses

while her tears cascaded onto his cheeks, as well. "Come, come in and sit by the fire. I can't believe—"

"Believe it, *querida,* believe in me. I am here to make you my wife," Lucas said, limping beside her to the hearth. Though his body had not yet healed, his voice was strong and purposeful. "If you'll have me, I would make my life at your side."

"How could you doubt it? I love you, Lucas del Fuentes." Alanna's smile was radiant, her excitement clearly mirrored in her newly energized step and her sparkling blue eyes, her earlier weariness faded as if by magic. Settling Lucas in a chair where he could enjoy the warmth of the fire, she perched beside him, unwilling to stop touching him, afraid he might disappear again. "I don't understand, though, how you came to be here. Oh, Devlin, you are responsible for bringing him to me, aren't you?" Alanna whirled around to throw her arms about the gallowglass again and hug him tightly. "Oh, Devlin, I *do* love you!"

"Aye, so you've said." He grinned ruefully, his lone dimple appearing as he finally acknowledged the hopelessness of his heart's crusade. "But don't worry, Alanna. It's clear you've chosen the better man."

"No! Not better, just more fortunate," protested Lucas. He owed his life to the care Devlin had given him over the past week. The Irishman had fed him, nursed his fever, bound his wound and broken the news of the *Girona*'s loss. He had never left Lucas's side, healing the one man whose claim on Alanna was deeper than his own. Few men could be so strong and honorable, and Lucas was not at all certain he would be one of them. Devlin had no right to denigrate himself, but before he could continue to voice his objections, Alanna's soft voice overrode him.

"No," she said firmly, stepping back to meet Devlin's gaze. "I would never say that, Devlin. But I did choose the man who owns my heart, whose soul is joined to my own, and I'll not apologize for that."

"Nor would I ask you to," the gallowglass answered, "though I'll not deny I would have preferred your devotion belong to me. See to him, woman, he's still not well, and I fear my efforts at nursing were rather clumsy."

"I'd say they were more than adequate. I am in your debt," Lucas said, extending his hand to the other man, who hesitated but a moment before he took it.

"Oh, Lucas, how did you escape? Alonso and all the others..." began Alanna. She needed to know every detail, now that she had assured herself he was real.

"I know. Devlin told me."

"By why weren't they able to reach safety if you were?"

"Since I have already heard the story, and the one detailing MacSweeney's villainy," interrupted Kevin's lieutenant, "I will leave you two alone and report my return to the O'Donnell. I daresay he'll be glad I brought him a new son-in-law."

"Devlin," called Alanna softly, "since it is so late and Kevin has probably already retired, why don't you wait until morning to see him? I am certain both you and Lucas could use a sound night's sleep."

"Aye, lass, but I'm not sure you'll be letting Lucas have one," he teased. He did not miss the fact that Alanna's hands were once more caressing the Spaniard, however unobtrusively. "Asking him about his adventures, I mean."

"All the more reason to afford us some privacy." The target of her attentions chuckled. "Consider it a last favor, Devlin Fitzhugh. Alanna and I need some time to speak together before we converse with the others."

"Aye," Alanna concurred, her deep blue eyes fixed on the sorrow lurking behind the gallowglass's expression. "But that doesn't mean that you are not welcome to remain with us for a bit."

"And if you keep me here talking much longer, your restful night will be over," chided Devlin, his voice gruff with emotion. "Take care of each other."

"Happily," Alanna agreed. She rose to walk her loving friend to the door, where she embraced him once more.

"Thank you again, dearest Devlin. I can imagine how difficult this must have been."

"Not half as hard as it would have been watching you pine your life away, mourning him," Devlin refuted hoarsely. "Just know, if you need me, you've only to ask."

"Good night, then," said Alanna, already anxious to return to Lucas's side. After planting a quick kiss on Devlin's cheek, she turned and hurried back to the man who had never left her thoughts, the wonderful Spaniard whom she would never again permit to leave her.

Noting with an ironic grimace the rightness of the lovers sitting by the fire, Devlin exited the solar, his mind made up. He would return to his quarters and gather his things together before retiring. In the morning before anyone arose, he would depart the keep that had been his home for so many years. There was no longer any place for him here. He knew that now. And goodbyes would only be tiresome and upsetting. No, he would slip quietly away and perhaps cast his lot in with the rebel O'Neills in the north. Then, too, someone should take MacSweeney to task for his behavior, but Kevin would most likely claim that pleasure, he supposed.

Walking down the cold stone passageway, Devlin wondered if Alanna's smiling gratitude for his part in del Fuentes's appearance would be payment enough for his own loss, his sorrow in the years to come. Stoically shrugging his broad shoulders, he decided it would have to be, and continued purposefully on his way, leaving his once-sweet dreams behind.

When she had watched Devlin leave the room, Alanna knew the only sadness that could mar her reunion with Lucas. Yet surely, she told herself, a man as handsome and caring as Devlin Fitzhugh would one day find a love of his own, if only he would permit it to happen. Then she put thoughts of all others aside and turned her attentions to her beloved once more, reveling in the sight of the face she had thought forever lost to her.

"While you tell me what happened to you, I'd best ten
to your knee," Alanna said, kneeling gracefully befor
Lucas and beginning to peel away the coarse dressing so sh
could inspect the wound. Though there were other thing
she longed to do, she would not lose this man to recurrin
fever now that Devlin had brought him back to her.

"Ah, but there is something else that aches quite terri
bly, *querida,* and demands your more immediate consid
eration," Lucas said with a roguish smile, stroking his long
strong fingers lightly across the crown of Alanna's hea
before allowing them to settle on her shoulders.

"That can wait for *later,* when you've regained you
strength," Alanna retorted determinedly, pushing hi
playfully descending hands aside. "Dear God, Lucas, yo
can hardly stand."

"I beg to differ, milady. I stand hard enough," he ar
gued in his most charming manner. He bent forward unti
his face was only an inch above Alanna's own. Then his lip
found hers and fiercely claimed them as his possession, s
that Alanna knew *later* had arrived much sooner than sh
would have ever thought possible.

Author Note

Alonso de Leiva was a character who did, in fact, exist. A distinguished member of Philip II's court, de Leiva was an experienced soldier and a knight in the Order of Santiago. Indeed, the twenty-four-year-old was held in such high esteem that Philip named him second in command of the Spanish fleet, answering only to Medina Sidonia. Had the great Enterprise been successful against the English, he would have led the Spanish ground forces in the subsequent land invasion of Britain.

Instead, history confirms that of the more than twenty-one ships that foundered off Ireland, three different vessels were captained by de Leiva, as our story recounts. Between September 21 and October 28, 1588, the treacherous Irish waters claimed those we referred to, the *La Rata Encoronada*, the *Duquesa Santa Ana* and the *Girona*, finally stealing de Leiva's life in the third disaster.

As a dynamic, if impulsive, leader, de Leiva had attracted the brightest and most promising of young Spanish aristocrats, for every family craved the honor of their sons' serving with such a renowned commander, especially when the prospects of success were so high. The tragedy of the *Girona*, which cost over thirteen hundred lives, is said to have touched every noble house in Spain.

Since some accounts of the period refer to a handful of *Girona* survivors who were sheltered by the Irish and even-

tually did return to Spain, we like to think that a man li
Lucas Rafael del Fuentes and his Alanna may indeed ha
descendants in Ireland today.

* * * * *

Harlequin® Historical

First there was **DESTINY'S PROMISE**...
A woman tries to escape from her past on a remote Georgia plantation, only to lose her heart to her employer's son.

And now **WINDS OF DESTINY**...
A determined young widow finds love with a half-breed Cherokee planter—though society and fate conspire to pull them apart.

Follow your heart deep into the Cherokee lands of Georgia in this exciting new series from Harlequin Historical author Laurel Pace.

If you missed Destiny's Promise (HH #172) and would like to order it, please send your name, address, zip or postal code, along with a check or money order for $3.99 plus 75¢ postage and handling ($1.00 in Canada), payable to Harlequin Reader Service, to:

In the U.S.	**In Canada**
3010 Walden Ave.	P. O. Box 609
P. O. Box 1325	Fort Erie, Ontario
Buffalo, NY 14269-1325	L2A 5X3

Please specify book title with your order.
Canadian residents add applicable federal and provincial taxes.

1994 MISTLETOE MARRIAGES
HISTORICAL CHRISTMAS STORIES

With a twinkle of lights and a flurry of snowflakes, Harlequin Historicals presents *Mistletoe Marriages,* a collection of four of the most magical stories by your favorite historical authors. The perfect way to celebrate the season!

Brimming with romance and good cheer, these heartwarming stories will be available in November wherever Harlequin books are sold.

RENDEZVOUS by Elaine Barbieri
THE WOLF AND THE LAMB by Kathleen Eagle
CHRISTMAS IN THE VALLEY by Margaret Moore
KEEPING CHRISTMAS by Patricia Gardner Evans

Add a touch of romance to your holiday with
Mistletoe Marriages Christmas Stories!

HARLEQUIN®

MMXS94

Relive the romance.... This December,
Harlequin and Silhouette are proud to bring you

by Request™

Little Matchmakers

All they want for Christmas is a mom *and* a dad!

Three complete novels by your favorite authors—
in one special collection!

THE MATCHMAKERS by Debbie Macomber
MRS. SCROOGE by Barbara Bretton
A CAROL CHRISTMAS by Muriel Jensen

When your child's a determined little matchmaker,
anything can happen—especially at Christmas!

Available wherever
Harlequin and Silhouette books are sold.

HARLEQUIN® Silhouette®

HREQ1194

This November, share the passion with *New York Times*
Bestselling Author

(previously published under
the pseudonym Erin St. Claire)

in

THE DEVIL'S OWN

Kerry Bishop was a good samaritan with a wild plan.
Linc O'Neal was a photojournalist with a big heart.

Their scheme to save nine orphans from a hazardos
land was foolhardy at best—deadly at the worst.

But together they would battle the odds—and the
burning hungers—that made the steamy days and
sultry nights doubly dangerous.

Reach for the brightest star in women's fiction with

MIRA™

MSBDO-R

HARLEQUIN®

Georgina Devon

brings the past alive with

Untamed Heart

One of the most sensual Regencies ever published
by Harlequin.

Lord Alaistair St. Simon has inadvertently caused
the death of the young Baron Stone. Seeking to
make amends, he offers his protection to the
baron's sister, Liza. Unfortunately, Liza is not the
grateful bride he was expecting.

St. Simon's good intentions set off a story of
revenge, betrayal and consuming desire.

Don't miss it!

**Coming in October 1994,
wherever Harlequin books are sold.**

REG2

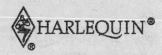

HARLEQUIN®

EDGE OF ETERNITY
Jasmine Cresswell

Two years after their divorce, David Powell and Eve Graham met again in Eternity, Massachusetts—and this time there was magic between them. But David was tied up in a murder that no amount of small-town gossip could free him from. When Eve was pulled into the frenzy, he knew he had to come up with some answers—including how to convince her they should marry again...this time for keeps.

EDGE OF ETERNITY, available in November from Intrigue, is the sixth book in Harlequin's exciting new cross-line series, **WEDDINGS, INC.**

Be sure to look for the final book, **VOWS,** by Margaret Moore (Harlequin Historical #248), coming in December.

WED6

"HOORAY FOR HOLLYWOOD" SWEEPSTAKES

HERE'S HOW THE SWEEPSTAKES WORKS

OFFICIAL RULES — NO PURCHASE NECESSARY

To enter, complete an Official Entry Form or hand print on a 3" x 5" card the words "HOORAY FOR HOLLYWOOD", your name and address and mail your entry in the pre-addressed envelope (if provided) or to: "Hooray for Hollywood" Sweepstakes, P.O. Box 9076, Buffalo, NY 14269-9076 or "Hooray for Hollywood" Sweepstakes, P.O. Box 637, Fort Erie, Ontario L2A 5X3. Entries must be sent via First Class Mail and be received no later than 12/31/94. No liability is assumed for lost, late or misdirected mail.

Winners will be selected in random drawings to be conducted no later than January 31, 1995 from all eligible entries received.

Grand Prize: A 7-day/6-night trip for 2 to Los Angeles, CA including round trip air transportation from commercial airport nearest winner's residence, accommodations at the Regent Beverly Wilshire Hotel, free rental car, and $1,000 spending money. (Approximate prize value which will vary dependent upon winner's residence: $5,400.00 U.S.); 500 Second Prizes: A pair of "Hollywood Star" sunglasses (prize value: $9.95 U.S. each). Winner selection is under the supervision of D.L. Blair, Inc., an independent judging organization, whose decisions are final. Grand Prize travelers must sign and return a release of liability prior to traveling. Trip must be taken by 2/1/96 and is subject to airline schedules and accommodations availability.

Sweepstakes offer is open to residents of the U.S. (except Puerto Rico) and Canada who are 18 years of age or older, except employees and immediate family members of Harlequin Enterprises, Ltd., its affiliates, subsidiaries, and all agencies, entities or persons connected with the use, marketing or conduct of this sweepstakes. All federal, state, provincial, municipal and local laws apply. Offer void wherever prohibited by law. Taxes and/or duties are the sole responsibility of the winners. Any litigation within the province of Quebec respecting the conduct and awarding of prizes may be submitted to the Regie des loteries et courses du Quebec. All prizes will be awarded; winners will be notified by mail. No substitution of prizes are permitted. Odds of winning are dependent upon the number of eligible entries received.

Potential grand prize winner must sign and return an Affidavit of Eligibility within 30 days of notification. In the event of non-compliance within this time period, prize may be awarded to an alternate winner. Prize notification returned as undeliverable may result in the awarding of prize to an alternate winner. By acceptance of their prize, winners consent to use of their names, photographs, or likenesses for purpose of advertising, trade and promotion on behalf of Harlequin Enterprises, Ltd., without further compensation unless prohibited by law. A Canadian winner must correctly answer an arithmetical skill-testing question in order to be awarded the prize.

For a list of winners (available after 2/28/95), send a separate stamped, self-addressed envelope to: Hooray for Hollywood Sweepstakes 3252 Winners, P.O. Box 4200, Blair, NE 68009.

CBSRLS

OFFICIAL ENTRY COUPON

"Hooray for Hollywood"
SWEEPSTAKES!

Yes, I'd love to win the Grand Prize — a vacation in Hollywood —
or one of 500 pairs of "sunglasses of the stars"! Please enter me
in the sweepstakes!

This entry must be received by December 31, 1994.
Winners will be notified by January 31, 1995.

Name _____

Address _____ Apt. _____

City _____

State/Prov. _____ Zip/Postal Code _____

Daytime phone number _____
(area code)

Account # _____

Return entries with invoice in envelope provided. Each book
in this shipment has two entry coupons — and the more
coupons you enter, the better your chances of winning!

DIRCBS

OFFICIAL ENTRY COUPON

"Hooray for Hollywood"
SWEEPSTAKES!

Yes, I'd love to win the Grand Prize — a vacation in Hollywood —
or one of 500 pairs of "sunglasses of the stars"! Please enter me
in the sweepstakes!

This entry must be received by December 31, 1994.
Winners will be notified by January 31, 1995.

Name _____

Address _____ Apt. _____

City _____

State/Prov. _____ Zip/Postal Code _____

Daytime phone number _____
(area code)

Account # _____

Return entries with invoice in envelope provided. Each book
in this shipment has two entry coupons — and the more
coupons you enter, the better your chances of winning!

DIRCBS